MW00479356

49 Days

The DMT Series: Book 1.

by Erik Hamre

49 Days

The DMT Series: Book 1

Copyright © 2015 by Erik Hamre

All rights reserved. No part of this book may be reproduced in any form by any electronic or mechanical means including photocopying, recording, or information storage and retrieval without permission in writing from the author.

Cover art by Twinartdesign
Edited by Mike Waitz
Interior design by Erik Hamre

www.erikhamre.com

Give feedback on the book at:
eh@erikhamre.com

First Edition

Printed in the U.S.A

For my wife, who told me to go for it.

Part 1

Prologue

The wind was blowing hard against the old and worn weatherboards of the Middletons' holiday house on Hedges Avenue. It almost sounded like the storm was gaining strength for every passing minute, like it was determined to create as much damage as possible, to wreak havoc on the beachfront properties of the Gold Coast.

Like it was out to get someone.

Dr Robert Middleton shifted uneasily in his reading chair; he knew whom it would be after. If nature had a way to correct its own mistakes, to unleash plagues to control population growth out of control, to bring life to new species when needed, then it would be after him tonight.

It would be out to get Dr Robert Middleton.

He thought back on the events that had led up to this situation. Should he have done something differently? Should he have contacted the authorities? Spilled the beans and saved himself? It would have been easy, a lot easier than the choice he had made.

But he was comfortable with his choice, it was the one that felt right, the one that made sense in a world that gradually made less and less sense.

"Could you be a darling and bring me another glass of wine," he said to Glenda, his wife of almost twenty years.

She smiled and nodded to him. She was decorating the Christmas tree with their daughter, who giggled and danced around in her PJ's.

They were a happy little family, the Middletons.

The sound of the storm mixed with the voice of Elvis Presley singing Christmas carols on the radio, and it reminded Dr Middleton about his own Christmas celebrations, growing up in Nungarin, a small town in Western Australia with fewer than a thousand inhabitants. Christmas had always been his favourite holiday. Everybody seemed so happy at Christmas.

Then of course, with the prospect of time off work, good food and presents, it was almost impossible for anyone to be grumpy.

But he knew from his own line of work that Christmas could be a hard time for a lot of people. There always seemed to be a peak in the deaths of his older patients around Christmastime. He wasn't exactly sure why, but he assumed it had something to do with thinking. Old people spent way too much time thinking at Christmastime. Thinking about what they had and hadn't achieved in their lives, thinking about lost loved ones, thinking about how lonely they were.

Too much thinking wasn't good for anyone.

He had been a lucky man, Robert Middleton. Married to the same woman for twenty years. Blessed with a beautiful child four years ago, a baby girl. He had worked in a rewarding job since he had graduated from Med school. He didn't have any regrets, or at least he had very few.

Mostly regrets he could live with.

The only big regret he would have in his life would be what he would have to do in the following days. It would impact on all the people he held dearly. It would make them hate him. But there was no other way.

He did it for them.

To save them.

At least that was what he told himself.

Glenda arrived from the kitchen, balancing two full glasses of red. She had that look in her eyes – the look he knew meant that she would let him have his way in bed tonight. It had been a while. Glenda didn't particularly like sex, not after the kid came along. But she knew that he needed the intimacy, that it was important for him to feel like a man now and then.

There had never been any danger that he would leave her or have an affair. He saw enough vaginas at work – the need for a thrill really wasn't there. But sometimes he needed to have sex, to feel like a man.

He would like to feel like a man one last time before he did what he had to do.

The doorbell rang, and it felt as if his heart instantly stopped. Who could it be? Ten o'clock the day before Christmas Eve. Was it a drug addict who had managed to figure out that there was a doctor living in the old beach house? Looking to force himself in, on the hunt for prescription drugs? It had happened before. Not at the beach house, but at home in Melbourne.

Glenda rushed the kid upstairs to the bedroom, while Dr Middleton got up from his chair and walked into his home office. He found the key to the desk drawer and grabbed a full box of bullets from the top of the filing cabinet. He unlocked the drawer and loaded the bullets into the gun before returning to the door.

The knocking increased in intensity.

"Coming," he shouted, stuffing the gun down his pants, pulling the sweater down to cover the bulge. "Who is it?"

"Dr Middleton, we are from the Australian Federal Police, we would like to have a word with you," the voice from the other side of the door barked.

It was as if all the colour immediately drained from Dr Middleton's face. How could they be here already? He thought he at least would have Christmas before they found out what he had done.

"Just a minute," he replied before unlocking the door. The wind was howling. And he struggled to keep the door open. "Come in," he said, holding the door just wide enough for the two police officers to slide inside.

A few minutes later they were all sitting in his office, Dr Middleton behind his solid oak desk, and the two federal police officers seated directly opposite him.

Glenda had served them all tea and biscuits.

"So how can I help you officers?" Dr Middleton asked, doing his best to conceal his nervousness.

"We would like you to come down to the station with us," the most senior of the police officers replied. His name was Greg Kingston. He had a skinny face and piercing eyes.

"Down to the station, the day before Christmas Eve? What has happened, is someone sick?" Dr Middleton asked.

"No, no. No one is sick." Officer Kingston shook his head. "We would just like to ask you a few questions."

"Go ahead. Ask them here."

Dr Middleton reached for his glass of red wine. He didn't particularly feel like a cup of tea, not this late at night. He rolled the wine in the glass, held it close up to his left nostril, and while he closed his eyes – inhaled the aroma.

The senior police officer almost rolled his eyes. Bloody pretentious Melbourne doctors. Beachfront holiday house at Hedges Avenue. Rolling the red wine like it was some kind of magic potion. He didn't know what the doctor was guilty of, just that they were under strict orders not to leave without him. Someone from the government wanted to talk to him, someone important. It would be fun to see how the doctor rolled the glass of water he would get for breakfast in the morning, he thought.

"Did you treat any patients from the train crash last Wednesday?" Officer Kingston asked.

"It is my understanding there were no survivors," the doctor replied, before he took a large sip of the wine. He kept it in his mouth for several seconds before swallowing.

"There was one," the police officer said.

"Ahh. So that's why you're here. The dead boy."

"Where is he?" the police officer asked.

"Do you know who he is?" Dr Middleton replied.

"Who?"

"The boy you are looking for, do you know who he is?"

"Doesn't matter who he is. He is wanted by the police. He's a criminal."

"Far from," said Dr Middleton. "He hasn't done anything illegal."

"Enough of the mumble jumble. You're coming with us." Officer Kingston got up from his chair.

"I don't think so," Dr Middleton said, and pulled out the gun he had concealed in his pants. He pointed it straight at Officer Kingston's face.

"Are you insane? We are federal police officers."

"I don't care who you are, I am not going with you. Not tonight."

Dr Middleton indicated with the gun that Officer Kingston should sit down again.

Officer Kingston and his colleague were unarmed, and now they wished they had taken some time to study the file of the doctor more closely before going to pick him up. Dr Middleton was handling the gun like a pro. Maybe the doctor had some kind of military background? In any case, Officer Kingston knew better than to do anything stupid. He would talk himself out of the situation, like he had done several times before. He was a police officer, the law. The doctor was an educated man, he would understand that there was only one way this could end, and that was with him going down to the station with them. The only difference was that he could now kiss red wine and his fancy beach house goodbye for the next ten to twelve years. Threatening federal police officers with a lethal weapon, he was going down big time.

"Glenda," Dr Middleton called out for his wife.

"Yes, darling. More tea?" she asked.

Dr Middleton shook his head. "We're fine. I will have to go down to the station with the officers for a few hours, they are in desperate need of a doctor."

"And they can't get a local?" She sounded upset when she walked into the office.

"It's not a problem, Glenda," Dr Middleton said, smiling. "But could you bring Mimi down, I would like to say goodnight before I leave."

Glenda nodded, smiled, and backtracked out the door.

When she had left, the doctor's face again changed. Gone was the smile and what remained was a determined face. Someone who knew exactly what he was doing.

But what exactly was he doing? What was his game plan? Officer Kingston was uncertain. And he didn't like uncertainty. What could the doctor possibly hope to achieve by holding them at gunpoint? Why was Dr Middleton so afraid of being taken down to the station?

The room was filled with tenseness when the four-year-old girl walked into the room. The two police officers were just sitting there, staring at Dr Middleton who discreetly kept one hand concealed under the table. In that hand he held a gun. And it was facing Officer Kingston's crotch.

"I love you, Mimi," Dr Middleton said and gave his daughter a big kiss on the forehead.

She smiled and looked up on him with true love in her eyes.

"Can we go to the beach tomorrow?"

"Sure we can," he replied.

Officer Kingston wasn't sure, but he thought he could see a

teardrop form in the corner of the doctor's eye. Was it a teardrop? Was he crying? If so, it was not a good sign.

Dr Middleton patted his daughter on the head, before a bewildered Glenda walked her out again.

"Ok. You have said good night to your daughter. Would you please now stop this nonsense? Come down to the station, and we will forget about this whole incident," said Officer Kingston. There was no way in hell he would forget about the incident, but he always told perps what they needed to hear.

"What's the charge?"

"Excuse me?" said Officer Kingston.

"You heard me. What's the charge? What am I supposed to have done?"

The two police officers looked at each other. Neither of them had been told about a formal charge. It was just imperative that they took the doctor into custody. Tonight.

"We just want to talk to you."

"About the boy?" the doctor asked.

Officer Kingston nodded. "I guess so."

"The problem is that I can't talk about the boy," Dr Middleton said.

"Why not?"

"I just can't."

"Is he still alive?" Officer Kingston asked.

Dr Middleton smiled. "You guys don't know what you have gotten yourselves into."

"Just tell us where the boy is," Officer Kingston said.

"I'm sorry. Sorry for everything," Dr Middleton said, and before Officer Kingston realised what was happening, Dr

Middleton had put the barrel of the gun inside his own mouth, and pulled the trigger.

Pieces of brain and blood covered the white wall behind Dr Middleton's desk. His wife Glenda came running into the room, and started screaming hysterically when she saw her husband sitting lifeless in his office chair, with the back of his head gone.

In the background Elvis Presley sang about jingle bells and reindeer. And the smell of gunpowder mixed with gingerbread filled the room.

Nobody noticed the little girl in the doorway. A four-year-old girl staring at her dad. She hugged her teddy bear with all her strength, the teddy bear her daddy had given her the Christmas prior.

And although she was too young to understand what had just happened, she understood that her daddy wouldn't take her to the beach the following day.

She understood he would never, ever again, take her to the beach.

Part One

–1–

April 2012,
Central Park, New York City

Dr Julian Kovacks stared at the monitor in front of him. Something had to be wrong; there had to be some sort of bug in the software, or maybe it was a hardware problem? The equipment had surely seen its heyday. The MRI machine was more than ten years old, an eternity in the industry in which he worked. He tapped his finger gently on the monitor, but the image remained the same.

It was an image of a brain, more specifically it was an image of the brain belonging to test subject MDTTA-67, a 43-year-old janitor from Brooklyn.

Dr Kovacks remembered skimming through his file the previous night. There was nothing special about test subject MDTTA-67. He was healthy, a divorced father with two teenage daughters, a little bit overweight, but not obese. He had volunteered for Dr Kovacks' study because his father had been diagnosed with Alzheimer's two years earlier, and he wanted to do his share to help science find a cure. The problem was of course that Dr Kovacks' study had nothing to do with Alzheimer's research, but that didn't seem to matter for test subject MDTTA-67, as he was determined to help science, to help understand how the brain worked. Dr Kovacks suspected this wasn't his real motivation. The study attracted a certain type of people, people who wanted to experience something new in their boring, stagnant lives. Dr Kovacks' study gave them just that.

"Turn off the machine. Prepare nitro-glycerine," he said with a firm voice. He preferred to use a minimum of words in the test room, it was easier that way. Although he was a bit rusty he had his routine nailed down. A long time ago he had discovered that the more precise his orders were, the less risks there were for any misunderstandings, for any mistakes. And that was his concern when he looked at test subject MDTTA-67, that someone had made a mistake. The image didn't look like it was supposed to. It didn't look like anything he had seen before. It only took two more seconds before an alarm bell started ringing. The blood pressure had elevated past 230/140, and it kept rising. Test subject MDTTA-67 started shaking uncontrollably inside the MRI machine. The research nurse on call, Bernadette Shaw, pressed the stop button on the MRI machine, but it didn't seem to work.

"No! No!" the test subject yelled.

Dr Kovacks was concerned that the loud yelling would be heard down the hallway of the hospital. He had spent a whole year getting approvals from the FDA and the DEA to conduct his study, the first study into psychedelics since the early nineties. They had warned him of something like this happening. Previous studies had always been conducted on persons with a documented history of using narcotic substances or psychedelics. This was the first study on subjects with no prior history of using drugs. The risk of them going into shock, having a bad trip, or just plainly getting addicted were enormous, and both the University and he were potentially open for massive lawsuits although lawyers had spent months preparing the waiver and consent papers the volunteers had to sign.

They were supposed to be bulletproof.

But not for this incident.

Not for malpractice.

"Please stay still," Dr Kovacks said into the microphone system he used to communicate with patients inside the MRI machine. It was important that the patient remained calm. If he started panicking he could hurt himself.

"I'm going in," nurse Shaw said, and opened the door to the MRI room.

It all happened so fast that Dr Kovacks didn't even have time to protest. All he could see was a projectile shooting out of the research nurse's breast pocket. It went flying through the air before entering the mouth of the MRI machine. The MRI machine had a magnet of 1.5 Tesla, or more than thirty thousand times the magnetic field of the earth. Whatever it was that had flown out of the research nurse's pocket could potentially kill the patient.

With horror Dr Kovacks watched as the patient started screaming. With incredible speed the flying object bounced violently from side to side inside the MRI machine before coming to a standstill at one of the walls. It had cut and sliced the patient's skin as it passed him. The research nurse screamed and covered her face. Dr Kovacks pressed the stop button again and let out a sigh of relief when the rumbling noise subsided and the magnets of the MRI machine turned off. He pressed another button and the tray with the bloodstained patient slowly slid out of the MRI machine.

The patient was almost out now. Only his upper body and head were still inside the tunnel of the MRI machine. The research nurse ran over and grabbed the patient's hand.

"Let his hand go," Dr Kovacks yelled to the research nurse, who immediately let go of MDTTA-67's hand. But it was too late. Test subject MDTTA-67 swooped his right hand to the side, and hit her in the stomach. Then he arched his back and threw his chest upwards. His head hit the opening of the MRI machine with a loud bang.

A few blood drops hit the research nurse in her face, before the patient's body collapsed lifeless back onto the MRI tray. Another big bang was heard when the back of his head hit the MRI tray.

The time was ten thirty when test subject MDTTA-67 finally opened his eyes. Dr Kovacks preferred injecting his patients early in the morning and it was now two and a half hours since they had injected just over 1.6 mg/kg of human grade DMT into a vein on the patient's right arm. The injection had taken 60 seconds followed by a 15-second injection of saltwater to flush out the remaining fluid in the syringe. Normally the test subjects had come down 30 minutes after the injection and were fine to have a conversation with after 45 minutes. Most of them were actually fine to talk to during their experience.

This was not an ordinary day.

"How are feeling, John?" Dr Kovacks asked nervously.

Test subject MDTTA-67 looked confused. He blinked twice, to

get his bearings it looked. And then he just said:

"Wow, that is the weirdest thing I have ever done."

"Can you tell us what happened, what you experienced?" Dr Kovacks asked.

"I am not sure if you will believe me, I am not sure if anyone will believe me," test subject MDTTA-67 said.

"Try me," Dr Kovacks replied, and sat down in his black rocking chair. He opened up his notepad, adjusted his glasses, and looked anxiously at test subject MDTTA-67.

=2=

The phone had been ringing for the last ten minutes; someone was very eager to get hold of Adam Mullins. He excused himself from his client, who was doing deep squats. The second he walked away the client started to relax. It was typical for his personal training clients. They almost needed him to stand on top of them and bellow out orders to complete a decent exercise.

"Adam," he said into the hands-free attachment that stuck out from his ear. It looked dorky, but it allowed him to have his hands free when he talked on the phone.

"She has surfaced," the voice on the other end said.

"Where?"

"Are you sitting down?"

"Yes," Adam lied.

"Have you heard about the airplane crash in Brisbane, Australia last night?"

"No," Adam replied. He rarely watched TV, and even more rarely the news.

"She was a passenger."

A cold shiver went through Adam's body.

"Is she ok?"

"All passengers died on impact," the voice said. It was the voice of his old army friend, Matthew Parks. He had helped Adam try to locate his wife for the last seven years. So far to no avail.

Until today.

And now he told him she was dead.

Adam fell down on his knees. In the corner of his eye he could see his client now lay flat on the ground, breathing heavily.

"Matt, no bullshit, tell me the truth. Was she on board?"

"I don't know. Your wife checked in alone, but there was a girl sitting in the seat next to her that is a match when it comes to age. She checked in alone as well. I have tried to check her identity, but it seems to be fake."

Adam Mullins' heart sank to the bottom of the sea. He was in the middle of a busy park in New York, but it was as if everything around him had just ceased to exist. He wanted to scream, he wanted to cry, but nothing came out.

"Adam, are you there Adam?" his friend Matt asked.

"I'm still here," Adam replied. "Thanks for calling. Thanks for your help."

"What will you do now?" Matt asked.

"I will go find her," Adam Mullins said, and got up onto his feet.

Then he turned around, and walked away.

His client, the forty-four-year-old CEO of a small advertising agency, looked bewilderedly at Adam's back as he started sprinting through the park. She wondered if she should call his name, but decided against it. He was a former marine, some kind of special forces guy. That was why she had hired him. He was ruthless, he pushed her way beyond her boundaries, and she had never been in better shape than after she took him on as a personal trainer two years ago. But in those two years she had never seen him smile, never seen him happy or sad. Always the same disconnected face. As if he just went through life without feeling anything. She wasn't sure, but just before he got up, just before he took off, she thought she had seen a tear in his eye.

What had the person on the phone told Adam Mullins? What message had broken through the shield he always surrounded himself with?

- 3 -

"**H**e could have died."

The director of research at New York State Hospital, Dr Martin Drecker, was genuinely concerned. "He and his family can potentially sue us for millions."

"They won't sue," Dr Kovacks said.

"How do you know?" The research director asked.

"He wants to go back in again," Dr Kovacks said.

"What? He wants to do it again? That's insane."

"I know, but that's the only way he won't sue us. He is willing to sign an airtight waiver, with the new dosage included."

"That's blackmailing," the research director said. "We can't let it happen."

Dr Kovacks scratched his chin. "Any other suggestions?"

Dr Martin Drecker rested his head in his hands. He was only four years away from retirement. He had known Dr Kovacks would be trouble the first time he set foot at the university. He had a reputation, he had baggage, lots of baggage. But Dr Martin Drecker had decided to give him a second chance. Everybody deserved a second chance, didn't they? After the morning's events he wasn't so sure anymore.

"No, I don't have any suggestions."

"So we proceed," Dr Kovacks said.

Martin Drecker thought he saw a hint of a smile on Dr Kovacks' face. It wouldn't surprise him if this was all a staged event. Dr Kovacks had from the outset wanted to test higher dosages, and now he would be able to.

"We don't have approval from the FDA to increase the dosages, it is outside the protocols we have established. If they find out we intentionally increased dosages without approval we could face prison time."

"So, you want to risk the university getting sued?"

Martin Drecker considered his options before he finally answered.

"Yes, it may mean I lose my job, but at least I haven't done anything illegal."

"This is a unique opportunity in history Martin, we are on the cusp on revealing something extraordinary."

"You will report today's incident, following the normal protocols. Then you will finish your study with the predetermined dosages. If there is merit you can apply for funding for another study, on higher dosages, but I would say it is unlikely it will ever be accepted. The risks are too high."

"You know what happened in room 762 earlier today, and yet you are willing to let this go?"

"All I know is that you made a mistake. You were supposed to give your volunteer a dosage of 0.3mg/kg pure DMT. Instead you gave him more than five times that amount. And then your research nurse enters the room with a pen in her breast pocket, enters the MRI room with a metallic object. Your incompetence is unbelievable."

"My incompetence? My patient had a 4-centimetre open cut in his left temple at 8:40. At 9:05 the cut had healed itself. No scar, no sign of any tissue damage. I literally saw the wound close by itself."

"Then write that in your proposal for new funding, because this trial is over. I have changed my mind. You are not fit to continue this trial. I am shutting you down effective immediately." Dr Martin Drecker knew he was making the right decision. He could see it in Dr Kovacks' eyes. He wasn't objective anymore.

"You can't do that," Dr Kovacks said.

"It has already been done," said the research director.

When Dr Kovacks had left his office, Dr Martin Drecker picked up the phone. He called HR and asked for Dr Kovacks' personnel file. He noted it was urgent. It was delivered six minutes later.

When he perused the file he was astounded that he had actually given Dr Kovacks a second chance. It was around the time his own wife had found out he was having an affair, and he had been all about giving people second chances for the following months. He now knew it didn't work. His wife had still left him, as he hadn't been able to contain himself when a new research assistant had been hired three months later. It was then he had realised what everybody else had known for all these years; he wasn't cut out for monogamy. And by the same token, Dr Kovacks wasn't cut out for science studies.

Dr Julian Kovacks had been unemployed for several decades before he joined New York State University. Or sort of unemployed. He had been drifting around; spent a few years in a monastery, managed a health and wellness centre, those sorts of things. Nothing academic. Not since the Connecticut Prison Study.

Dr Martin Drecker turned the page. He remembered the Connecticut Prison Study almost from memory. Dr Kovacks had received approval to treat psychopaths in a maximum security prison with LSD, a mild psychedelic. The intention was to ascertain if psychopaths, whose illness really was that they lacked emotions and empathy, could open up to these if they were exposed to LSD. The study was clouded in controversy. Families of the victims murdered by the psychopaths participating in the study were disgusted by the thought that these people were getting high on taxpayers' money. Instead of being punished for their crimes, they were being rewarded with free drugs inside the prison. One could even argue that the prisoners could let their minds escape the prison walls when they got high, that they again were free men for the duration of their LSD trips. But the experiment had produced some astounding results. Psychopaths, who previously were considered incurable, were now being cured in scores. They learnt how to deal with their feelings, they learnt compassion. It was almost unbelievable to see how stone cold murderers turned into soft-spoken, considerate citizens. The alarm bells only went off a few years later. It turned out that the psychopaths didn't turn into kind compassionate people, they just learnt how to act that way. And they used this skill, the skill Dr Kovacks had taught them through his LSD sessions, to persuade the parole boards to let them out early.

And once out, they recommitted in droves.

The statistics were undeniable. None of them had been cured;

they killed within weeks of being let out of prison.

And now Dr Kovacks had found himself a new pet project: High-dosage DMT experiments on normal people. He claimed that test subject MDTTA-67, who by accident had received more than five times the prescribed dosage, had self-healed during the session. That a self-inflicted cut had healed before the very eyes of Dr Kovacks and the research nurse Bernadette Shaw.

It was ridiculous.

The guy was delusional.

Dr Martin Drecker had read Dr Kovacks' notes from the interview of test subject MDTTA-67 after the episode. It was complete madness, rambling from a person high on narcotics. Stories about a different world, about doctors fixing him up, about doctors putting probes in him.

Dr Martin Drecker closed the file, and looked over at the window.

He could see a bird landing on the windowsill.

That was reality, that was life.

What he could see with his own eyes.

Not this crazy stuff people experienced under the influence of drugs.

He knew he was right shutting down Dr Kovacks.

The guy didn't know what was best for himself.

-4-

A dam Mullins had arrived with an early flight from Seoul. The route from Newark International airport via Los Angeles and Seoul was the quickest one he had found. It was also the most expensive one, by far. The tickets had set him back more than six grand. But money didn't matter in this instance. He had been searching for his wife and daughter for the last seven years, and less than forty-eight hours ago he had been given the first real lead he had ever received in all those years. His wife had been a passenger on an Airbus A330 from Singapore Airlines, on route from Brisbane to Singapore, that had crashed forty minutes after take-off from Brisbane International Airport.

He had been to Brisbane Airport on several occasions over the last few years. Australia was one of the countries he had suspected that she might be hiding. But it was such a god damn big country that it was almost impossible to find anyone there. Not if they wanted to stay hidden, not if they were resourceful. And his wife had always been resourceful, very resourceful.

He was now standing in the reception of the Royal Albert Hospital in Brisbane. This was where most of the passengers initially had been taken for identification. All 237 passengers had died on impact from the crash, and most of them were burnt beyond recognition.

"Are you a relative?" a doctor in a white coat asked.

Adam Mullins nodded. "I'm looking for a girl, sixteen years old. She was on-board flight SQ138."

The doctor cleared his throat. "There were no survivors. All the passengers are down at the morgue. If you want to go down there to make an identification I can organise it for you."

Adam Mullins nodded slowly.

"Wait here, I'll get a nurse to take down your details," the doctor said.

He had barely turned around before the doors swept open and a woman dressed in an expensive suit walked briskly into the hallway.

"Doc, we have a survivor from the plane crash, badly burnt. Operating theatre 23 is ready. Go and get scrubbed down."

"What age is she?"

The woman in the suit looked at Adam, before she turned towards the doctor.

The doctor shrugged his shoulders. "He is not a journalist, he is a relative. Looking for a sixteen-year-old girl," the doctor said.

The lady faced Adam before continuing. "It's a teenage girl. But she is badly burnt. She might not make it."

There was a glimmer of hope in Adam Mullins' eyes.

"Can I come along?"

"You can't come to the operating theatre, but you can stay in the waiting room. I will get you processed. Is it your daughter you are looking for?" she asked.

"Yes." Adam answered. "My wife and daughter were on the plane."

-5-

Dr Kovacks stared at the key. He wasn't stupid, he knew that his career was over. Dr Martin Drecker had given him a second chance, he was the only one who had even considered doing that in the last twenty years. Most research directors for the hospitals Dr Kovacks had applied for hadn't even bothered to return his calls, let alone send a reply after rejecting his applications. What would he do now? He had loved being back in action, on the frontline of scientists who sought to change the world. But they hadn't learnt from their mistakes. Back in the early 1970s, when they had terminated his Connecticut Prison Study, they had used the reoffending psychopaths as evidence that his LSD treatments didn't have a rehabilitating effect. But they hadn't realised that it was the termination of the project itself that was the cause of the prisoners reoffending, of their killing innocents when they were let out on early parole. They had done it for him, for Dr Kovacks. They had done it because they were angry that the prison study had been shut down, angry for the way the research committee had treated him, treated Dr Kovacks.

And now history would repeat itself.

Yet again his research project would be shut down prematurely, before it could prove itself, just when it was on the cusp of providing incredible scientific breakthroughs.

He needed that key, he thought. He couldn't go back to his old life. Meditating and singing hums with bums and hippies. He was a scientist, he had always been a scientist.

A New Age Scientist.

But a scientist.

"Good weekend?" he casually asked the pharmacist.

He was glad he had maintained a good relationship with her over the last two years, always smiling when he bumped into her in the canteen, or striking up a quick talk when he caught her in one of the hospital lifts. Maybe it was his subconsciousness that had known he would need that rapport at some stage, that he would need her help at some stage.

"Pretty boring, mostly housework," she replied.

He glanced at her nameplate. Maria it read. He thought that sounded right, but he was terrible with names. Couldn't remember if he tried.

"Get yourself a cleaner, life is too short to do laundry on the weekends," he said with a smile, and moved closer to the cabinet on the wall behind her. It held the key for the narcotics vault. It was where they kept his stock of DMT, in a special locked freezer.

"If I could afford one, I would, believe you me," she replied.

"Thought they were paying you the big bucks down here."

"Yeah right," she said and looked up from her desk. "Can I help you with anything today, Dr Kovacks?"

"Thing is….," he started. "I need a favour."

Her eyes narrowed. "What kind of favour?"

"I'm spending the day with my nephew tomorrow. He is twelve and wants to become a doctor when he grows up."

Her face seemed to loosen up.

"He's supposed to go to a dress-up party on the weekend, and I've promised him I would get him an outfit. But unfortunately all the costume shops I've been to were sold out. So I was wondering if I could buy one of the surgery outfits from the pharmacy, extra small size." Dr Kovacks gave Maria the biggest smile he could muster.

"Don't be silly. You don't have to pay for it. Wait here and I'll get you a full outfit. How cute, does he need a mask as well?" she asked.

Dr Kovacks nodded.

As soon as Maria had turned the corner to collect the clothing from the storage room, he leant over her desk and unhinged the key for the locked freezer. He already had access to the room with the narcotics vault; the only failsafe they had put in place was to not give him a key to the freezer itself. The lady from the DEA had told him that it would be for his own good. If some of the DMT went missing, nobody could blame him, because he didn't have a key. But of course, if something did go missing, and didn't resurface, they would blame him anyway. They always needed someone accountable, someone to point the finger at.

He wasn't too worried about putting Maria in a bad spot. One thing was that he didn't really care, he didn't really know her apart from the casual small talk they, from time to time, engaged in. And once the Research Director reviewed the film from the narcotics vault it would be clear that Dr Kovacks was a lone perpetrator, that he alone was guilty.

But by then, it wouldn't really matter, for by then Dr Kovacks would have proven his theory. There was a risk that they could deny him a Nobel Prize, due to the risks he was taking, due to the laws he was breaking. But hadn't all great scientists in history taken great risks? Hadn't most of the discoveries we today took for granted been discovered by people willing to experiment on themselves?

The x-ray was a result of Pierre and Marie Curie's tinkering with radioactive elements.

Jonas Salk had conducted the first trials of the polio vaccine on himself.

Michael Faraday, the father of electromagnetism, had poisoned his own body and ruined his eyes experimenting on himself.

Even Albert Hoffman, the first person to synthesise LSD, had used himself as a laboratory rat.

Nobody in the academic community looked down on those distinguished scientists for experimenting on themselves, for not using double blind tests and placebos. Sometimes the circumstances called for extreme measures, for someone to rise to the occasion.

He smiled when he closed the key cabinet, the key safely placed in his left pocket.

"You should really consider getting a cleaner," he said to Maria, who had returned from the storage room with a green surgery outfit. "Life's too short to only do what people expect of you."

-6-

There was a controlled madness outside operating theatre 23. Doctors kept swarming through the doors, and they all seemed to whisper amongst themselves. Adam Mullins had tried to get some information, but he had been met with a wall of silence. Nobody could or would tell him how the girl in theatre 23 was doing. He turned on the TV in the waiting room, and he could see that reporters were queuing outside the hospital reception. The miracle survivor, the passenger who had been found alive three days after the crash! It was a story of hope in all the devastation and sorrow that had rippled through the nation of Australia when the Singapore Airlines flight had crashed shortly after take-off from Brisbane International airport. Adam didn't like the prospect of attention. If it really turned out it was his daughter who had been on-board flight SQ183, his daughter who had survived the horrific crash, what would the press write about him? Would they make a story on him, Adam? He couldn't risk that. He had to stay under the radar, somehow he had to stay under the radar.

"Mr. Mullins?" A stern-looking woman was standing in the entrance of the waiting room. He was the only other person there.

"Yes," he answered.

"There seems to be a mistake. We have gone through the

passenger manifest. Your daughter wasn't on the plane."

Adam sighed. He knew this was going to happen.

"She wouldn't be travelling under her own name," he said.

"Excuse me?" the woman said.

"My wife was on that plane. Andrea Mullins. Travelling under her maiden name."

He helped the stern woman locate his wife's name on the piece of paper she held in front of him.

"My wife abducted my daughter when she was nine years old, I haven't seen her since. I know there was a teenager sitting in the seat next to my wife. She was travelling under a false name."

"How do you know this?" the woman asked sharply.

"I just do," he replied. "I have been looking for my daughter since the day she disappeared. I believe she may be the person you have in the operating theatre."

"And why do you believe that, Mr. Mullins?"

"Because I am a survivor, and I believe my daughter is a survivor too," he replied.

"I'll see what I can do," the lady said before leaving. Adam knew what that meant. She would confer with her superiors, possibly make a few phone calls to check out his story. But he had seen it in her eyes. The doubt that always came when he told women that his wife had abducted his child. Why had she done that, was he an abusive father, a wife beater, a paedophile? They couldn't comprehend, or rather didn't want to comprehend, that he had been a good father and a good husband. That it had come out of nowhere. That he had been on his third and final tour in Afghanistan when it suddenly became impossible to get hold of his wife. The military police had sent someone over to check on his family and found an empty house. She had vanished into thin air, and she had taken his daughter with her. The fact that he had been a soldier didn't help. Everybody had read about fucked-up war veterans returning from Iraq and Afghanistan. PTSD, Post-Traumatic Stress Disorder. They all put that label on him the second they heard the story. Well, fuck them, fuck them all, he thought while he considered his options. There was no way in hell he would let his daughter slip away again, if it really was his daughter of course. He had been kept in the waiting room for more than six hours now, he had hardly eaten or slept the last thirty hours, and nobody gave him any information.

He got up from the couch, his legs aching from all the sitting down, and walked over to the reception. The three women behind the reception counter were chatting excitedly to each other.

"Can someone please tell me what's going on here, is my daughter ok?"

"Is that your daughter in there?" one of the women asked.

"Yes it is. But nobody is telling me what is going on."

"Haven't you heard? It is a miracle. She is going to live," the woman behind the counter said.

-7-

Dr Julian Kovacks placed the knife on the night-table next to his bed. He positioned the camera so that it would have a clear view of his right arm when he lay down on the bed. He knew there was a risk that he wouldn't remember anything from his DMT trip. Memory loss had been a frequently cited side effect of large DMT doses in the past. The early DMT pioneer Dr Stephen Szara, who in the mid-1950s had discovered the psychedelic effects of DMT by injecting himself in his own laboratory in Hungary, had stated that his patients had a total loss of memory if the dosages of DMT were too large. The well-known psychologist, Dr Strassman, had recorded the same result in the early 90s. And after Dr Strassman, nobody had really done anything with DMT. The research had stopped almost overnight.

Those old studies had however been conducted on much lower doses than the one that Dr Kovacks accidentally gave to test subject MDTTA-67. And Kovacks was in the firm belief that this was the reason for his astonishing results.

He had crossed another threshold with his dosage of more than 1.6mg/kg.

He knew from previous studies that the "psychedelic threshold", the point where there was a separation of consciousness from the body and the effects of the drug completely consumed the mind of the test subject, was achieved at much lower levels. Nobody had ever been able to go higher than about 1mg/kg without ending up with test subjects who couldn't recollect anything useful from their psychedelic trip.

Dr Kovacks' dose was the magic number, and he had only found out due to a clumsy research assistant.

That wasn't entirely correct though.

He had always wanted to try higher dosages, and it was he himself who had prepared the dose they had used on test subject MDTTA-67.

He just hadn't planned to use it yet.

It was something he had considered using later in the study.

After they had collected more data on the lower dosages.

But the research nurse, Bernadette Shaw, had accidentally picked up the wrong syringe from the DMT freezer that morning.

And thus he had achieved his breakthrough.

He had proven his theory.

But he had not expected the results.

Not at all.

He had expected something entirely different.

He knew he was lucky, but he also knew that a lot of the scientific breakthroughs in history were made just like that, made while looking for something entirely different.

He lifted the knife from the table and held it against his skin. He had to ensure that the cut was deep enough to be visible to the camera, yet not deep enough that he risked having too great of a blood loss if he passed out during the DMT-trip.

With a swift movement of his left hand he drew blood.

It was a perfect cut.

He had avoided any arteries, yet he had a gaping wound on his arm. One that would leave a five-centimetre scar.

On a normal person of course.

He inserted the syringe with DMT into the IV he had placed next to his bed, and lay down flat on his back. The setup wasn't ideal; he knew that there were three important things when testing out drugs: set, setting and drug.

He was alone in his crappy apartment. A big painting of the Hindu elephant god Ganesh covered most of the wall he was looking at. He had just self-administered a massive dosage of a psychedelic drug into his vein. He had been clean for almost a year, only getting high on the occasional mushroom. If something went wrong, if he had a bad trip or a cardiac arrest, there was nobody there to help him.

But life was too short not to take any risks.

He felt the rush of the DMT going into his vein.

"Here it comes!" he shouted into the empty room before he lost his breath, and the world around him seemed to squeeze into a black hole.

Thirty seconds later he was floating above his body, he could clearly see his body down there on the bed, lifeless, so insignificant, an empty shell.

He had expected this effect, as several of his test subjects had told him that after the initial rush it was as if they were dying. You could either fight it or let go, the body would automatically go into a fight or flight mode and all the vitals would peak – heart rate, blood pressure, you name it. It was those vitals that had been his largest worry when going for increasingly larger dosages. If a patient fought too hard, didn't let go, then it could potentially lead to a cardiac arrest.

Dr Kovacks decided to let go, to let go of his earthly body and float into oblivion.

What came next he didn't expect.

There were none of the bright colours he had experienced during LSD and magic mushroom sessions.

There was just this loud humming, this incredibly loud humming.

It was as if his head was about to explode.

He could feel his whole body vibrate.

Vibrate to the loud humming.

Then it was as if his head popped.

He opened his eyes, or at least he thought he did.

He found himself in an operating theatre. There was a group of doctors surrounding the bed he was lying on. They were busy, busy operating on him.

Observing him.

Talking to him.

Then it all turned black.

Black as the night.

Black as the deepest depths of the universe.

Black as a hole.

–8–

A dam Mullins had just closed his eyes for a second when he sensed a presence in the room. He opened his eyes and looked straight at the stern-looking woman he had spoken to earlier in the day.

"We would like to do some tests," she said.

"On me? Why?" he asked.

"Just a blood sample, for now. We need to ascertain that you are who you claim you are."

Adam Mullins understood immediately. The teenage girl was badly burnt. The only way to determine if she was related to Adam was by checking his blood type, maybe even comparing DNA samples.

"You can do as many tests as you want," he said.

The woman handed him a consent form, which he completed in less than a minute. He was a healthy man, never been a smoker, wasn't on any medication, even though he sometimes had considered taking sleeping pills to get through the night. Nightmares from Afghanistan had been replaced by nightmares about his daughter being abducted. But he had wowed to never take the easy solution. Prescription drugs were an invention of psychologists; the easy way to solve your problems. Hell, if he had been born today he would probably have been diagnosed with ADD and a range of other disorders. The need for an adrenaline kick that had served him so well on three consecutive tours in Afghanistan would have been medicated out of his personality, and he would have grown up to become a shadow of the man he actually was.

The woman held out a syringe, while Adam Mullins pulled up his shirtsleeve. She hesitated when she saw the burns and scarring on his arm.

"An old accident," he said casually. His body was covered with them.

She had no problem finding a vein. After he returned to New York and started working as a personal trainer, to pay the mounting bills he had accumulated in the search for his daughter, most of his arteries were on the outside of his muscles.

She capped the tube with the blood sample, and got up.

"This won't take long. If it is your daughter, you will be able to see her shortly."

"Is she ok?" Adam asked.

The woman was about to say something, but hesitated.

"I'll let you know when the results are ready," she snapped. Then she simply turned around and left the room.

What the hell was going on? Everybody acted awkwardly around him. Nobody told him anything. He could understand that they had to make sure there was no doubt it was his kid who was in the operating theatre before they let him see her. But they could at least give him some information, tell him there was no new information available.

In the corner of his eye he could see a journalist being escorted out by a security guard. He had managed to get all the way to the reception area before getting caught. This was what they had to deal with, the people who were saving lives. Shameless reporters trying to sneak into a hospital, to get the first picture of the lone survivor of flight SQ183. The tragedy reduced to entertainment. He held up his hand to cover his face and ducked behind the corner. The reporter hadn't held a camera, so he wouldn't have taken a picture of Adam, but he had seen his face. He had looked straight at him. And Adam knew that the reporter had realised Adam had something to do with the kid in the operating theatre, the lone survivor of flight SQ183.

He had seen that glimmer of excitement, that moment of realisation, through the bespectacled face of the reporter.

And Adam knew that he couldn't stay around for too long.

If he stayed at the hospital, one of those vultures would find out who he really was.

The stern-looking woman re-entered the room twenty minutes later. If possible she looked even sterner than before; her skin was pulled tight over her face, her legs skinny, her fingers pointy. A smoker.

"I am sorry to inform you that the patient is not your daughter," she said.

"You sure?" Adam asked while his heart sank. He had been so certain. After all these years he thought he had finally found her.

"Yes, I'm sure. The patient's blood type is B. That is not a possible outcome given you and your wife's blood types. You can't be her father. I'm sorry."

Adam nodded. It was a nod of defeat.

"I understand if you can't tell, but out of curiosity: How is the kid doing? Will she live?"

The woman smiled.

"I am not allowed to tell. But watch the news tomorrow, something extraordinary happened here today." And with that comment she left the room.

Adam picked up his bag of clothes from the salmon-pink floor. He had only brought the bare essentials to Australia. One pair of extra underwear, a toothbrush and a deodorant. When he threw the green military bag over his shoulder, he felt the force of sleep deprivation set in with full force. He had a sore throat and his body ached as he walked out of the waiting room.

To the left of him, the door of the operating theatre bounced open, and a stream of doctors in surgery outfits came rushing out. Behind them four nurses rolled a hospital bed.

He glanced over at the patient.

A kid.

A teenager.

"Cameron," he said in reflex.

"Dad," the patient answered with a clear voice.

–9–

"What on earth was he thinking?" asked the agent from the Drug Enforcement Agency, the DEA. She was viewing the video of Dr Kovacks' experiment on the screen in front of them. The Director of Research, Dr Martin Drecker, was sitting to the left of her.

"I guess he didn't see any point in going on. I feel partly responsible."

"Well, you shouldn't," said the DEA agent. "Dr Kovacks was a loose cannon. I am just glad he did it to himself, and not another patient."

Dr Martin Drecker nodded.

She was right. It could have been worse, much worse. Dr Kovacks had taken a massive dose of DMT, a potentially lethal dose. This incident would be written down as a suicide, a tragic and unfortunate event. If he had given the same dose to a patient it would have been murder.

On the screen in front of them they could see Dr Kovacks get up from his bed. He looked like he was in a daze, then he focused on the camera. It was as if he had a moment of clarity, before he disappeared out of the picture. There was just a picture of an empty bed on the screen, but one could clearly hear the sound of shattering glass, the moment when Dr Kovacks jumped through the window of his apartment on the tenth floor of a building in Queens.

The sheet on the empty bed moved slightly – it was the wind from the now smashed window. One could hear it on the video. It was like static background on a TV, that noise one used to get, before all the TV signals went digital.

The DEA agent got up and walked over to the screen. She turned off the camera, and ejected the memory card.

"I'll hold on to this. It will go into the evidence bag, but I don't think you have anything to worry about. You did everything by the book."

Martin Drecker tried to put on a smile. But he wasn't able to muster one.

He had done everything by the book.

He had terminated Dr Kovacks' study when he was informed they had given an unauthorised dosage to one of the volunteer test subjects.

He had prepared the papers for the proposed termination of Dr Kovacks' employment at the hospital.

He had followed the book.

But why did he still feel guilty?

He knew.

He hadn't cancelled Dr Kovacks' access to the narcotics vault.

And that was the reason Dr Kovacks was now dead.

There was a reason Dr Kovacks had never been given a key to the locked freezer where the narcotics were kept. DMT was a narcotic, it was classified as a category 1 drug. That was the same category as Heroin and Cocaine. And now Dr Kovacks had broken into the narcotics vault, pumped his body full of human-grade DMT and committed suicide by jumping straight through the window of his apartment. He had landed on the roof of a parked car below. It had somehow softened the fall, but his body was still a mess. Dr Martin Drecker had been the one who had to identify him. It had been hard when the face was almost unrecognisable, a mere pulp of blood.

But there was no doubt.

Dr Kovacks was dead.

Dead because Dr Martin Drecker had terminated his study.

"There is nothing more we can do today. I'll stop by your office tomorrow. Collect all his files from the study. His notes and protocols."

Dr Martin Drecker nodded again.

He was still in shock. But that wasn't the problem. There was this thought that wouldn't go away, this thought that didn't make any sense.

Why did Dr Kovacks cut himself on the arm just before he injected the DMT?

"Can we run the video one more time?" he asked.

"Don't torture yourself," the DEA agent replied.

"No, it is not that. I just want to check something."

The agent put the memory card back into the camera and pressed play on the video.

He struggled to contain his excitement when he saw what happened. At seven minutes and forty-five seconds into the video, it was as if the wound on Dr Kovacks' arm had not just stopped bleeding. It was as if it had disappeared. The gaping wound closed by itself and it was all done in seconds. There was still blood on his arm, so unless you actually looked for it, you wouldn't notice.

What was it Dr Kovacks had claimed earlier in the day?

"You know what happened in room 729. The wound healed itself."

Could it be?

Could Dr Kovacks have stumbled upon a way to self-heal wounds? Did DMT have unknown properties?

"You OK?" the DEA agent asked.

"Yes. Sorry. It was nothing. It just seems so unreal," he answered. "I'll have all his notes and protocols ready in the morning."

"Thanks, I probably won't come by until after lunch."

They shook hands and Dr Martin Drecker let her out of his office.

He waited for twenty minutes before he headed down to Dr Kovacks' office. If Dr Kovacks had stumbled upon an unknown effect of DMT, the consequences could be unimaginable. But he would have to act quickly. He would need to go through all the notes from Dr Kovacks' study before the DEA agent arrived. He couldn't hand over a potentially ground-breaking discovery. He would have to contain the information.

After four hours, seated in Dr Kovacks' comfortable black leather chair, he had read enough. Dr Kovacks had not been honest with him when he applied for a position at the university hospital. He had told Dr Martin Drecker he had matured since the Connecticut Prison Study, that his New Age methods were a thing of the past.

When reviewing the interviews of the test subjects who had been given the smaller dosages of DMT, it became clear that Dr Kovacks had been searching for something. He hadn't been content to just catalogue the test subjects' experiences under the influence of DMT.

"What did they ask you? Did they do anything to your body?"

Dr Kovacks had been asking the test subjects leading questions. The study was worthless from a scientific point of view. But what had he been searching for? Dr Drecker located the pile of notes relating to the test subjects who had been given the strongest dosages.

It was remarkable how similar the stories of the test subjects were. Was it because Dr Kovacks had been coaxing them, asking them leading questions? There was no way to be sure. Unless one had been present at the interviews it was hard to determine how much of the test subjects' stories were actual experiences, and how much was due to Dr Kovacks' questioning.

He looked at the entries:

"They were there, waiting for me."

"Who, who were there waiting for you?"

"The reptiles."

Dosage too low. Test subject MDTTA-23 had vision of reptiles again. A large alligator shape communicated with him telepathically.

What the hell was this? This wasn't science. This was crazy-talk. This was organised insanity.

There were dozens of similar recordings. Test subjects claimed to experience different worlds, inhabited by reptiles, aliens and humanoids. They claimed to arrive on space stations, in operating theatres. They claimed that the reptiles raped them, that the humanoids put probes into them. It was pure craziness. This was the study of a madman.

Dr Drecker closed the file he had open. He leant back in the chair and let out a big sigh. What the hell had Dr Kovacks been searching for? He knew he wouldn't find the answer in the study notes, they had been prepared for a situation like this. They might look crazy when read out of context, but this was a study of the effects of psychedelics. Of course some subjects would have crazy experiences. They were tripping on a category 1 narcotic for fuck's sake. But it was clear from what Dr Drecker had read that there had been a purpose behind Dr Kovacks' questioning. He had been searching for something.

The question was, What?

-10-

It was still the middle of the night when Dr Martin Drecker arrived at Dr Kovacks' unit. The car Dr Kovacks had crashed through the roof of, just a few hours earlier, had been towed away. Just some pieces of shattered glass on the ground bore witness that something terrible had happened there. The road and pavement were wet. The fire department had hosed them, cleared any remnants of Dr Kovacks' bodily fluids.

Dr Martin Drecker stood outside for a while, uncertain whether to go through with it or not. He had found Dr Kovacks' spare key in his office, the spare key to his apartment. The apartment where he had committed suicide. Was it technically still a crime scene? The agent from the DEA had said it was a closed case. It was a suicide. But then again she wasn't the one who would investigate the suicide. Some local cop would have to do that. And if Dr Drecker entered Dr Kovacks' apartment now, could he become implicated, could he become a suspect?

No, he had seen the video. There was no doubt what had happened. If somebody found out he had been inside the apartment, he could always claim he had been there to collect something for the study, in order to hand it over to the DEA agent.

He inserted the key into the door of the apartment building

and pushed the door open. His heart was racing in his chest, but he wasn't really scared. He was excited. Dr Kovacks might have been a crazy New Age scientist, a mere amateur. But sometimes amateurs got lucky.

And maybe Dr Kovacks had stumbled upon something, something big.

Dr Martin Drecker was sitting in Dr Kovacks' living room. In front of him he had laid out thousands of pages of notes, Dr Kovacks' notes. It appeared that Dr Kovacks had never given up his studies of psychedelics after he was sacked from Connecticut University and the failed Connecticut Prison Study. He had continued to study the effects of psychedelics, but now with himself as the test subject. He had spent more than a decade in South America, in the Amazon. Interviewing tribes that used Ayahuasca, a brew made out of local plants to achieve heightened states of consciousness. He had spent time in Mexico, trying mescaline, magic mushroom. Time in Amsterdam, doing LSD. If there was a psychedelic in this world, Dr Kovacks had tried it.

But he hadn't found what he was looking for, a drug that sent the user back to the exact same place every single time.

A drug that was consistent.

He had theorised that these places people visited under the influence of different psychedelics could be alternative worlds, hidden worlds. He had dozens of books outlining quantum theory and the possibility of other dimensions, the possibility of parallel universes.

Dr Martin Drecker looked over at the window, the window that hours earlier had been the only thing that could have saved

Dr Kovacks. The only thing that had stood between him and certain death ten stories below. But it had been too fragile, it had succumbed under the pressure of Dr Kovacks' moving body, and it had let him through.

Dr Martin Drecker had hoped Dr Kovacks would have had a theory of DMT as a healing molecule. That there would be something in the DMT molecule that could potentially have a healing effect on human skin. He knew that lack of serotonin had the effect of contracting blood vessels, thus limiting the blood flow. But that wasn't what he had seen in the video. He had seen the gaping cut in Dr Kovacks' arm close by itself.

As if by pure magic, the wound had healed itself.

He sat up in the chair. Life only gave you a few chances. You could either grab them or not. He was well respected within the university and in four years' time he would retire on a good pension. He would travel; see all the places he had never had time to see when his son was growing up. Instead of taking the annual vacation to Disneyland, he could go to South America and see the sunrise at Machu Picchu.

He took a deep breath.

But had he done enough? Had he really used all his abilities in life, had he achieved what he wanted academically? Would they still talk about him ten years after he was dead?

No they wouldn't.

He had never done anything remarkable.

Just what was expected of him.

This was his chance.

His chance to do something remarkable.

To become a name people remembered.

To be remembered for decades.

He picked up his mobile phone, and dialled a familiar number.

"Cody, I need a favour," he said.

"Do you know what time it is?" his son asked.

Dr Martin Drecker looked at his watch. "Yes, it is four o'clock."

The answer didn't surprise Cody; time and etiquette had never been his dad's strongest quality. His academic colleagues had received calls at all different times of the night. If something was on Dr Drecker's mind, he called. He didn't wait.

"What do you want?" Cody asked.

"Bring your van, I need to move a bunch of boxes from an apartment in the city to the summerhouse."

-11-

A dam Mullins dropped his bag on the floor and started walking after the nurses rolling the hospital bed.

"Cameron! Cameron, are you ok?" he hollered as the nurses rolled the bed through the doors of the lift.

"Dad," the patient called again before the doors of the lift closed.

"Where are you taking her?" Adam Mullins asked with a bristling voice. The question wasn't directed at someone in particular. It was directed at the five doctors standing in front of him, two of them still wearing their green surgery masks over their mouths.

"She is not your daughter," a voice said to the left of him.

It was the stern-looking woman.

"Are you kidding me? I saw her. It was Cameron."

"How long is it since you have seen your daughter? Seven years? Would you even know what she would look like now?"

"You heard her, she recognised me."

"The kid has just been through an enormous trauma. She has survived an airplane crash that killed all of the 236 other passengers. She is in shock. She has been asking for her mum and dad for the last hour."

"She responded to her name."

"She might not even remember her real name. She acted out of reflex."

"What the hell are you saying?"

"I am saying that we tested your blood. We tested it three times. It is not a match. You are not her father."

"Bullshit," Adam cried, and pressed the up arrow on the side of the lift door. He noticed the lift had stopped at level 4. That was where they were taking his daughter.

"I have to ask you to leave the hospital," the stern-looking woman said.

"Leave? Why?" Adam asked with a frown on his face. In the corner of his eyes he could see two security guards rapidly approaching them from the reception area. One of them had what appeared to be a Taser gun in his hand.

Adam threw his hands up into the air. "I won't make any problems. I will leave now. All I ask for is for you to test my blood again."

"It won't matter. You are not the kid's father," the woman said.

"Just test it again. And give me a call when you have the result." He handed her his business card.

Adam Mullins, Personal Trainer, NYC.

She looked at the card, and nodded.

"I will ask the team to do another test. And I will personally give you a call about the outcome, either way it swings."

"I would appreciate that," Adam Mullins said.

He walked over to where he had dropped his overnight bag,

and picked it up while measuring up the security guards. Buffed up, walking like they had cactuses under their arms, protein supplements and gym muscles. It would take him less than thirty seconds to knock them both out cold.

"Is there another way out, I would prefer not to have to leave through that," he said pointing at the TV screen on the wall in the waiting room.

It looked like all the TV stations of the Western world had sent a team to the Royal Albert Hospital of Brisbane. The reception of the ground floor was buzzing with people and reporters.

"Take him out the back way," the stern woman said to the security guards.

Half an hour later Adam Mullins was drinking a ginger beer and eating a chicken sandwich at one of the local coffee shops across the street from the Royal Albert Hospital. He had just called his old army friend Matthew Parks. Due to the time difference he had woken him up. It was the middle of the night in NYC, but Matthew hadn't seemed to care. In fact he had seemed relieved to hear from Adam.

"You need to be careful," he said.

"Careful. Why do you say that? I just want to see Cameron."

"What if the hospital is right? What if it isn't Cameron? It's been over seven years, Adam. The kid was probably in shock. Scared and alone. Crying out 'dad' is exactly what you would expect a kid like that to do."

"I know," Adam said. "But I saw her eyes. It was Cameron. I'm sure of it."

"What about the blood test?"

"Screw the blood test. Doctors get it wrong all the time."

"Amen to that," Matthew Parks said.

"I'm not giving up. Not this close. I'm going in to get her."

"Please don't Adam. Please don't."

"I saw her, Matt. They said she was badly burnt. She didn't look burnt at all. She looked fine. Sedated, but fine."

"She just survived a plane crash for Christ's sake. She wouldn't be fine."

"I'm telling you, Matt. She looked totally fine."

There was a pause on the line. Adam could hear Matt breathe heavily. And he knew what it meant.

"What is it you're not telling me?"

"Nothing," Matt replied.

"Matt. Don't bullshit me."

There was another long pause. Adam knew he had to wait, wait for Matt to come to the table. Let him come there by his own will.

"This can't come out."

"You know you can trust me," Adam said.

"I have a friend in Virginia."

"CIA?"

"Yes," Matthew Parks replied. "He told me, off the record, that they dispatched a team of three agents to Australia a few hours ago."

"For what?" Adam asked.

"To interview and bring back the kid," Matthew Parks said.

"Shit, they think she is behind it. Cameron and her mom have been off the grid for the last seven years. Then she resurfaces, as the only survivor of plane crash that kills 236 passengers. They think she is a fucking terrorist, don't they?" Adam asked.

"I don't know," said Matthew Parks. "But it wouldn't surprise me if the suckers did."

-12-

D r Martin Drecker studied the face of the person sitting across his desk. He hadn't really noticed the first time they met, but she was quite a nice-looking woman. Truth be told he hadn't noticed much at all the first time he'd met her. He had been in a state of shock. One of the research professors, Dr Kovacks, had committed suicide only hours after Dr Drecker had shut down his research project.

And then she had shown him the video.

The video of Dr Kovacks injecting himself with DMT.

The video of the empty bed, with the sheet that was blowing in the wind.

The video of the wound that healed itself.

He was more in control now. More his usual calm self. She was in his office, in his domain. Where he reigned.

She reminded him of Franceska, the intern from Romania. How long was it now? Must have been almost eight years since he had to let Franceska go. She wasn't very good at her job, but she had the most delicious ass one could ever imagine. That ass had been worth it all. And if it hadn't been for the fact that his wife had started getting suspicious he would have kept her on, at least for a few more years. She had only been twenty-four, young and ripe.

"Did you get everything you needed from my assistant?" he asked.

"Yes," she said. "Your assistant has been very helpful."

"So what can I do for you?"

"It is my understanding that Dr Kovacks had worked on getting funding for his study for more than a year, and that he had been testing volunteers for more than three months."

"That is correct," Dr Drecker answered.

"Well, it is just a little bit odd. Your assistant only gave me three boxes of files. Not a lot for a year's worth of work."

"Is there any information missing?" he asked.

"Yes. Interviews with test subjects, protocols. Even the correspondence with me."

"Wouldn't most of that be in the electronic files?"

"Dr Kovacks sent letters. He took handwritten notes from the interviews. He was an old-school scientist. You should know that."

Dr Drecker nodded. "That he was indeed."

He scratched his chin before continuing. "I can have my assistant ask around the premises. Maybe Dr Kovacks used some of our storage facilities."

"That would be appreciated," the DEA agent said. "It would also be appreciated if it could be done urgently."

"Sure," Dr Drecker answered.

He got up and followed the agent to the door.

"Out of curiosity: Why is the DEA so interested in the files? I thought the case was closed. That Dr Kovacks committed suicide."

"It may be more complicated than that," the DEA agent said.

"It turns out Dr Kovacks didn't just steal the DMT he injected himself with. He stole all of it. DMT is classified as a category 1 drug. It is the same as if somebody stole a kilo of heroin from the government. This case won't be closed until we recover the DMT."

"Oh shit," Dr Drecker blurted out before making an apology for his language.

"Have you checked his apartment?" he asked.

She nodded. "Someone got there before I did, though. It has been cleaned out. Drugs and files."

"Any suspects?" Dr Drecker asked.

"We've got some leads. You shouldn't worry too much, when there are drugs involved somebody always talks. This case will be solved."

"I hope so. For the university's sake," he said. "We don't need this sort of publicity."

The DEA agent stared straight at him, as if it was a pissing contest and she wanted to see who ran dry first.

"I'll keep in touch," she said before turning around, leaving his office.

He closed the door and let out a big sigh. That had been close, very close.

But he was in the clear.

In the clear to make the discovery of the century.

-13-

Adam paid for the sandwich and left a five-dollar tip. The waiter wished him such a beautiful day that he considered continuing tipping like he was still in New York for the rest of his stay in Australia. It was great to actually get a smile when you left a tip, and not just feel that it was expected.

He stood outside in the sunshine, took a sip of his coffee, and looked at the five buildings that constituted the Royal Albert Hospital of Brisbane. He had googled the hospital on the phone while he ate his sandwich. It was recognised as the best hospital in Australia for the treatment of burns. That was part of the reason they had set it up as the emergency hospital for the crash victims of flight SQ183. That was of course before they realised that there were no survivors.

Until one passenger was found.

Three days after the crash.

What were the odds of something like that? What were the odds of somebody being a lone survivor of an airplane crash?

Adam Mullins had told the stern-looking woman he thought his daughter was alive because she was a survivor like her dad. And that was partly true. Adam had survived missions in Afghanistan that he shouldn't have.

He had fought himself out of impossible situations, survived ambushes where some of his best friends were slaughtered standing right next to him.

Adam had faced death so many times he had stopped counting.

People talked about near-death experiences, where life was replayed before their very eyes, where they saw a light in a tunnel.

Suckers. There was no time to look for a light in a tunnel.

When you were facing death, you stood up and you fought back.

You kicked death in the face.

You motherfucking put a grenade down its throat.

That was the only way you survived.

He looked at the parade of news crews standing outside the hospital. It would be hard to get into the hospital; security was maxed up because of all the news crews and the lone survivor of flight SQ183.

He had said that his daughter was a survivor like her dad, because that was what he wanted to believe. That was what he had been telling himself for the last seven years. That one day, one day he would find Cameron. That one day he would be reunited with Cameron. But he knew in his heart that survival had nothing to do with being his daughter. Death struck randomly. Adam had been lucky to survive three tours in Afghanistan. He hadn't stepped on a landmine, the bullets had just grazed him instead of killing him, and his mind was still uncorrupted – he didn't have nightmares about all the terrible things he had seen. He didn't have problems settling in to a suburban life, because he had a mission, a mission to find his daughter.

He walked over to the hotel facing the Royal Albert Hospital and booked a room for two nights. He probably didn't need it for that long, but if he was going to be successful he had to do his homework. He had to treat this as a mission.

-14-

I t wasn't much of a summerhouse, the hundred and ten square metres of wood and bricks that had been in the Drecker family since Martin Drecker's grandfather had built it more than forty years ago. The summerhouse at the Hamptons, that's what he called it when colleagues asked where he was going for the weekend. It wasn't really at the Hamptons; it was in the area, but it wasn't anywhere near the beach, nor the millionairess row where hedge fund managers and investment bankers were spending their weekends of debauchery. But he had seen too many of his university friends strike it rich. Starting up biotech companies, patenting genes, just being plumb lucky. So saying he had a summerhouse in the Hamptons made him feel good.

It levelled the playing field a little bit.

He had used to take Franceska and all the other girls out to the summerhouse. Told his wife he would have to work at the hospital all through the weekend. That was one of the perks of being a doctor. The wives were so used to doctors working odd and long hours, when they tried to establish their careers, that when they finally made it, when they started managing instead of working, when they started working regular hours instead of nights, they had all this time on their hands, all this time they could use chasing tail.

But this weekend Dr Drecker didn't intend to chase any tail. Not that it mattered anymore. He was divorced. The wife had taken the house and most of the money. All he got was the so-called summerhouse in the Hamptons, probably not worth much more than the hospital director's car. But he loved it.

His useless son had arrived at Dr Kovacks' apartment fifteen minutes after Dr Drecker's call. He knew he would. All he had to do to make his son jump was to dangle some money in front of him. He was twenty-five and unemployed. Still living at home with his mum, Dr Drecker's ex-wife. Wasting his days playing videogames and getting high. All her, none of the Drecker genes.

But he had come through yesterday. For the first time in a very long time, Cody had impressed his father. He had parked the van around the corner, found all the angles of the CCTV cameras in the area, and loaded up the van with all of Dr Kovacks' files in record time. It was as if he had done something similar before.

Dr Drecker shrugged it away. Maybe his son was a dopehead, but he wasn't a burglar.

Dr Drecker opened the first box of files from Dr Kovacks' apartment. "Outline of the DMT Study", the label on the box read.

DMT, N, N-dimethyltryptamine, a short-acting and strong psychedelic. First synthesized by Canadian chemist Richard Helmut Fredrick Manske in 1931. Dr Drecker skimmed through the objective and lifeless description of the drug that Dr Kovacks had written in his proposal for funding. He remembered how different the language had been when Dr Kovacks had pitched the proposed study in his own office. He had acted like a born-again Christian, like someone who had just seen the light.

"DMT has a presence in all of our bodies. I believe that the source of the DMT is the pineal gland. That the pineal gland produces DMT so that we can experience the world as it is." Dr Kovacks had preached.

"The pineal gland?" Dr Drecker had remarked. "I believe Descartes called the pineal gland the seat of the soul."

Dr Kovacks had smiled, as if he just had found himself another convert, another born-again Christian.

"He may have been right," Dr Kovacks had answered.

Dr Drecker should have ended the interview there and then. First rule of Science was to always be objective, and it had been clear from the start that Dr Kovacks wasn't objective. He'd had some ulterior motive for conducting the DMT study.

But instead of shutting him down, he had helped Dr Kovacks. Mentored him, advised him on how to write the proposal without all the colourful language, without all the passion and New-Age jargon.

To the surprise of both of them, Dr Kovacks had received the funding he had asked for, and he had been able to focus full-time on the research instead of teaching for the last three months.

But what was it that had been Dr Kovacks' ulterior motive? What was it that he had been looking for when he decided he wanted to study the effects of DMT on humans? Dr Drecker knew it wasn't the purpose described in the proposal, "To determine the effect of DMT as a suitable treatment for death anxiety." The thought had been that terminally ill patients could possibly benefit from a spiritual experience, that if it was possible to send patients on a safe psychedelic trip, a trip where they experienced being part of something bigger, then death wouldn't seem as such a scare anymore. The problem was of course that it was impossible to send someone on a safe trip with any psychedelic, DMT included. They could end up in a nightmare or they could end up in a blissful paradise. The problem wasn't only the dosages. Any psychedelic was as dependent on the set and the setting as the drug itself. The ultimate goal of Dr Kovacks' study was to figure out whether it was possible to come up with a perfect dose of DMT, a dose that sent a user back to the same place every time. Dr Drecker knew that wouldn't be possible, because the set and setting would always change, and thus the outcome would be corrupted. But that was how science worked. Dr Kovacks' study had to be completed to determine who was right.

Dr Drecker noticed a worn notepad at the bottom of the box. He remembered having seen it on several occasions. Dr Kovacks used to have this habit of carrying it around with him when he was at the hospital or the university. It had always seemed out of place, as it was too big to be carried around like a diary. Dr Drecker picked it up and laid it on the kitchen table. It had a brown leather covering with a small imprint in the leather itself. It looked like an eye.

Dr Drecker opened the notepad and looked at the first page.

He now understood.

He now understood why Dr Kovacks had wanted to do the DMT study.

-15-

It was dark outside, and the sky was clear. Adam Mullins looked up at the stars above him. He always found comfort in looking at the stars. It reminded him of how insignificant we were, that there wasn't anything scary about this world we lived in. We had been given an opportunity to live, maybe for eighty to a hundred years if we were lucky, and we had to make the most of it. When we died, we were no more. But if we lived our lives being scared of death we weren't really living. The only thing Adam had been scared of the last seven years was the thought of never seeing his daughter again, never hugging her, kissing her, never seeing her grow up.

Now he wasn't even scared of that. He had seen her, and he knew in his heart that they would be together again. But he had to act quickly. Matthew Parks had told him that the CIA had sent three agents to interview and bring Cameron back to the US. Most likely they would figure out that Cameron had nothing to do with the crash of flight SQ183, and let her go. But Adam couldn't risk that they took her.

Adam couldn't risk his daughter disappearing again.

He crossed the road with a brisk walk, a fresh cup of coffee in his hand. He had maxed out the withdrawal limits on all his credit cards earlier in the day. VISA and MasterCard had first declined the transactions and he had to call them up to explain that he was putting down a deposit for a time share unit in Australia. Reluctantly, they had removed the withdrawal restrictions, and Adam now had more than twenty-five thousand Australian dollars available. He figured that would be enough to stay under the radar for a while, at least until he figured out his next move.

The hospital seemed like a different place at night time. There were still a few reporters hanging out in the reception area, but most of the news crews had left for the night. They would probably be back in the morning though. People just loved air crashes with westerners involved. It was one of those accidents everybody could relate to. The fear of being stuck in an airplane when it plummeted out of the sky, the fear of sitting in the same cabin as hundreds of other doomed, screaming souls, a flying casket on the way to the ground.

Adam bumped into a tall, slender guy dressed in Lycra, rolling his expensive bike out from the reception of the hospital. He excused himself before stepping through the revolving door of the Royal Albert Hospital. He had scouted the place for several hours. This meant that the police probably wouldn't have any problems finding out who was responsible for what was going to happen in the next few hours or so – they could just review the CCTV footage – but he didn't have much choice. Security was too tight. It would have to be dramatic.

He kept his head high, and smiled to one of the nurses who passed him. It was an advantage that he didn't have to conceal his identity. It allowed him to act more naturally, to blend in without attracting attention. He had studied the blueprints of the hospital on his laptop. His friend Matthew Parks had been able to get hold of them, through the deep web. There were several ways to reach level 4, the level where they kept the emergency burn victims, but it wouldn't be easy.

Security was on high alert.

And like most hospitals, the Royal Albert Hospital of Brisbane was built like a maze. It was a good thing Adam was trained to memorize maps, to know how to move around a building based purely on what he had pre-planned, to resist the urge to follow his own intuition. Because it would be easy enough to get stuck in a dead-end in the Royal Albert Hospital of Brisbane, and he hoped to minimize the use of violence.

He walked past a cop and two security guards. They were busy arguing with a reporter.

Adam tried to visualize the blueprints of the hospital in his head as he walked down the hallway from the reception. He knew the hospital had recently built a gym for its employees, with showers and a sauna. A lot of doctors were not only workaholics, some of them also spent most of their precious hours of downtime exercising. Usually endurance sports, they seemed to thrive on pain, doctors. Adam had a few doctors as PT-clients and they all just seemed intent on punishing themselves.

Never relaxing.

Like life was supposed to be hard, like life was supposed to be filled with suffering.

Adam could relate to doctors.

He turned left and arrived at the glass door that marked the entrance to the gym. It looked like one of the many 24/7 gyms that had popped up everywhere over the last couple of years. Neat and tidy, and almost deserted. He pulled out the key card. The one he had casually nabbed from the cyclist he had bumped into outside the hospital. The cyclist had been an easy target; Lycra suit, expensive bike and helmet, and a thin, tall and scrawny body: A doctor. Probably a surgeon. Cycling home or doing a bit of exercise after having saved people's lives for fourteen hours straight.

Adam looked at the key card. It just had a name, no picture. And it would only take him into the gym. If the owner hadn't left his belongings in his personal locker, Adam would have to move to plan B.

It turned out plan B wasn't necessary. The doctor had left all his belongings at the gym. When you spent a thousand dollars to shed 500 grams of weight from your bike, you probably wouldn't want to carry non-essential items on your body. And the doctor had basically left everything in his locker. His ID, his white robe, even his wallet.

Adam undressed and slipped into the doctor's clothes. He knew the size would be a bit of a squeeze. The doctor had been the same height, but a fair bit skinnier. Luckily, he had been one of those doctors who enjoyed loose-fitting clothes. On Adam, the white robe was anything but loose-fitting. His chest was threatening to burst out of the jacket, but Adam reckoned it didn't look suspicious.

The next step in the plan was to get to level 4, not to the burn victims unit, which was in lockdown, but to the adjoining head trauma unit. He knew he wouldn't be able to pretend he was Dr

Nick Meade, as his ID-badge now read. The doctors and nurses probably all knew the surgeons, and he would probably have been better off stealing the identity of a janitor or a male nurse. But he didn't have much choice. With the restrictions that had been put in place after the arrival of the lone survivor of flight SQ183, he had to take some chances.

Adam knew that if one acted cocky enough, if one acted with enough confidence, then most people shied away from a confrontation. He had used the same strategy on covert operations in the past. Walked straight into places he shouldn't have been allowed to walk into.

People just didn't expect people with bad intentions to do that.

They expected them to be nervous, to act suspiciously.

If someone walked into a building with a smile on his face, like he belonged there, then most people let him pass.

Adam put on the light blue Crocs he had brought in his backpack. They were the only item he didn't gamble on fitting. He had large feet, and he didn't want to have to flee in small shoes. He closed the locker, attached the ID card to his breast pocket, and walked over to the dirty clothes hamper. He ruffled through the items. A few towels, a couple of white doctor coats, and what appeared to be a patient robe. He grabbed the patient robe and held it up. It looked dirty, but it would do. One less item to think about, he thought. Adam folded it up, placed it in the backpack and walked out of the gym's wardrobe.

It took him around seven minutes to find the lift to level 4. A security guard perused his ID badge before letting him in. Another security guard was permanently stationed in the lift.

Adam exited at level 4 and made his way towards the east end of the building, the head trauma department. He knew he didn't have a lot of time. He had no idea how long it would take the doctor to ride home on his bike, but he knew that when the doctor did arrive home, he would notice that his gym key card was gone, and he would most likely call it in due to the increased security at the hospital. Thus cancelling Adam's access to the doors.

Adam held out his ID-card and the indicator light on the wall turned green. Hopefully, the doctor was taking a long trip.

"Can I help you?" A voice behind him asked, just as he walked through the door.

He turned around and smiled. Instead of clipping the ID card back on his breast pocket, he clipped it onto his left front pants pocket. It would be harder for people to get a good look at it then.

It was, after all, impolite to stare at somebody's crotch.

-16-

Four hours had passed since Dr Drecker found Dr Kovacks' leather-bound notepad. It seemed like only ten minutes to Dr Drecker. He had been totally consumed by Dr Kovacks' notes, and hadn't eaten or drunk anything since he had found it. Now he realised that he was starving.

He walked into the kitchen, still carrying the notepad. He remembered having read a study about DMT by renowned psychologist Dr Richard Strassman several years ago. Dr Strassman had called DMT the spirit molecule. He had also claimed that there was a very odd coincidence between the release of DMT into the body and certain important stages in human life. He had proposed that a release of DMT from the pineal gland, forty-nine days after conception, marked the entrance of the spirit into the foetus. The same forty-nine day interval marked the point in time when the foetus differentiated into male or female gender, and the first signs of the human pineal gland started to appear.

Dr Kovacks had quoted The Tibetan Book of the Dead in his notepad. "It takes forty-nine days for the soul of the recently dead to reincarnate. Seven weeks for the soul to find a new body."

Normally Dr Drecker would have laughed it all away.

Crazy preaching by a New Age scientist.

Probably some propaganda that anti-abortion people had come up with to scare people.

But he knew what he had seen on the video. He had seen the gaping wound in Dr Kovacks' arm heal itself. What if there was more to the DMT and the pineal gland than we knew? It was a part of the brain that hadn't really been studied in depth. And why would one study the pineal gland? It wasn't even made out of brain tissue. It stemmed from specialized cells originated in the foetal mouth, and then it migrated to the middle of the brain of humans during pregnancy. The only part of the brain that wasn't really part of the brain.

The pineal gland of lizards and amphibians, evolutionary ancient animals compared to humans, was called the third eye. As the reptiles' seeing eyes, the third eye possessed a lens, cornea and retina. In humans the pineal gland didn't have any lens, cornea or retina. It was stuck in the centre of the brain. Apparently with no other function than to produce melatonin when it was dark, so that people could sleep. Why did it produce DMT? What was its real purpose in humans?

If it also was a human third eye, what was it meant for people to see?

Dr Drecker realised this was the real motive for Dr Kovacks' study of the DMT molecule; this was Dr Kovacks' ulterior motive. He wanted to know what the human third eye was meant to see. He wanted to find out whether he could fine-tune the dosage of DMT so that he could send his test subjects back to the same place every single time.

He had described it as fine-tuning an analogue TV-set, one of those TVs that people used to have before everything went digital.

If you knew the exact frequency, you could easily set the channel on any TV. But if you didn't know the frequency you would risk getting only white snow on your TV, or by accident end up on a totally different channel than the intended one.

Dr Drecker knew that some researchers, in 1964, had stumbled upon the discovery that about one percent of all the static noise on an analogue TV set was radiation from the big bang, a distant echo from the creation of the universe. When a person searched for new channels on a TV he would sometimes only get that static noise. Was Dr Kovacks suggesting that the reason people had different experiences under the influence of DMT was a tuning problem? Dr Drecker couldn't believe what he was reading. Dr Kovacks had theorized in his notepad that it was a possibility that these different worlds the DMT test subjects claimed to experience could be real, that they quite possibly could be different realms of existence.

Parallel worlds, dark matter, dark energy. He hadn't seemed sure what they really were. But he had seemed certain that they existed.

That they were real.

The problem was to get a consistent outcome. To send someone back to the same place, to fine-tune the DMT dosage so that the user ended up in the same world every time, like he'd fine-tuned a TV set to lock in the same channel every time.

And Dr Kovacks had come up with a theory on how to fine-tune the DMT dose.

He had known from the outset that he would be breaking all the rules of the DMT study.

He had come up with the number.

The magic number.

-17-

"Yes, I am looking for the bathrooms," Adam said, turning around to face the voice behind him.

"Are you new here?" the nurse asked. She was a Scandinavian looking blonde, with a big rich smile.

"Yes. First day of my secondment. I am supposed to work with Dr Stavos at level 4," he answered and took a sip of his coffee. He had googled the burn victim specialist of the Royal Albert Hospital earlier in the evening.

"The toilet is right down the hall, and to the right. But you are too late and in the wrong department if you are here to see Dr Stavos. He left two hours ago, and he is usually in the burn victims unit. I work there too. When you exit the toilets, you will have to continue down the hall and take two rights. It is impossible to miss it. Lots of security," the nurse said.

"Ah, the surviving passenger," Adam said.

The nurse nodded. "Yes, it's been a very interesting day. Nice to meet you. And I must say you've got a good taste in coffee. Blackfire is my favourite. I live next to one of their outlets. Can't function without it, " she said before walking off.

"See you around, Susan," Adam said to her back. He had

noticed her nametag read Susan Carr. She turned around and gave him an even bigger smile. "The name is Nina. I've just finished doing a shift for a friend today, at the burns unit." She smiled, unclipped her nametag and raised her right index finger to her lips. "I'll be back tomorrow, doing my own shift. I might see you then."

Adam smiled before continuing down the hall to the toilets. He stopped for a second, looked around to see if anybody was watching, and when he had established that he was alone, he entered the bathroom.

He realised that he had been reckless. He shouldn't have said he worked at the burn victims unit. If Susan, or Nina, or whatever the nurse's real name was, decided to go back to the burn victims unit she might start asking around about him. That could potentially spell trouble. She had however said that her shift was over, and hopefully she was going straight home.

The bathroom smelt of industrial soap, and the salmon-pink walls reminded Adam of the hospital in which he had spent six months recovering from his first tour in Afghanistan. God how he had hated that place. Those six months were the longest six months in his life.

He found a cubicle and locked the door. The bathroom was empty except for him.

He put his backpack on the toilet lid and opened it. He pulled out the green patient robe he had just taken from the gym's dirty laundry basket and put it on. He then stuffed the white doctor robe underneath two massive pieces of what appeared to be green clay. A pair of red and blue cables stuck out of the clay and was connected to a timer. He set the timer for three hours and left the backpack open. He then jammed the lock to the toilet cubicle from the inside, and reached his hands up to the ceiling while standing on top of the toilet seat. With a gentle push he was able to lift the mesh covering the air vent. He had studied the blueprints of the Royal Albert Hospital for hours at the hotel room. He was directly next to the serious burns unit at level 4, which shared an air flow system with the head injuries department. If there were no obstacles in the air vents, he could theoretically follow them all the way to the burns unit.

Theoretically.

Adam had been on enough missions to know that theory and practice did not always walk hand in hand.

But at least the plan had worked this far. Now he just needed to get to the toilets in the burns unit without anyone realising that there was a man crawling around in the hospital's air vent system.

It took him almost thirty-five minutes to crawl the fifteen metres he needed to get above the toilets in the burns department. He was dripping with sweat and his stomach felt like it had been through a cheese shredder. When he had done his research on the building, he hadn't been able to figure out whether the hospital could monitor airflow and temperature. He hoped they weren't able to because he was certain that he had pretty much blocked most of the airflow when he wormed himself around in the narrow tubes that constituted the Royal Albert Hospital's air duct system.

He stopped moving and held his breath for a second.

He thought he had heard a voice.

There. He heard it again. And then the flushing of a toilet.

He realised that he was directly above the toilets of the burn victims unit.

Now it was time for the tricky part.

How would he get out of the air duct system, down to the toilets, and from the toilets to the room where they kept Cameron without getting noticed?

And how would he find Cameron?

He didn't even know which room they kept her in.

He didn't even know if they still kept her at level four.

Cameron could have been moved, she could even have been moved to another hospital.

But given the level of security outside level four, Adam was pretty certain he was in the right place.

He lifted away the plastic grid covering the air vent and peeked his head down.

The toilets were empty.

He would have to go head first, there wasn't enough room to get out any other way.

When he was dangling from the roof, half his body still inside the air vent and the rest covered by the smelly and dirty patient robe he had stolen, he only had one thought: This is going to hurt, he thought as he let go and fell towards the toilet bowl. He hit the side of the toilet bowl with his shoulder and he could have sworn he heard something crack.

But when he got up on his feet, he realised that no bones were broken. He was just a bit banged up.

He sat down on the toilet bowl, pulled his knees up under his jaw, locked the door and waited.

He had made quite a big bang and he wouldn't be surprised if somebody came to have a look what was going on in the toilets.

But nobody came, and five minutes later he felt safe enough to put his feet back onto the ground.

He looked at his watch.

3:45.

The timer was set forty-five minutes ago. It meant he didn't have much time.

He walked over to the door, and slowly, trying to be as quiet as possible, he opened the door and stuck his head out into the corridor. It looked deserted. It was the middle of the night and most patients hopefully would be asleep. He could see some shadows far down the hall, behind a glass door, but they didn't seem to move. Probably some nurses chatting.

He stepped out in the hallway and made his way to the first room. He would have to check every single room to locate Cameron, and the risk of getting caught was too great for his liking. He was in the burn victims department, patients here were severely incapacitated, they were susceptible to infections and needed constant monitoring. Adam wouldn't be surprised if at least half of them had parents or relatives sleeping in a chair or on the floor of their room, not willing to leave their side for a second. Adam knew that was how he would have been.

That was why he was here now.

He didn't care if the bitch of a hospital director refused him to be near his daughter.

Nobody could stop Adam from being with his daughter.

Nobody.

He checked his watch again.

Time was ticking too fast, he had to speed up.

He opened the first door and tiptoed in. A plastic sheet covered the bed and made it difficult to see who was lying there, but Adam knew immediately that it wasn't Cameron.

It was almost as if he could feel it.

He checked five more rooms without any result, and he was now closer to the glass door separating him and the chatting nurses than he preferred. He could hear them through the door. One of them said that any interrogation would have to wait until the morning, the patient needed sleep.

With a sudden sting of fear Adam realised it wasn't a couple of nurses chatting on the other side of the door. It was the CIA agents wanting to speak to Cameron, it was the CIA agents wanting to take his daughter away. The only thing that stood in their way was a doctor who insisted on the patient having some sleep.

Adam looked up at the door number.

Room 478.

It was almost as if he knew it was the room before he opened the door.

He slipped in, barely making any noise, closed the door gently behind him, and walked slowly over to the bed.

The same plastic covering encircled the hospital bed, but the patient in this bed wasn't asleep.

She was sitting upright, as if she was waiting for something, waiting for Adam.

Adam walked over to the bedside and gently drew away the cover.

The patient, a teenager with short black hair and a face that was so pretty that it was almost criminal, looked straight at him without smiling.

"I have been waiting for you. Dad."

"Cameron? Is it really you?" Adam whispered.

Cameron looked angry. "Where have you been all these years? Mom told me you were dead."

"Please keep it quiet Cameron, I will explain everything later. You just have to come with me."

"Where is mom?" Cameron asked. Still angry.

"Everything will be explained. For now it is just important that you trust me," Adam could hear the voices in the hallway through the door now.

"There is somebody after us. We have to get out of here as soon as possible. Are you well enough to walk?"

"I feel totally fine," Cameron said. "I don't understand why I'm in a hospital. Did I have an accident?" she asked.

Adam looked dumbfounded at Cameron. She had obviously no memory of the plane crash. Or had she even been on the airplane? She looked fine. She looked unharmed. How was that possible if she had been on-board a plane, a plane that had exploded and killed all the 236 other passengers?

An explanation would have to wait though. There were three CIA agents standing outside in the hallway. They were most likely unarmed, but still dangerous. And the hospital was crowded with police and security guards.

Adam had planned a spectacular exit. He would call in a bomb threat, they would find the dummy bomb he had planted in the toilets at the head trauma unit, and in the commotion of the evacuation he would slip away with Cameron.

Two patients just wandering off.

There was no bomb of course, just two blocks of military-green clay with a couple of electrical cables attached to a digital alarm clock. Harmless, but for an amateur it looked surprisingly like the Semtex they had seen in the movies.

Plan B had to be to pull the fire alarm, and force an evacuation of the hospital. Both plans had depended on him locating Cameron first, so that he could lead her out and disappear in the chaos.

After having gone through the rooms of the burns unit, Adam had however realised that both plans were faulty.

The patients in the burns unit were kids who had just been through a traumatic experience, possibly a fire that had killed friends or family. If he set off the fire alarm he would make them all relive that fear.

And the same went for a bomb threat evacuation.

Some of the patients here would even be at risk of dying if they were evacuated. Burn victims were at high risk of getting infections, they had to be kept in completely sterile areas. Evacuating them would jeopardise their lives.

"We have to use plan C," Adam said.

"What is plan C?" Cameron asked.

"I have no idea," Adam answered.

-18-

D r Drecker took a big bite of the sandwich he had just made himself, and chewed. He could taste the cheese, the pepperoni sausage, the lightly toasted Turkish bread covered in salty butter. The taste of the sandwich felt real to him, as real as anything else in the world. But he knew that it was all an illusion. It was the brain making sense of the different spices he had just eaten. Even when he looked out the window, he didn't really see what was outside. The big tree in the garden, the old white fence and the overgrown lawn. It was all an illusion. His brain would make sense of incomplete pictures. What his eyes really saw was a big black dot in the middle of the picture, and a blurry landscape around it. The lens would send that information to the brain, upside down, and then the brain would start to get to work. It would flip the picture around so that he saw the garden the way it was supposed to be seen, and it would start rendering the picture, fill in the gaps, get rid of the blurriness, complete the big black dot in the middle of the picture with green grass and flowers. That was how the brain worked, it made everything seem effortless, but it did a job a billion computers couldn't copy. It was the most amazing machinery in the world.

What if the pineal gland, the only part of the human brain that wasn't made of brain tissue, had a bigger role to play than previously thought? What if Dr Kovacks had been right, that

DMT could be the key to unlocking unseen worlds? NASA Scientists talked about building rocket ships that could travel at speeds close to the speed of light, that this would be our way to explore the galaxies in a couple of centuries. But what if there was another way to travel, a way that didn't involve spaceships, a way that didn't involve our physical bodies?

What if the pineal gland and DMT was the solution?

Dr Drecker walked over to his fridge and opened the door to the freezer. He reached in and grabbed a plastic container.

'100% Human grade DMT' the label read.

Dr Drecker had the means to continue Dr Kovacks' studies, but he lacked one important thing. He didn't have any test subjects, and he knew from watching the video that he didn't want to test his theory on himself. That was where Dr Kovacks had failed. He had forgotten the two other essential elements of drug testing; set and setting. Something in his apartment may have scared him, maybe that hideous poster of the elephant god Ganesh he had plastered on his wall, maybe the sound of an ambulance rushing past the building? It was impossible to know. All Dr Drecker knew was that Dr Kovacks hadn't been careful enough. So he would make sure that he was extremely careful.

And that left only one choice.

One choice only.

-19-

A dam walked over to the door, put his ear against it, and tried to listen. He couldn't hear anything, the voices were gone. That could mean one of two things: Either the resident doctor had been successful in persuading the CIA agents to return in the morning, or they had simply retreated to somewhere else in the hospital where they most likely would contact someone high up in the system to get authorisation to release the patient. If Adam had to bet, his money would be on the latter alternative. CIA agents were like vultures, they just kept on pushing.

"We will have to move straight away," he said to Cameron.

Cameron jumped out of her bed. They were both wearing matching green patient robes.

Adam had planned to be evacuated along with Cameron, he had already checked the fire assembly points for the building, the predetermined places where the patients would be evacuated if faced with a bomb threat or a fire drill. And he had placed a getaway car stashed with plain clothes and food in close vicinity. With the options of setting off the fire alarm or calling in a bomb threat gone, he had to improvise.

"There is an old elevator down in the west end of the corridor.

One of the nurses, Susan, told me that they used it to send food up from the kitchen before the building was renovated a few years ago," Cameron said.

Adam looked with surprise at Cameron. There hadn't been any old elevator in the blueprints Matt Parks had sent him. But those blueprints only included the layout the way the hospital was now, not how it had been historically. It was possible that the elevator, if it existed, could still be operational. "It's worth a try," Adam said, and opened the door out to the hallway. He hadn't mentioned it, but it worried him that Cameron hadn't asked more about her mum. Just accepted Adam's word when he told her they had to flee. What had Cameron and her mum been hiding from the last seven years? What sort of lies had her mum told her that she would immediately accept that someone was after her, that they had to flee?

Cameron had been waiting for Adam. Waiting for Adam to break her out of the hospital. What the hell had she and her mum been up to all these years?

"Keep your head low, and stay behind me," Adam said as they entered the hallway. It was dark, only lit up by a few exit and fire extinguisher signs in bright neon colours. They moved quickly down the hall, staying close to the wall. Adam had no idea what had happened to Cameron, but one thing was for sure: She had never been on SQ183, the plane that crashed and killed his wife and 235 other passengers. She moved with grace, almost like she had been military trained. Silently, fluidly.

Like a shadow behind Adam.

When they finally found the old elevator shaft, next to a maintenance room, just as the nurse had told Cameron, Adam stopped to listen for sounds. Satisfied that there were no immediate threats, he picked the lock and slid open the elevator doors. It was a cramped space, barely one by one meter.

"You go," Adam said to Cameron. "The lift will take you to the kitchen."

He handed Cameron the small backpack. "It contains a pair of thongs, a shirt, some shorts and some cash. The kitchen is located next to the general admission. There should be minimal security there. See if you can make it out and meet me by the southeast entrance, next to the Coles shopping centre. I have a car there. A Ford."

"Shouldn't be a problem," Cameron said confidently. "I'll be there in ten," and with that remark she entered the lift. Adam closed the door and pressed the down arrow, marked "kitchen".

The elevator started moving.

Something wasn't right, though. Cameron hadn't even asked why Adam wasn't going to take the lift. She had intuitively understood that the lift wouldn't be able to fit Adam or even hold his weight, and had moved on. His daughter acted more professional than some of his colleagues from the military, and she was barely sixteen years old.

Shit, Adam blurted out before heading back towards the toilets. He couldn't use thirty-five minutes to get through the air ducts this time; he would have to move a lot faster.

It only took him twenty minutes to get back to the toilets in the head trauma department. He made a lot more noise, but he wouldn't want to risk Cameron being stuck outside by herself for too long. He could have asked Cameron to flee through the air ducts with him, but it was less risky if they split up. Adam had left a fake bomb in the toilets, and he had no idea whether someone had already discovered it. If they had, he would most likely be caught. But Cameron would have a relatively easy way out from the kitchen. Adam had studied the blueprints, Cameron had to go through three separate doors before she reached the stairwells that led to the basement. From there it was an easy run. She would be out in less than twenty minutes.

The only problems she could possibly encounter would be that the kitchen was manned, which was unlikely at this hour, or that the entrance to the elevator in the kitchen was blocked. If that was the case she would be stuck there. Potentially stuck in a small one by one meter room with enough air to last her a few hours.

He had to stay positive though. If she got stuck he would get her out.

Adam slid away the plastic grid and stuck his head down. The toilet was empty.

He had learnt from his less than graceful last descent, and managed to grip on to the back of the toilet before lowering himself down. He quickly changed back into his white doctor's robe before zipping up the backpack with the fake bomb.

And then he casually wandered out the toilet door.

"May I see your ID, please?" A big Maori of a security guard was blocking the hallway.

Adam was unsure whether they had found out Cameron was missing, whether the nurse had sounded the alarm of a fake doctor walking around in the hospital halls, or whether the doctor with the bike had arrived home and realised his key card was stolen. It didn't matter though. Whatever the reason was, Adam now had to fight his way out.

He walked towards the security guard while unclipping his ID card. The security guard held one hand on his Taser, the other hand on his walkie talkie just under his chin.

"Here you are," Adam said and handed the big guy his ID card. The security guard had to let go of the Taser to check the card, and Adam took the opportunity to launch himself on top of the Maori, while bringing down his palm with full force on the security guard's neck.

A normal person would have been knocked out cold. This guy was however anything but normal. He looked like he could have walked straight on to the All-Blacks, New Zealand's famous rugby team. He hit Adam in the stomach with an uppercut that left Adam gasping for air. He cracked his neck, and launched a kick towards Adam's head. Adam rolled to the side and the size-13 boot narrowly missed his head. Adam was now lying on the floor. This was not going as planned, he would most likely not be able to win a fight against this guy in a fair manner. Why hadn't one of the other security guys been there? One of the gym-junkies he had seen in the morning. Like corn-fed cattle they looked stronger than they were. This guy was pure muscle, genes of steel. Adam swirled around and kicked the back of the big-guy's ankles. The security guard's legs lost contact with the floor and 140 kilos of muscle went airborne before landing on the floor with a bang. Luckily he had a massive neck and back, otherwise he would have cracked his skull right open when he landed. Now he just looked confused, uncertain how this guy in a doctor's robe had been able to floor him. Adam moved quickly, and before the Maori realised what was happening Adam had the Taser two inches from his face.

"I don't want to hurt you, but I will if I have to," Adam said, unclipping the walkie talkie from the Maori's jacket.

"You won't get far," the Maori said. "The whole hospital is filled with security."

"I'll take my chances," Adam said before standing up. He could hear footsteps in the hallway around the corner. Somebody came running.

"You tell them to keep their distance," Adam said and strapped his backpack to his chest. He halfway unzipped it. Just enough to let the Maori see that there was a timer and what appeared to be two large chunks of Semtex inside.

"All I want to do is to get out. Don't come after me and nobody gets hurt."

The big Maori nodded. Probably scared for the first time in his life. In front of him was a threat his big muscles had no way of fighting.

A bomb.

Adam turned around and started running. He tried to visualize the blueprints of the hospital in his head. Left, right, through the door and two rights. Down the stairs and to the right again. He should be able to get out, but he would be exiting on the wrong side of the building. The opposite side from where Cameron was waiting, the opposite side from where he had left the getaway car. And there would probably be a dozen cops and security guards waiting for him. This was going shitface.

The only positive was that he was leading them away from Cameron. He had left some cash in her backpack. Enough for her to stay hidden for a couple of days, but after that she would be on her own.

On her own, with the CIA on her tail.

If she had gotten out.

Why the hell had he tried to break her out of the hospital anyway? If the CIA had interviewed her they would have realised that she had nothing to do with the plane crash.

Now, after trying to escape, she would look as guilty as O.J. Simpson.

Adam burst through the doors to the stairwell, he jumped four steps in one before sliding the railing to the bottom. He kicked open the fire door and felt the fresh night air caressing his face. He could hear shouting and people's running feet from nearly every direction. He was trapped. The only way to get out of this situation was to fight his way out.

But he wouldn't be fighting Afghan terrorists. He wouldn't be fighting military trained personnel.

He would be fighting cops and security guards.

Honest, hard-working people with ordinary jobs.

He couldn't justify potentially killing an innocent person. And that was the only way to get out of this situation.

To be ruthless, to only focus on the mission and let everybody who stood in his way be acceptable collateral damage.

He dropped his backpack to the ground and walked out into the road.

He wasn't like that anymore, he couldn't do it.

He would give himself up. Give himself up before he killed someone.

He hardly had time to jump out of the way before a black car came speeding around the corner of the building.

It looked like the Ford Falcon he had rented earlier in the day.

The getaway car he had parked on the opposite side of the hospital, on the side where Cameron was supposed to wait for him.

The door burst open and he could see Cameron sitting in the driver seat.

"Jump in," she said, looking straight ahead.

Adam did as he was told and jumped into the passenger seat.

Before he even managed to shut his door, Cameron had put the car in reverse and spun back towards the delivery area of the hospital.

"How did you know where I was?" Adam asked.

"Heard it on the radio," Cameron said. Next to the gear stick there was a walkie talkie. The same brand the big Maori had used. Had Cameron taken out one of the security guards? She was sixteen years old, how could she have possibly taken out one of the security guards?

-20-

Cody Drecker, Dr Drecker's only son was slouching on the couch in the summerhouse in the Hamptons. He was fidgeting, picking and biting his nails, scratching the label of his beer bottle. It was one of the many things Dr Martin Drecker truly regretted. He had seen it coming since Cody was a toddler. Kids took after their parents, and Cody took after his mum. He always blamed others for his own mistakes, never took responsibility. Dr Drecker had tried to crack down on the fingernail-biting as soon as he saw the first the signs – he had smeared Cody's fingers with chili pepper, put gloves on him, he had tried everything. But the little shit had continued to bite his fingernails. His ex-wife had said he would grow out of it, and in the end Dr Drecker had just given up.

It was too hard to fight it alone.

The kid had of course never grown out of it, and it still annoyed the hell out of Dr Drecker. The twenty-five-year-old deadbeat with his whole hand in his mouth. Who would ever employ him? Cody had no qualifications. He had chosen to follow his passion, to draw and paint. But what job would that skill provide for a person in the twenty-first century? Being good at drawing portraits didn't pay the bills.

Dr Drecker took a deep breath. He had to distance himself

from the negative thoughts, from all the built-up resentment. He was dependent on having Cody on his side, on trusting him, on really trusting him.

"Thanks for the help the other day. I really appreciated it," Dr Drecker said.

"No worries," Cody replied. He didn't even look up from his task of removing all the skin around his left thumb. The thumb looked red and painful.

"I was hoping to ask you for another favour," Dr Drecker started.

Cody looked up. "Yeah. What sort of favour?"

"It's a bit different from what you did for me the other day. More enjoyable I would say."

Cody's eyes narrowed.

"But before I decide whether I can give you the job, I need you to be totally honest with me."

"Ok," Cody said.

"What sort of drugs are you using?"

"Fuck off," Cody shouted, and threw his left arm in front of his face.

"Cody, Listen, I'm not an idiot. I know you are using something. I just need to know what it is."

"I'm not using anything."

"Cody, I grew up in the sixties. I have probably tried a lot more things than you have. Just be honest with me, it is not going to affect your inheritance." The comment about the inheritance was a bit below the belt, and Dr Drecker regretted it immediately. He didn't want Cody to go on the defensive.

But it didn't seem like Cody cared. He took a few seconds

before he answered.

"I smoke weed, that's all."

"You sure?"

"Of course I'm sure. I smoke weed. That's fucking all." Cody answered.

"Ok, no need to get loud. Have you tried any heavier drugs, any psychedelics?"

Cody looked at him.

"Is that what this is about? My trip to Argentina? Fuck you dad."

"What? Trip to Argentina? What the hell are you talking about?"

"I know you, Dad. Always an agenda. You have heard that Tommy and I did some psychedelics on our trip to Argentina three years ago, and now you want to question me about it. Unbelievable."

Dr Martin Drecker looked bewildered. He didn't even know that Cody had been to Argentina. Three years ago. That was when he had had the affair with Mia, the Swedish student, he was hardly home for several months. Was it possible that he had missed that his son had gone to Argentina?

"How long were you there for?"

"Two weeks," Cody answered.

Dr Drecker wiped his face with his right hand. He was tired, he needed some sleep. But it could wait.

"You didn't even know I was away, did you?" Cody said. His voice sounded hurt.

Dr Drecker shook his head. "I haven't always been the best father, Cody. I know that."

Cody smirked. "Not the best father? You have hardly been a father at all."

"I know. I've always worked too much. And I have never included you in what I do. In my work."

"That's ok. I am sure it is pretty boring," Cody said with a crooked smile.

"Argentina. You took Ayahuasca, didn't you?" Dr Drecker asked.

Cody nodded. Curious that his father knew about Ayahuasca.

"How was it?"

Cody looked a bit wary, unsure of what was happening. Finally he said: "Amazing. Got a bit sick. Threw up a few times, but the visions. For a moment I realised that I was part of something greater, something greater than myself."

"But the feeling didn't last, did it?"

"No. I thought it would though. I was so inspired the first two days. I had this whole new way of looking at the world, it was as if the true meaning of my life had finally revealed itself."

"What happened?"

"I got home, and I realised that everything was just the same. Nothing had changed. I wasn't part of anything greater, I'm just me. It is me against the world," he said, laughing.

"What if you can go back there?"

"What do you mean back there?"

"Back to that feeling, the feeling of being part of something bigger."

"Are you offering to buy me a ticket to Argentina?"

Dr Drecker grinned. "No. You don't have to go to Argentina for that. Everything is better in America."

Half an hour later Cody Drecker was lying on the couch with closed eyes. Dr Martin Drecker had just injected his son with a relatively small dose of DMT. It had been a fortunate coincidence that his son had tried Ayahuasca, or Yage as the locals called it, on his trip to Argentina in 2009. That gave him some familiarity with what to expect when he got the DMT dose. Dr Drecker had decided to give him a small dose to begin with. To get a bearing on his tolerance level, and to check whether he had any adverse reactions to the drug. DMT was considered a non-lethal drug, it was almost impossible to overdose on it. One needed to inject something like six litres to do that. And it didn't cause any craving or withdrawal symptoms. Cody would never get addicted. Dr Drecker always had thought it was strange that the United States, through the Controlled Substances Act of 1971, had classified it as a class 1 drug, the same classification as heroin and cocaine. Why would they? It didn't cause drug addiction or the compulsive behaviour that other class 1 drugs did. But he now started to wonder whether there could be other reasons behind the classification.

Other agendas.

Cody started to move his fingertips, and he briefly opened his eyes.

"Just take it easy, I'm here if you need to talk," Dr Drecker said.

He was also pleased with the fact that Cody hadn't smoked any weed for almost six weeks, and had never tried any stronger substances after the trip to Argentina. That meant that his body was clean enough to try the DMT straight away.

And Dr Drecker was anxious to test his theory out. There would probably be people who would criticize him, using his own son as a test subject. But he knew it was safe. If he controlled the drug, the set and the setting. There wouldn't be any problems. And tomorrow he would try the higher dose, the dose that Dr Kovacks so ingeniously had come up with.

He took another look at Cody's blood pressure. It was perfect. Cody's body had accepted the DMT dosage without any problems. He suspected that the previous experience with Yage had prepared Cody for the experience. A lot of people would get the feeling of dying when the consciousness separated from the body, and the natural instinct was to fight it. If one knew what to expect it was easier on the body. If one didn't fight but tried to take the whole experience in, it would be less of a constraint on the body. He knew, from Dr Kovacks' notes on previous test subjects, that it would probably take another fifteen minutes before Cody was ready to talk about his experience, so he picked up Dr Kovacks' worn notepad and started to read about Szara's tests in the mid-1950s. The problem, both Szara and later Dr Richard Strassman had encountered, was that the test subjects couldn't remember anything of their experiences if the doses were too high. Szara had tested schizophrenic patients, thus further clouding his results. Dr Kovacks theorized that if you moved beyond the threshold where the memory loss kicked in, you could reach another plateau, another threshold where the patients again would have memories of their experience under the influence of the DMT drug.

And it was at this level he had tested test subject DMTTA-67, the janitor from Brooklyn.

It was at this threshold he had injected himself that day he had jumped out of the window of his ten-story apartment.

And it was at this threshold Dr Drecker would inject his son, Cody, tomorrow morning.

"Holy crap," Cody exclaimed.

He was awake.

-21-

A dam looked at Cameron. He knew it had been seven years, but it felt like it was just yesterday Cameron had been playing outside in the garden on her ninth birthday. An innocent kid. Totally oblivious to all the pain and suffering in the world. Jumping up and down on the trampoline. The trampoline her mother had insisted needed a net. Adam had argued against it, he felt that it was important that kids learnt from their mistakes, that they got hurt when they fell off their bike or climbed a tree. How else would they learn? Kids who wore a helmet every time they got onto their scooter or needed to hold someone's hand when they walked to school, would never learn to take responsibility for themselves. When he looked at Cameron now, the once-innocent kid he had feared her overprotective mum would make weak, he realised that he had been wrong. Cameron was stronger than he could have ever imagined, and he just wished he himself would have been more protective when Cameron grew up, that he had listened for the signals, seen what was coming, and maybe then he could have prevented his wife from abducting Cameron, maybe then he wouldn't have lost the last seven years of his life.

Cameron opened an eye and looked at her dad.

"What's the time?"

"Five thirty. You don't need to get up yet. I am just a morning person, can't sleep in even if I tried."

"I'm the same," Cameron said, and wiped a bit of tiredness out of her red eyes. It was obvious that she was still tired, but she wanted to get up, she didn't want to be alone.

"I am proud of you, Cameron. You have grown up to become a wonderful person."

Cameron smiled awkwardly. She wasn't good at receiving compliments, but the words felt good.

"Who were those guys at the hospital?"

Adam considered for a moment whether he should lie; make up a story for Cameron. But he decided against it. Cameron's mum had lied to her for the last seven years, told her that Adam was dead, killed on a secret mission in Afghanistan. If Adam started lying he wouldn't be any better.

"They were from the CIA," he said.

"Why would the CIA be after me?" Cameron asked.

Adam shrugged. "I haven't figured it all out yet. But I think it may have something to do with your mother."

"They believe she was a terrorist, that she was behind the airplane crash," she said.

"That's one theory."

Adam had told her about the airplane crash before they went to sleep the previous night. That all the other passengers, including her mum, had died in a fiery explosion. At first she hadn't believed him, but then Adam had turned on the TV. She had seen with her own eyes the reports from the crash site, and she had collapsed. She had cried for almost two hours before finally falling asleep.

"It is totally ridiculous. I've been with her the whole time, for the last seven years. I swear: She was not a terrorist."

"Where have you guys been for the last seven years? I have been looking everywhere. And then suddenly, out of nowhere you show up on a plane that explodes mid-air. A wanted fugitive and her daughter travelling with a fake passport. That is the reason they think your mom was a terrorist."

"We had to travel like that. There were people after us. We've been hiding on a sailboat for the last few years."

"What people? Who were after you?"

"Mom didn't say. Just that we had to stay under the radar."

"That was me she was hiding from, Cameron. I was the one searching for you guys. I've been looking everywhere for the last seven years. I never gave up. Never."

Adam could see Cameron was about to cry again. It wasn't fair that he badmouthed her mother. Cameron had just lost her mum. She might have lied to her all those years, but she was still her mum.

"I'm sorry, Cameron. I didn't mean to talk bad about your mom."

"Did you still love her?" Cameron asked.

Adam thought about it. He wasn't really sure. Initially, when she disappeared, he wasn't even sure if she had left out of her own will. There was no goodbye letter, there had been no warning signs. She could have left because she thought they were in danger. Adam had worked a lifetime for the military on covert operations. Naturally he had acquired some enemies. They could have been abducted by one of them. As time passed and more and more clues suggested that she had abducted Cameron, that she had just packed up and left, he had started hating her, he had been so angry, so incredibly angry. But it hadn't ever stopped him from loving her. He had always secretly wished that he would find her and Cameron, and that she would explain what she had done, and why she had done it, and he would understand, and everything would be as it once had been.

A fairy-tale ending.

He nodded. "I still love your mom, I always will."

"So you haven't found yourself someone new, a new girlfriend in all these years?"

Adam shook his head. "It was never on the agenda. You are my family, Cameron. Your mom was my family. I couldn't just start over, I had to find you guys."

"And when you finally found us, mom was dead," Cameron stated the obvious fact.

Adam nodded silently. There were no words that could describe what he felt. The joy of finding Cameron, and the sorrow of realising his wife was dead, the love of his life was dead and he hadn't received an explanation for why she had done what she did.

There was no fairy-tale ending.

"How was she, how was she these last years?" he asked.

"She was brilliant. I didn't have what you would call a normal upbringing, I couldn't go to school, couldn't go into the system, but she organised private tuition for me, and we saw a lot of places."

"On a sailboat?"

Cameron nodded. "The sailboat has basically been my home all these years. I have seen most of Asia. We only arrived back in Australia three months ago. Grandy was sick and mom wanted to see her one last time before she passed.

Adam nodded. He had been to visit his mother-in-law several times over the last seven years. She had also been bewildered, couldn't possibly begin to understand why her daughter had done what she did. But it was two years since he'd last seen his mother-in-law. Travelling to Australia was expensive.

"How is Grandy?" he said.

Cameron smiled. "She is fine. Still a chatterbox."

They both laughed. She had always been a chatterbox. A chatterbox like her daughter.

Cameron got out of bed and joined Adam on the couch in front of the TV.

"So what do we do now?" she asked.

Adam looked at her.

"First we get to know each other again, and then we figure out a way to get the CIA off our back."

-22-

The sun was shining, and a stream of light gently touched Dr Martin Drecker's face, as it lay on a pillow on the worn grey couch. He opened his eyes, and peered at his watch. Seven o'clock. He normally woke up at five thirty every day, regular as clockwork. He had slept in for the first time in years. He sat up on the couch and stretched his arms towards the ceiling. His body still felt tired. But he felt good, he felt happy.

For the first time in God knows how many years, he had actually spent some quality time with Cody. And the kid wasn't as stupid as he had thought. He was actually quite like Drecker had been at Cody's age. It was just that Martin Drecker had forgotten how he was when he was a teenager, how he was in his early twenties.

He had been a rebel, a rebel just like Cody.

Searching for something, something meaningful. It wasn't until he met his wife that he had changed pace, started becoming serious, gotten a job and studied medicine on the side. Sacrificed himself to provide for his family. Sacrificed his time to climb the ladder.

Always thinking about the future.

Always thinking about his career.

He got up and walked into the kitchen, made himself a cup of coffee. A strong one.

He smiled, recounting Cody retelling his experience with DMT.

"Dad, it was amazing. I left my body. I realised how insignificant our bodies are. How they are empty shells. How everything is connected."

Cody was under the same presumption as Dr Kovacks. That what he experienced under the influence of DMT was real. A hidden realm of existence. That it was more real than the reality of his own life. Dr Drecker, of course, knew that they were both wrong. Dr Kovacks was nothing but a New Age scientist, a spiritualist who saw what he wanted to see.

And by some fluke, Dr Kovacks had stumbled upon a scientific discovery.

A discovery that was going to make Dr Drecker famous.

He had discovered that if you released the exact right amount of DMT into the bloodstream of a human being, the body gained the ability to heal itself.

One didn't travel to a different world, a parallel universe or any other of those ludicrous theories Dr Kovacks had written about in his notepad. One just plain and simply gave the body the ability to heal itself.

This wasn't uncommon in nature. If one cut off the tail of a lizard, a new one would grow out again. It could take a while, but a new limb would eventually replace the old one.

Reading through Dr Kovacks' notepad, Dr Drecker had realised that the function of DMT production in the pineal gland may not be to allow the mind to see different worlds. Dr

Kovacks had studied the stages in human life where the DMT release into the body was at its highest; when the gender of the foetus was decided, at birth, at death. And he had inaccurately predicted that this was due to the fact that the spirit travelled between bodies at these points in time. The DMT production had nothing to do with the souls of humans though. That was a massive misunderstanding. The pineal gland would produce DMT at these particular points in life to attempt to heal the body, to generate the gender, to protect the foetus at birth, to try to salvage the body at death.

The DMT production of the pineal gland was our species' counterpart to the regeneration of limbs in lizards.

And he was about to prove it on his own son.

"Cody. You awake?" he shouted from the kitchen.

He could hear a rustling from the bedroom. Cody was awake. He was probably eager to try another dose of DMT. To go back to feeling part of something bigger.

Well, after this day, he would be part of something bigger.

He would be part of Dr Drecker's breakthrough discovery.

The point in time when Dr Drecker revolutionized how we would treat human injuries.

The most important discovery in humanity since the discovery of penicillin.

"I'll be out in two seconds dad," Cody said.

And for the first time in many years, Dr Drecker was glad to hear Cody call him dad.

For the first time in many years he was proud of his son.

For what he was about to do.

"Wake up, Cody. God damn. Wake up."

Dr Martin Drecker was shaking his son, slapping his blue face.

"Can I get your location?" the voice on the phone asked.

"77 Hillcrest Avenue, Southampton Village," Dr Martin Drecker shouted to the phone lying on the floor, next to the couch. The hands-free was on, and a woman from 911 was on the other line.

"We will have someone there shortly. Just hang in there, and try to open your son's airways," the voice said calmly.

Dr Drecker put his hand on Cody's chest and felt for a heartbeat. There was none. White foam started coming out of his mouth.

"Shit, his heart just stopped," Dr Drecker shouted.

"Do you know how to do CPR?" the voice asked. Still calm.

Dr Martin Drecker didn't answer. He rolled Cody off the couch so he landed on the wooden flooring. He needed a harder surface underneath him when he started the CPR.

"1, 2, 3," He started calling out the times he pushed Cody's chest. Keeping count.

"You are doing well, we will have someone there shortly," the voice said. But Dr Martin Drecker wasn't listening. He didn't even notice that one could hear sirens in the background.

All he could think about was that he had just killed his only son.

He had killed Cody.

And for what?

To become famous?

To become rich?

A tear fell down on Cody's blue chest.

Dr Martin Drecker hadn't even noticed, but for the first time since he saw Cody being born, he was crying.

-23-

Adam and Cameron had talked together for the last three hours. Cameron had talked about how she and her mum had been sailing through Indonesia, the Philippines and Thailand, looking for this Shaman who was supposed to live there. Her mum had never really explained why she was looking for this Shaman, just that it was important that they found him. Adam was astounded to hear about everything Cameron had experienced, living with local farmers, trekking into the jungle with elephants. She had lived the life of an explorer, an adventurer. But he also realised that Cameron had missed almost her entire childhood. Never had any long-term friends, always been on the move, never staying more than a few months in each place.

"Do you miss them, your friends from New York?" Adam asked.

Cameron smiled. "Sometimes. I sometimes wonder how their lives have been, if we would still be friends if I went back."

"Of course you would still be friends," Adam said.

Cameron shook her head. "I would be so different from them. I realised a couple of years ago that I have stopped playing with other kids. I gravitate towards the adults. I don't see myself as a kid anymore. I haven't in years."

How sad, Adam thought. But he realised it was the sacrifice of living a life on the run, to never settle down, to never allow yourself to set roots or have friends. His daughter had been robbed of her childhood.

"Well, it's about time for us to move. I'm just going to make a phone call, and pick up a few things from the store. Watch some TV and I will be back in half an hour."

Cameron nodded and turned on the TV.

Adam let himself out of the motel room, and walked down the alley towards the rental car he had organised the day before. He had paid in cash and used fake names when he booked the room, but the owner had insisted that he brought down the passports in the morning. It was the law. It meant they had to leave straight after breakfast. He didn't have any fake ID's they could use, and it wouldn't take the CIA long to pick up on any trail Adam and Cameron left behind.

He picked up his phone and dialled the number to Matthew Parks, his old friend from the military.

Cameron was watching the news on channel nine. A reporter was standing outside the Royal Albert Hospital of Brisbane. Dozens of ambulances were parked outside. A bomb had gone off inside the hospital the night before, and killed thirty-seven people – four patients and thirty-three staff.

Cameron turned the volume up.

"It is a sad day here at the Royal Albert Hospital. Shortly after five o'clock this morning a big explosion rocked level four of the hospital. Thirty-seven people are so far confirmed dead and four critically injured. In a twist of fate the sole surviving passenger of flight SQ183 is confirmed as one of the deceased. At this point in time the authorities are not certain what caused the explosion, but they are said to be investigating the possibility of a gas leak."

The live broadcast was cut and the broadcast continued from the studio. A broad-shouldered man in a grey suit was interviewed about the possibility that the explosion was linked to the airplane crash.

"It is a curious coincidence that there has been an explosion in the same hospital, in the same building and on the same level on which the sole survivor of flight SQ183 was being treated. No terrorist organisation has so far claimed responsibility for the crash of SQ183, but I expect that to happen shortly. This was a demonstration of power. A statement. The terrorists have basically said, you cannot escape from us, we will hunt you down, we will get you."

Cameron turned the TV off, and got up from the couch.

"What do you mean, Matt?"

"I can't talk to you anymore, Adam. It's not safe. If we ever talk again, you have to assume that I have been corrupted."

"Why?"

"Because they will find the leak, they will figure out I was the one who told you they were coming for the kid."

"Coming for Cameron, my daughter's name is Cameron."

"She is not your daughter, Adam. You should get out of there as soon as possible. Give up, hand her over to the authorities."

"Are you insane?"

"Trust me Adam. Trust me on this," Matthew Parks said, and hung up.

-24-

The police station smelt like old mould. No, it was something different, like a wet dog, it smelt like a wet dog. They had kept Dr Drecker in the interview room for almost two hours. He had hardly said a word. They had asked if he wanted to see a lawyer, but he had waved them away. He would confess to whatever they charged him with. He had just killed his son. He didn't care.

It was obvious they considered him a suicide risk. They had removed his belt and anything else in the room he could potentially use to end his miserable life. And that was what he intended to do as soon as he got a chance. He would end his life.

Put himself out of his own misery.

What did he have to live for anymore?

He had no wife, she had left because he was always whoring around.

He had no job or career. The minute the university found out what he had done he would be sacked and stripped of all respect.

He didn't even have a son anymore.

Cody may not have always made him proud, but he had been his son. Although he always criticised him, deep down he loved him more than anything in this world.

He realised that now.

And he had just killed him.

Given him a drug overdose.

Killed his own son.

His own flesh and blood.

He didn't deserve to live.

"Has he said anything?" a tall man in a black suit asked. His features were fine. Broad shoulders, thin waist. A chiselled jaw.

The police officer shook her head.

"He doesn't want to talk, doesn't even want to see a lawyer. But there shouldn't be any problem getting a confession out of him. He keeps mumbling to himself. Saying he deserves to die. Saying he killed his son."

"We will take over from here. Thank you for your assistance, Officer."

The police officer shrugged her shoulders, and handed the brown manila folder to the CIA agent. If they wanted the case that was ok by her. She had more important cases than a deranged university professor killing his own son in a failed drug experiment. But she did wonder why the CIA was interested. Almost as soon as she had entered the case file into the system, she had received a phone call. And she had been asked to stall the interview until some agents arrived. She hadn't listened to the request of course, it had piqued her curiosity, and she had gone straight into the interview room and started to ask Dr Martin Drecker about what had happened. He had just been rambling. Said that he had wanted to solve human healing, to enable the body to regenerate, maybe even create immortals. Then he had shut down. Stopped talking. Just started mumbling to himself. That's when she decided to strip him for his belt, and remove any other potential hazardous equipment from the interview room. This guy was a nutcase, a suicidal nutcase.

"Dr Martin Drecker?" The tall CIA agent had, almost without making a sound, entered the interview room.

Dr Drecker looked up. But he didn't answer.

"I work for the government, I work for the CIA."

Dr Drecker looked up. DMT was a category 1 drug. He had expected to see the DEA, not the CIA.

"I want you to come with me."

"Just give me a statement, I will sign it, I don't care. I stole the DMT. I killed my son. I don't deserve to live," Dr Drecker shouted towards the CIA agent. He had always constrained himself, never lost control. He had lived his whole life like that. But it didn't matter anymore. His life was over.

"I know you are having a tough time. I might be able to make it a bit better."

"Are you able to give me my son back? Are you able to undo what I have done?" Dr Martin Drecker looked back down at the table.

"Maybe, maybe I am," the CIA agent replied.

Dr Martin Drecker lifted his head from the table and stared at the agent. Trying to figure out whether the CIA agent was having fun with him.

He couldn't tell from the CIA agent's expression.

It was cold and emotionless.

And for the first time since he'd injected the fatal DMT dose into his son's vein, his mind was clear.

Clear as ice.

Had the agent just said he might be able to give him his son back?

Was Cody still alive?

Had the hospital been able to resuscitate him?

-25-

Cameron was already packed and ready to leave when Adam walked into the room.

"We don't have time for breakfast," Adam said.

"I know. I'm ready," Cameron replied.

Adam looked at his daughter, studied her. Was she tricking him? Was it possible that the person in front of him wasn't Cameron? It had been seven years.

Nah, he shrugged it off. It was Cameron. He could see it in her eyes; it was the same eyes he had been longing to see for all these years. And the stories she had told, how she and her mum had travelled around in Asia, looking for some Shaman. The story was just too incredible to make up.

"Everything ok?" Adam asked.

"You should have a look at the news before we go," Cameron replied.

Ten minutes later they were buckled up in the car, and on the highway. Adam realised that his friend Matthew Parks had been honest when he told Adam to get out of the situation as soon as possible. Whoever it was that were after his daughter, whoever it was that were after Cameron, had just killed thirty-seven people and wounded dozens more. Who was it Adam's wife had been trying to hide Cameron from all these years? Who was it who would kill thirty-seven innocent people? And Adam knew that they had been killed, he knew a good cover-up when he saw one. The news report had said that Cameron, the sole survivor of flight SQ183 had been killed in the explosion. They hadn't used her real name of course, they had used the fake ID she had booked her ticket under. And when they listed all the other casualties from the explosion, Adam had noticed another familiar name.

Dr David Savos, the burn victim specialist that the nurse had told him left the hospital just after one am. Why would he be dead in an explosion that happened several hours later? Someone was cleaning up, someone was covering their tracks. Did they think Cameron had seen something on the airplane, that Cameron could represent a threat to whoever was behind the explosion on-board flight SQ183? Was it really a terrorist act, or was it something else?

He had no idea, and he had just lost his only source of information. His friend Matthew Parks had basically told him that there was no point contacting him again, if he did, he should assume the information was corrupted.

Cameron was sleeping in the passenger seat, it had only taken her a couple of minutes to fall asleep. The kid was exhausted. Adam looked at his green military bag in the back seat. After the call to Matthew Parks he had stopped by a pharmacy. In a moment of doubt he had picked up two DNA self-test kits. He had decided not to use them though. He didn't care what Matt had said, he didn't care what that bitch of a woman at the hospital had said. Cameron was his daughter. There was no question about it. But he needed to know what had really happened last night, he needed to find out who was after them, and why they were after them. And during the last few minutes he had come up with a plan. It wasn't a good plan; a good plan would have been to put as many miles as possible between himself and whoever was after them. To drive north or west, into the big outback that no one had overview over. Instead, he found himself driving back towards Brisbane, back towards the Royal Albert Hospital. He thought back on how he had been able to get into level 4, the nurse who had told him the way to the toilets. He had called her Susan, and she had said that it wasn't her real name. That she was just finishing a shift for a friend.

That she would be in the next day for another shift.

Her name tag.

'Susan Carr'.

The name had been on the list of deceased people from the explosion. But she was about to finish her shift, she would have gone home a long time before the explosion went off. The people who supposedly were killed in the explosion, they were all people who had dealt with Cameron, they were all people who had dealt with the lone survivor of flight SQ183.

Why was that?

What had they seen that could be so dangerous for someone?

-26-

The big grey building seemed to rise out of nowhere in front of them. They had only been driving for four hours, but they seemed to be so far away from New York City that they might as well have been in a different country.

"What is this place?" Dr Drecker asked. It was the first time he spoke for more than an hour. He had been sitting in the back seat, consumed by his own thoughts, riddled with guilt.

"It is your new home," the agent in the front passenger seat replied casually. He had been silent as well. He hadn't made any promises, just hinted that there was a chance Dr Drecker might be able to see his son again. Dr Drecker didn't understand what it really meant. Cody was either dead or alive. Why couldn't they tell him which it was? But he also understood why they might choose to keep the facts from him, it was a big difference in the charges if Cody ended up dying, as it would be manslaughter. If he survived, Dr Drecker might only be charged with the drug theft. Cody would be able to confirm he had willingly taken the drug. Or would he? Dr Drecker had told him that it was totally safe, that it was non-toxic, non-lethal, didn't cause addiction, withdrawal or craving. He had sold his own son the fairy tale story of a class 1 drug.

What kind of dad did a thing like that?

What kind of sick fuck did a thing like that?

The agent had said that the building in front of them was his new home. It didn't look like a prison, more like a hospital. Was that where they were taking him? To an asylum? Had he turned mad? Did they think he was insane?

He looked down at his hands, down at the handcuffs. They were tight around his wrists, had made small spots of red come through his skin when he had tried to wriggle his hands out. It was of course impossible. He had learnt that lesson when Franceska, the crazy Romanian intern, had tied him up to the bed post in the summerhouse one weekend. She had humiliated him, taunted him, tortured him. At first he had been afraid, he didn't know what she was capable of, what was really going on in that crazy brain that sat on top of that divine body. Then he had let himself go, he had immersed himself in the experience, and he had learned that it was what he had longed for all those years. To be dominated, to not be the boss for once, to not be the one who had to make all the decisions, to be the one who was told what to do.

It had brought them even closer, Franceska and him, but it had also made her more dangerous. Suddenly their relationship was different, they were more equal, and that was never a good thing.

The driver parked the car, stepped out and closed the door. The CIA agent turned around and faced Dr Drecker. It was only the two of them left in the car.

"I shouldn't have to tell you that what you will see here today, and over the next few weeks, is top secret. We have brought you in because we find ourselves in a bit of a conundrum, and we could need your help."

Dr Drecker looked confused. He didn't understand what the agent was talking about. Was he about to be put in jail, a mental hospital? Or was there something else going on?

The CIA agent reached over the centre console and grabbed Dr Drecker's handcuffs.

"Don't do anything stupid," he said, and unlocked the handcuffs.

Dr Drecker nodded. Still confused, but at least he was rid of the handcuffs.

"This building was erected in 1974. It is part of a program called MKULTRA. Have you ever heard about it?"

Dr Drecker nodded. He had heard about MKULTRA before. It was a classified project that was started by the CIA in 1953 and cancelled in 1973, after the Watergate scandal. Its mission had been to explore fringe ideas, bizarre experiments like mind control and telekinesis. At one point in time almost six percent of the CIA budget went to MKULTRA, and during its heyday it had funded 44 universities, and a range of hospitals, prisons and pharmaceuticals. But for all the billions of tax dollars that were spent on the black projects of MKULTRA, not one single piece of practical applicable science ever emerged.

"I thought MKULTRA was cancelled in the early 1970s," Dr Drecker stated, matter-of-factly.

"Officially yes. The original program was a disaster. No accountability, no adult supervision of the scientists. One part of MKULTRA was, however, never closed down, it couldn't be. It was kept off the books, and supervised by the CIA. It was to address one matter only, a new threat to America."

Dr Drecker looked at the CIA agent with fear in his eyes. What had really happened this morning? Did Cody take the drug, or had Dr Drecker taken it himself? Was he having a bad trip, was he getting paranoid? This was how mad people talked. About conspiracies, about secret government agencies.

Oh my god! It just dawned on him. He was going mad, he was going complete nutters.

He decided not to say a word more. If he was going mad, if this guy in front of him wasn't a CIA agent, but maybe a nurse in a mental institution, or a prison guard, the best thing he could do was to keep his mouth shut. To not say another word, and then to take the first opportunity he had to off himself, to kill himself before the madness took full control.

"I can see that you have problems grasping what I'm trying to tell you. So let's just jump into it. Let me give you a guided tour."

The CIA agent stepped out of the car and walked around to Dr Drecker's side. He opened the door and a ray of light hit Dr Drecker's face. He could feel the warmth of the sun, it felt so real. How was it possible that everything could feel so real in this state of madness he found himself in?

"This is where we keep our patients," the CIA agent said. They were standing on a ledge and peered down at two rows of glass cages. Dr Drecker could count five people dressed in white robes inside the first row of cells. The second row was empty. The people were all standing straight up inside their own glass cage, facing Dr Drecker and the CIA agent. They were wearing white robes that covered them from top to toe, and their hair appeared to have been shaved off. They didn't move. Just stood there and observed the CIA agent and his guest. They didn't seem drugged, and they didn't seem like they were dangerous. But Dr Drecker understood something was wrong. It looked more like a hospital than a mental institution. But that was what it was. Dr Drecker had understood as much. He had gone mad, and was being put into an institution.

"So where am I going to live?" he said.

"You will be staying with the rest of the scientists, we have another building next to this one. It is quite luxurious. You won't be wanting for anything."

Dr Drecker nodded again.

"And these patients. Why are they here?"

"I thought you had understood that by now," said the CIA agent. "They have all taken DMT. They have all seen it."

-27-

"Why do you think she lives here?" Cameron asked, peering out of the window of the Ford her dad had hotwired at an abandoned parking lot two hours earlier.

"She said that she could smell my coffee, that it was from the same coffee shop near where she lived."

"And?"

"I bought that coffee from the coffee shop across the road from the Royal Albert Hospital, from a chain called Blackfire. They only have five shops in the Brisbane area. I googled it. If you take away the coffee shop outside the hospital, which is in the middle of a high density office area, and the three shops that are located inside big shopping centres, you are left with this one: The only Blackfire coffee shop you could possibly live close to."

"Who would have known. My dad is a detective," Cameron said with a smile.

Adam laughed, but he knew it was a longshot. The nurse could have mistaken the smell of the coffee, she could be at the hospital, working another shift, or she could possibly be dead, with the authorities mistakenly identifying her as Susan Carr, as she was the one who was supposed to be at work.

"Well, let's get to work," Adam said, and opened the door. He wore a black baseball cap, a pair of dark-blue shorts that stopped just before the knees, and a Quicksilver T-shirt. Just a regular Aussie bloke.

Cameron stepped out as well. She was dressed in an almost identical outfit, but it hadn't been intentional. They had walked into two different clothes shops, and come out dressed the same. She dressed almost like a boy. To Adam that was evidence enough. There was no doubt. Cameron was his daughter.

"Were do we start?" Cameron asked.

"We start in the coffee shop. If she can remember the smell of coffee, odds are that she is a regular," he said, and pointed towards the Blackfire coffee shop.

They had already agreed that Cameron would do the talking. Adam had an imposing figure; he didn't look like a bodybuilder, more like a professional swimmer. Broad shoulders, slim and slender waist. But he had those eyes, those clear, blue eyes that could see straight through people. It was a good quality to have when you wanted information, but not when you asked for the whereabouts of a woman you only had a vague description of. It could look like he was trying to track down an ex, or something like that.

Cameron walked over to the coffee shop and straight up to the counter. There was no one else in the queue, so she ordered a long black and a cappuccino.

The young, male barista smiled to her when he prepared the coffees.

"A colleague of my dad told me you guys have the best coffees in Brisbane," Cameron said, leaning over the counter.

"That is so nice to hear. We try our best. We even source or own coffee beans from Columbia," he said, smiling.

"Wow, that's amazing," said Cameron, before she continued. "She also said that you make cracking banana bread."

"Sure do. Do you want to try some?" the barista asked.

"Actually I might get some. My dad's friend Nina lives just down the road. She is a nurse at the Royal Albert. My dad and I were supposed to pick her up this morning. But we don't have the exact address, and the battery on my phone is dead."

"He is a friend of Nina?" the barista asked.

"Yes. Do you know her?"

"She is a regular."

"Do you know which building she is in?"

Suddenly the barista became a bit cautious. It was ok to mention a customer's name. Not so ok to tell a stranger where the customer lived. But she was just a kid. Probably not more than fifteen. And she had known Nina by her first name.

"I am not sure, but I have seen her go into the building across the street. That grey one on the corner," the barista said, pointing out the window.

"Thanks heaps. I'll get my dad to ring the doorbell. Saves me getting late for school."

"You don't have to wear a uniform to school?" the barista asked.

Cameron realised her mistake. All schoolkids wore uniforms in Australia.

"No, it's Mufty day. Can dress however I like," she said, paid for the coffees and the banana bread, and walked out. She could feel his gaze at her back when she closed the door to the coffee shop, but she thought she had gotten away with it.

It only took her a couple of minutes to find a 'Nina' on one of the doorbells. There were two other names on the nametag, so she probably shared the apartment with some friends. Cameron walked back to the car where her dad was waiting.

"There is a Nina Winter living in apartment 12. She is a nurse at the Royal Albert Hospital."

"Great work, Cameron. I'm impressed."

"As I said, I haven't gone to school the last couple of years, but mom did home-school me. I have a different set of skills than most kids my age."

Adam saw that the mentioning of her mum had struck a chord in Cameron. Her eyes teared up a little bit before she turned her head away. And it dawned on Adam that he hadn't really let Cameron grieve the loss of her mother. Instead he had abducted her from the hospital, told her that someone was after them, and they had been on the run since. He had done the exact same thing his wife had done.

He was no better than his wife.

He scratched his chin.

Adam felt sorry for Cameron, but there was nothing he could do about that right now. Priority one was to find out why someone was chasing them. Why someone had eliminated all the hospital staff who had been in contact with his daughter.

And the answer was right in front of them.

Nina Winter.

The nurse who had been working Susan Carr's shift yesterday.

The name of the nurse who had been on the list of casualties from the explosion at the Royal Albert Hospital of Brisbane.

"It is too dangerous to wait around here. We will have to get into the building, get into her apartment," Adam said.

"Easy peasy," Cameron said.

It only took fifteen minutes before someone exited the apartment building and Cameron got the opportunity to sneak through the open door. Five minutes later Adam and Cameron stood outside the apartment door of Nina Winter.

Adam knocked on the door. There was no answer. He knocked again. Still no answer. He pulled out a paperclip and a screwdriver from his left pocket. He had come prepared for this. He had picked his fair share of locks in his military career.

Just as he inserted the straightened-out paperclip into the lock they heard a noise from inside the apartment; it sounded like glass breaking. Adam immediately realised that he wouldn't have enough time to pick the lock. If Nina Winter was inside, she would be calling the police right now. He took one step backwards and lunged against the door. It was a relatively thin fire door and it caved in like there was no resistance. He went straight through it and tumbled across the floor. When he looked up, a woman in her pyjamas holding a big meat knife in one hand and a mobile phone in the other stood staring at him. She looked scared to death. "You..." she said, frantically pressing the buttons on her phone.

"Put down the phone, Nina," Adam said as calmly as he could, rising from the floor.

"It's you," she repeated. It didn't appear that she was listening to Adam, and he knew he had to take action. He lunged forward and grabbed the knife. With a quick flick of his wrist it dropped out of her hand. With the other hand he grabbed her phone and hung up. It looked like she had just dialled 000, but he was unsure whether she had actually managed to get through.

"We don't have much time, Nina. You have to come with us."

"You murdered them. You murdered them all," she screamed. And then she froze.

It was as if she had just seen a ghost.

Cameron had entered the room. And she just stood there, gazing at Nina with her big innocent blue eyes.

Seven minutes later they were hurtling out of the quiet suburb of Western Brisbane when they noticed the lights. Two police cars were heading straight for them. Instead of stopping, though, they raced straight past them and didn't stop until they hit the curb of the grey building on the opposite corner of the Blackfire coffee shop. The young barista looked out the window and knew that his gut feeling had been correct. There had been something off about that schoolkid. No uniform, too young to drink coffee. He had kept an eye on her when she left the shop. Watched her walk over to the grey building, then study the nametags for a while before returning to a parked car where a tall man had been waiting. He looked like a police or something, but he wasn't wearing a uniform. He was dressed almost identical to the young kid. In dark-blue shorts and a white T-shirt.

When they had snuck inside the apartment building, when one of the other residents had gone out, he definitely realised that something was off. But what could he do? He was still in his probation period at Blackfire coffee shop, it wouldn't look good if he called the police, and nothing wrong had happened.

He had decided to look the other way.

When he saw the four policemen, with weapons drawn, exit the police cars, he realised that he had made the wrong choice.

-28-

D r Drecker had finally concluded that he wasn't going mad. It was the American government that had gone mad. He had been on a guided tour of the MKULTRA complex for the last two hours. First he had to sign a stack of papers, confidentiality agreements, security clearances. It all seemed so organised, as if they had expected him for months.

"We kept an eye on Dr Kovacks when he started at your university. He was part of the LSD group here at MKULTRA in the late 1960s and early 1970s."

"So the Connecticut Prison Study was part of MKULTRA?"

The CIA agent nodded.

"A disaster like most other projects the organisation did at the time. But we learned a lot about psychedelics. They may not have cured the psychopaths, but they had other benefits."

"Like what?" asked Dr Drecker.

"They allowed us to have a glimpse of potential threats."

They walked over to a wide door, and the CIA agent keyed in a code before he faced a camera that scanned his iris. The door opened and they entered a white room.

"Stephen Hawking once said that if we ever encounter an alien civilisation it will be more advanced than our own, and hence pose a threat to our very existence."

Dr Drecker nodded. You only had to look at human history to confirm the hypothesis. The Spanish invaders annihilated the South American Aztecs in a matter of months in 1521, and the way the English had colonised the rest of the world didn't leave a lot of hope for humans to ever meet a friendly alien species. And that was how humans treated other humans. If we looked at how we treated species we thought were beneath us on the food pyramid, like chickens or cattle, Earth would be a very hard place to be if we ever encountered aliens with human traits.

"You are in the belief that psychedelics can give humans a glimpse of alien worlds?" Dr Drecker asked. He understood that the CIA agent had the same belief as Dr Kovacks. That the visions of people who tried DMT were real, that they actually visited other realms of existence.

"We are way past beliefs. We have evidence," said the CIA agent, and opened another door.

"Look at your son," he said.

In front of them was a hospital bed. On top of it was Cody, Dr Drecker's only son. He was naked, and had multiple instruments connected to his chest.

"What are you doing with him? What are you doing with my son?" Dr Drecker cried as he ran towards the bed. He grabbed Cody's hand and squeezed it. It was freezing cold.

The CIA agent looked at his watch. "It has only been 24 hours. You need to wait another 48 hours. Then you will have your son back. And then you will start working for us."

-29-

The traffic was running smoothly. They were on their way out of the city, while most commuters were on their way into work.

Adam looked over at Nina Winter, the nurse from the Royal Albert Hospital. She was still shaking, still sobbing, but she had calmed down.

It had taken Adam almost ten minutes to convince her that she would be safer with them than with the police. They had been dangerously close to getting caught. He realised that he would have to act quicker in the future, make tougher decisions. Her reluctance to believe she was in danger could have put them all at risk, and he couldn't afford for that to happen.

"Take it easy. Take deep breaths," he said.

"I can't," she sobbed. "They are all dead. They are all dead."

Adam nodded. Calming down a hysterical woman was not one of his best skills. The last time one of his colleagues in the army had a panic attack, Adam had punched him in the face. The shock of the punch was exactly what his colleague had needed. He had lost his leg in an explosion, but it didn't help sitting down screaming. Screaming wouldn't get his leg back. The important thing was to focus on the mission. To complete the mission and get back to base as uninjured as possible. The foot was gone. Nobody could change that. He considered slapping her in the face. Not a punch like his colleague had received. Just a gentle slap. A slap to get her to focus. But he rejected the idea.

"What happened at the hospital yesterday? Did you see anything special?"

Nina Winter laughed a hysterical laughter.

"I saw the kid in the back seat. That's what I saw."

Adam frowned.

"What do you mean?"

"The list of deceased people. The list of dead people from the hospital. It's the whole team who looked after the kid you've got in the back seat."

"Why on Earth would someone kill everyone who was in contact with a survivor of an airplane accident?" Adam asked.

The nurse turned around.

"Why don't you ask her that question?"

"What do you mean? Did something special happen yesterday?"

"You mean, did someone wake up from the dead?"

"What the hell are you talking about?"

"Tell him. Tell him what happened," the nurse said to Cameron.

"I don't know what you're talking about. I woke up at the hospital. I don't remember anything from the airplane crash."

"Well, that's convenient."

Adam stepped on the brake, and the car skidded to a halt in the middle of the deserted road.

"No more bullshit. Tell me what you saw yesterday," he said, facing Nina.

She wiped a tear away from her eyes, before turning her head to face Adam.

"At first I thought it was a miracle. A survivor from the crash. Then I realised that she had no injuries. Who survives a plane crash without a single injury?"

She sobbed, before continuing. "They said she was brought in with burns. That she was close to dying. They were wrong, weren't they? She didn't have any burns. When we started cleaning her wounds, the blood just washed off, and the skin underneath was fine. It was new."

"What are you saying?"

"I'm saying that whatever you have in the back seat is not your daughter. It's not even human."

PART 2

-30-

D r Drecker was still in shock. There was no way he would have believed the CIA agent if it wasn't for the fact that he had shown him Dr Kovacks. The CIA agent had taken Dr Drecker to another room, packed with another ten prison cells made out of glass. Dr Kovacks had been sitting in one of the cells, dressed in a white robe. He had been wearing handcuffs and looked tired. When he saw Dr Drecker he hadn't even met his eyes, just turned his head away – as if he was ashamed.

The CIA agent had explained that the bureau had kept tabs on everyone conducting experiments with psychedelics since the 1960s. They had been surprised when Dr Kovacks had received approval for his study to test whether psychedelics could be used to ease death anxiety for terminally ill people. The DMT study had slipped through the cracks and had somehow been approved without the CIA being able to intervene. As the proposed dosages of DMT had been lower than 0.5mg/kg, the CIA had considered it less risky to let the study proceed than to create possible media attention by retracting an approval already granted by the FDA. Considering Dr Kovacks' history, the monumental disaster he had created with his LSD project in the Connecticut Prison Study, the bureau had however decided to keep a close eye on him, and on the study itself. They had in fact caught the whole incident, when Dr Kovacks injected test subject MDTTA-67 with a dose of more than 1.5 mg/kg, on film.

"So why didn't you intervene? If you knew Dr Kovacks was going to breach protocol, why didn't you stop him?"

"We wanted to see what happened."

"Wanted to see what happened. How insane is that? You knew he could possibly kill civilians, and you still let him go through with it?"

"Look around you, Dr Drecker. There are a lot of empty glass cages here. We don't have a lot of volunteers in this hospital. The five patients you saw earlier today were test subjects from an MKULTRA study conducted in the early 1970s. After that study not a single US president has allowed any new test subjects. The only new patients we have received since then are Dr Kovacks' test subject MDTTA-67, and your own son."

Dr Drecker looked at the CIA agent.

"Did you know I was going to inject Cody with DMT?"

The CIA agent shook his head. "No, we didn't even know that you stole the DMT. We had Dr Kovacks under surveillance, but the agent on call didn't pick up on the significance of what happened that morning. He had listened to so many strange stories from test subjects over the last three months that he simply thought that test subject MDTTA-67, the janitor from Brooklyn, was yet another lunatic. Talking about alien abduction stories or visiting heaven. All that crazy stuff."

"So what happens with Cody now? You claim he will wake up from the dead. Do you really want me to believe that?"

"You saw Dr Kovacks' body four days ago. Do you doubt he

was dead? You were the one identifying him at the morgue."

"His whole face was smashed up. I can't be sure. It could have been someone else."

"Fair enough. You deserve an explanation."

The CIA agent pulled out a folder and put it on the table in front of them. "The US government started experimenting with DMT back in the early 1960s. We didn't, however, get a breakthrough until 1974."

"Phi?" Dr Drecker asked.

The CIA agent nodded.

"Yes, we had been trying out different dosages for years. The aim back then had basically been to attempt to see whether we could awaken something dormant in the human brain. The ability of telekinesis."

"You thought you could get people to move objects with the power of thought?"

The CIA agent smiled. "It sounds silly now, but those were the priorities back then. People high up in the government were convinced that the Soviet Union was doing the same, so they spent billions on beating them to the mark. The studies were of course worthless. We understood quite quickly that telekinesis would be impossible because it contradicts basic laws of the universe."

The CIA agent sucked on a toothpick.

"So how did you come up with Phi?" Dr Drecker asked.

"It was actually Dr Kovacks who gave us the idea. Back then he was busy with his LSD study."

"The Connecticut Prison Study," Dr Drecker said.

"Correct. We funded the study, but kept in the background. It was off the books. The study was considered fringe from the outset, but we needed to focus broadly."

"So the CIA was responsible for all those psychopath murderers being released from prison, just to go out and kill again?"

"That was the unfortunate part of it. Nobody had actually considered that any psychopaths would be released. Being a psychopath was not considered a treatable mental illness back then. These guys were supposed to remain in jail indefinitely, until they died. But with Dr Kovacks' help they started to appear in front of parole boards, and with the learned behaviour, with the ability to fake emotions and empathy, they were let out one by one. They were set free."

"You are saying it was the parole board's fault?"

"Who cares whose fault it was? The important thing is that we learned one crucial thing from that experiment."

"And that was?"

"To never let a psychologist lead a science project. Dr Kovacks became emotionally involved. He wanted the best for his test subjects."

"And you don't? You just look at them as test subjects?"

"I am not a scientist, Dr Drecker. You however, are. You are a neurologist. A brain scientist, trained to make decisions based on logic, not wishy washy feelings."

"What makes you say that?" Dr Drecker said.

"Why else would you use your own son in an experiment," the CIA agent said bluntly.

Dr Drecker didn't know what to answer, and there was an awkward silence between them.

It was the CIA agent who finally broke it.

"We look at them as opportunities. We look at the test

subjects as opportunities to solve the enormous tasks that will face humanity in the not-so-distant future."

"And what tasks would that be? What tasks are so important that human life doesn't seem to matter?"

Half an hour later they were standing outside Dr Kovacks' cell.

"Dr Kovacks came up with the theory that Phi, the Divine Number that is found so many places in nature, could have other special properties. He theorized that a dose of LSD, measured based on Phi, could possibly create the same LSD experience every time." The CIA agent laughed. "Of course, an LSD dose based on Phi would kill an elephant so he quickly scrapped his plan. But we used his theory on a new DMT experiment and the results were astonishing."

The CIA agent knocked on the glass window to Dr Kovacks' room.

"We had already learned from his mistakes. We couldn't take the risk that any of the test subjects were ever released from prison, so we tested the theory out on prisoners on death row."

"You gave prisoners on death row DMT?"

"Don't act so surprised, Dr Drecker. You helped Dr Kovacks write up his DMT study proposal. In fact you convinced him to write that the purpose of the study was to see whether it was possible to ease death anxiety for terminally ill patients. We gave DMT to people who knew they were going to get executed within months. What's the difference?"

Dr Drecker shrugged his shoulders. There really wasn't much of a difference.

The CIA agent continued:

"We gave them extremely high doses, up to 3 mg/kg without any breakthroughs. And then we gave them Phi, we gave them exactly 1.618 mg/kg, and we had our epiphany."

"You saw them self-heal?" Dr Drecker asked.

The CIA agent shook his head, and smiled.

"No. I believe that Dr Kovacks was very lucky when his test subject hurt himself during the experiment. None of our test subjects hurt themselves. They just died."

"Died?"

"Yes, like Cody. Most of them died about half an hour into the experiment."

The CIA agent took a long pause.

"And then, three days later, they scared the shit out of the morning shift at the morgue."

Dr Drecker stared at the CIA agent with a confused look.

The CIA agent continued:

"They all resurrected three days later." The CIA agent said.

"They returned from the dead?"

"Yes," the CIA agent said. "Like our saviour Jesus they stood up three days later and walked out of their grave. But let me tell you: These guys were not like Jesus."

"I don't believe you," Dr Drecker said.

"You don't have to. You will witness it with your own eyes." He looked at his watch. "What time did you do the DMT experiment with Cody?"

"Nine thirty," Dr Drecker said.

"Well, we should head back up then. You don't want to miss this."

-31-

They had been driving for almost two hours. No one had said a single word. Adam was fuming inside. He was angry with Nina, the nurse. She had no right to accuse Cameron the way she did. He should have thrown her out of the car, head first. That's how the old Adam would have handled the situation – made a quick decision, the right decision without hesitating. Instead he found himself thinking about consequences. If they dumped Nina, she would most likely be dead within a few days. She had no training in hiding from whoever blew up the hospital, no skills that would help her stay under the radar. He would in reality be handing her a death sentence. And he wasn't willing to do that.

It was his fault that the CIA, or whoever else it was that had killed all the hospital staff from level 4, was after her. If Adam hadn't broken out Cameron they would probably still all be alive. Or would they? He couldn't understand why someone had killed all the hospital staff. What could they possibly have witnessed that could justify such an operation?

Why go through the immeasurable risk of killing so many people?

He turned on the radio, to get a bit of relief from the silence. Cameron was sleeping in the back seat, she was sleeping a lot.

"I'm sorry," Nina Winter said.

Adam looked at her. She looked frail. "It's ok. We have all had a tough day. It is easy to say things you don't mean when you're tired."

Nina nodded. "I am just so afraid. I don't understand why this is happening. Why someone would kill all my colleagues."

"I'm still trying to figure that out myself," Adam said. "But I can assure you that there is nothing alien about my daughter in the back seat. She is one hundred percent human."

Nina laughed a nervous laughter. "I guess it is natural to fear the unknown. We were all so excited when she arrived, the survivor. Then it turned out she was unharmed under all the ash and dead skin. All her vitals were normal. It was a bit creepy. And then we heard rumours that she had woken up at the morgue. That the corpses from flight SQ183 were lined up in a refrigerated room when one of the body bags just started to move. It is just too hard to comprehend. Nobody wakes up from the dead," she said.

Except one, Adam thought. They had argued about this often when Cameron grew up, he and his wife. Adam was an atheist, and his wife a Catholic. Adam didn't want Cameron to be brainwashed by religious teachers before she was old enough to make up her own mind about creation or evolution. But his wife had wanted to put her into a Catholic private school. It was a tough decision. The private schools were better, but they did preach a lot to the kids. The public schools were not as good, but at least they were a bit more open-minded about religion and science. In the end his wife had won the argument, and they had sent Cameron to Kings Cross Private School.

Adam was afraid his worst fears had come true when Cameron

one day, barely six years old, started preaching about Jesus. His wife had laughed it away. Kids that age change their mind every week, she said. And she had been right. The next week Cameron came home and said she didn't believe in Jesus anymore, that it was all a made up story. And so it went on. She kept changing her mind. One day a believer, the next day not.

The story Nina Winter had just told made Adam wonder. He didn't believe in Jesus or the creation myth. But was it possible that some people could resurrect, that someone could come back from the dead? Cameron seemed unharmed. Except for sleeping and eating a lot, and having some extraordinary abilities when it came to breaking out of hospitals, she seemed totally fine. Like just any other teenage girl. How was that possible if she had been in an airplane that had exploded ten thousand metres above the ground?

"There must be other lone survivors of airplane crashes. Other incidents where only one survived and beat the odds," he said.

Nina Winter nodded. "That was the first thing I did when I got home from my shift. I looked up lone survivors from airplane crashes on Google. It turns out there are less than sixty lone survivors from plane crashes around the world, and no one has ever survived a crash with more than two hundred fatalities. Your daughter is a statistic impossibility."

"The fact that it has never happened before doesn't make it impossible," Adam said.

"Flight SQ183 didn't crash. It blew up in the air. Do you know what sort of forces an explosion mid-air set in motion? The plane would go from 800 kilometres an hour to an almost standstill, the deceleration alone would be enough to kill the passengers.

Then you have hypoxia, the plane was at a height of 10,000 metres when it blew up. They would lose consciousness or die within seconds. And then you have the blast itself, the moment flight SQ183 blew up and the following impact when the plane hit the ground. Four separate reasons why no one would be able to survive the crash. Four separate reasons that this was an unsurvivable accident."

"People have survived unsurvivable things before," Adam said.

"Maybe, but how do you explain her waking up in the morgue?"

"I have no idea," Adam answered.

Nina Winter looked out the window.

"I know one thing though. She might seem strong now, but all this sleeping. It is her way of coping with the stress on her body."

"What do you mean?"

"Lone survivors have a very difficult time adjusting to normal life after their accidents. There is no one they can relate to, there are no survivor groups, no support, nothing. We've had a few of them in the burns unit over the years I've been there. I would say that almost all of them suffer from survivor guilt, blaming themselves for surviving when no one else did, blaming themselves for what they did or didn't do when the accident happened."

"But Cameron doesn't remember anything from the accident. She says she just remembers waking up at the hospital."

"That's her mind trying to shield her from reliving the terror of the accident. But her memory will come back. And you will have to be there to support her when it does."

Adam stared out of the windshield, lost in his own thoughts.

"Were there other kids? Were there other lone survivors who were kids?"

Nina Winter turned towards Adam before replying. "A few. Statistically, flight crew and kids have a higher probability of being a lone survivor."

"So kids are more likely to survive an airplane crash?" Adam asked.

Nina Winter nodded.

"Nobody knows why though. Maybe their will to live is just stronger," she said, and stared out the window.

-32-

Tears were rolling down Dr Drecker's cheeks. It was as if the crying, the crying when he thought Cody had died three days earlier, had opened up something inside him. Before that it had been twenty-five years since he had last cried; he hadn't even cried at his parents' funerals. And now twice in a week.

"I will let you have some time together," the CIA agent said before leaving the room.

Dr Drecker looked up at him with gratitude in his eyes. The CIA agent hadn't lied. Regular as clockwork, Cody's heart had started to beat again at 9:34. The exact same time his heart had stopped three days ago.

Dr Drecker wasn't religious, but today he had witnessed a miracle. Something unexplainable. Something that contradicted the laws of the universe. His son Cody had come back from the dead.

"How are you feeling?" Dr Drecker asked.

"Tired," Cody said before attempting to sit up in the bed. He pulled on some of the cords that were attached to his chest.

"Don't. Just rest," Dr Drecker said.

"Where am I?" Cody asked.

"I think the question is: Where have you been?" Dr Drecker said.

-33-

The sun was setting when Adam pulled into a driveway along the Bruce Highway. Red dust swirled up around the car while he navigated it up the bumpy road to an old Queenslander house.

"Do you know the people who live here?" Nina Winter asked.

Adam shook his head. "No."

"Then why are we stopping? Shouldn't we be moving, getting as far away from Brisbane as we can?"

"We can't continue in this car. The police probably already have an APB out for it."

"You're planning to steal this family's car?" Nina asked. She had a terrified look in her eyes.

Adam nodded towards the green and rundown shed in the overgrown garden.

"If Walter White hasn't used that motorhome, I think it might be our new home for the next couple of days."

Nina looked out the side window and saw a grey motorhome, with a big FOR SALE sign in the window. It looked old and rusty.

"You want to buy that?" she asked, pointing.

"Think about it. We won't need to check into any hotels, we

can stay out of populated areas. We can stay off the grid long enough to figure out why all this is happening."

"I'm not sure," Nina said.

Adam could see it in her eyes. She didn't know either him or Cameron well enough to appreciate the thought of sleeping in the same room at night, let alone the same car."

"Don't worry. I'll pick up a tent as well. You can sleep in the motorhome. I'm used to sleeping outside," Adam said. It was the biggest understatement of the day. He had slept more nights outside than most avid campers. So much so, that he almost preferred the hard surface of a paddock than a cushy hotel room bed."

Nina smiled, to show that she appreciated his consideration.

It didn't take Adam long to negotiate a good deal with the farmer. A decade of drought had put a strain on farmers in the area, and cash-in-hand was well appreciated. Adam handed over eleven thousand two hundred dollars, almost half of his cash, and got the keys and a can of oil in return.

It struck him that he was doing exactly the same his wife had done. She had kept Cameron stowed away on a sailboat for the last seven years. Always moving around, never staying long enough in one place to get comfortable. Would this be Cameron's new life? Moving around in a motorhome? Crossing the deserted towns of Australia in an old rundown motorhome?

"What do you think?" Adam asked Cameron.

Cameron didn't smile. "What's our plan? I have been hiding for most of my life. From what I have no idea. But I know one thing. I'm dead tired of running. I want to know what I'm hiding from."

Adam folded his arms across his chest.

"I can promise you one thing, Cameron: I won't let anybody hurt you. I will find out why someone is after you, and who they are. And when I find them, Cameron, I will take care of them."

Cameron looked at her dad with a distrusting face before turning around and stepping into the motorhome. She had probably heard the same speech before.

Nina Winter followed Cameron inside and closed the door.

Adam was left outside by himself. He walked over to the black Ford Falcon, opened the door to the driver seat. He pushed down the accelerator with a piece of wood and jammed it up against the seat. The engine revved and the sound of 260 horsepower, waiting to be let loose, filled the air. He leant in and pushed the automatic gearstick into drive, and the car took off. He watched it pick up speed, for a good thirty metres, before disappearing over the edge of the cliff they had admired the view from only moments earlier. He could hear the splash when it hit water, a good fifty meters farther down, and he knew that it would take weeks, maybe months before someone would find the wreckage.

He walked over to the motorhome and slid into the driver's seat. Cameron had been right though. They couldn't just continue to run. They had to find out who was after them, and why they were after them.

He knew that the CIA wanted to question Cameron. But maybe the CIA was in Australia for a particular reason? Maybe they also were after the people who had been hunting his wife and daughter for the last seven years? Maybe the CIA was hunting the very people who were behind the explosion at the hospital and the killing of all the hospital staff?

-34-

"Thank you. Thank you so much for giving me my boy back," Dr Drecker said to the CIA agent. He was still teary although he had left Cody almost an hour ago.

The CIA agent tightened his tie, and straightened a pile of documents on the desk in front of him.

"Don't thank me just yet," he said.

"What do you mean?"

"I mean: Don't thank me yet. Your son is not safe yet."

Dr Drecker stared confusedly at the CIA agent. Was he threatening him?

The CIA agent pushed the pile of documents across the table before he started to talk.

"As I said, we kept tabs on Dr Kovacks and the study. And that means we also kept tabs on you," he said, pointing the finger towards Dr Drecker. "There is a reason you are not already in jail for what you have done."

The CIA agent started to list all the possible charges:

"Breach of science protocols, theft of a category 1 drug, breaking into a private property, simple theft, obstruction of a police investigation, administering a category 1 drug to your son.

Do you want me to continue?" he asked.

Dr Drecker stared down at his feet. He had almost forgotten that his life was over. He would lose his job at the university, he faced bankruptcy and jail time. But at least he had Cody. He hadn't killed Cody. That was the saving grace, the only thing that kept him going.

"No, please stop," he said. "I know what I've done. And I'm ready to take responsibility for my mistakes."

"Here is what's going to happen," the CIA agent started. "You will resign from the university immediately. You will not speak to anyone about your reasons for quitting, and you will start working here tomorrow."

"Working here?"

"When I said we had kept tabs on you, I meant it. We have had our eyes on you for a while. The director has kept mentioning your name. Saying that we needed a good neurologist, a new research director on our team. And now the opportunity has presented itself." The CIA agent smiled.

"What would I be doing?" Dr Drecker asked.

"You would be saving your own son," the CIA agent said.

Dr Drecker felt drained of energy. He was used to being in control, to always having control. That was why he had craved those weekends away with Franceska, the Romanian intern. Her role plays, her dominant alter ego, had given him a brief refuge from his compulsive need for control, his need to control every little detail of what went on at his research division. Right now he was craving that control again. He had never been more confused than he had been for the last few days. Not knowing what the CIA agent was talking about, not knowing whether Cody was dead or alive, not knowing what was reality or not. He felt he was going mad. It was as if his head was about to explode.

"What do you mean?" he asked.

"Have you heard about The Book of The Dead?" the CIA agent asked.

Dr Drecker nodded. The book he had found in Dr Kovacks' files. The Buddhist book that claimed the spirit left the body after death.

"Then you know that the cycle of death is 49 days. It is 3 days since Cody died. You have 46 days left to save him."

Dr Drecker stared at the CIA agent.

"What do you mean? Are you saying that Cody will die in 46 days?"

The CIA agent nodded.

"I told you about the prisoners on death row, the MKULTRA DMT Experiment. We didn't have to execute those prisoners. They may very well have come back from the dead after three days. But 46 days later they were definitely in hell. Back in the hell where they belonged." The CIA agent smiled.

-35-

Adam found a phone booth in the next town they were driving through. He knew it would be under surveillance. Unless one was a drug dealer or a hit man there really weren't any reasons not to use a mobile anymore. If the Australian police had half a brain they would have CCTV coverage of all the phone booths in Australia. He keyed in the phone number to his friend Matt Parks and waited for the dial tone. Matt had said that Adam should assume that he was compromised the next time he called, that somehow they would have found out that Matt had been speaking to Adam.

"Adam," Matt answered. He probably didn't receive too many calls from Australia.

"Just a quick call, Matt. Just wanted to say thank you for being my friend all these years. I have found Cameron. We are together now. I am happy now. Goodbye my friend," Adam said, and held the phone out from his body.

He could still hear Matt on the other line. Repeating his name several times. With an increasingly worried voice.

Adam hung up the phone and walked over to the bus station. He had checked out the CCTV camera earlier, and it was conveniently positioned to show both the phone booth and the ticket office. Adam bought three tickets to Sydney with the Greyhound Express and paid in cash. He then wandered over to the local Tavern. Well inside, he walked straight through the gaming area and into the toilets. He mounted one of the toilets and manoeuvred his 190 centimetres of muscles through a rectangular window. He was out in the back alley within minutes, and proceeded to jog quickly over to the motorhome which was parked nearby with the engine running.

"I gave my friend the message. He will most likely try to contact me within a few days. Until then we need to stay under the radar. Any suggestions?" he asked. Nina Winter was Australian and probably knew the area much better than he. And Cameron was already a seasoned fugitive, having been on the run with her mum for the last seven years.

"We can probably stay with Grandy," Cameron said.

"I thought you said she was dying."

"She recovered when mom and I went to visit her," Cameron answered.

Adam laughed. "Is she still at the farm?"

Cameron nodded.

"Nearly eighty years old and she still runs a farm. She has always been a machine."

Nina smiled. "Hiding out on a farm sounds better than driving around in this crap. Cameron has my vote."

"Then to the farm it is," Adam said, and put the motorhome in gear.

There was a risk that the CIA had figured out that Cameron's grandmother was living in Queensland, and that it was one of the most likely places they would try to hide out. But Adam also knew his mother-in-law. She had always been suspicious of authority. Adam had known what he'd married into. His mother-in-law had been off the grid for several years when Adam met Cameron's mum. She didn't pay taxes, she produced her own electricity from solar panels, and she got water from her own well. Adam should have known that it was in his wife's genes. This need to stay hidden, this need to be off the grid.

-36-

The blinds were almost fully closed, and only a few small stripes of sunbeams hit the desk in front of Dr Drecker. He had always preferred to work without a view, without any distractions. His best office had been at a now-demolished building in East Village. A small hospital where he had started his career in the medical profession. The office had been located in the basement, in an old bomb shelter. He would arrive early in the morning, before the sun got up, and leave late in the evening, a long time after the sun had set again. He wouldn't have a clue whether it had rained or been a sunny day, whether people had been eating ice creams or drinking hot chocolates. And that had been the way he liked it. Sealed off from the rest of the world, allowed to completely immerse himself in his work. He had wanted to change the world back then; he had envisioned himself as someone who would make a breakthrough discovery. Then eventually he had realised that it wouldn't happen, that his mind hadn't been built for discoveries, that his real talent had been in management. Management of other brilliant people. And at that he had excelled, rapidly moving up the ranks until he was officially rewarded with the title Director of Research.

That was more than twenty years ago. That was the last promotion he had ever received. His life had stagnated after that. And now these CIA guys, these MKULTRA guys, wanted him to do practical research on DMT. He who hadn't done practical research for decades.

He wasn't optimistic.

But they had given him an incentive.

A very good incentive.

If he didn't figure out a solution, his son would be dead in 46 days.

He looked at the chart in front of him. It was a PET scan of a brain. The brain of somebody just labelled Patient E.

It looked normal, with the exception of the enlarged pineal gland in the middle of the brain. Dr Drecker had seen thousands of brain scans throughout his career, but he had seen nothing like this.

He held up the scan of Patient D. Almost identical. The pineal gland seemed to be twice, maybe three times the size of a normal pineal gland.

He looked through his notes again. He knew that the pineal gland shouldn't grow in an adult human. Yet these patients, whoever they were, all had grossly enlarged pineal glands. The CIA agent had explained that there had been no new test subjects available after the MKULTRA project in 1974, where they had tested injections of 1.618 mg/kg DMT on five death row prisoners. Injections of Phi, just as Dr Kovacks had done on himself and the janitor from Brooklyn, just as Dr Drecker had done on his own son Cody.

He punched in Patient B on the computer screen, and got a list of all the tests that had been conducted on him. The list went on for several pages. The poor guy had been tested since the early 1970s. Who were these patients? The CIA agent had said that the death row prisoners all had died after 49 days, so it couldn't be them. There had to be other test subjects. Other test subjects whom the CIA agent hadn't told Dr Drecker about.

He pulled out the image of his own son's brain. And put it next to the two other ones. It was almost identical.

Somehow the DMT injection, if measured at exactly 1.618 mg/kg, led to a rapid growth spurt of the pineal gland. The DMT that rushed through the body had proven to have a healing effect on at least two subjects, Dr Kovacks and the janitor from Brooklyn, test subject DMTTA-67. In all the cases, at least according to the CIA agent, the DMT injection was also lethal. All the death row prisoners and Cody had died almost instantly and Dr Kovacks had committed suicide. But what had happened to the janitor? Test subject DMTTA-67? The test subject Dr Kovacks first injected with the lethal dose of DMT?

Dr Drecker grabbed the PET scans and walked over to the door. The CIA agent had told him he would be a pair of fresh eyes in MKULTRA. Instead of briefing him on all the events that had happened over the years of study, information that could lead him into the same thought pattern as the other scientists working there, they would keep Dr Drecker in isolation. Let him make his own discoveries. And when needed they would brief him on his exact questions.

"What happened to the janitor?" Dr Drecker asked. He had barged straight into the office of the CIA agent.

"What happened to knocking?" the CIA agent asked.

"Won't happen," Dr Drecker replied. "Occupational hazard. Haven't knocked in thirty years. Won't start now. And don't expect any apologies if I call you at night either."

The CIA agent smiled. "Fair enough. The janitor is in cell twelve. Three cells down from Dr Kovacks."

"But the janitor didn't die from the DMT injection. He survived. He holds the answer."

The CIA agent shook his head. "None of the test subjects died from the DMT injection."

"What are you saying?" Dr Drecker asked. "I was there. I saw Cody stop breathing. I felt his heart stop."

"Cody didn't die from the DMT injection. He died from swallowing his own tongue. The janitor died ten minutes after leaving your hospital. Walked straight out in front of a semi-trailer."

"Are you saying they all committed suicide?"

The CIA agent nodded.

"The same thing happened with our death row prisoners. They all committed suicide. And there was nothing we could do about it. The research team tried to strap them down, remove any dangerous objects. Nothing helped. Within a few hours of the DMT injection they were all dead. They were all dead by their own hand."

"But why?" Dr Drecker asked.

"Honestly, we don't know. We have a theory, but we want to hear your thoughts first. That is the whole point of bringing you in. A fresh pair of eyes."

"What I think? How can I have an opinion? I never met any of the death row prisoners."

The CIA agent got up from his chair and grabbed his keychain.

"Let's see what we can do about that," he said, and walked straight past Dr Drecker.

-37-

I t would take them another eight hours to get to Adam's mother-in-law's farm. They were all extremely tired, and Adam decided that it was best that they called it a night. He turned into a caravan park and parked the motorhome next to a large RV. He could have just found a spot along the road and parked there, even an empty parking lot next to a supermarket. But he found it safer to stay out in the open, to hide in plain sight. Drunk drivers always made the mistake of taking the less trafficked roads home from the pub. They were all deceived by the false assumption that there were also fewer cops on those roads. They were of course wrong. If you tried too hard to hide, you would eventually be found. Those chasing you weren't stupid. They always tried to anticipate your next move. So if you wanted to stay hidden you had to act irrational, do things they didn't expect. Adam had another motive as well. He needed to use the internet. They had worked out this system, his old army friend Matt Parks and he. If one of them at any stage in their lives happened to be in trouble and needed the other one's help, they should just say a final goodbye on the phone. The goodbye was the signal to only communicate electronically from then on. They had set a system up for this specific purpose a few years back. Adam knew that electronic correspondence probably wasn't safe either. It had been revealed that the NSA was listening in on most phone and email correspondence throughout the world. If they used the wrong words in their messages, it was likely that their correspondence would be intercepted by some automated program trawling through billions of messages every day, looking for the right keywords. But he had no other options. He needed to find out why the CIA was chasing Cameron. It couldn't be because they thought Cameron had been involved in the airplane crash. If that was the case, who was it who blew up the hospital? It didn't make sense. No, there had to be something more to it.

It had to be more complicated.

He left the motorhome and sat down outside on the steps. He took out the iPad he had bought from the son of the farming couple who had sold him the motorhome. The kid had happily accepted the payment of five hundred dollars; it probably meant he could upgrade to a newer version and still have some leftover change. Adam hadn't cared. All he needed was something to access the internet with. The kid had said that he had installed a free VPN service, Hola, on the iPad, so that it looked as if he was based in the US whenever he accessed the internet. Adam didn't think it would be enough to fool the NSA, but he left it on.

You never knew.

He accessed the free WIFI of the caravan park and logged on to Spideroak, a cloud storage company like Dropbox, but with the increased security of user access only. Even if the NSA wanted to check out Adam's files, Spideroak wouldn't be able to access them. In fact Spideroak would have to go to a judge to obtain a warrant to get the unique encryption key directly from Adam. And the account was also of course set up with a fictitious name, so Adam would have a long time to delete files should they ever try to get hold of the fake accountholder. Adam trawled through the folders before finding the document he was looking for. It was over four hundred pages long, more than a hundred thousand words. He found the top of page 126 and wrote his message. Then he saved the update and logged off.

When Matt Parks logged on, he would read the message and reply on page 94. It was a cumbersome system, but he hoped that the text would be concealed by all the other useless information in the document. There were no emails going back and forth, just a shared document being updated by two different users. And the document being updated was in a format that didn't allow tracking of changes.

The caravan park was rundown, but had a prime location. It was one of the many things that amazed Adam about Australia. How they had managed to leave most of the prime locations to caravan parks, to cheap accommodation for people without massive travel budgets. In most other countries these parcels of land would have been auctioned off to developers, who would have turned them into luxury apartment blocks or hotels for the rich and famous. Not so in Australia. The best spot on the beach always belonged to the caravan park. He got up from the steps and stretched his legs. He had picked up a tent from a BCF outlet a few hours earlier and he looked forward to a nice sleep under the stars. Nina and Cameron could have the motorhome. There were two beds in there, so they would have plenty of privacy.

"Can I have one of those?" Nina said pointing to Adam's six-pack of VB stubbies.

He smiled and handed her the one he had just opened. It sat in a small stubby holder with the Australian flag on it. The stubby holder had come with the motorhome.

Adam folded out three green camping chairs and lowered his body into one of them.

Cameron came out a couple of minutes later and asked if she could have a stubby too. Adam wasn't sure what to say. He hadn't been a dad for the last seven years. There had been no need for him to set ground rules for Cameron as she ventured into her teenage years. And now she asked for a beer. She was only sixteen, but she had been through more than most sixteen-year-olds had been through. She had just lost her mum, and just rediscovered her dad. What was the appropriate way to say that she would have to wait another two years before she could have a beer?

Luckily, Nina beat him to it. "It's probably best you don't drink any alcohol. We don't want to attract any attention. And you're still under the legal drinking age."

Cameron nodded before going back inside. There was no point in arguing. They had to stay as inconspicuous as possible, to attempt to blend in with the rest of the campers.

"Is she ok?" Nina asked.

Adam shrugged. "I think so, I'm a little bit out of practise with this parenting bit. When Cameron disappeared with her mom, she was only nine years old. She is a teenager now. I have no idea how to treat her."

"It will come to you," Nina said, and placed a hand on his shoulder. "Children don't come with instruction books, you just have to do what comes naturally."

"That's the problem," said Adam. "It doesn't feel natural anymore." He got up from his chair and folded it up. "I'm going to call it a night. We've got a big drive ahead of us tomorrow." He grabbed the tent and walked off to the side of the motorhome.

Nina was sitting by herself, looking at the stars.

Wondering why she felt so lonely.

-38-

"So they've been here the whole time since 1974?" Dr Drecker asked.

"The DMT injection causes the patient to commit suicide. Sometimes immediately, sometimes delayed, but always within a few hours. The other effects are more predictable. Exactly three days after a person dies from a Phi injection of DMT, he will resurrect. For the next 46 days he appears to be normal, with the only exception that his body has gained the ability to heal faster. Not as fast as the janitor and Dr Kovacks, who both cut themselves when the DMT levels in their body were close to the divine level of Phi, but a lot faster than normal people."

"And what happens on day 49? You asked me if I had read the Buddhist Book of the Dead. I have, and it says that the spirit leaves the body on the 49th day. But that is not true, is it? The death row prisoners are still alive. It is their files I have in my office. They are the patients with only an alphabetical identifier."

The CIA agent smiled. "Yes, you are correct. Patient B, which you hold the PET scan for in your right hand, could be said to still be alive. At least his body could be said to be alive. Now let us go through his file on the way down to see him."

It took them barely ten minutes to walk down to Patient B's room, enough time to go through the entire file.

Patient B, Douglas Eugene Brown, was born in 1945 and was of African-American origin. He had been on death row for almost five years when he was enlisted for the DMT project in 1974. He had been found guilty by an all-white jury for strangling his son and ex-girlfriend in front of his former mother-in-law. When he had finished suffocating his family he had put a bullet in his mother-in-law's head and torched her house. The mother-in-law miraculously survived, with a calibre .22 bullet lodged in her left temple. There had been no doubt about his guilt. People had been cheering in the streets when he was handed the death penalty.

"This can't be the right person," Dr Drecker said. In front of them stood a young athletic African-American, Dr Drecker would guess his age was about thirty.

"On the 49th day all our death row prisoners died. But their bodies didn't die a normal death. Somehow, something else, something we don't yet know what, occupied their bodies. And their bodies stopped aging."

"Are you saying that the person in front of me, the person behind that glass is an alien?"

The CIA agent shrugged his shoulders.

"All we know is that it isn't Douglas Eugene Brown anymore. It is something else."

"Can I talk to him?" Dr Drecker asked.

"Sure. You have free access to talk to the patients. As long as they stay in their cells. We have safety protocols in place for a reason. Just follow them and you will be fine. But don't get your hopes up. The patients stopped talking a long time ago. They chose to stop talking," the CIA agent said, and walked off.

Dr Drecker knocked on the window and stepped closer to the microphone.

Patient B turned around and fixed his gaze on Dr Drecker.

There was something purely animalistic about the way his eyes glowed.

Like a predator.

Like a predator staring at its prey.

And suddenly it dawned on Dr Drecker that he was the prey.

-39-

"Where is Cameron?" Adam asked. He was standing in the door of the motorhome with some fresh croissants and coffee.

Nina Winter rubbed her eyes. She had hardly slept through the night, tormented by nightmares about her friend Susan Carr getting killed, and the killers now chasing her.

"Isn't she in her bed?" she asked.

Adam shook his head. The bed, or rather the couch which Cameron had slept on last night was empty. "Are you dressed? Can I come in?" he asked.

"Sure," she answered, and sat up in her bed.

Adam put the breakfast on the table in the middle of the motorhome and walked over to Cameron's empty bed. "She's probably just gone for a walk. I did the same thing myself this morning," he said.

Nina Winter looked at her watch. "When did you get up?"

Adam laughed. "Can't sleep past 4 o'clock, occupational hazard," he said.

"What exactly is your occupation? I hardly know anything about you or Cameron," she said.

"I've been working as a personal trainer in New York for the last few years. Before that I was in the army," he said.

Nina Winter pulled the sheet closer to her body.

Suddenly Adam stopped in his tracks, and with a horrified look in his eyes he grabbed his green army bag.

It was open.

He emptied the contents on the couch, swearing. "Shit, shit, shit."

"What's wrong?" Nina Winter asked. Suddenly nervous.

"I'm an idiot," Adam said. "That lady at the hospital. She kept saying Cameron wasn't my daughter. That we didn't have the same blood type. And then my friend said the same thing."

"Which friend?" Nina asked.

"Doesn't matter. What matters is that I started doubting, doubting whether Cameron was my daughter. So I picked up one of those new DNA self-testing kits. It was in my bag and now it's gone."

"You think Cameron found it, that she has run away?" Nina asked.

"She has been on the run for the last seven years with her mom. Been taught not to trust anyone. Yes, I think there is a good chance she has run away."

"So how do we find her?" she asked.

Adam looked at her. For the first time it didn't look like he had an answer.

-40-

I t was freezing cold in Dr Drecker's office. He walked over to the wall and turned up the heating. He had spent the last three hours interviewing his own son, questioning his own son.

It had gone better than expected. It was as if his son had matured since he was injected with the fatal DMT dosage, as if he had instantly grown up. Even his vocabulary seemed more advanced. More reflected.

But apart from this increased level of maturity, it had still been Cody sitting there in front of him. There was no doubt in Dr Drecker's mind.

Cody had realised that something bad had happened. He was kept in isolation, away from the other patients, the death row prisoners. Even Dr Kovacks and the janitor from Brooklyn were kept away from Cody. Dr Drecker knew that this was just a temporary situation. If the CIA agent was correct, if Cody would die in another 46 days, and his body would be taken over by something unknown, something alien, then Cody would soon be joining the rest of the patients.

Confined to a glass cage.

A test animal the MKULTRA scientists would experiment on for the next decades to come.

Dr Drecker skimmed through his notes.

There was nothing that really stood out.

He had read through most of Dr Kovacks' interviews with the DMT trial test subjects. Everything Cody had experienced could be found in parts of those interviews as well.

The humming.

The vibration.

The feeling of separation of body and consciousness.

And then the awakening.

To find yourself in a different world.

An otherworldly world.

The only difference was that Dr Kovacks' patients had been under the influence of DMT for around thirty to forty minutes.

Cody had been dead for three days.

But for Cody it hadn't felt like three days.

He spoke about being in a place where time lost its meaning.

He initially thought he had been away for several years, he even asked which year it was.

When Dr Drecker asked Cody where he had been, Cody just answered "Heaven."

He had been to heaven.

Dr Drecker tapped his fingers on the tablet in front of him. The CIA had come up with the idea to use a DMT dosage based on Phi after spying on Dr Kovacks' Connecticut Prison Study. What was it with the number Phi that made it so special?

Dr Drecker of course knew that the number Phi was roughly

1.618. It was an irrational number that went on forever. A rectangle, whose sides were proportional to the golden ratio, was said to be aesthetically pleasing, and this ratio was found numerous places in nature. Great composers, architects and artists were said to have based some of their best works on the ratio, and you could find the ratio in anything from the structure of the DNA molecule to the way the leaves of a tree were distributed. The reality though, Dr Drecker knew, was that there was nothing special about the number Phi. The reason artists used it in paintings was that the proportions looked good, but so did a lot of other proportions like the square root of two or three. Nobody claimed that those numbers were magic.

It was all pseudoscience.

He could agree that there was a clear relationship between Phi and another famous and mythical mathematical number, or sequence of numbers if you will: The Fibonacci series. By definition the first number in the Fibonacci series was either 0 or 1, and then each subsequent number would be equal to the sum of the previous two, in example 0,1,1,2,3,5,8,13,21,34,55 and so on. As this series continued infinitely, the ratio of each number to the previous one would approach Phi. But it would never quite get there because the Fibonacci series was in itself infinite. So, to Dr Drecker, Phi was only another aesthetically pleasing number that of course would show up in nature and human creations now and then. This was purely a result of its efficient properties.

This was also a well-accepted explanation of Phi in the scientific community. People who liked to see magic, wonders and miracles wherever they looked would of course be able to find situations where the number Phi seemed to have divine properties. If one searched hard enough for something, one always found randomness that seemed magic. It didn't, however, make it true.

One could just ask the numerous people trying to predict stock market movements and secrets in the Bible based on Phi. They were all convinced that they had solved the mystery, that Phi was a magic number. But the harsh reality was that it was just another number, just another ordinary number.

So why did it have this unexplained effect on the DMT dosages?

There had to be something special about it. And Dr Drecker had to find out what it was.

-41-

"She can't have gone far," Adam said. "We're just on the outskirts of town. She may have caught a ride with someone leaving the caravan park, but I think that's unlikely. It's a beautiful day and most people will probably not be on the move until after breakfast."

"So she would have walked into town?" Nina asked.

"That's not my guess. She has no cash. The only way she can manage to be on the move, and she knows she has to, is to catch a ride. I think she might have walked towards that truck stop we passed just before driving into town. If she can catch a ride with a truck she can make serious headway."

Adam walked down the stairs of the motorhome.

"Do you want me to come?" Nina asked.

"No. I'll go by myself. You stay here in case she returns."

Nina Winter nodded and got out of bed.

Two minutes later she stood outside with a fluffy head of bed hair and a toothbrush in her hand. "Don't forget me," she said to herself as Adam drove the motorhome out of the caravan park.

A million thoughts were racing through Adam's head as he was driving towards the truck stop. He kept looking out the window, hoping to spot Cameron walking down the road somewhere. But the road was empty.

He could understand why Cameron had left. She had lived the last seven years in the belief that her dad was dead, and then one day Adam had just appeared out of nowhere. Instead of appreciating finding his long-lost daughter Adam had questioned whether he was Cameron's real dad.

It must have hurt.

It must have hurt badly.

When he found Cameron he would ask for forgiveness, he would do whatever it took. And finally it dawned on Adam that it didn't really matter if the lady at the hospital was right or not. Cameron had always been his daughter. Adam had been with her since she was born. Who cared whether they had the same blood type or not? Wasn't it the connection they had made that mattered?

He had heard a story when he was stationed in Afghanistan. Two babies had accidentally been switched at birth, and it hadn't been discovered until they were four years old, as one of the mums had to get a DNA test in a maternity case. The shocking fact in the case wasn't that the babies had been switched, however; the shocking fact was that one of the mothers wanted to get her biological baby back. She was happy to give up the baby she had nurtured for the last 4 years. It had sent a chill down Adam's spine. The dilemma, what would you do? Would you want your own blood back or would you want to hold on to the baby who had been part of your life for the last 4 years? Most people would want both, but that was of course not an option. Adam and his wife had discussed the dilemma for hours, and they both had agreed that they would have wanted to keep the baby they had raised, and ask to be a part of their biological baby's life. To see how his life turned out.

The real effect of the conversation, though, had been that his wife had been almost obsessive in her fear of Cameron being switched with another baby at birth. She had asked Adam to always keep an eye on her, to never let her out of his sight, and he never had. One thing he knew for sure was that Cameron was their baby. He had never let his guard down at the hospital, not once.

But now, sitting in the car, searching for Cameron, he knew that he had let his guard down. He should never have left that DNA kit in his bag, he should have known how Cameron might react if she found it.

He tapped his indicator stick and took the exit to the truck stop. It wasn't like an American truck stop with semi-trailers lined up in big lines, but there were maybe twelve trucks there. Some already had their engines running, the morning fog clouded with diesel smoke.

Adam parked next to the first truck and jumped out of the motorhome. He quickly walked over to the cab of the truck and asked whether the driver had seen a teenager asking for a ride. The truck driver shook his head, but told Adam that most of the trucks had already left. They preferred to start early to beat the traffic.

Adam grew more and more concerned as truck driver after truck driver shook their heads. No one had seen a teenager asking for a ride.

There were only two more trucks in the row and Adam started

to wonder whether Nina had been right. Maybe Cameron had walked into town instead? She was a seasoned fugitive, she knew that the truck stop would be the first place Adam would look. Maybe she therefore had done something unexpected.

Adam knocked on the window of a large blue semi-trailer. A tired face, with a cigarette that was down to the filter, popped his head out of the bunk above the driver's cabin.

"Can I help you, mate?"

"Looking for my daughter. Teenage girl, sixteen years old with dark hair and grey hoodie. Had an argument last night down at the caravan park, and I think she may have run away."

The truck driver slid out of his sleeper cab, and sat down in the front seat. He was wearing a pair of boxers and a dirty white singlet.

"You don't look too concerned. Happened before?" the truck driver asked.

Adam nodded. "She's an independent girl. Likes to cause a bit of drama. Seen anybody fitting the description asking for a ride?"

The truck driver sized Adam up before he responded.

"I saw a kid matching your description go into a red truck about half an hour ago. I was out taking a leak. Can't tell for sure if it was her or not. But the kid wore a grey hoodie."

"Thanks so much," Adam said. It wasn't just the fact that he had a good lead. He also understood that Cameron wanted to be found. That this wasn't a deliberate attempt to run away, it was an attempt to see how much her dad cared.

To see how much her dad wanted her.

-42-

D r Drecker stood on top of the roof of the MKULTRA building. He was having a cigarette. He looked at the surrounding buildings and realised the scope of MKULTRA's deception. The building that housed both the death row prisoners and his son, the building that the CIA agent claimed housed a new threat to humanity, was located in the middle of a suburban area. About two kilometres south Dr Drecker could see a couple of rows of houses, and to the west he could see several industrial buildings. Dr Drecker remembered he had thought the grey building that housed the DMT patients had looked like a hospital when he first arrived, and that was what they had disguised it as. To every neighbouring property the MKULTRA building looked like a boring old grey concrete block; a hospital. There were no military guards stationed outside, no tall electrical fences. It appeared that there was nothing to hide. But that's exactly what they did. They were hiding in plain sight. There were so many conspiracy theorists in the US that if the government had placed the MKULTRA building inside a military camp, someone would have started to ask questions. Nobody asked questions here.

It looked too boring.

Dr Drecker knew that what was going on inside the building was far from boring though. He had tried to interview the death row prisoners that morning, and the experience had scared him. It had scared him in a way he had never been scared before.

First Dr Drecker had printed out a list of all the death row prisoners. There were only five of them:

Patient A: Andrew Mortimer. White Caucasian. Raped and strangled two women. Death penalty in 1971.

Patient B: Douglas Eugene Brown. Afro-American. Killed ex-wife and son. Given death penalty in 1970.

Patient C: Eddie Morales. Hispanic. Raped and killed three boys aged four to sixteen. Death penalty in 1969.

Patient D: Oba Davidson. White Caucasian. Raped and strangled mother (37) and her two daughters (14 and 16). Death penalty 1970.

Patient E: William Jones. Afro-American. Tortured and killed a white couple (23 and 25 years) after carjacking their vehicle. Death penalty 1972.

He had quickly read up on their files, something that had been a rather unpleasant experience. These guys deserved to die. There was no doubt about it. Then he had brought a plastic chair and his notepad, and entered the sealed area of the glass cages, the prison cells where the DMT patients were being held. He had placed the chair outside the glass wall of the first cell and knocked gently on the window. Patient A had walked over to the glass wall and only stopped when a few centimetres separated his face from the glass.

Dr Drecker had felt intimidated, but the CIA agent had assured him that the cells were impenetrable. It was impossible to break out.

Dr Drecker had shuffled through his papers and found the list of questions he had prepared. He had asked seven of them, but the patient hadn't answered a single one. He had just stood there. Immovable.

His face expressionless.

Dr Drecker had moved on to the next death row prisoner, but the result had been the same. Patient B had acted exactly as Patient A. He had mimicked his movements. In the end Dr Drecker had prepared to leave. There was no point. The CIA agent had been right. The patients had simply chosen to stop speaking.

Then, as he was packing up his things, the patient in front of him had suddenly moved away from the glass wall. He had walked to the middle of the cell and knelt down. Facing northeast he had started to lower his hands and upper body to the floor. It looked like he was praying, but no words were uttered. Intrigued, Dr Drecker noticed that it wasn't only Patient B who had started praying. All the Patients seemed to be doing it, in complete unison. Dr Drecker moved closer to the glass cage. Trying to hear if they were saying anything.

But no words were uttered. They were just chanting. It almost sounded like they were chanting Aum, Aum. Like the Hindus and Yoga fanatics.

It all lasted for less than five minutes. Dr Drecker looked at his watch; they had all started at exactly noon. And afterwards the death row prisoners had just walked back to the fronts of their cells. They had remained standing there, just staring at Dr Drecker.

He felt a cold shiver go through his body.

Then he grabbed his things, and left the room in a hurry.

-43-

It didn't take Adam long to drive back and pick up Nina. She looked relieved that he actually returned. Had she also started doubting him? They filled up the motorhome with a full tank of fuel before taking up the chase of the red semi. Adam thought he knew where Cameron was going. She was heading in the direction of her grandmother's place, the same way they had all agreed to go anyway. This wasn't a serious attempt to run away, just a statement. The truck driver had said that most trucks were travelling along the same route. Heading north on the highway until they got to Rockhampton, the beef capital of Australia. There they stopped for lunch, a smoko and a stubby. And then they continued farther north along the Bruce Highway. He was at least forty-five minutes behind the truck carrying Cameron, and the motorhome was hardly equipped with a turbo engine. But if he continued without any more delays, and stayed just above the speed limit, he should be able to catch up with Cameron's truck in a few hours.

"What is that?" Nina asked. The traffic had come to a complete halt a few hundred metres in front of them. The line of trucks and cars appeared to be several kilometres long. Adam steered the motorhome off the road and onto the curb, and continued driving at just forty kilometres per hour. Red dust swirled up around the motorhome, and small rocks kept banging against the skid plate of the car. A few drivers honked angrily, as small rocks and gravel hit their cars, but Adam didn't care. He couldn't stay stuck in this pileup, not if Cameron was on the highway.

"This is crazy. People are going to report us to the police. They will be looking for the motorhome," Nina said.

"That's a risk we will have to take. We have to make ground," Adam said.

Nina didn't object anymore, and Adam was glad she didn't. She didn't make everything about herself. She had only known Adam and Cameron for a day or so, and her life was just as much in danger as theirs were, but she accepted that locating Cameron was important for Adam. Something that trumped their own safety.

"There is a red semi on the side of the road just ahead of us," Adam said. He had noticed it a couple of seconds earlier. It was the semi that the truck driver had described; red chassis with a white hanger.

Nina squinted out the window. It was hard to see anything with all the dust being whirled up by the motorhome. "Is it on its side?" she asked.

"Looks like it," Adam replied. He couldn't believe it. Cameron had just survived an airplane crash, what were the odds she would be involved in a car accident just a few days later?

Adam eased off on the accelerator, and turned on his emergency indicator. There was an ambulance standing on the curb of the road. Lights flashing, but no sound.

"What do we do now?" Nina asked.

"We wing it," Adam replied, and drove straight up to the back of the ambulance. A police officer came walking over, still talking on his radio, frantically waving his arms.

"Let me do the talking," Adam said. He turned off the engine and stepped out of the motorhome.

"What the hell are you doing? You can't park here," the police officer hollered.

"I believe my daughter may have been a passenger," Adam said, pointing at the semi.

"Can't have been," the police officer said. "There were only two people inside, the driver and another male passenger. The driver is dead, and the paramedics are working on the other guy."

"Can I talk to him?" Adam asked.

"Get the hell out of here," the police officer replied. "You should be glad I'm not booking you. One person is dead, the other one is fighting for his life, and you have the nerve to drive up here, just to have a peek."

Adam looked at him, a bit dumbfounded. Did the police officer believe he was there to have a perv at the accident? That he would pull out a camera, that he got off on car accidents? He knew there were a lot of sick people in the world, but surely not that sick?

"Officer, over here," one of the ambulance officers bellowed to the police officer. "We need some help, urgently."

"I'll be right over," the police officer said, before shooting Adam an angry stare, and walking off.

Adam was wandering back towards the motorhome, when he heard a sound from the high grass next to the road.

"Psst...Dad."

"Cameron?" Adam replied, immediately stopping. "Are you

ok?"

There was no answer.

Adam tried to listen where the sound had come from, but he couldn't hear anything.

"Park closer to the grass and leave the door open for ten seconds. I'll make my way over," the voice whispered.

"Ok," Adam replied, starting to speed up. The semi had veered off the road, killing the driver and critically injuring a passenger.

Had Cameron been a passenger in the semi, had she survived yet another fatal crash?

What the fuck was really happening?

–44–

Dr Drecker was chewing on the tip of his pen. He felt like standing up, but remained seated. The CIA agent was on the phone, and had asked him to sit down. It would be rude to stand up, wouldn't it? It would imply that he wanted the CIA agent to finish his phone conversation, which was exactly what he wanted.

The CIA agent could obviously sense Dr Drecker's impatience, and apologised to the person on the other end of the line.

"Sorry, James, something has come up. Can I call you back in twenty?"

Then he hung up.

He turned towards Dr Drecker, who was almost trembling with excitement.

"They were all chanting. They were all praying."

The CIA agent glanced at his watch before nodding.

"Yes, it's that time of day."

"You said they hadn't spoken for several years."

"And I meant it. I don't count chanting as speaking."

"So they've been doing this for some time?"

"Since they stopped speaking," the CIA agent replied, before standing up. He walked around the office desk and over to a large

TV screen on the wall. "Could you hear what they were saying?" he asked.

"No, I couldn't make out any words."

The CIA agent turned on the TV and walked back to his desk. He sat down and pointed a remote towards the screen.

"I'll show you what they were saying," he said, turning up the volume.

On the big TV screen Dr Drecker could see one of the patients. It looked like Patient B, the guy who had killed his ex-wife and his own son. The patient was down on his knees, and started to lower his head and upper body to the floor.

The sound was crisp and clear. They must have recorded it with state-of-the-art equipment, he thought.

Oh you great son of heavens, blessed be your return.

Oh you great son of fire, blessed be your wrath.

His eyes cut out by evil, his soul darkened by injustice.

On the eve of Venus' second passing of the sun,

Our saviour, the long lost son will return,

On this blessed day the army of the undead will rise from the depths of hell,

On this blessed day the earth will burn and millions of souls will fly into the sky.

On this blessed day our saviour will return and we will all be set free,

Oh how we long for this blessed day, our saviour.

Oh how we long for our revenge.

"What the hell does that mean?" Dr Drecker asked when the

CIA agent turned off the TV.

"We've had several specialists trying to decode the meaning, and they all come to the same conclusion. The patients are talking about a coming apocalypse, the end of our world as we know it. The army of the undead is the patients and their fellow beings, whoever they are. And they are coming here to destroy us and our world."

"But that can't be right," Dr Drecker said.

"Then you tell me how we are supposed to interpret those verses."

Dr Drecker didn't reply. He didn't have anything to say.

Then he asked.

"The eve of the second passing. Is that the date I think it is?"

The CIA agent nodded.

-45-

"What the hell happened back there?" Adam asked. In the rear mirror he could see the lights from the ambulance getting dimmer, and a tow truck pulling the semi up from the field with a winch gradually got smaller and smaller.

"I don't know," Cameron replied. She was staring at the floor. "Am I some kind of a freak?" she finally asked.

"No, don't you even dare to think that thought," Nina said, putting a hand on Cameron's shoulder. She had no idea what Cameron was or wasn't, but she knew one thing for sure; Cameron was scared – scared shitless.

She could see it in Cameron's eyes. Deep down she was just another scared teenager, a little girl who had lost her mum and survived two terrible accidents. A little girl who now feared she was the reason everyone around her died.

"Do you remember anything from the crash?" Adam asked.

"No, I woke up in the field. More than a hundred meters from the semi. I have no idea how I got there. I must have been thrown out the window."

"You have no injuries," Adam said.

Cameron didn't reply.

Nina looked at Adam with an angry expression on her face, and he stopped the interrogation.

"I'm sorry, Cameron. I know you found the DNA kit," he said after a pause.

"Why did you get it? Don't you believe I'm your daughter? Do you believe I'm some kind of alien?"

"Don't be ridiculous, Cameron. I was just stupid. The hospital kept saying you weren't my daughter, and then my friend back in the US said the same thing. I bought that kit in a moment of stupidity."

"Why would a friend back in the US know whether I am your daughter or not?" Cameron asked.

"Long story," Adam replied. "He has helped me the last few years trying to track you and your mmomum down. He has access to government channels, and information that is closed off for me. He was the one who told me the CIA was coming to interview and bring you back to the US, and he was the one who told me you might have been on the plane."

"So he is working with the same guys we are trying to hide from?" Cameron asked.

"We don't know whether it was the CIA that blew up the hospital or someone else. But until we know who it was we have to treat everybody as a potential suspect."

"Even the police?" Nina asked.

"I think it is safe to say that the Australian police are not involved. But they may hand us over to the wrong people. Thus we have to stay away from them. But the point is that my friend said the same thing, that you weren't my daughter."

"How could he even claim to know such a thing?" Nina asked.

"We'll know soon," Adam answered. "I sent him a message from the caravan park. Once he replies we might get a greater understanding of why the CIA is so interested in Cameron."

Cameron looked out the window. The sun was glaring, and heated up the windows of the motorhome. She missed her mum, and couldn't really fathom that she was gone. That she would never be able to see her again. It was nice to have her dad back, but nothing could replace her mum, nothing could replace the person she had been travelling with for the last seven years. When she found out who was responsible, who was responsible for flight SQ183 blowing up, she would kill them, she would kill them all.

-46-

It was three am, and the office building seemed deserted. Dr Drecker sat in front of his computer screen, alone with his thoughts, alone with his guilt. Four days had passed and he was basically back where he had started.

Why did a DMT injection of 1.618 mg/kg cause all these effects? They had tried to inject higher and lower dosages, but none produced the same result. A higher dose than 1 mg/kg led in most cases to total amnesia from the experience, and even if they administered patients up to 2 mg/kg, there were no other unusual effects. The patients woke up and went on with their daily lives; they may have had a scary experience, they may have seen reptiles or angels, but there were no physical changes in them.

If, however, a patient was given the exact dosage of 1.618 mg/kg, the divine number of Phi, the patient would die or commit suicide within hours of the injection. Then he would resurrect three days later, only to die again exactly after another forty-six days.

Forty-nine days.

What was it about these forty-nine days?

Upon the second resurrection, the test subject's personality would be totally different, and he would now have acquired the ability to self-heal from small injuries, and stopped aging. Or at least aging would have slowed down drastically.

All because his pineal gland had grown.

Dr Drecker scratched his head.

There were no other physiological changes. The enlarged pineal gland didn't produce any more DMT than before. The levels were as before the injection.

It was as if the stories that the old mystics preached about, about humans possessing a dormant third eye, were all true. That somehow this third eye had awakened in all these patients.

But what did they see, and what did it mean?

And why had they stopped talking?

Before they had stopped talking, they had all kept reciting this prophecy about a forthcoming apocalypse. Now all they did was chant two times a day. Nothing else. Not a single word for decades.

Dr Drecker glanced at the Bible in front of him. He had felt compelled to start skimming through it, to see whether he could find some clues in this old book that so many people believed in.

Wasn't it true that Christians believed in resurrection? That they believed Jesus had died for our sins, only to resurrect three days later?

He pushed the Bible away. He couldn't allow himself to look for simple solutions.

To look for faith where there was none.

Jesus had been a con man.

A clever con man.

Dr Drecker had always found it funny that religious people

could believe in Jesus and God, in Mohammed and Allah, and still consider themselves sane.

If, on the other hand, someone believed he was Jesus resurrected, he was deemed insane.

Did the fact that millions believed the same, make it sane?

In the level below his office, Dr Drecker had five patients, and they had all died and resurrected after three days.

They had all acquired the ability to self-heal, and never grow old.

It had even been considered that they were immortals, as none of them had died since the experiment was concluded in 1974.

Were they gods?

Were they prophets?

Dr Drecker opened the search engine on the laptop. He had an idea.

What if the Bible didn't lie about Jesus?

What if Jesus had lived, and what if he had resurrected after three days?

The rest of the stories in the New Testament could still be just that, made-up stories, myths about a man who beat death.

Dr Drecker punched in 'resurrection after three days'. He wanted to see whether there were more recorded incidents in ancient history.

Whether other religions made the same claims.

He got a lot of hits. Some claiming that the story of Jesus was made up. That there was nothing original about Christianity, that it was simply a copy of older Pagan religions.

Horus in Egypt, Tammuz in Mesopotamia, Adonis in Syria and Attis in Asia Minor. There were articles claiming that they all had resurrected after three days, that they all had died and returned to life. There were also claims that they had possessed healing powers.

Dr Drecker scratched his head. Many scholars took this as evidence that Christianity was a made-up religion, that it was a copy of the old Pagan religions, with their made-up gods.

But what if they were all wrong? What if Christianity wasn't just a copy of old Pagan religions? What if all these people had lived, or at least some people with the ability to resurrect had lived?

Evolution worked in increments, not in big jumps. All the death row prisoners had experienced the same result from their DMT injection. They had died and resurrected. But they had also changed personalities forty-nine days later. They were no longer the same people. Why was that? It could mean that the ability to self-heal and resurrect was something that was latent in all humans, that the DMT injection just set something free. But it could also mean another thing.

A much worse thing.

Dr Drecker packed up his things. There was something he needed to check.

Something he urgently needed to check.

-47-

It was three o'clock in the morning when they drove up the driveway of Cameron's grandmother's old farm. The sky was clear and hundreds of stars littered the black canvas above them. Adam turned off the headlights and continued the last few metres, with only the light from the stars as guidance. He knew the driveway faced his mother-in-law's bedroom, and he didn't want to scare her by lighting up the whole room in the middle of the night. Although she was a tough woman, she was still an old lady.

"We'll stay in the car until morning. Then we go over and introduce ourselves," he said.

His fear of waking up his mother-in-law proved to be unfounded. She appeared on the front deck, with a shotgun in her hand, in less than a few seconds.

Adam laughed. "Should have known it. Farmers get up early."

He opened the door and stepped outside. "Glenda. How are you?"

"Adam? Adam is that you?" His mother-in-law cried out.

"Yes it is," he replied.

"You won't believe who showed up not so long ago!" she said.

Adam didn't answer. Instead he watched her eyes tear up as

she saw Cameron stepping out of the motorhome.

"Cameron, what a wonderful surprise. Is your mum there too?" she asked.

Neither Cameron nor Adam answered. Instead, Adam started walking towards her with a sad face, shaking his head almost unnoticeably.

He could see that she almost immediately understood what it meant. Although she didn't want to, she understood what it meant.

"No, no. It can't be," she said.

Adam reached his hands out and hugged her. He could feel her body throbbing, while he held her tight.

Four hours later, Nina and Cameron's grandmother were sitting in the kitchen drinking coffee when Adam returned. He had driven to the closest town to see whether they had any WIFI access. Luckily, the Australian Labour Party had started rolling out broadband to remote areas, so he had been able to locate an unsecured network outside a residential house just on the outskirts of town. He had downloaded the updated Spideroak document in a few seconds. Adam had just read the message from Matt Parks. It made no sense.

"How did it go?" Nina asked.

Adam put his head in his hands and wiped his eyes. "I've got no idea what's happening. And it doesn't seem like my contact has any idea either."

"What did he write?" Nina asked.

"I asked him why the CIA was after Cameron, and why he claimed Cameron wasn't my daughter," Adam said.

"What's this about? Cameron is not your daughter?" Adam's mother-in-law asked.

"It's a long story, Glenda," Adam replied.

"Anyway, all he wrote back was two words. Two words without any meaning."

"What were the words?" asked Nina.

"He wrote 'Patient F'," Adam said.

The sound of shattering glass broke the silence in the kitchen. Adam turned around and saw his mother-in-law standing in the middle of the kitchen with a mortified face; it was as if all the colour had been drained from her body. As if somebody had sucked her dry of blood.

"What's wrong?" Nina asked, and rushed over to grab Adam's mother-in-law's hand before she fell over. Nina led her out of the kitchen and sat her down in a reading chair.

Adam brought her a glass of water.

"What's going on, Glenda?" he asked.

She didn't answer.

She just started sobbing.

-48-

"What was your plan? What did you think you would achieve by administering patients 1.618 mg/kg of DMT?" Dr Drecker asked.

Dr Julian Kovacks was sitting in front of him, on a cheap, white, plastic chair. A wall of thick glass separated them, and Dr Drecker immediately felt sorry for Dr Julian Kovacks. His cell was covered with small cameras, he had no privacy whatsoever. No dignity. They might as well have put him in a Big Brother house.

"You know what my plan was. I wanted to prove that the earth isn't the only world in the universe," Dr Julian Kovacks said. He almost spat the words out.

"So you believe that you visited an alien world when you injected yourself?"

"I don't believe. I know. I was there and that world was much more real than the world I see before my eyes right now."

Dr Drecker leaned forward, closer to the glass wall. He knew there was no point. Everything he said was probably recorded anyway. But it felt more intimate. Felt more personal.

"Why did you jump out of that window, Julian? Why did you take your own life?"

Dr Julian Kovacks smiled. He looked away, gazed at the naked white wall in his cell before returning his look to face Dr Drecker.

"Why live life in this empty shell of a body?"

"So you prefer this life? Stuck in a cell?" Dr Drecker asked.

"You're the one who is stuck. You're the one who is a prisoner of your own body."

"What do you mean?" Dr Drecker asked.

"Ask your son. He knows what's coming."

A cold shiver went down Dr Drecker's spine. "What do you know about my son? Have you spoken to him?"

"Ask your son," Dr Kovacks said with a smile on his face. Then he rose from the white, plastic chair and walked over to his bed.

An hour later Dr Drecker sat down in front of the bed in Cody's room. Dr Drecker was still allowed to enter Cody's cell, to touch his son and talk to him face-to-face. But he knew it was just a matter of time before they sealed off Cody's cell too. They had been nervous about giving Dr Drecker access to his own son, but Dr Drecker had argued that this was a once-in-a-lifetime opportunity. If Cody had 46 days before he changed into someone else, they should make the most out of those 46 days. Putting him into a glass cage like the rest of the patients would be a wasted opportunity. He was therefore being held in a separate glass cage.

Cody and a row of four empty glass cages.

"Are you feeling ok, Cody?" Dr Drecker asked.

Cody shrugged. "I guess so. It is kind of boring here. I have asked to get an Xbox, but they won't let me have any electrical stuff," he said.

Dr Drecker nodded. They were probably afraid that the

patients, if they were from an alien world, would be able to make a bomb or an invisibility cloak from basic computer electronics. He had heard about paranoid people, but the guys at MKULTRA were extreme. They took no risks at all; it was as if they feared these patients more than a Muslim extremist with a nuclear bomb strapped to his chest.

"I'm sorry. I'll see what I can do about it," Dr Drecker said. It was a lie, but at least it gave Cody some hope.

"How long are they going to keep me?" Cody asked.

"For a month and a half," Dr Drecker said. "They just need to be sure that you are healthy."

"Ok." Cody said, and gave his dad a smile.

Dr Drecker coughed before he straightened up his back.

"Have you had contact with anybody else here in the facility?"

"What do you mean?" Cody asked.

"Any other people?" Dr Drecker clarified.

Suddenly it was as if all the air in the room disappeared. Cody's eyes got darker, as if all the white disappeared, and only the black pupils were left.

"You've spoken to Julian," Cody said.

Dr Drecker didn't know what to respond. There was no way Cody could know about Dr Kovacks. Dr Kovacks had been held in a different part of the building the whole time.

"Yes, I have. Dr Julian Kovacks was one of my employees. What I don't understand is how you know him," Dr Drecker said, pulling the chair a bit farther away from the bed.

"I've met them all," Cody said.

"Met whom?"

"All the patients here. I met them the first night. We all talk at night."

"What do you mean talk at night? There are no other patients here."

"You don't have to pretend with me, Dad. I know what is coming. I am ready for it. I've always been ready for it."

-49-

Adam was pacing back and forth in the kitchen while Nina held a wet cloth to his mother-in-law's forehead. She had gotten some of the colour back, but she still looked pale.

"How are you feeling?" Nina asked.

"A little bit better," his mother-in-law answered.

She took a big sip of water and turned around facing Adam, who stopped in his tracks.

"I swear I didn't know," she said.

"Didn't know what?" Adam asked.

"Keep your voice down. You may wake up Cameron," she replied.

Adam walked over to his mother-in-law. He loved her, he always had. But now he started wondering what secrets she had kept from him all these years. Had she been honest when she claimed she had no idea where Cameron and his wife were hiding, had she lied when she claimed she didn't know why his wife had disappeared? And how did she know what 'Patient F' meant? How did she know what the two words his friend Matt Parks had responded with meant?

"You need to be honest with me, Glenda. You need to tell me

everything you know."

His mother-in-law nodded. "I'll tell you everything, everything."

Adam felt betrayed when he heard his mother-in-law tell the story about how his father-in-law had committed suicide more than thirty years ago. Why had his wife never told him the truth? She had claimed that her father died in a car accident when she was four. On his way home from a patient visit. On a windy night the day before Christmas, he had fallen asleep behind the wheel and his car had run off the road and collided head-on into a tree. It had been the reason she always was a bit moody around Christmas time, never able to really enjoy herself.

"So your husband shot himself because he didn't want to give up the location of this Patient F?" Adam asked.

Glenda nodded. "I found his diary a week after the suicide. He wrote that he had received a patient at the hospital after the big train accident in Melbourne in 1980. That the patient didn't have a name, that he had just called him 'Patient F'."

"But why did your husband hide him? Why did he kill himself instead of telling the police where this patient was hiding?"

"I don't know," Glenda said, tears streaming down her cheeks. "The diary entry just said he knew he had done the right thing. That he had to hide this patient without a name for the sake of everybody. That his own life was worth sacrificing for the betterment of humanity."

Adam stared out the window. The sun had come up and the sky was filled with red glare.

"But I don't understand how this relates to Cameron," Adam

said.

Adam's mother-in-law stared out the window, fighting the tears, before returning her gaze to Adam. "Do you remember when you and Mimi came to visit in 1995? Mimi had been trying to get pregnant for more than two years, and your American doctor had recommended that she needed a break, a break away from the hustle and bustle of New York?"

Adam remembered. It had been the most wonderful vacation. They had stayed at the farm, lived the simple life. Helped herding the cattle and farming the land. He had stayed there for two months before he got called back into action. Deployed to a war zone somewhere in the Middle East. Playing world police for uncle Sam.

"It was a nice break," he said.

"Before you left, you went to see Doctor Mason in Cairns. You signed up for IVF trials," Glenda said.

Adam nodded. He was getting nervous now. Where was she going with this? "Yes, Australia had a good reputation for IVF back then. And Dr Mason was recognised as the expert. What's your point?" he asked.

"A week after you left I was going through some of my late husband's belongings. I had kept boxes and boxes of his stuff. Some of it I had never, ever opened. It had travelled with me, unopened, as I moved around bringing up Mimi."

"Yes..." Adam said. Both eager to hear what came next, and fearing it.

"I found a key in one of his old jackets. I didn't know what to do with it so I put it away. A couple of days later Mimi came home from the IVF doctor, all broken down in tears. She said it wasn't working, she said the IVF had been a failure."

Glenda coughed.

"I didn't know what to do. But I knew that the only way I got through what happened to my husband, was by focusing on something else, by having a purpose. So I gave her the key, and asked her if she could figure out what it was for."

Nina Winter leaned in closer. She was totally enthralled by the story.

"Did she find out what it was for?" she asked.

Glenda nodded.

"She travelled to Melbourne, was away for more than a week. And when she came home she was happy. Happier than I had seen her in years."

"What did she find?" Adam asked.

"I honestly don't know," Glenda said. "But she went back to Doctor Mason, and a few weeks later she was pregnant."

"What the hell?" Adam said, jumping up from his chair.

"Keep quiet. Cameron is still asleep upstairs," Nina said.

Adam sat down on a chair. "What does it all mean?" he asked, anger filling his voice.

"I'm not sure. My husband was a brilliant doctor. Maybe he came up with a new method to cure infertility. Maybe Mimi found his notes and gave them to Dr Mason."

"That doesn't make any sense," Adam said.

"Well it is worth a shot," Glenda said.

"What's worth a shot?" Adam asked.

"Talk to Dr Mason. He is still here. He is in the aged care facility in Cairns."

Adam got up from his chair. "It's the only lead we have. We

need to find out who this 'Patient F' was. We might as well go and see Dr Mason."

"I don't think Patient F is a person," Glenda said. "I think it is just a codename."

"Why do you say that?" Adam asked.

"Because the great train accident in Melbourne never had any survivors. How could my husband have treated and hid a survivor, when there were none?" She asked.

-50-

"So you don't want to have access to your son's cell anymore?" the CIA agent asked.

"No, I think it's too dangerous. I think we should move him into a closed cell like the others," Dr Drecker said.

"Why the change of heart?"

"He knows about the others."

"The other patients? Impossible. We have kept him in complete isolation."

"They talk at night. Apparently he sees them at night."

"In his dreams, you mean?"

"I don't know. I assume so, but I didn't ask. In all honesty I got a bit freaked out. For a second it was as if Cody had left the room. It was as if someone else took over his body for a brief moment."

"But that doesn't make any sense. The changeover doesn't happen until after 49 days," the CIA agent said.

"I can only tell you what I saw. Play the tapes. You've got the whole cell rigged with cameras. I'm sure you got it on film."

The CIA agent looked a bit concerned.

"What is it?" Dr Drecker asked.

"Dr Drecker, something happened down in that cell today. For a moment we lost the connection. It has never happened before, but for about ten minutes we only have white noise on the cameras."

"For ten minutes? I can't have been there for more than a couple of minutes," Dr Drecker said.

"You were there at least ten minutes," the CIA agent said. "We have you on film going into the cell, and leaving. But nothing in between. Just white static."

"What does that mean?" Dr Drecker asked.

"We don't know. But we will need you to complete some tests."

-51-

"What do you think?" Adam asked.

Nina Winter was unsure what to reply. She could sense the fear in Adam's voice. He was afraid he was about to learn something he didn't want to know.

"I don't think 'Patient F' is a code word. The blood samples the hospital took were not a match, and it sounds like this Patient F, whoever it may have been, survived a train crash in 1980. There are too many coincidences. I think you should prepare yourself for being told that Cameron is not your biological daughter."

Adam didn't answer. He had already prepared himself. If it was possible to prepare yourself for being told that most of the things you had believed in life were a lie, he had prepared himself.

"Whatever the doctor tells us today, I don't want Cameron to know. I don't want her to ever know that we spoke to the doctor. And if it turns out Cameron is not my daughter, I don't want Cameron to know."

"Then why are we going? Why are we making this trip?" Nina Winter asked.

"Because I need to know. It doesn't matter whether Cameron is my biological daughter or not, but I need to know. I need to know."

"Why?"

"I don't know. Maybe because I believe it may help me understand why my wife kept secrets from me all these years, why she took Cameron and ran away."

"You have to prepare yourself for the possibility that knowing won't change anything," Nina said. "That finding out whether Cameron is your blood or not won't change the real issue: That you are still mad at your wife."

Adam looked out the window.

"Have you ever wanted kids?" Adam asked.

Nina Winter looked at him. "Sometimes. But I don't think it is a birthright to have kids. I think a kid should have a mum and a dad, or at least two people who love him or her. And until I find the right one, I don't really allow myself to think about it. I don't allow myself to want it."

"Well, they change you. That's for sure," Adam said.

"Kids, you mean?" Nina asked.

"Yes, when you get a kid, you realise that you are not the most important person in your own life anymore. The only thing that matters in life is to take care of your kids. To make sure they are safe."

"So you changed after Cameron?" Nina asked.

Adam shook his head. "I was one of the stupid ones. I didn't really understand until she was gone."

After driving for about two hours they arrived at the aged care facility Glenda had told them was Dr Mason's new home. It was a decent-looking building, newly renovated and with a large parking lot outside. Adam stepped out of the motorhome and asked Nina to follow. She was a nurse, and used to talking to elderly people. If Adam had problems extracting the information he wanted from Dr Mason, her experience could be helpful.

They walked over to the counter and asked to see Dr Mason. Their timing was good, as there was still an hour left of visiting hours. The receptionist called up to Dr Mason's room, and he willingly accepted the visit when he heard it was an old patient who was there to see him.

Adam had a feeling that Dr Mason wasn't too different from his own doctor PT clients. They all had stressful jobs and made good money. But what really drove them wasn't the money. Most of them lived and breathed their work. The responsibility of being the master over other people's lives, of healing people, of saving people. When one went from such a responsibility to being placed in an aged care home, where most of one's cohabitants were senile, or at least had minimal conversational value, one would long to relive some of one's old glory. Adam felt the same after he retired from the army. He had grown to disagree with a lot of the missions he undertook, but he had always treasured the camaraderie, the feeling of belonging.

"Do you remember me?" Adam asked, as he sat down in Dr Mason's small studio apartment. It looked like a five-star hotel room. One of the fringe benefits of being a doctor – they all worked so long, far longer than normal retirement age – was that most of them had enough super to enjoy the best possible treatment when they finally threw in the towel and moved to a retirement home.

Dr Mason shook his head, before he stopped.

"You're the American army guy. IVF treatment in the late 1990s?" he asked.

Adam smiled. "You've got a great memory, doctor."

"I have always had a great memory, it is just a bit short," Dr Mason said with a cheeky smile. He probably didn't get a lot of compliments about his memory anymore.

Adam laughed politely. "I wanted to ask you a few questions. I can understand if you don't remember, it was a long time ago," he started.

"Don't be shy kid. Fire away," Dr Mason said.

"Do you remember anything special about the IVF treatment you gave my wife?"

"I remember enough to know that the beautiful lady sitting next to you is not your wife. Is it your daughter?" Dr Mason said with the same cheeky smile.

Nina smiled. "Thanks for the compliment, but I am not his daughter. Just a friend," she said. She assumed he was a seasoned flirter with the old ladies at the facility.

Dr Mason crossed his legs and scratched the tip of his nose. Some skin came off, and left a red mark.

"I'm sorry. What was your name again?" he asked Adam.

"Adam, Adam Mullins."

"Well, Adam. I do remember your wife. She was a beautiful lady. Still together?"

Adam shook his head. "She has recently passed," he said.

"I'm sorry to hear that."

Dr Mason crossed his legs back again. He seemed uncomfortable.

"Are you ok?" Nina asked.

"Yes, thank you dear. I'm fine. I'm just pondering this situation," he said.

"What situation?" Adam asked.

"You coming here, asking me questions."

"Is there anything wrong with that?" Adam asked.

Dr Mason shook his head. "No, truth is I have always wondered if you would show up at one stage," he said.

"Why?" Adam asked.

Dr Mason folded his hands.

"I told your wife you couldn't have kids," he said. "I was told you had left Australia, that you had been shipped back to fight for mighty Uncle Sam. So when I got the results back I only spoke to your wife. She was very upset, and left my office in tears."

"I can't have kids?" Adam asked.

Dr Mason shook his head. "I'm sorry. The tests revealed you were sterile," he said.

"None of the other doctors told me that," Adam said in disbelief.

"I can't answer for them. But our tests were conclusive. You can't have a child."

"Then how did my wife get pregnant, how did the IVF work?" he asked.

"A few weeks after you had left, your wife came back with some new samples of sperm. I told her there was no point. But she insisted. The samples were frozen and she claimed that they had been taken before you were deployed to Afghanistan for your first mission."

"I never had any sperm frozen," Adam said.

"I didn't know that. We had used the elimination method and compared your sperm to other Australian war veterans. We had deemed it probable that your infertility would most likely have been caused by contact with depleted uranium, something which is almost unavoidable in places like Iraq and Afghanistan. So when your wife said she had samples taken before your first deployment we took her word for it."

"But it was a lie!"

"I realized that too. But by then it was too late, she was already pregnant."

"She used someone else's sperm. I am not Cameron's dad?" Adam asked.

"I'm afraid so," Dr Mason said with genuine sorrow in his voice.

Adam got up from his chair and walked towards the door.

"There is one thing more you need to know before you leave," Dr Mason said.

Adam turned around. He was fuming.

"What is it?"

"Your wife didn't have an affair,"

"How do you know?" Adam asked.

"The sperm samples I got, they were more than fifteen years old," Dr Mason said.

-52-

The dim light in Dr Drecker's office cast shadows on the white wall. If he made an effort, he could imagine all kind of shapes from the shadows. It had been one of his favourite pastimes when he was a little kid. Other kids his age had been afraid of monsters hiding under their beds or in the closets. Dr Drecker had never been afraid of the dark. He had loved it, treasured it. He couldn't wait for his foster mum to close the door at night, to leave him and his imagination alone. He had lain there in his little bed, dead-still, looking at the shadows on the ceiling, seeing the fan swirl around faster and faster, imagining he had special powers, that he was something very special.

He had focused on the fan, trying to get it to speed up by using the sheer force of his mind, his willpower.

He had wanted it to spin through the wall, smash through the bedroom of his foster parents, and cut them up into tiny little pieces.

The fan had of course never sped up. And when he had started high school he had realised that magic wasn't real. He had realised that the universe essentially was controlled by four fundamental forces: Gravity, the weak and the strong nuclear force, and electromagnetism. If something contradicted those four fundamental forces, then it would not be possible in our universe.

When he looked at the shadows on the ceiling of his office now he realised that he, for the first time in his life, was afraid of the dark. He didn't want to go to sleep tonight, not after what had happened.

What was going on inside Cody's body? Was it still Cody or was it someone, something else, taking over?

Was Cody a prisoner in his own head? Could he see and hear Dr Drecker, but was unable to scream out that he needed help?

It was a father's nightmare, not knowing whether you were doing the right thing for your son.

There was no way out. Dr Drecker had to make a decision. First he had to make up his mind whether the person he had talked to a few hours ago was still his son.

Whether it was still Cody or someone else, something else fighting to take over his mind and body.

And then he had to make a decision whether Cody wanted to change or not. If this world Cody had experienced when tripping on DMT was so fantastic, if it was heaven as Cody had described, what right did Dr Drecker have to take that away from him?

What right did Dr Drecker have to deny his own son heaven?

He started to go through the stack of folders in front of him, the death row patient files.

Cody had scared him today, with that brief moment of a distant soulless look in his eyes. But Cody was essentially a good boy. The other patients at MKULTRA were serial killers, paedophiles and rapists. They were the scum of the earth. What if this DMT injection transformed people into a worse version of themselves? He remembered having felt like prey the first time Patient B had cast his eyes on him. After that episode he had hardly visited the other patients. He had preferred to read their files, to study them from a distance, from his office.

He looked at the pile of folders in front of him again. The MKULTRA team had named Dr Kovacks 'Patient H' and Cody 'Patient I'. That meant that they basically used the alphabet and gave each patient a name based on when they were admitted. Dr Drecker refused to use the labels and still referred to Dr Julian Kovacks and Cody by their first names.

But there was something missing.

If the janitor was "Patient G', and Dr Kovacks and Cody H and I, where was "Patient F? Who was 'Patient F'?

Dr Drecker flipped through the folders quickly, to ensure that he hadn't made a mistake.

The CIA agent had been quite specific when Dr Kovacks arrived. He had said they had eight patients. That had included the three most recent ones, and thus there was a letter missing: F.

"Do you know what the time is?" the CIA agent asked.

"I told you that when I started," Dr Drecker replied. "I don't check the time when I have an idea."

"Here's an idea. Let's talk in the morning," the CIA agent said.

"Who is 'Patient F'?" Dr Drecker asked.

The line went silent for several seconds.

"I have been waiting for that question," the CIA agent finally replied.

"Who is he? Where is he?" Dr Drecker continued.

"I am not sure if this is the right time or place to discuss that matter," the CIA agent answered.

"When is?" Dr Drecker asked. "You have hired me as a pair of new eyes to look at this case. But you can't hide information from me. That's not going to work."

"I'll be there in fifteen minutes," the CIA agent said, and hung up.

Dr Drecker placed the receiver back into its cradle. He suddenly realised that there was hardly any light in his office. His mind had been too preoccupied, staring at the spinning fan on the ceiling, looking for monsters hidden in its shadow on the walls, to notice that he was sitting in almost complete darkness.

As he turned on the light he wondered what sort of monster 'Patient F' had been. Had he been one of the death row prisoners?

Another cold-blooded serial killer who had been randomly picked for the study?

A person nobody would miss?

And where was he?

If all the death row prisoners in the DMT study were still alive, or at least their bodies were still alive, where was 'Patient F?'

-53-

A dam was standing in the paddock, chatting with his old mother-in-law. The sun was setting and there was a chill in the air.

"I don't understand. Even if I'm not Cameron's biological dad, Mimi had no right to take her away from me. Why would she do that?" he asked.

"Mimi was a complicated person. I always wondered if it was due to the fact that she saw her dad commit suicide. An experience like that will always leave a mark."

"Did she get any counselling afterwards?" Adam asked. The comments Nina Winter had made about lone survivors and their need for counselling were still fresh in his mind.

"No, I took her to a therapist, but she thought Mimi handled the situation quite well. She said there was a risk that continued talking about the incident could cause more damage than good, so I just made up a story. Said her dad was killed in a car accident. That what she saw in our old beach house had just been a bad dream."

"You lied to her?"

"I did what I thought was right. This was back in the 1980s.

I didn't know any better, and I had no one to help me. My husband had bought all these investment properties over the years. Negative gearing was the future, his accountant had told him. Well, when Rob died I had no money to pay the mortgages with. The life insurance was declared invalid because he took his own life. And within twelve months Mimi and I were out on the streets. All alone, all our wealthy doctor friends gone."

Adam put his arms around his mother-in-law. Hugged her tightly.

"I never trusted anyone after that. It is probably my fault Mimi turned out the way she did. I taught her not to trust anyone."

"Mimi turned out well," Adam said. "I still love her, you know."

"Even after all she did to you? Even after she took Cameron?" Glenda asked.

"She must have had her reasons. Mimi was a wonderful person. The most wonderful person I have ever known."

Adam looked out over the paddock. It seemed so tranquil.

"I think she wanted me to know that she was on that flight," he said, breaking the silence.

"On the flight that crashed?"

"Yes, she had been able to stay hidden for more than seven years. There had not been a single trace of her. And then she books a ticket in her maiden name. She would have known I would find out."

"I thought her name was on the Interpol list, that she was a wanted fugitive."

"No, I withdrew my charges a few years back. I didn't want Cameron to be a wanted fugitive, and I thought Mimi would understand that I wasn't angry. That I just wanted them back."

"So you think Mimi wanted you to come after her. That buying a ticket in her maiden name was a signal?"

"It may sound silly, but yes I do. I think she wanted me to jump on a plane to Singapore, to track her down."

"Why Singapore?" Glenda asked.

"I assume that's where they had left their sailing boat. Cameron told me that they had been sailing around Asia for the last few years."

"The sailing boat is here in Australia, Adam. They sailed here to say goodbye to me. I was told I only had a year to live."

"Are you that sick? You look good."

"That's the strange thing. I have recovered. My doctor has changed the prognosis. He doesn't know what has happened, but my cancer is gone."

Adam hugged her tightly.

"I'm glad to hear that." He kicked a rock with his foot. The rock bounced off the fencepost.

"If they weren't going back to the boat, where were they going?" he asked.

"Why don't you go and ask your daughter?" Glenda asked.

-54-

The CIA agent walked into Dr Drecker's office exactly thirteen minutes later. His eyes were red, but otherwise he looked like normal. Neatly dressed in a blue suit and a grey tie. His hair combed back, and face clean shaven.

"Who is Patient F?" Dr Drecker asked. He hadn't forgotten how their conversation ended.

The CIA agent walked over to his desk and sat down.

"You asked me earlier why we won't let any of the patients outside the facility. Patient F is the reason for that."

"He escaped?" Dr Drecker asked.

The CIA agent nodded. "Back in 1980."

"So where is he now?" Dr Drecker asked.

The CIA agent shrugged his shoulders.

"We don't know."

The CIA agent adjusted his body in the chair.

"You have to understand that Patient F wasn't like the other patients."

"What do you mean?" Dr Drecker asked.

"Well, the other patients are all cold-blooded killers. They were convicted for murders and there were no doubts about their guilt."

"You're saying Patient F was innocent?" Dr Drecker asked.

The CIA agent brushed his hand over his face, felt his clean shaven jaw.

"It's not that simple," the CIA agent said.

"What do you mean?" Dr Drecker asked.

"Let me try to explain. When we initiated this experiment we had a problem with the uptake. Not enough death row prisoners signed on for the experiment. So we decided to give them an incentive, an incentive we knew would motivate them. We gave them access to prostitutes."

"You gave convicted killers access to prostitutes? You gave people who had possibly killed prostitutes access to prostitutes?"

"We had to do something. And it was a safe environment. The prisoners had sex with prostitutes under our supervision. And we had no major incidents."

"No major incidents. What does that mean?"

"Well, these were violent prisoners, and sometimes they got carried away. We had some bruises, some small physical injuries, but that was all."

Dr Drecker couldn't believe his own ears. He had thought Dr Kovacks' Connecticut Prison Study was crazy, but this was much worse.

"We had done a proper screening of the prostitutes. They had no reported illnesses, they were all in good health and they were all incapable of having children. In addition, they used protection."

"Oh my god," Dr Drecker blurted out.

The CIA agent nodded. "It turned out we didn't do a good enough job in screening the prostitutes, and somehow one of them ended up pregnant, the conception having been made sometime in the first few days after the first resurrection."

"Don't tell me she gave birth to the child," Dr Drecker said in disgust.

The CIA agent nodded. "Unfortunately the team responsible for the study were inexperienced. They had no idea of the implications of this experiment when they started, and when the prisoners started to die, resurrect and die again, they simply lost control over the experiment. If MKULTRA Central hadn't realised the gravity so quickly, the consequences could have been far worse. But the child issue slipped through the cracks."

"So who is Patient F? Is he the father of the child?"

The CIA agent shook his head. "Patient F is the child. We only found out by accident. Some of the prisoners started having weird dreams about kids, about play parks and duck feeding. Some bright young psychologist figured out that they could be sharing a kid's visions, and so MKULTRA decided to track down the prostitutes. The prostitute program had only lasted for thirty days, but MKULTRA was able to track them all down, and we got our Patient F. At this stage he was about one year old."

"You've got to be kidding me. Patient F is a child? You imprisoned a child here at this facility?"

"You still look at them as humans, Dr Drecker, but we do not know what they are. The reality is that Patient F, this person you think of as an innocent child, could potentially have the power to end our world."

"How can you say that? What basis do you have to be able to make such an outrageous claim?" Dr Drecker thought for a second before continuing. "You can't seriously believe that he is the saviour they are talking about in their prayers, that he is the returning son?"

"It's not only the prayers. It's because of what happened afterwards," the CIA agent said. He turned around and faced the wall.

"Patient F was special. He was not like the others, not at all. At first he seemed to be just a normal kid. He aged normally, he grew normally. We gave him everything he needed, we stimulated his curiosity, gave him puzzles and challenges."

"You put a child in a prison. That's what you did," Dr Drecker said.

The CIA agent seemed unaffected by Dr Drecker's criticism and just kept on.

"We kept him isolated from the other patients, the death row prisoners. But then one day something strange started to happen; the death row prisoners stopped being aggressive. In the first year of the study they had been very aggressive, expressing anger at being locked up, threatening the facility staff. But suddenly, almost overnight, it was as if they all had a religious experience. They started to sit in their cells meditating for hours. Our psychologists couldn't find an explanation. It was as if they just suddenly found something they believed in."

"And..." Dr Drecker asked.

"We didn't understand the connection until weeks later. The death row prisoners' religious epiphany coincided with the moment Patient F started to use words to express himself."

"What are you saying?"

"I am saying that they all view him as a god, a god with special powers, a god who one day will take them all away from this place."

"But you said that he was normal. That he grew and developed like a normal kid. That doesn't sound like a god."

"No it doesn't. And we couldn't figure out what they all saw in him. Not until we did some tests, and it turned out that he not only had acquired the ability to self-heal, but the ability to heal others."

"Are you trying to say he had the ability to heal sick people?"

The CIA agent nodded. "We don't know how, but somehow this kid had acquired the ability to heal other people. Several of our staff who interacted with him experienced physiological changes afterwards – they became stronger, smarter, and any illnesses they had disappeared."

"How is that even possible?"

"We have no idea. This was back in the late 1970s. We didn't have the tools to figure out what was happening. And we got scared."

"Then who is his father, who is Patient F's father?"

Darkness covered the CIA agent's face. He seemed to get a new level of seriousness over him.

"Patient F's father was a mean bastard. He was the original Patient F."

"Was? You mean he is dead?"

The CIA agent nodded. "Yes we started the study with six death row prisoners. One of them never resurrected the second time."

"Why?"

The CIA agent shrugged his shoulders. "Who knows? Things have happened in this facility, things that defy our traditional knowledge of how our universe is put together. If you want to help us, you need to forget about a lot of the things you have been taught, and you need to be open to the fact that everything is not as it seems. Look around you. We think we have solved most of the mysteries of the universe. We now know that Earth is not the centre of the universe, we now know that the Earth is not flat. But it wasn't that long ago we all had those beliefs. The reality is that we still know very little about the universe. More than ninety percent of the universe is made up of dark energy and dark matter, and we have no idea what those things really are. And we here at MKULTRA are the best poised in the world to figure out the answers to some of these mysteries."

"How?"

"Because the scientific world has been looking in the wrong direction for too long. They have been pointing their telescopes at the edges of the universe, while they should have been pointing them at themselves."

Dr Drecker understood what the CIA agent meant. He thought the human mind could hold the answer to some of the mysteries of the universe. He was one of those crazy ones who still thought humans were special, that the universe revolved around humans.

"But I still don't understand how I can help, how Cody can help," Dr Drecker said.

"One of the things we did learn about Patient F before he disappeared was that he wasn't a totally normal child. He was slightly autistic."

"Autistic, what has autism got to do with this?"

"We don't know. But that's why Cody is so important. He was diagnosed with Asperger syndrome when he was seven, am I right?" the CIA agent asked.

The blood drained from Dr Drecker's face.

Suddenly it dawned on him. They weren't after his expertise. They were after his son. Cody might hold the key to the DMT puzzle.

"You think Cody will act differently than the other patients? You think Cody won't die after 49 days?" Dr Drecker asked.

The CIA agent smiled. "We are stuck in an impossible situation here at MKULTRA. We are not allowed to initiate new trials. The only test subjects we have had for the last 30 years have been the death row prisoners, and none of them were autistic. Except Patient F."

"So now you suddenly have a fresh supply of test subjects. My son's reactions can be compared to that of the janitor and Dr Kovacks."

"In essence, yes," the CIA agent said.

"You set this whole thing up, didn't you? You knew what Dr Kovacks was planning to do. You didn't stop him because you wanted new test subjects," Dr Drecker said.

"No, I didn't," the CIA agent said. But Dr Drecker could see it on his face, he was lying, he was lying his face off.

"But why is the reaction of Cody so important? Why is it so important to find a way for the personality not to change?" Dr Drecker asked.

The CIA agent got up from his chair.

"Think about the opportunities, Dr Drecker. If we can figure out the secret of Patient F, then we will have broken the code to immortality."

"You already have the code to immortality. All your death row prisoners have stopped aging."

"But they are not the same anymore. They are different. Who wants immortality if you can't be yourself anymore?"

As the CIA agent walked away he thought back on the original Patient F, the father of the person they now called Patient F. He had been the last American war criminal to ever receive the death penalty. Guilty of slaughtering a whole village of innocent peasants in one of America's foreign wars. Forty-five defenceless women and children shot down in a killing spree that redefined how cruel humans could be. He had been the main instigator and had received the death penalty. His two accomplices had received long prison terms. It was a long time ago, the CIA agent thought.

A long time ago.

-55-

Cameron was lying on her bed, eyes closed, listening to music. She hadn't heard Adam knock on the door, so Adam had gently opened it, fearing that his daughter once again had run off. Adam walked over to the bed. Seeing Cameron lying there filled him with memories. His wife, Mimi, had always said Cameron looked like an angel when she was sleeping. She could be quite the devil when she was awake, running around creating havoc, but when she was asleep she looked like the most innocent person in the world.

"Are you awake?" Adam asked as he brushed some of Cameron's dark hair away from her closed eyes.

Cameron opened her eyes, and looked at her dad with true love. It was all the confirmation Adam had ever needed. It didn't matter who was Cameron's biological father. Adam would always be her dad.

"Yeah, just listening to some music," Cameron answered.

"I just wanted to ask you a question," Adam said, sitting down on the bed next to Cameron.

Cameron turned off the iPod she had borrowed from Nina, and removed the headphones.

"Sure."

"Do you know why you were flying to Singapore with your mom?" Adam asked.

"Mom didn't tell, she never did, but I think we were going to Vietnam."

"Vietnam? Why Vietnam? I mean why Vietnam if your boat was still here in Australia?" Adam asked.

Cameron shrugged her shoulders. "I had learned not to ask too many questions. Mom wouldn't tell me the truth anyway. But I saw her reading this article on the boat. It was about Vietnam. Two days later she booked tickets."

"Do you remember the name of the article?" Adam asked.

Cameron shook her head. "Nah, but if we go on the boat, I might be able to find it. Mom printed it out."

Adam considered the proposal. They had taken a huge risk seeking out Cameron's grandmother. True, she had managed to stay off the grid for the last ten years, no security numbers, no electronic traces the CIA could use to track her down. But they had probably figured out how Mimi had entered Australia by now. The sailboat, if it still was where they had left it, would most likely be compromised.

Then again. Staying at the farm would lead them nowhere. They couldn't keep running, that was not a sustainable plan. They either had to find out why someone was after them, or they had to figure out whether they could safely surrender to the police or the CIA. They had to find out who were their friends and who were their foes.

Adam got up from the bed and clapped his hands together. "We'll leave in the morning. Staying undetected for seven years has to count for something. We are probably safer on the boat than here at the farm."

Later in the afternoon, Adam drove back to the farm with the unlocked WIFI network. He sat outside in the motorhome and logged on to the shared Spideroak account. There were no more updates from Matt Parks, and Adam didn't update the document either. He didn't want to get Matt into any more trouble than he probably already was in. If Matt uncovered more information, and it was safe to send, he would update the document in his own time.

The simple system they had devised was based on New York Knicks' legendary 1969 season. Adam had written his comment on page 126 because that was the Knicks' score in their first regular game of the season. Ninety-four was their score for the second game. The next entry, by either Adam or Matt, therefore had to be on page 116, the score of their beloved team when they demolished the Chicago Bulls with twenty-nine points on October the seventeenth of 1969.

Adam looked at the iPad. Reluctantly he opened the Safari web-browser and found the Google website. He knew there was a risk any searches could be intercepted, but he couldn't help himself. He entered 'Patient F' in the search field. Only one relevant hit showed up in the search results.

It was a .org address, and it seemed legit. It looked like one of those conspiracy websites, websites with hundreds of conspiracy theories about governments around the world.

Adam clicked on the link.

It took some time before the website finally loaded, and Adam immediately regretted his actions. He had turned off the location services, and he was using a VPN service that would show the website owner that he logged on from the Hola server in the US. But if the NSA was listening in, surely they would have advanced technology that would surpass his amateurish circumventions a million times. And he had just heard the camera take a picture. Whoever owned the website had set it up to take a picture of the person who logged on. This was not a conspiracy website, it was a government website. A tracking website.

Most likely operated by the CIA, the very people they were trying to hide from.

Adam swore as he started up the engine. He quickly checked his watch. He had no idea what intelligence capabilities the CIA had in Australia, but he would be best off assuming they were well-equipped.

He stepped on the gas pedal and spun out on the road.

He had to get back to the farm as soon as possible.

They didn't have much time. The CIA would be there soon, and Adam wanted to have a quick look at that sailboat before they left Queensland.

-56-

D r Drecker was sitting by himself in his office. He couldn't see them, but he could hear birds outside the window, singing in the morning sun. He felt empty. The conversation with the CIA agent had drained him of strength, drained him of life.

He had thought MKULTRA had brought him in for his expertise, that he was the only person who could save Cody. Now it turned out it was only Cody they were interested in. Dr Drecker was only there to ensure that Cody behaved.

They had given him sort of meaningful tasks, let him interview the death row prisoners who didn't talk, let him come to his own conclusions about how the DMT affected the human body and brain. Rebuilt his self-confidence, let him remember how brilliant he had once been when he'd just started off as a scientist. But they hadn't been interested in his findings, not at all. He understood that now. He was there because of Cody only.

Because Cody needed someone familiar to relate to.

Someone who would let him open up.

Dr Kovacks had realised this several days ago. That's why he was so standoffish, so secretive. That's why Dr Kovacks didn't want to speak to Dr Drecker.

He knew that Dr Drecker was only a pawn in the game.

An unwitting spy for MKULTRA.

With a desperate cry he swiped his arm across the office desk. Piles of paper and documents went flying through the air. His coffee cup shattered in a thousand pieces when it hit the concrete floor.

He stared straight ahead for almost forty seconds before slowly tilting his head and looking up at the ceiling, up at the smoke alarm.

It didn't look like a normal smoke alarm. He had noticed that the first time he walked into the office.

"Sir, he has seen the camera. What do we do?" the guy in front of the video monitor asked. He was wearing a grey suit and a white tie.

"Keep it on. He won't do anything," the CIA agent replied.

-57-

The sailboat was anchored up in a somewhat sheltered river just outside Cairns. It was surrounded by several catamarans and houseboats. They all seemed abandoned. Adam was admiring the boat from the shore. "How do we get on-board?" he asked. The dinghy hung off the back of the sailboat, which was gently swaying in the wind in the middle of the river.

"We swim," Cameron replied, and started to undress.

"Are you serious?" Adam asked. "Aren't there sharks and crocodiles in these rivers?"

"Yeah, but sharks normally don't attack humans."

"What about the crocodiles?" Adam asked.

"Yeah, you gotta watch out for those. They'll kill you," Cameron replied, before diving into the river.

"Shit," Adam blurted out. He didn't want to, but there was no way he was standing back on shore when his daughter was swimming in a crocodile-infested river.

He jumped in, fully clothed, and started making his way towards Cameron, who was swimming on her back, laughing.

"What the hell are you laughing for?" Adam shouted. "Get your ass over to the sailboat as soon as possible. I don't want you swimming around here."

"There are no crocodiles in this river, Dad. You are more likely to win the lotto than encounter a crocodile here."

"You little shit," Adam said, with a friendly smirk. Then he started racing after Cameron. To his surprise though, he wasn't catching up. Cameron was a brilliant swimmer, although she didn't seem built for it. Adam had excelled in swimming at high school, he was built like a swimmer and had taught many of his PT clients how to improve their freestyle swimming. But he had no chance in hell of keeping up with Cameron, who kept gaining metres on him, and now almost had reached the back of the boat.

"How did you learn how to swim like that?" Adam asked while sitting on the stern of the boat, removing his wet clothes.

"Not much to do on a sailboat," Cameron said matter-of-factly, as she located the key to the cabin and unlocked the small wooden door. Water was dripping from her body.

The muggy air, the air one lived and breathed in on a sailboat, filled Adam's lungs as he followed Cameron down into the cabin.

"We'll have to be quick," Adam said.

Cameron nodded and moved swiftly. She found two brightly coloured, waterproof bags, dry bags, and started filling them with items. Adam didn't say anything. This boat had been his wife's and daughter's home for the last few years. It had been all Cameron had known. It contained all her possessions.

A normal girl her age would probably have a room full of electronic gadgets. She would have bikes and trampolines, closets full of dresses. Cameron had quickly filled up two small bags with clothes. That was all she owned.

"Do you know where mom kept her files?" Adam asked.

Cameron nodded and opened a secret door in the floor of the hull. She pulled out a waterproof plastic box, forty by forty centimetres. "She kept all her important stuff in here," she said.

"What's inside?" Adam asked.

Cameron shrugged her shoulders. "I don't know. I never asked."

-58-

D r Drecker walked down the stairs towards the patient cells, he was in a hurry. Behind him he could hear the sound of running feet on metal.

"Hold up, Dr Drecker, hold up."

It was the voice of the CIA agent, the familiar voice of the CIA agent whom Dr Drecker had begun to like over the last week or so. Now he knew it had all been a charade. All the kind words and flattering, it had all been a sham. He should have understood it sooner. The CIA agent had never introduced himself with a name, just told Dr Drecker that names were unnecessary at MKULTRA. He should have known. How could you trust a person who wouldn't even tell you his name?

"Where are you heading?" the CIA agent asked when he finally caught up with Dr Drecker.

"I'm on my way to see my son."

"I don't think that's a good idea," the CIA agent said.

"Why not?"

"Not the way you feel right now. I don't think it is a good idea to see your son the way you feel right now."

Dr Drecker stopped and turned around.

"Do you think I'm an idiot?" he asked.

"I beg your pardon," the CIA agent said.

"This bullshit story about Cody being the solution to immortality. Do you think I'm an idiot?'

"I don't understand," the CIA agent said.

"I had a long think about it up in my office. The office you have bugged with cameras."

"I'm sorry about that. But that's how all the offices here are. You do not have any privacy when you work for MKULTRA."

"And everybody just forgot to tell me that?"

"That was my fault," the CIA agent said. "I didn't want to overwhelm you with all the details. You have had a lot of information to take in, and the added stress of not knowing what's going to happen to your son. I guess I wanted to shield you from all that."

"I want out. And I want to take my son with me."

"That won't happen," the CIA agent said.

"You have no right to hold us here. This is not Guantanamo Bay, we are not terrorists."

"That's true. But you're not leaving this facility."

"People will start to ask questions. Wonder where we are."

The CIA agent cleared his throat.

"I am sorry to burst your bubble, Dr Drecker, but nobody will start to ask questions."

"What do you mean? I have colleagues, Cody has friends. They will start to wonder where we are."

"Cody is dead. His funeral was held a few days ago. You didn't make it."

"What do you mean, I didn't make it? Cody is alive, he is right down the hall."

"That is correct. But out in the real world Cody is officially dead. You resigned from the university the first day I brought you here. Don't you remember signing all those papers?"

"Yes, but..."

"You sold your summerhouse in the Hamptons. You took the money and moved to New Mexico. To start a new life. People will understand. It is hard to lose a son. It saves them from the awkward conversations, asking how you are dealing with it."

"You've erased my life?" Dr Drecker asked.

"We haven't erased anything. We have given you a unique opportunity. To be a part of something greater than yourself."

"And what is that? Finding a cure for aging? Creating immortals? No, thank you. I have thought through that scenario. It isn't right. Nobody should be able to live forever. If you came up with a way to create immortality it would ruin our planet. We already have a population problem. The Earth can't sustain its current population, what would happen if people stopped aging?"

"Finally, you get it," the CIA agent said. "This has never been about finding a cure for aging. This has been about fighting a war to allow our world to remain the way it is."

The CIA agent grabbed Dr Drecker's shoulder.

"Why do you think we closed down all the psychedelic experiments in the 1980s? We knew we could probably learn a helluva lot from them. Maybe even the secret of travel to distant galaxies."

"So the government believes we can travel to different worlds through the mind?"

"We know that we will never be able to travel to other stars if we are constrained by our bodies. And regardless the speed of light will always be another constraint. Even travel to the nearest stars would take several light years, and to travel to a possibly habitable planet system is inconceivable for humanity for the next few centuries." The CIA agent let go of Dr Drecker's shoulder again. "But our goal has never been to travel to other stars. We have to consider the facts, and the facts are that when we at one stage in the distant future finally encounter an alien civilisation, it will most likely be our doom. Look at how we treat animals we consider mentally inferior to us. Do you think a superior alien civilisation would treat us any differently?"

Dr Drecker acknowledged that the CIA agent had a point. It was unlikely that an alien civilisation would invite us over for tea and cupcakes.

"So you closed down the psychedelic experiments because you didn't want to risk finding out something you didn't like?"

"Partially correct. But there are other matters to consider. A government's primary objective isn't to foster scientific advances or economic growth. It is to create stability. If large masses of people started to take psychedelics in order to connect with the greater universe, to hunt for hidden worlds, then productivity would plummet. There is one massive side effect with psychedelics. They are not addictive or destructive like cocaine and heroin, but they are a hindrance for materialism. Have you ever met a hippie with ambition? Probably not, and that is the problem. Our whole society is built on people wanting and buying stuff they don't need. If we took that away, our society would collapse. That's why the most important war our government is fighting is not against the Taliban, Al Qaida or some other terrorist organisation, hiding in a mud hut in the mountains of Afghanistan. We're fighting a domestic war. A war against spirituality."

"You're saying that the US government is in a war against spirituality?"

The CIA agent smiled. "Spirituality causes lack of ambition and materialism, which are vital for our society and our very way of living. Spirituality could possibly lead to the discovery of other worlds, and open the gates for alien species to enter our world. We don't really know what the consequences could be. We don't want to know. But what we do know is that a society where people want stuff, a society where people have ambitions, a society where people work for fifty to sixty years, and then die a few years after retirement is a society that works. It is a proven system. Why mess with a proven system?"

Dr Drecker shook his head.

"But why do we study these patients, why do we study the death row prisoners if we are not looking for a cure for aging, a process for self-healing?"

"We are not studying them to find out how we can recreate them. We are looking for a way to kill them."

-59-

"Holy cow. That was close," Adam said. They had just passed the farm he had been stealing bandwidth from the last few days. Three police cars were parked outside in the garden. Undoubtedly the police officers were inside questioning the owners; had someone been stopping by, asking to use their WIFI? Adam thought back on the situation where he had noticed the picture being taken. Luckily he had been sitting inside the motorhome. His face had filled most of the screen, so it was unlikely the police could deduce, from the picture, that it was a motorhome he was driving. But one never knew. The CIA was clever, they had their methods. Somehow they would figure out how Adam, Nina and Cameron moved around, and then it would only be a question of time before they got caught.

There was, however, a positive: There had only been regular police cars outside the farm. That meant that the CIA probably didn't have a large presence in Queensland, and had to rely on local police for most of their intelligence. They would probably locate his mother-in-law's property and the sailboat within twenty-four hours. But by then Adam and Cameron would be long gone. And the mother-in-law wouldn't say a word. Couldn't say a word. Because Adam hadn't told her what his next step was going to be.

In all honesty he didn't know what it was going to be himself.

Three hours later they were still on the road.

"We might stop for a stretch and a coffee," Adam said. He had just seen a sign for a rest place coming up.

"That sounds like a good idea," Nina said. Cameron was listening to her iPod and probably hadn't heard Adam's comment, but she would be unlikely to protest. She looked bored, and a stop would at least mean a change of scenery.

Adam parked the car close to the toilets, and they all jumped out. "Stay close, and don't wander off," Adam said.

Nina turned around and smiled at him. She and Cameron were going for a walk down to the beach, while Adam was going to have a look at the contents of his wife's plastic box. The one from the sailboat.

He sat down at the dinner table in the motorhome and lifted the lid of the box. He struggled with mixed feelings. This was what was left of his wife, this was all there was.

He had lived in this fantasy world the last seven years, hoping that he eventually would find his wife and daughter. That his wife would explain why she had done what she did, and that everything would be fine again.

A happy ending.

Instead he had found a dead wife, and a daughter who wasn't his.

He had been living in a bubble all these years.

He should be more realistic going forward, he should be more pragmatic.

He wouldn't find the answer in the box. There would be no

letter from his wife explaining her reasons. There would be no closure.

Instead he found himself just wishing for that.

Wishing for an explanation, wishing for a closure.

He first pulled out the pile of papers that filled the top half of the box. Some papers were held together by beige manila folders with red rubber bands, and some were just scattered around. There didn't seem to be any system in his wife's filing. He laid the documents out on the small kitchen table in the motorhome. It seemed like most of them were just old paper clippings or printouts from the internet. Some of them were yellow in colour, and a sailboat full of moisture had probably not been the ideal storing place all those years.

Adam skimmed through a couple of pages; they were mostly about large accidents and terrorist actions in South East Asia. A cold shiver went through his body. Could the CIA possibly be right in their suspicion that Cameron and her mum had something to do with the explosion on-board flight SQ183? Could his own wife and daughter be terrorists?

No, he dismissed the idea.

If that had been the case, Cameron would never have led him to the boat, led him to the plastic box with all these news clippings.

They had to be innocent.

He stacked the papers together in a big pile. His wife must have been collecting news clippings over several years, as some of them dated back to the late eighties. A long time before he and his wife met.

He pulled the plastic box closer. On the bottom there was a small, grey, metallic chest. Adam immediately recognised it, his wife used to keep it next to her night table. She used to keep her jewellery in it, but when she disappeared she left all her jewellery at home.

He reached for the metallic box with anticipation.

He placed it on the table and gently opened the lid. He couldn't believe his eyes. Inside were a stack of letters, letters he recognised very well, letters he himself had authored.

His wife had kept all the letters he had written when he was stationed in different war zones around the world.

A tear crept up in the corner of his eye. Was it possible? Was it possible that she had still loved him all these years?

He picked up a few letters and skimmed through them. He didn't really need to read them, he knew them by heart. When you were stationed in a foreign country, when you saw friends and strangers getting killed every week, it did something to you. You became hard. You hid your emotions.

But you still had to let the steam out somehow, still had to feel like you were a human being. Adam's way of coping with this problem had been to write letters. He had poured his emotions into those letters. Told his wife how much he loved Cameron and her, told her how he would never leave them. It was only when he was home that he was incapable of showing emotions, it was only at home that he put on his stone face, only at home that he never acknowledged how happy he had been.

On paper he had allowed himself to be another Adam, allowed himself to feel. He put the letters away and picked up a brown envelope. He didn't recognise it, it didn't look like one of his own.

It looked official.

He pulled out the letter from the envelope and started reading.

It was as if his whole world came crashing down.

This was the reason she had left.

This was the reason she had been running all these years.

-60-

D r Drecker stared at the CIA agent in disbelief.

"Did you say you were looking for a way to kill them? To kill the patients?"

The CIA agent nodded. "I can understand that this may come as a shock to you, but we have to do what is best for our country. What is best for our planet."

"Are you crazy? Do you want me to help you find a way to kill Cody? To kill my own son?"

"You are not looking at this in a rational way, Dr Drecker. That person down in the cell is not your son anymore. You said it yourself, you saw something change in him. Something that scared you. You even requested that he be put into a cell."

"There is a difference. I asked if he could be kept in a cell so we had more control. I didn't ask for him to be killed."

"You have to understand that these are unprecedented times. We have a possible new enemy, an enemy stronger than anything we have ever encountered before in all of human history. And this enemy has the ability to walk among us undetected. To blend in where they want to. To take on any identity."

"If you are right, if these personalities that have taken over the patients are from a different dimension or a different realm of existence, what wrong have they done? We were the ones who opened the gates, we were the ones who injected our test subjects with DMT."

"That's true, but we can't allow ourselves to be fooled by their seeming lack of aggression. We can't forget Dr Kovacks' LSD-study, and how all his psychopaths pretended to have become gentle and compassionate, only to murder and rape when they were let outside the prison. The fact is that all the patients have an apocalyptic ideology. They pray twice a day. Always the same verses, about the world burning and its inhabitants being slain. It doesn't matter that they are no longer using words. We know how they think. Doesn't that scare you?"

"We are not comparing apples with apples," Dr Drecker said.

"How so?"

"I don't care what you do with the death row prisoners. They were sentenced to death and probably deserved it. Whether they are the killers they once were or something else doesn't really matter. I don't care if you kill them all. But my son Cody has done nothing wrong. He is the only innocent in this whole situation. You have to let him go," pleaded Dr Drecker.

"You know we can't do that. And Dr Kovacks and the janitor are in the same boat as your son. They are not murderers either."

"They are not my son," Dr Drecker yelled before calming down. "Do you have kids?" he asked the CIA agent.

"No."

"So you can't possibly understand what I am going through. You can't possibly comprehend that there is no way I can let you kill Cody."

"We are not going to kill Cody."

"I thought you said you were looking to find a way to kill the patients, I thought you said that was the purpose of this facility."

"That's true. But Cody might be an exception. If he follows the pattern of Patient F, then he might provide us with the answers we need."

"Follow the pattern of Patient F? I don't understand. You never explained to me what happened with Patient F. How did he escape and where is he?"

"The first question I can answer, the second I want Cody to help us with," the CIA agent answered.

-61-

There was a knock on the door of the motorhome and Adam quickly rose from his seat. He put the official-looking letter back in the brown envelope, folded it and stuffed it down his left back pocket.

He opened the door and to his relief it was only Cameron standing outside.

"I think we should get going," Cameron said. "We just listened to the police radio, and they are talking about being on the lookout for an RV or a motorhome."

"How did you listen to the police radio?" Adam asked.

"There was a kid over at the toilets. He let me borrow his phone for a while. Just wanted to check the news, but it turned out he had this mobile app that lets you listen to the police radio. It's pretty cool," Cameron said.

"Can we use your iPad to do the same?" Adam asked.

"Nah, we should assume that it will be tracked. I slipped it into the kid's backpack. They were on their way to Cairns. Hopefully he won't find it until they get there. It may lead the police in the wrong direction," Cameron said.

Adam smiled. "Don't even tell me how you come up with these ideas," he said and let Cameron and Nina back into the motorhome.

"Do you get carsick, Nina, or do you think you can go through some documents while I'm driving?" Adam asked.

"I'm fine. Never been carsick in my life. But what am I looking for?" she asked.

"Something about Vietnam. I had a quick look myself, but I couldn't find anything. Might need a woman's eyes."

"Isn't it best Cameron has a look? I mean, if she has seen the document before?"

Adam checked his rear mirror. Cameron was lying in the back of the motorhome, listening to music with closed eyes.

"I'd prefer if you did it."

"Ok," she said without pursuing for a reason. She unclipped her seatbelt and climbed back towards the pile of news clippings in the plastic box.

"I think I have something," she said half an hour later. She had moved back to the front passenger seat and was going through the last few pages of the news clippings.

"What is it?" Adam asked.

"It seems to be a short article about this Shaman in Vietnam who supposedly has healing powers."

"I don't get it," Adam said. "My wife has obviously gone through a lot of effort to collect all these news clippings, but why? They are either about terrorist actions or dodgy prophets hiding in the mountains."

"There must have been something she was looking for. According to Cameron they have been sailing in most of the waters these clippings are about. Vietnam is probably one of the few countries in Southeast Asia they haven't visited," she said.

"But why? And why take the risk of leaving Australia by plane when they have managed to stay under the radar for so long?" Adam asked.

"I think you should ask your daughter that question," Nina answered.

Three hours later Adam pulled off the main road and parked the motorhome at one of the rest stops. When Cameron returned from the toilets, Adam called her over.

"Is this the article your mom was reading?" he asked, handing over the printout of the article about Vietnam.

"I'm not sure, but it looks like it," Cameron answered.

"Why was she collecting articles about Shamans and terrorist actions?" Adam asked.

"I told you I don't know," Cameron replied, with cold bitterness in her voice. "Mom wasn't really the most open person."

"Well, there has to be a reason," Adam said.

"I've got no idea about the terrorist actions, but she did have this fascination with Shamans. We visited a lot of them over the years, people claiming they had healing powers, people claiming they could tell the future. They were all crooks of course. Mom was quite good at sussing them out. Didn't take her long before she knew whether they were fake or not. All of them were."

"And what did you do then?"

"We just moved on to the next one. She didn't expose them or anything. She just got a bit disappointed, and then we would leave the next day. I think that she was hoping to find one who was real one day," Cameron said.

Adam thought about it. His wife had been sailing throughout Southeast Asia for the last seven years, searching for Shamans. Always staying under the radar, not once slipping up. And then, out of the blue, she had bought tickets for herself and Cameron to fly to Singapore, and planned to travel to Vietnam from there. Why this sudden recklessness? Why the urgency?

She must have known that Adam would find out where she was going, and had that been the purpose? Did she intentionally buy her ticket in her maiden name so Adam would come after them?

There was only one way to find out what had been going through his wife's head.

They had to go to Vietnam.

They had to find this Shaman.

"Are you crazy?" Nina said. "We've got everybody from the police to the CIA after us, and you want to go to Vietnam."

"We are getting nowhere just hiding out here on the road. At some stage they will find us, it is inevitable."

"How do you even plan to get out of Australia? The moment we show our passports at the airport we will be arrested. Oh hey, I forgot, I don't even have my passport. I had to leave it in my apartment when you and Cameron abducted me."

"Abducted you? Don't be ridiculous. If we had left you in Brisbane you would be dead by now."

Nina looked at Adam with anger in her eyes. Her life had been perfectly normal until Adam and Cameron had shown up. She knew Adam was right though. They had probably saved her life.

All the other hospital staff who were on duty the night Cameron was admitted were dead. But she also secretly blamed Adam for it all. If it hadn't been for Adam and his daughter, if it hadn't been for the airplane crash, her life would have still been perfectly normal.

Boring, but perfectly normal.

"Sorry, I didn't mean that," Nina said.

"I know. We are all in the same boat here. I have no idea why these people are hunting us either. But we have to do something. Waiting for the problem to solve itself is not going to work."

"I agree. But how do we get into Vietnam? To leave Australia we will need passports."

Adam turned to face Nina, and smiled. "I am not sure, but I've got a feeling my daughter has got some ideas."

-62-

"So you think Cody can help you find this Patient F?"

"You heard what he told you. He has been held in total isolation, yet he has been able to communicate with the other patients. He has been able to communicate with Dr Kovacks."

"Yes, but they are only separated by a few hundred metres. We have no idea where this Patient F is located."

"Do you really think distance matters? These patients have acquired capabilities way beyond our understanding, Dr Drecker. We are best off assuming nothing."

"Ok," Dr Drecker said. "But what is in it for Cody? Why would you be willing to give up Cody if he can deliver Patient F?"

The CIA agent smiled.

"Because Cody is Cody, and Patient F is Patient F. Your son is not a mass murderer. We may be able to live with Cody having extraordinary abilities, under your supervision. We can't live with a mass murderer having them."

"Mass murderer? I thought you said Patient F was different. That he was a kid, the son of one of the death row prisoners?"

"That is correct," the CIA agent said. "But it turned out Patient

F wasn't that innocent after all. He may have been innocent when he was here at MKULTRA, but we have evidence he is behind the deaths of almost a hundred people."

"So once again the US has created their own enemy. Turned a patriot into a terrorist?"

"I can see the irony," the CIA agent replied. "That is how most of the terrorists we fight have been formed. They respond to the injustice they feel in their hearts by attacking our very way of living. But we will bow for no terrorist, and we will not make excuses for thugs. Because that is what he is, Patient F, – a criminal who wants to spread fear in the hearts of every American."

Dr Drecker lay down on the couch, and closed his eyes for a few seconds. He had a massive headache that wouldn't go away, it had been years since he was plagued with a migraine, and he hoped this wasn't the first sign of a relapse.

"Are you ok?" the CIA agent asked.

"I'm fine. I just need some water." Dr Drecker stood up and walked over to his desk, grabbed a half-full bottle of water and downed it in one big drink.

"Do you want a break, or do you want me to continue?" the CIA agent asked. Dr Drecker was still lying on the couch.

"Please continue," Dr Drecker replied. The CIA agent was prepping him for the next meeting with his son, Cody.

Dr Drecker had agreed to the CIA agent's plan. He wasn't sure whether the CIA agent would honour his word. Wasn't sure if he even had the authority to offer a deal. But Dr Drecker didn't have a lot of choice. He had to try whatever he could to save Cody, to save him from a future in this facility, a life without a future, a life stuck in a glass cage.

Or for Cody, possibly eternity in a glass cage.

"So how was Patient F able to escape? How was a kid able to escape?" Dr Drecker asked.

"We didn't know the full extent of the patient's abilities back then, and we did take larger risks in assessing them. The patients were initially allowed to mingle among themselves, and we interviewed them face-to-face on a regular basis until they stopped talking. Patient F, however, was kept in isolation; he was about to turn sixteen and appeared to go through some sort of a change."

"Puberty, he was probably going through puberty," Dr Drecker said.

"I wish it was that simple, but it wasn't. He started to get sick and his body started showing signs of shutting down. It was decided to send him to Australia."

"To Australia? Why Australia?"

"There was this expert on genes who was based in Melbourne. We had to send Patient F to his lab. We couldn't complete the tests here in the US. We sent him on a special flight, security was top notch and everything seemed to go as planned. But on the way to the lab disaster struck. The train that carried Patient F and his minders the last leg of the trip collided with another freight train. More than eighty people dead. Everybody on board the passenger train died."

"And Patient F?"

"Patient F died too. But three days later he woke up at the morgue. He was rushed to the hospital and some religious doctor thought he was Jesus resurrected and helped him escape."

"So he is still out there?

"He is very much still out there."

"And you're afraid that he being out among the general population is a threat?"

The CIA agent laughed. "I don't think. I know."

"Well, if we are going to have any progress with these patients we need to remove them from their normal surroundings. Part of the reason they have stopped talking is probably that they know there is no point. Whatever they do, they will still be stuck inside a cell the next morning. You need to offer them some incentives."

The CIA agent smiled. "Incentives? These are not normal patients. At one time in their life they were stone blood killers. Patient A strangled two women, Patient C raped and killed three underage boys. These are not normal people."

"But they are not these people anymore. It is clear when you observe them that they are not these people anymore."

"Remember what happened with Dr Kovacks' Connecticut Prison Study. Don't get fooled by how they appear."

"Are you suggesting that this is a play? That they have all managed to keep this going for almost forty years, five patients, without anyone slipping up?"

"Remember Dr Kovacks' study," the CIA agent repeated, walking away.

Dr Drecker remembered Dr Kovacks' study all too well. He had studied it in detail before accepting Dr Kovacks' application to work for the university. And it was true that Dr Kovacks' opinions had changed during the study. Initially he had been sceptic, he had even written a book about psychopaths and how the diagnosis wasn't a mental disorder it was possible to cure. One was either born a psychopath or not. But he had grown attached to his test subjects, seen them flourish in the study. Seen them progress from hard and closed off personalities, to passionate humans with consideration for their fellow humans. Seen them comfort each other, seen them share experiences. He had been fooled.

Was the same thing about to happen with him? Had the sceptic Dr Drecker finally been convinced? As far back as he could remember, he had never had any faith, never fallen for the lies and hypocrisy of religion. He had attended church and been amazed how grown people could sit there and listen to a pastor preach that people were supposed to disregard everything they saw, and instead live life by blind faith.

Now he was proposing the same himself.

Proposing that there was more to the brain than we could see through the scans, more than we could see through the microscope.

More than we could see through science.

He rested his head in the palms of his hands. They felt warm against his cold face.

He knew there were many things that were invisible to humans. We couldn't see infrared light, UV light, X-rays nor gamma rays. Did this fact make those things less real?

We couldn't see thoughts, but we still had them every day.

Maybe he should be open to the possibility that there were things right in front of us that we couldn't see. Maybe there were overlapping universes, different realms of existence, and that

Carl Sagan had been right when he once said that we might be living in a world surrounded by alien civilisations, and just not have the technology to realise it.

Maybe the CIA agent was right when he feared that the patients had been taken over by aliens.

Dr Drecker shrugged it off.

He was a man of science, and his son's life depended on him.

His son's life depended on Dr Drecker approaching this problem as a scientist. That was also the reason the CIA agent had included him in the project. He realised that their own scientists had been compromised by the isolation of their work, compromised by the patients.

Stuck in a dead-end thinking pattern.

It was up to Dr Drecker to break this thinking pattern.

It was up to Dr Drecker to come up with new ideas.

-63-

"So it's that easy? They don't check the passports?" Nina asked.

"Why would they? Nobody has reported them stolen," Cameron said.

"And we don't need visas?"

"Not if we plan to stay under fifteen days. Holiday visa is fine."

"I'm not going to feel safe on a plane ever again. If it is this easy to get onto a plane using a fake identity I mean."

"It's even easier." Cameron said. "Most airports don't even check stolen passports. It's too time-consuming. That's how illegal immigrants get to Europe. Nobody bothers to check the databases. We've got valid passports. We should have no problems."

Adam shook his head.

"I still think it is risky. What if they find out that the passports are missing?"

"How often do you check your own passport? There are no signs anybody has ever broken into their home. Nothing is missing, except for their passports, which I by the way found hidden in the dad's home office. Trust me, they won't find out until they start planning their next overseas holiday, whenever that is going to be."

"I'm still not convinced," Adam said.

"Any better ideas?" Cameron asked as she laid the three passports on the table in front of them.

Nina picked one up. "It kinda looks like you," she said, looking at Adam. Age is right, eighty-five isn't it?

"Let me see," Adam said, and snatched the passport from her fingers.

"Ah, I have been to the Middle East twice in the last two years, and I had my big trip overseas in 2010. Visited three countries in Europe," he said flipping through the pages of the passport.

Nina and Cameron giggled.

"Ok, it is the best option we have. We need to get out of Australia anyway. It is only a matter of time before they start putting up posters of us," Adam said.

"Why do you say that?"

"Because I know how these things work. We've been on the run for more than a week now. The longer it goes, the harder it will get for them. So they will start to tighten the screw. Make it harder for us to hide. The motorhome is not an option anymore, neither is the sailboat or Cameron's grandmother. Our best option is Vietnam. At least I know some people over there."

"Do you know people in Vietnam? You haven't mentioned that before," Nina said.

"There was no need to. But yes, I do know a few people over there, or at least one guy. Southeast Asia is a popular place for retired military personnel. Cheap alcohol and cheap girls, and none of the stigma the vets are met with at home in the US."

He hadn't intended it to, but Adam realised that the comment came out with a sting of bitterness. He could sympathize with the soldiers who moved to the Far East, and if it hadn't been for Cameron he would probably have done the same. It was hard to get on with life in American suburbia. Nobody knew what you had been through; nobody could even start to comprehend what you had been through. In the Philippines and Indonesia there were at least other people with the same experiences, people who knew how it was to have taken lives and have to live with it afterwards.

People who had been to war.

"Ok, it's agreed. We go to Vietnam." Adam said, rising from the table.

-64-

"How are you feeling, Cody?" Dr Decker was seated in a white, plastic chair in Cody's room. Cody was lying on his bed, pretending to read a book. It looked like a Penguin Classic.

"I'm ok," Cody answered. He didn't look up from the book.

"What are you reading?" Dr Drecker asked.

Cody turned his head and shot his dad an uncertain look. "War and Peace," he said.

"Wow, didn't realise you were into that heavy stuff," Dr Drecker said, trying to lighten the mood.

"Have you looked at the selection we can choose from in the library? Even China doesn't censor this much," Cody said. "And besides, the title seemed appropriate."

"What do you mean?"

"I have realised that I am not a patient here. I am a prisoner. You and your friends from the government think I am a threat, somebody they have to keep locked up."

"That's not right. You have to stay under observation for the next month or so, but after that you will be free to go."

"Really," Cody said with a sarcastic tone in his voice. He made it abundantly clear that he realised Dr Drecker, his own father, was telling a lie. The realisation hurt Dr Drecker in ways he had never imagined. He had been so happy when he had seen Cody rise from the dead, when he had reconnected with the son who had been lost to him for so many years. Now Cody was about to slip away yet again. Cody knew Dr Drecker wasn't telling the truth, Cody knew he wouldn't be released in less than a month. It was Dr Drecker who was delusional, thinking that the CIA, thinking that MKULTRA and CIA would honour their word and let Cody out under his supervision. It would of course never happen, it could never happen.

They were both already dead, Dr Drecker just hadn't realised until now.

If MKULTRA found a way to kill the death row prisoners, if they found a safe way to exterminate them, they would. And afterwards they would clean up. They couldn't risk any civilians blabbering to the public about the black DMT operation. Dr Drecker had already been told too much information, seen too much.

Truth be told, he wouldn't be surprised if, officially, he was already dead, buried in an empty grave next to his son Cody at the local cemetery in the Hamptons.

How could he have been so stupid? How could he have believed the promises of the nameless CIA agent, the man who kept feeding him dribs of information whenever it suited his needs? Cody was the smart one, Cody had realised what he hadn't: That he was suffering from hope, hope that everything would sort itself out.

Hope that Cody and he would be free to go as soon as they provided MKULTRA with this Patient F.

It was of course impossible.

They were already doomed.

Dr Drecker wiped a tear away from the corner of his eye, and looked away from Cody. He didn't want him to see him crying again.

And while he was sitting there on the white, plastic chair, staring at the white wall in front of him with eyes full of tears, he realised that there was only one possible solution.

He realised he had to give MKULTRA Patient F to save Cody.

-65-

The stewardess from Singapore Airlines handed Adam his headphones. He hadn't minded paying the few hundreds extra the Singapore Airlines flight had cost compared to Air Asia X and the other low-cost carriers. At least they got some free meals and entertainment on-board. The main reason he had booked Singapore Airlines, however, had been that it was probably the safest airline at the moment. They had just had an accident, on the very same route, where all passengers had perished. It was human nature therefore for the airline to be extra cautious with safety measures, and it was human nature for passengers to avoid Singapore Airlines like the plague. Adam, Cameron and Nina therefore had a whole row of seats each. Economy class had turned into first class with excellent service and plenty of leg space. Adam plugged in the headphones and turned on the entertainment system. He flipped through the movies without being able to decide what to watch. Instead, he removed the headphones and picked up the stack of papers the hostess had handed him when he entered the plane. It had been ages since he had read an actual paper, an actual paper made out of paper. He quickly ditched the purple one, he didn't even have to look at the title to know it was the financial paper, something that didn't interest him at all. Instead he picked up one of the tabloids, Brisbane News, and started flipping through the pages while chewing on some peanuts. At page eleven he almost choked on them.

The top quarter of the page had a picture of Adam. He closed the paper and looked around, trying to assess whether any other passengers had seen what he had just seen. It was a blessing that the plane was almost half empty. The only other passenger who had a clear view of what he was reading was already curled up in a blanket sound asleep. Adam shifted over to the window seat and opened the paper to page eleven again. With horror he read the text underneath the picture.

He had been correct when he had wondered whether the reporter at the hospital had connected the dots, he had been correct when he had worried that the reporter had suspected Adam could have some sort of relation to the lone survivor of flight SQ183. But how had the reporter been able to take a photo of Adam? He was certain he hadn't seen any camera.

"Shit," he blurted out. The glasses! The reporter had worn glasses. Probably some cheap imitation of the new Google glasses. That must have been how he had been able to snap a picture when he was being led away by the security guards.

The picture was of poor quality, it was grainy, in black and white, and half of Adam's face was covered by the door to the waiting room. But the poor quality, and the fact that Adam quite obviously tried to conceal his face made the impact even greater.

'Who is the mystery man in the waiting room?' read the tabloid headline. It was followed by a short speculative story of who Adam could be. The reporter had no sources, no identity, no story at all. Nevertheless the editor had somehow allowed him to publish the picture.

"Fucking tabloids," Adam swore. He was glad they had left Australia and were on their way to Vietnam. Moving around in Australia would probably be impossible in a few days. Someone somewhere would recognise him – the internet was like that. And the demand for news involving the crash of flight SQ183 was still going strong in Australia. As long as no conclusion had been made whether it had been an accident or a terrorist action, the story would keep bouncing around in the media. It was human nature. And now they had a possible culprit. Who was the man in the grainy picture? What was his business in the waiting room of the operating theatre that was working on the lone survivor of flight SQ183? Could he have been involved in the explosion later that night, the explosion that killed thirty-six hospital staff and the lone survivor?

Adam closed the paper and waved for the air hostess. He needed a drink.

Ten minutes later, while he was enjoying his whiskey, he pondered how easy it had been to leave Australia. The officers in the passport control had hardly glanced at the passports. It was obviously easier to leave a country than to enter one. But Adam didn't fear that they would have any problems in Singapore or Vietnam either. Singapore was just a transit airport and Ho Chi Minh City, which was their final destination, would most likely be a breeze too. The passports Cameron had stolen were relatively inconspicuous. Adam wasn't an exact replica of the guy in the picture, but he was pretty close. And Adam knew that Asians to a certain degree viewed westerners the way westerners viewed Asians. They had more difficulties distinguishing the facial features. Westerners often joked about Asians looking alike. Well, for Asians westerners looked alike.

For once a little bit of racism would work in Adam's favour.

PART 3

-66-

"I am so sorry Cody. It's all my fault." Dr Drecker couldn't help himself. He started sobbing uncontrollably.

Cody got out of bed and walked over to his dad. He put his right arm on Dr Drecker's shoulder, a consoling touch. "It doesn't matter, Dad. What's done is done."

The comment just made Dr Drecker sob even harder. He knew Cody was right. There was not even a point to say the socially expected 'It's not just your fault. It's my fault too', because Cody was totally innocent in this whole ordeal. Cody had been living his own life. He didn't have a good job, a fancy education or a lot of prospects for the future. The most he could have hoped for was probably a low-level job in construction or retail. A low-income life with not a lot to live for. But at least he had had a life, his own life. Dr Drecker had taken all that away from him. And who was Dr Drecker to judge what a good life was? He hadn't been happy with his own life. He had divorced his wife and hardly spent time with his son when he grew up. For what? To get a fancy job title and a massive mortgage, to have power to boss around his underlings and intimidate his pretty assistants into having sex with him? Dr Drecker's life had amounted to nothing, it was shallow, empty. The university research programs would go on without him, everybody would go on without him. They probably wouldn't even notice he was gone.

"It's ok, Dad," Cody said.

"It's not ok, Cody. I have failed you. I have failed you on so many levels."

Cody leant in closer and whispered into Dr Drecker's ear. "It's not over yet," he said.

"What do you mean?" Dr Drecker asked.

"I've seen him."

"Seen whom?"

"The saviour. And he is coming here. Coming here to free us."

Dr Drecker pulled back from Cody.

"Impossible. That's impossible. You can't talk to him. Telepathy is impossible."

"I don't talk to him. I don't talk to any of them. I just see what they see. I feel what they feel. And they can feel him. They can feel him coming."

"You see what Patient F sees?" Dr Drecker asked.

Cody nodded. "Through the others."

"Where is he now?" Dr Drecker asked.

Cody shrugged his shoulders. "I don't know. I only know that he is underground. In some sort of tunnel or something. It's dark. It's hot. It's scary."

"Can you draw it for me?" Dr Drecker asked.

"Sure," Cody said."

Dr Drecker pulled out a pencil and pushed his notepad over to Cody.

Cody started immediately. He had always been an artistic

boy. It had been part of his Asperger syndrome. When he was a toddler he could sit for hours just colouring in or making doodles. And when he grew into a teenager he could draw almost exact replicas of what he had seen at some point in his life. If Cody's mum took him to the Zoo he would draw every single animal over the next few weeks. And he wouldn't just draw them, he would draw them in the exact position he had seen them the day they'd gone to the Zoo. In the exact same position, with even an insignificant detail as how the leaves had been swaying in the wind on that particular day, perfectly captured. Dr Drecker had always despised this quality with Cody. Artists didn't make any money. Drawing pictures wouldn't pay the bills and he had strongly discouraged Cody from pursuing his hobby. Instead he had enrolled Cody at a school that focused on maths and physics, courses that he himself had excelled in when he was a teenager. It hadn't worked out well. Cody had dropped out early.

It turned out his eidetic memory, or photographic memory as most people called it, didn't apply to any practical stuff.

Watching Cody draw the underground tunnels he had seen in his dreams made Dr Drecker for the first time in his life really appreciate Cody's talent. The pen raced elegantly over the page, it was almost as if it caressed it. And although the drawing wasn't even half finished, Dr Drecker knew where Patient F was hiding. He had seen those tunnels before on a television program. He knew exactly where they were.

And he had noticed something else when Cody was drawing.

Something he didn't know the reason for.

But something he understood was important.

Very important.

-67-

The mercury was close to forty degrees as Adam downed his second Tiger beer for the day. The time was only ten thirty, but it felt like mid-afternoon. They had walked around for several hours already, asking for a man who just went by the name Hayburner. He was one of Adam's contacts from his time in the military, and had received his nickname because he was fast as hell and built like a racehorse.

"How long has it been since you spoke to this guy?"

"About ten years," Adam replied.

"How do you know he is still here? How do you even know if he is still alive?"

"He's alive, and he's here," Adam replied bluntly, without even trying to offer an explanation. Instead he started flipping through the menu in front of him. "Snake porridge, fried waterdragon…. don't they have anything decent?"

"Try the last page," Cameron said.

With a sigh, Adam flipped through to the last page, and found some more appealing meals. He decided to stick to a vegetarian dish. The restaurant wasn't among the most hygienic-looking on the street, but a local vendor had told him that it was the place to go if you liked whiskey. No other place in Ho Chi Minh City had a better selection of imported whiskey, and if good old Hayburner ever had a vice, it was expensive whiskey. Whiskey and cheap women. But the whiskey habit seemed an easier lead to follow.

"Ten million dongs, a meal here costs a few paltry dollars and they charge you ten million dongs for a bottle of Johnnie Walker Blue Label." Nina said with a surprised tone in her voice.

"Supply and demand," Adam said. "And ten million Vietnamese dongs is only around five hundred dollars, a fair price for that bottle."

"It just doesn't look like a place where you would spend five hundred dollars on a meal," she said.

"That's exactly why someone like Hayburner would be going here," Adam smiled.

"How do you know?" Nina asked.

"Because I served with him for almost a decade. This is his kinda place. If he is still in Saigon, he'll be here." Like most of the locals, Adam still used the old name of Saigon when he talked about Ho Chi Minh City.

"I think it is best that we eat before I start my enquiries, so have you guys decided what you want?" he asked.

Both Nina and Cameron nodded. Nina stuck to a vegetarian dish like Adam, while Cameron ordered something exotic from the menu. Adam wasn't even sure what it was, but it didn't look like it was of earthly origin.

The meal was surprisingly tasty and when they had finished, Adam walked over to a table with two teenage girls and a woman in her mid-thirties, faces glued to their mobile phones, to pay the bill. The oldest of them dragged out a calculator with a sigh, and started adding the menu items they had just eaten. In the corner of his eye, Adam noticed two Vietnamese men staring at him. They were sitting at a table in the far corner of the restaurant. The table was covered with small empty plates, a bottle of Whiskey prominently placed in the middle of the table.

"Who are those guys?" Adam asked the woman with the calculator.

"No, no can't say. You should leave," she replied.

Instead Adam took out a bunch of notes, close to a million Vietnamese Dong, which roughly equated to fifty US dollars, and left them on the table in front of the calculator. "Take a break," he said, and walked over to the table with the two Vietnamese men. The two girls popped their heads up from their mobile phones, then quickly followed his advice. The woman with the calculator remained seated.

Cameron and Nina had already left the restaurant when Adam pulled out a chair and sat down opposite the Vietnamese men.

"Yankee?" one of them asked, his yellow and brown teeth sticking out of his mouth like spears. A white cloud of spit formed in the lower corner of his mouth when he talked.

"Yes," Adam nodded.

"What do you want?" the Vietnamese man asked, moving his hand underneath the table.

Adam didn't show any fear. The movement had been too obvious. It was a test, a test of his courage.

"I'm looking for an old friend."

"What makes you think you will find him here?"

"He shares your good taste in whiskey," Adam said, and nodded towards the bottle on the table. It was a Chivas Regal, aged for twelve years.

"No yanks come here," the Vietnamese said. Almost spitting the words out.

"Who said he was a yank," Adam said.

He pulled out a stack of bills, and placed them on the table.

"I'm not looking for any trouble. My friend's name is John Waters, but he only goes under the name Hayburner. I'm not even sure if he is still in Saigon, but if he is I would imagine somebody like you would know him. He's Australian."

"Somebody like us? What do you mean by that?" the Vietnamese man asked, the spit now almost foaming in the corner of his mouth.

Adam put both his hands flat on the table, to ease the tense situation.

"Listen, I'm not going to waste your time. You look like important people, somebody who would know my friend. If that's not the case I'm sorry I have wasted your time," he said, and removed his hands from the table, indicating he was ready to leave. He let the money be.

"How do you know Hayburner?" the older of the men asked. Adam assessed his age to be around sixty-five, old enough to have experienced the war.

"I served with him ten years ago," Adam said, sitting back in the red, plastic chair.

The young Vietnamese guy almost jumped out of his seat. "You're a yank soldier. Get the fuck out of here."

The older man put his hand gently on the younger one's shoulder, and he sat down again. Silent.

"Where did you serve with him?" the older one asked.

"Can't tell you," Adam replied.

The old man smiled, and poured Adam a glass of the Chivas. "That's the same answer Hayburner always gives me when I ask."

Adam nodded as a thank you and downed the glass in one drink.

"Where can I find him?" Adam asked.

"I don't know, I haven't seen him in weeks."

"Where did you see him last?"

"Here. He said he had been offered a job. A well-paying job."

"Did he mention where?"

The old man looked at the younger one, before turning his head to face Adam again.

"It is not safe here at the moment. You should leave before you get into trouble."

"I can't do that," Adam said. "I have to find my friend."

"Believe me when I tell you this. Hayburner is no longer your friend. He is your enemy."

"What do you mean?" Adam asked.

"I have already said enough," the old man said, the younger one looking down at the table. He was obviously angry at the older one, but out of respect he didn't allow himself to show it.

Adam thanked for the glass of whiskey and got up.

He was about to leave the table when the old man leant over and grabbed his hand. "Your daughter, the young one at the table?" he asked.

"Yes," Adam replied.

"Leave now," he said. "If not for yourself, then for your daughter."

Adam gave the man a nod, and left the table. When he walked

past the woman with the calculator she quickly handed him a piece of paper.

"Your receipt, Sir," she said, slightly bowing her head. Adam put the receipt in his back pocket, before proceeding down the stairs of the restaurant.

-68-

Dr Drecker studied his day planner. He counted the days from the date he had injected Cody with DMT. It was now sixteen days ago. That meant he had just over thirty-three days left to figure out how to save Cody.

He had noticed something strange in Cody's cell earlier, something that had happened when Cody drew the picture of the underground tunnels he claimed Patient F was hiding in.

Cody had always been right-handed, he had used his right foot to kick soccer, his right hand to write and play tennis. Dr Drecker couldn't remember having ever seen him use his left hand for anything important, especially not something as important as drawing a picture, his major talent in life.

But down in that cell twenty minutes ago, Cody had been using his left hand to draw. There had been no hesitation when Dr Drecker handed him the pen and paper. He had just started drawing, and he had used his left hand, as if he had always used it.

Dr Drecker wasn't sure what this meant. Did the transformation start earlier than they had thought? Was there a possibility that Cody was already someone else? Or could this provide a possible explanation to what had happened to the death row prisoners back in 1974?

There was only one way to find out. He needed to learn more about what caused people to become left-handed, and he needed to do it without the CIA agent knowing why he was looking into the matter.

He pressed the speed dial for the CIA agent.

It rang three times before somebody picked up.

"I know where Patient F is," Dr Drecker said.

"I'll be over in a sec," the CIA agent answered.

"So where is he?" the CIA agent asked.

"You listened to me, and you turned off the cameras in Cody's cell. That is the only reason I have this information right now."

"I'm still listening," the CIA agent said.

"We can't continue to treat the patients as idiots. If we do then they will give us nothing. If you want me to find out what happened to all the death row prisoners, if you want me to find out what is happening to my son, then you have to let me inside with them."

"Let you inside their cells?" the CIA agent asked.

Dr Drecker nodded.

"You know that I can't do that. If you have any physical contact with them then we can't know for sure whether you have been compromised or not."

"I can live with that risk," Dr Drecker said.

The CIA agent studied the man in front of him. He knew people often would be willing to make big sacrifices for their kids, but this was something different.

"I don't think you understand, Dr Drecker. I don't think you understand what entering the cells would mean."

Dr Drecker smiled. "I do understand. And I'm ok with it. If I can't save Cody, I won't have anything to live for anyway."

The CIA agent studied Dr Drecker. He knew he wasn't supposed to have any feelings for the people MKULTRA employed; he couldn't have any feelings for them. But when he stood in front of this once broken man, he couldn't help feeling admiration for him. He couldn't help feeling respect for him.

"I only have one request. I understand that once I enter the cells I can't leave. I will be locked in with the others. So I want to see the blue sky one last time before I go in. I want to see the blue sky with my son Cody, one last time."

"I'll see what I can do," he said. "Now tell me where Patient F is."

"He is in Vietnam," Dr Drecker replied.

-69-

"How did it go?" Nina asked when Adam caught up with her and Cameron at the hotel.

"I'm not really sure," Adam said. "I know he is here. The old man confirmed as much. But he may have gotten in over his head."

"How so?"

"I just got that feeling. And the old man told me to get out of Saigon as soon as possible, saying that the city wasn't safe."

"Not safe? Have you tried crossing the road here, hell yea it is not safe. They are all fucking crazy."

Adam smiled. Nina was right though. Adam had been to many distant corners of the world, but he had never experienced more crazy traffic conditions. There were no traffic lights, no zebra crossings. To cross the road you just had to step out into the road and hope that everyone avoided you. You might as well close your eyes and start walking, because if you stopped, if you hesitated, then everybody got confused. The system only worked when everyone was moving, when everything was in constant movement. And that was the only way they could have any hope to find Patient F as well, they had to keep moving, had to be in constant movement.

"It's a bit like that," Adam said. "But I'm not sure what the best way to proceed from here is. I was hoping to find Hayburner right away. He would have been able to provide us with some new identities, some safe ones. Now we will have to be very cautious. If those guys Cameron stole the passports from figure it out and report them stolen, it won't take the CIA long to realise where we are. And they have a large presence here."

"They have a large presence here in Vietnam?"

"It's one of the few communistic countries left in the world. And it's in close proximity to China. It's important to the US."

"So what are our options?"

"Well, we can't continue to stay here. If the passports get compromised then they'll find us."

"Homestay," Cameron said.

"What?" Nina asked.

"That's how mom and I used to travel. We stayed with local families."

"Don't they have to be registered?" Adam asked.

"You just offer them cash-in-hand. There are no paper records, no handing over passports or anything. You are just relatives visiting for a short time."

"Ok, that's a good idea. I want you and Nina to sort something out. Find a family where you can stay for a few days. The more remote the better."

"Me and Nina? Where are you going to be?" Cameron asked.

"I have something I have to attend to," Adam replied. He was looking at the note in his hand, the receipt from the restaurant.

It just read, 'I know where Hayburner is. Come alone at eleven pm," and underneath an address was scribbled in capital letters.

-70-

The CIA agent studied his boarding pass. He was due to leave JFK Airport in one hour. He could have requisitioned a private jet, but he didn't want to risk the attention. Although a busy airport, Ho Chi Minh City was still a poor city, and flying in with a private jet could cause speculation. He was better off on a commercial flight. His three colleagues, the three colleagues who were behind the disaster in Brisbane, were flying in from Australia to meet him. He couldn't believe the mess they had been able to create. MKULTRA had managed to operate in the shadows for almost four decades. That was no coincidence; it was because they always made rational decisions. They weighed up the risks and the potential gain, and then they chose the solution with the best prospects. It had been clear that they could never let the hospital staff who dealt with the lone survivor of flight SQ183 talk to the press. But there had been a multitude of ways to deal with that problem. They could have isolated them, dispersed them to faraway hospitals where they would never talk about what they had seen. They could have planted small seeds of disinformation in the press. There were a million ways to divert the story into wrong directions. And that had been the plan of the agents. They were planning to use the story of the Maori security guard, the guard who had seen Adam with a bomb wrapped around his chest, to create a manhunt for

Adam. The plan had been to set off a small bomb in Cameron's room, to invent the scenario that a lone lunatic had set off a bomb to kill the lone survivor of flight SQ183. The team had prepared themselves well. They had done everything correctly, except for one massive mistake. The blueprints of the building they had acquired didn't include the old drawings, they didn't include the old gas tank next to Cameron's room. When they blew up Cameron's room they also blew up half the floor of the hospital. Then panic struck, and in an effort to contain the situation, the agents had killed three other staff. Staff who weren't present at the hospital when the bomb went off, but staff who had seen Cameron, staff who had witnessed the resurrection.

It was only due to the gross incompetence of the press that the public hadn't figured out there was something more sinister to the hospital explosion than a gas leak. The stories about a terrorist group being behind both the airplane crash and the hospital explosion were just too incredible to be believed. They fell straight into the same bucket of conspiracy theories as the ones about the man who was the namesake of the airport the CIA agent was currently at. There had been multiple theories about the CIA being involved in the murder of John F. Kennedy. But the more theories were put forward, the crazier they got. One could hardly find anyone these days who didn't doubt the official story, but it was a long leap from there to believing one of the conspiracy theories. In the end, most crazy assassinations were done by lone nutters.

And that was how the story of flight SQ183 would go down.

Adam Mullins was the lone nutter.

The lone nutter who had come back from Afghanistan with Post Traumatic Stress Disorder, a guy who was so abusive that his wife had taken their daughter and disappeared seven years ago.

He had managed to track them down to Australia and in a wild act of revenge he had planted a bomb on their airplane. And when his daughter had miraculously survived the crash, he had decided to blow up the hospital too.

He was an explosives expert.

His story was well-documented. They had pictures of him sneaking into the hospital, they had official records of his training with explosives, hell they even had pictures of him showing his chest strapped with explosives.

It was all ready to be released to the press once Adam was dead and they had control of Cameron.

They had been taken by surprise by Brisbane News publishing the picture of Adam, standing in the waiting room of operating theatre number twenty-three.

They had wanted to wait publishing his face.

But luckily the quality of the picture was pretty poor.

They had bugged the phones and computers of the reporter in question, and no one had yet recognised Adam and responded to the request.

The CIA agent thought it was most likely caused by loyalty.

Some of his friends would surely have recognised him, but there was no way anyone who knew Adam was going to give him up.

They knew that from how Matt Parks had dealt with the situation.

He had allowed them to strip him of his job and pension, but he still hadn't been willing to talk about Adam. Not one single word.

He was willing to let his own life go down the drain rather

than ratting out his friend.

Even when they discovered he had used a file-sharing site called Spideroak to send Adam a coded message, he had refused to reveal their system of pages on which to insert the next comment.

The CIA agent could respect that, the honour in it. But he still had to do what he did. These were traitors they dealt with. America depended on him, and Matt Parks would never see the light of day again.

-71-

Dr Drecker stared at the computer screen in front of him. In exactly ten hours he would be allowed to conduct face-to-face interviews with some of the death row prisoners, to do face-to-face interviews with the people who hadn't aged since they were injected with DMT back in 1974. It would be the first time in all those years that the prisoners, or patients as they called them at MKULTRA, had been allowed contact with another human being.

Dr Drecker was putting the finishing touches on his hypothesis. The one he wanted to test when he now entered the cell block.

The idea had only come to him when he asked Cody to draw where Patient F was. Cody had started drawing with his left hand, his left hand!

And when Dr Drecker had started to think back on whether he had seen any signs of changing behaviour in Cody since he had resurrected, he realised that he had noticed some small changes. There was the episode when Cody's green eyes seemed to turn dark, when something else was fighting to take control of him. In fact, when he thought about it there had been tens of minor changes in his behaviour. He had stopped picking and chewing on his fingers. He had become more mature in his conversations, more calm, more content.

He had changed.

The CIA agent had said that the death row prisoners had all died, for the second time, 49 days after the DMT injection. And that when they resurrected again they had totally different personalities, they were totally different persons. They talked about a different world, a world far away from Earth. Initially the CIA and MKULTRA had believed that the patients were delirious, that they talked nonsense. But then they had started to fear that the death row prisoners were telling the truth. What if they really were someone else, what if the DMT injection was able to send people to another dimension, and what if the death row prisoners' bodies had been taken over by inhabitants from one of those dimensions? What if the prophecy they talked about was true? What if an army of undead, an army of aliens led by Patient F, the Son, would come and unleash hell on Earth? It was a risk far too great to ignore. If this was the case the patients could never be let loose into society again. Luckily, the decision hadn't been hard for the White House at the time. The patients had already been condemned to death for their crimes, life in jail could hardly be described as an inhumane sentence.

And so it had come to today's situation.

The remnants of an ancient department in the CIA, the MKULTRA, was still in operation, and five death row prisoners were still held in cells.

The real reason they were scared was of course the extent of damage their only runaway patient had been able to cause.

The CIA director had told the story about Patient F, and what he had done. But unlike the CIA agent, Dr Drecker hadn't felt threatened by Patient F.

He had felt respect.

He had felt admiration.

And soon he would be here.

The illusive Patient F.

The only one who could save Cody.

But before he was going to interview the death row patients he had something he had to do. The CIA agent had come through on his promise. He would be allowed to take Cody outside for one last time, to see the blue sky one last time. Afterwards, Dr Drecker's and Cody's destinies would be intertwined. The date of the prophesised apocalypse was coming up shortly. And Dr Drecker understood that this was the reason for the CIA agent's rush. He wouldn't risk leaving any of the DMT patients alive when the date came. He might not be totally convinced they were aliens from a different world, but he was afraid of their abilities. They had to be killed before the date of the apocalypse, they had to be killed so that the prophecy could never materialize.

"Are you ready?" Dr Drecker asked Cody.

Cody was sitting on his bed. "Ready for what?"

"Ready to get some fresh air?"

-72-

Adam arrived at the address just before eleven pm. Cameron and Nina had found themselves a family willing to earn some extra cash, and in exchange for a few dollars a day they had a roof over their heads, food on the table and the safest possible hideout in Ho Chi Minh City. Adam sent a text to Cameron. It was just a short one. "At meet. Everything seems ok."

They had picked up some cheap mobile phones from the market. They were unregistered and as long as they only used them to send inconspicuous messages there was no risk that anyone could link them to the phones.

"Mister, over here, mister."

Adam turned around and saw a young kid standing on the corner of the alley, an unlit cigarette hanging out of his mouth. The young kid nodded to Adam and indicated that he should follow him as he started walking down the alley.

Based on the determination of the nod Adam had understood that this was the guy he was supposed to meet, he wasn't just there to try to sell him something. But Adam immediately felt uneasy. He had expected the woman from the restaurant to meet him, not some unknown kid. Should he abort the whole thing?

After a second of hesitation he decided to follow the teenager. Fuck it, even if it was a trap this was the only chance he had. Without Hayburner he had no sources he could use to get information about where this mysterious Patient F could be. The only information they had at this stage was a news article his wife had found on the internet a few weeks earlier. About a man with healing hands. They needed something more, and this was his best shot.

The teenager moved quickly through the streets, and Adam had problems keeping up without having to run. Roughly a hundred meters in front of him, the teenager stopped in front of one of the local Pho restaurants. The thirty or so miniature red, plastic chairs were almost all filled up by locals chatting and eating soup. A few tourists were also scattered around the big pot of brewing Pho. The teenager sat down on one of the chairs just as Adam recognised the woman from the restaurant. She was now sitting on a concrete block counting money.

Adam walked over and sat down on the red chair closest to her.

"You know my friend?" he asked without looking at her.

"Yes," she answered, and indicated for one of the other girls to give Adam a bowl of soup.

"Do you know where he is?" Adam asked.

"You have to help him. He's in trouble."

"Trouble...what sort of trouble?" Adam couldn't really imagine Hayburner not being in trouble, he always was, but the tone of the woman's voice told him that it was serious.

"He has gotten himself involved with some very bad people," she said.

"How can I help?" Adam asked.

"You can get him out. You're Adam aren't you?" she asked.

Adam nodded. A bit surprised that she knew his name.

"Hayburner has mentioned you. Said you were a good friend."

The noise of the other Vietnamese customers drowned their conversation, and Adam suspected most of them didn't even understand English. That was probably why she had chosen this place for the meet.

"I still am," Adam replied.

"She nodded over at the teenager from the alley. "My son. He will take you to Hayburner. Just promise me you bring him home."

"I can't promise that," Adam said. And he wondered whether he should decline the offer straight away. He didn't have time to sort out problems one of his old army pals might have gotten himself into. And Hayburner normally didn't need any help to get out of trouble, it was usually the other way around. Hayburner solving other people's problems. But he couldn't decline the request either. You never left anyone behind. It was a rule he had lived his whole life by, and he wasn't about to change that now.

"His son?" Adam asked, looking at the teenager. He was sitting crouched together in one of the plastic chairs, wolfing down a bowl of soup.

For the first time the woman raised her eyes from the pile of paper money in front of her. She briefly looked Adam straight in the eyes. The brief look was enough. It told him he was right. The teenager was Hayburner's son.

-73-

D r Drecker was reviewing the scientific literature available on left-handedness. It wasn't much. Most of it was pseudo-science or conclusions based on small and unreliable studies. He did however find it interesting that the word sinister originated from the Latin word for left, and that left-handed people throughout history had been forced to convert to use their right hand instead of the one that felt natural. It seemed that left-handedness was an obvious advantage in many sports and wars, as right-handed people had greater difficulties adapting to left-handed opponents. And if one absolutely had to fight with a sword it couldn't hurt to hold it in a hand that was unexpected. But mostly, being left-handed appeared to be a disadvantage. There were no conclusive results that left-handed people were more artistic or analytical than right-handed people, something Dr Drecker had hoped to find evidence for in his review.

He stared at the numbers on the computer screen. It said that 8-10% of the population was left-handed. Why was it so? How did people become left-handed? Had this 8-10% always been the case?

A study of hand paintings in Western European Palaeolithic caves indicated that the distribution had been roughly the same thirty-five thousand years ago. There were some formal countries, like China and Japan where right-handedness was strictly enforced in schools, which as a consequence had very low numbers of left-handed inhabitants. But otherwise the 8-10% seemed quite consistent. Both around the world, and throughout history.

Now that he had established that it wasn't possible to deduce a clear reason for left-handedness based on origin or abilities, Dr Drecker tried looking for other reasons that could cause left-handedness. He found his answer in a couple of surveys conducted in the late 1980s. The surveys had found that infants who had undergone birth stress were significantly more likely to be left-handed. One study found that more than a third of four-year-olds who had been born prematurely were left-handed, whereas another found that more than half of children with extremely low birth weights were left-handed. He knew that such births often resulted in long-term neurological damage, and that hypoxia, the lack of oxygen to the brain, could thus possibly be the culprit for left-handedness. Or could it be something else? He remembered having read in Dr Kovacks' notes that the human body released DMT naturally at certain points in time. One of those times was at birth. Could it be that a stressful birth caused the body to release an extraordinary amount of DMT into the bloodstream, and that this caused the left-handedness?

He wasn't sure, but he knew he was onto something. The problem was that one statistic seemed to work against his hypothesis. The DMT patients had become left-handed after their injections. There was no doubt about it. But they had also acquired the ability to self-heal and had almost stopped aging. Left-handers, on the other hand, lived on average nine years shorter than right-handed people. That was an undeniable fact. It could of course be explained by the fact that it was more dangerous for left-handers to live in a world that was mostly designed for people using the other hand on a day-to-day basis. Work tools, cars, even the insides of homes. Everything was designed for right-handed people. No wonder the left-handers had more accidents.

But the discrepancy could also be explained by something else.

Dr Drecker packed his things together.

It was time to meet the death row patients face-to-face.

It was time to go directly to the source.

-74-

The sun was glary, it was hot and sticky, and the smell was unbearable. Unlike at home in the US, where everything smelt fresh and clean after a bout of rain, in Vietnam it just started to smell. The warm rain only lasted for about twenty minutes, and it didn't clean up the streets nor freshen the air, it just washed everything out to the middle of the road. The CIA agent lowered his sunglasses. He was dressed in beige chinos and a white short-sleeved shirt. A few black and grey chest hairs were visible behind the buttoned down shirt.

"How is it possible, with all the damn analysts working for us, that no one made this connection?"

"Maybe it was too obvious?" one of the agents who had flown in from Brisbane said. One of his two colleagues nodded.

"It dates back to the sixties and seventies. When we tried to look for connections we looked for more recent events," the other colleague said.

"He was a known communist. Hell, he was even stationed here in Vietnam, right here in Saigon. This is where it all started. Still none of you managed to see the connection, to see the god damn obvious."

None of the agents answered. They had no answer, no answer

that could take away the embarrassment they felt. Patient F was hiding in Vietnam, a communistic country. The bureau had spent thousands of hours, probably tens of thousands of hours and certainly millions of dollars, to figure out where he could be hiding. And then it turned out he had been hiding in the most obvious place of all.

Still, not a single one of the highly paid analysts at CIA had made the connection to Vietnam, not one of them had made the connection to Agent Orange.

Agent Orange, or Herbicide Orange which it also was called, was one of the herbicides and defoliants used by the US military as part of its herbicidal warfare program in Vietnam, operation Ranch Hand. The aim of operation Ranch Hand had been to destroy crops, bushes and trees so that Vietnamese insurgents would starve and have no places to hide. In reality the spraying of more than 75 million litres of herbicides had mostly affected civilians. It had led to famine and severe health problems for several million Vietnamese, and one could still witness the effects by walking around in Ho Chi Minh City where beggars with birth defects acted as a reminder of what the US had done.

"Well, it's too late to do anything about it now. We have to focus on our goal, and that is to apprehend two targets: Cameron Mullins, the girl who survived flight SQ183, and Patient F."

"How do we know they are here?" one of the CIA agents asked.

"A good source has told us that Patient F is hiding right here in Saigon, and we already know that Adam Mullins and his daughter Cameron arrived in Saigon a few days ago. It was a tedious task, but our London office reviewed all video images from the main airports in Australia over the last few days, focusing on passengers travelling to Bangkok, KL and Singapore, the normal hubs if you intend to travel to Vietnam. We got a confirmed hit on Adam Mullins in one of the images. It turns out he has managed to steal some passports without the owners realising. Thus the passports have not even been reported stolen yet. The last sign of them was at a five-star resort, The Equatorial, which they checked out of yesterday. After that there is no sign of the three of them."

"Three?" one of the other CIA agents asked.

The CIA agent looked straight at him, disappointed. "The nurse you killed in Brisbane, Susan Carr. She wasn't the one who looked after Cameron Mullins at the hospital, was she? Another nurse by the name of Nina Winter breached regulations and did Susan Carr's evening shift. You killed the wrong nurse. But you already knew that, didn't you?"

The other CIA agents didn't say anything. They knew they had blown the operation in Brisbane, and were all embarrassed.

"Do we focus on Patient F or Cameron?" one of the other agents finally asked.

The CIA agent smiled. "We focus on Cameron, if we catch Cameron, Patient F will come out of hiding, Patient F will come to us."

-75-

"So you're sure that's where he is?" Adam asked.

The Vietnamese teenager, Ahn, nodded. "He told me that's where he was heading."

Adam considered the situation. Ahn had just told him that his dad, Adam's friend Hayburner, had headed into the jungle nine days ago. It had been supposed to be a three-day trip, but he had never returned. Ahn didn't know what sort of business his dad was involved with, but his dad had assured him that it wasn't drugs. And he had made the trip several times the last five years without any problems. That assurance was the only reason Adam still considered the proposal to join a search and rescue effort for his old friend. He did, however, have two other mitigating circumstances: Without Hayburner's help, without his local experience and contacts, there was very little hope for Adam to find out more about this Shaman whom Cameron and her mum had been on their way to find. The article his wife had printed off the internet was quite sparse on information. It had only said that a reportedly blind man had gotten his vision back after seeing the Shaman. The article was six months old and there was no further description of the event. The main thing that had piqued Adam's interest was that the so-called healing had occurred in a relatively small area between Saigon and the Cambodian border, almost the exact same area that Hayburner was supposedly missing in.

Could there be a connection, Adam wondered.

He put the tiny empty tea cup back onto the wooden table, and pointed his right index finger on the map that lay spread out on the table.

"What's in this area?"

"Jungle," the Vietnamese kid said. "And tunnels. Lots of tunnels."

"Viet Cong tunnels you mean?" Adam asked.

Ahn nodded. He put his finger on the map and traced a route. "This is where the tunnels start. The Cu Chi province was bombed heavily during the War of Yankee Aggression, and the only way for the local population to survive was to live underground."

Adam took a deep breath. He had read about the Vietnam War, the longest war the US had ever been involved in. It took them seventeen years and a loss of almost sixty thousand troops to end the war, and yet they had not won. The estimated loss of human lives was more than three million.

"That's a tourist area now?" Adam asked.

Ahn nodded. "There are two sites open for the public in the Cu Chi province. Here and here," he pointed at the map. "These sites allow tourists to enter the tunnels and see how life was for the Vietnamese soldier."

Pretty crappy, Adam thought. The life of a Vietnamese soldier must have been pretty crappy. "And the rest of the area?" Adam asked, pointing at the map.

"Closed to public. Of strategic importance for our government."

"So it's guarded by soldiers?"

Ahn shook his head. "Too dangerous for soldiers. Landmines and booby traps everywhere."

"So why is it of strategic importance? If the army doesn't even control it?"

"You have to understand. The War of Yankee Aggression wasn't the first time Vietnam was attacked. The tunnels were originally built to fight the French."

Adam wasn't exactly a historian, but he knew the back story of the Cu Chi tunnels. They had originally been built to fight the colony power of France, and then they had proven essential in the guerrilla warfare against the US. Ahn probably meant that an extensive underground tunnel network would be beneficial in any war threat Vietnam would face in the foreseeable future. He nodded. "I understand. But I've got the distinct feeling that there still might be people in the area. Who are we likely to meet?"

"Bad people. People hiding from the government."

Adam wiped his face with the sleeve of his shirt. It was 38 degrees, and he had a throbbing headache.

"Do we have any weapons?" he asked.

Ahn shook his head. "No guns, just knives."

Adam smiled.

This could very well be the most ridiculous mission he had ever undertaken. They were about to enter an area riddled with landmines and booby traps from the Vietnam War. It was a restricted area, so they basically broke the law just by entering it, and if they were lucky enough to meet any people, they would most likely be criminals, heavily armed and with minimal desire to ever be found.

"Ok, we start at dawn. I'll prepare a list of items you need to acquire. We don't go unless you get all the items, understood?" Adam said.

Ahn's face broke out in a big grin, as he nodded frantically. His two friends, slightly older by the look of their facial features, didn't smile. It wasn't their father who was missing, maybe they had secretly hoped for the American to turn down the plan. To tell Ahn that it was an insane plan that was doomed to fail.

Well, that hadn't happened. They now had to follow through.

"Thank you, thank you so much," Ahn said.

You shouldn't thank me yet, Adam thought as he studied the map in front of him.

The mighty force of the American Army never managed to penetrate that jungle, and now he, along with some teenagers, was about to walk straight back into it.

-76-

"I think we've got them," one of the CIA agents from the Brisbane team said. His name was John Fowler.

"Is it confirmed or not?" The CIA agent asked.

"It's not confirmed, but I would say it is an eighty percent chance it is them."

"Ok. At the moment it is the best lead we have so we'll move forward."

"How many people do you want in the extraction group?"

"Max six people. And only people we know. If this operation goes south, on Vietnamese ground, we could be in real trouble."

"Understood. I'll have a team ready in four hours."

"And agent Fowler…"

"Yes sir?"

"If you mess up this operation, like you did in Brisbane, your career is over. Understood?"

"Understood, Sir."

-77-

They were a strange sight, Adam and the three boys walking through the village. Ahn had been successful in acquiring the items that Adam had requested. Adam had to pay though, as neither Ahn nor his two friends seemed to have any money. The two friends were introduced as Ho and Nguyen, and seemed friendly enough. Adam didn't need any friends on this trip though; he needed people he could trust, people who knew how to follow orders if they accidentally walked into some trouble. And he had his doubts about Ahn's friends in this regard. They were obviously a bit reluctant to be part of the search party for Hayburner, and Adam had started to wonder whether Ahn had told him the full story about the area. If it was closed off to the public, and none of the locals or government people ventured in there because of the threat of old landmines and booby traps, it would be an ideal place for drug smugglers and other shady people to hide out. The border to Cambodia was only a few hours away, and the area stretched all the way from the Cu Chi province to the border.

"Listen up boys. I only have one rule: When I tell you to do something you listen. You don't try to come up with a better plan, you don't think it through. You do what I tell you to do. And if you have a problem with that rule, you are better off staying here. You do not want to cross me once we enter this jungle."

Ahn and his friends nodded. Adam studied them. It was quite possible that they wouldn't meet any hostiles in the jungle, that they would walk straight to the point on the map where Ahn's dad, Hayburner, had said he was heading nine days ago, and find him safe and sound. Maybe he had been injured, walked into one of those old booby traps and hurt himself? Maybe he was incapacitated or maybe even dead? But one thing was for sure. If these boys didn't listen, some of them could possibly end up in body bags. They weren't trained to look for booby traps, they weren't trained to look for tracks. They were amateurs. This might be their country, but these kids were no Viet Cong soldiers. They were just kids.

"Ok then. We walk during daylight. It may be hot, but we can't risk walking without perfect sight, as we don't know which areas have been cleared."

The boys nodded again.

"I walk front. You guys in a line behind me."

One of Ahn's friends, Ho, raised his hand.

"You don't have to raise your hand to speak, Ho. This isn't school," Adam said.

"I have worked two years for the UN, clearing mines. I know how to spot them."

"Did you also look for VC traps?" Adam asked.

Ho shook his head.

"Then you stay back in the line. This is no game. If there are still old landmines and booby traps in this area, you could potentially lose a leg, or worse. All it takes is a moment of less than one hundred percent concentration. We know that it will take us roughly eight hours to get to the area where Ahn's dad was heading. That is one day of full concentration. One day of full concentration is not a bad sacrifice if it can save your life. Now let's head out."

Adam thought the small pep talk seemed to have worked as he observed Ahn and his friends obediently fall back in line behind him. He set the timer on his watch and glanced up at the sky. It was still early morning, only five thirty, but he wanted to get going as soon as possible. He hadn't spoken to Cameron or Nina since the previous night, when he told them he was going away for a few days. He felt bad about leaving Cameron, but there was no way she could come along with the search party. It was much too dangerous, and she wasn't by herself anyway, she still had Nina. They seemed to get along quite well, at least given the circumstances. Adam had realised, over the last week or so, that he had started to grow affectionate about Nina. It was the first time in several years he had allowed himself to spend time with a woman over a longer period of time, without feeling he was cheating on his wife, and he had started to wonder what Nina felt about him. She was a fair bit younger than he, and a massive amount prettier. But there could potentially be something there, he thought. He would have to be patient though. He had to be extremely careful around Cameron. She had just lost her mum. Seeing her dad making the move on another woman this soon could set her off again, and he didn't want to relive the situation where she ran away from the caravan park. He had enough trouble trying to locate Hayburner and this mysterious Shaman his wife had been looking for, without having to chase Cameron as well. He had even gone to the extent of buying Cameron a present the other day, a nice watch from the market. It had some extra equipment though. It had come with a GPS tracker. The range was only about one kilometre, but it made Adam feel a little bit better. He didn't want to lose her again.

While they trekked into the jungle Adam thought back on the episode with the rolled-over semi-trailer, the dead driver and the critically injured passenger. How was it that Cameron had managed to survive that accident without a scratch? How was it possible that she had been the lone survivor of a plane crash? Was she responsible for the accidents? Had she somehow caused those accidents?

Nah, she couldn't have.

Cameron had never mentioned what had really caused the semi-trailer accident though, and Adam hadn't pursued the matter any further. Nina Winter had explained that his daughter would need time, lots of time, but at some stage he would have to talk to her about those accidents. Otherwise Cameron could suffer permanent psychological damage. He didn't look forward to the talk.

"Nine o'clock. Three hundred metres ahead." It was Ahn's voice. Adam almost let out a laugh, but he was able to constrain himself. They all started to use military lingo around him, even his personal training clients back in New York. They would pick something up from watching a Rambo movie and then they would casually mix it into their conversation with him. Like it was part of their normal vocabulary.

Adam looked up ahead. Nine o'clock, 300 metres. It was more like eleven o'clock and 450 metres ahead, but it was well-spotted by Ahn. Adam crouched down to get cover.

Ahn had spotted a Vietnamese straw hat; it didn't seem to move though, and it could potentially just be a hat sitting on top of some branches. Adam checked his watch again. The timer showed eight hours and twenty-five minutes. They had ventured a fair few kilometres into the restricted area, but the pace was much slower than anticipated. Even though they had yet to see any landmines, they had discovered several booby traps.

He held a flat hand up, to signal to the others to duck down and stay quiet. And then he ventured off the track.

-78-

Dr Drecker dragged his rocking chair up to the front of the glass cage housing Patient A, Andrew Mortimer. He remembered Andrew's crimes from having read his file a week earlier. Andrew Mortimer was a rapist and a killer, he was the scum of the Earth.

"Good morning Andrew," Dr Drecker said with a big smile. "I'm Martin Drecker. I would like to ask you a few questions."

As expected, Andrew Mortimer didn't reply. He just stood there, staring at Dr Drecker.

Dr Drecker opened the metal suitcase he had brought down to the cells. He had initially asked the CIA agent if he could give the death row prisoners pen and paper, but the request had been denied. It had been deemed too dangerous. Especially now that the date was nearing.

Instead he had been allowed to give them scrabble letters, and a small piece of black cloth. He put the items into the drawer that was used to send food through to the death row prisoners, and pushed a button. The drawer opened on the other side.

Andrew Mortimer studied Dr Drecker intently, but Dr Drecker didn't seem fazed. He just sat there in his rocking chair. Rocking slowly back and forth.

Eventually, Andrew Mortimer walked over to the drawer and pulled out the contents. He dropped it all onto the floor and sat down with crossed legs.

"Here is what I want you to do," Dr Drecker said. "I want you to cover your left eye with the piece of cloth."

Andrew Mortimer peered suspiciously at Dr Drecker. Dr Drecker didn't press him, however, but just sat there in his rocking chair. Letting Andrew Mortimer take his time, letting Andrew Mortimer make his own decision.

After two minutes he did exactly that. He held the black cloth up to cover his left eye.

"Thank you," Dr Drecker said. "Now I want you to do me one more favour. I want you to read the question on this note," he said, and held up a note in front of the glass cage.

"It simply read: "Who are you?"

The death row prisoner, Andrew Mortimer, stared with his one eye at the note for several seconds. Then he averted his gaze and looked down at the floor.

Dr Drecker didn't say anything. He needed to let the prisoner do this of his own free will, without any leading questions. That was the only way he could prove his theory.

And so they sat there. Dr Drecker in his rocking chair and the death row prisoner, with his legs crossed on the floor.

Nobody said a word.

-79-

Cameron was woken up by a loud bang. She immediately got up from the mattress on the floor, her bed for the night. She looked at her watch. It was four am. She gently pulled the blanket covering the window to the side. It was still almost pitch-black outside, but she could hear people chatting.

"What is it?" Nina Winter asked. She was also awake now, and sat upright on her mattress, rubbing the sleep out of her red eyes.

"Don't know," Cameron replied, while she tried to listen to what the voices outside said. "I heard a loud bang. Could have been a car crash or something."

"It's probably nothing," Nina Winter said. "Go back to bed. You need the sleep."

Cameron glanced over at Nina Winter. She didn't mind her, she was actually quite cool, but Nina had started to act more and more like a mother over the last day or so. And it pissed Cameron off. She knew she was only sixteen years old, and still a kid in most people's eyes. But they had no idea what she had been through. They had no idea what sort of life she had lived. Nina had refused Cameron a beer at the caravan park, just because she was underage. Cameron hadn't lived by the laws of society for many years. It didn't matter whether she was old enough for a beer or not, the normal rules didn't apply for her.

"I'm just going to have a look," Cameron said, and slipped into a blue flowery dress she had picked up from the local market the day before.

As Nina Winter watched Cameron step into her flip-flops, she was amazed by her natural beauty. Up until this morning Cameron had almost always dressed like a boy, and with her short, dark her and relatively flat chest, it was sometimes hard to notice that she was a girl. Especially from a distance. But as Cameron stood there, in the dim light of the bedside lamp, she was one of the most beautiful girls Nina had ever seen. She almost looked like an angel.

An explosion of light ruined the sight. Nina covered her eyes by reflex, but it was too late. She was blinded and disoriented. He ears rang and she felt nauseated. "Cameron," she yelled out, as she tried to stagger to her feet. Instead she fell over and hit her head against the hard concrete floor.

Cameron hadn't heard Nina's scream. Her own ears were ringing so loudly that everything else was blocked out. She clenched her fists and waited for the first attacker. She could feel him even before he tried to grab her shoulders. With a swift movement of her hips, she channelled all her strength into an elbow blow. Although she couldn't see the attacker, she knew she had hit him hard. She had felt the soft skin of his face, or maybe it had been the side of his head, give in when she drove that elbow with full force against it. Then she felt more hands against her body, maybe two more persons. She kicked her ankle against the shin of one of them, but she knew it wouldn't do much damage;

she had flip-flops on, and her feet were not hard enough to do much damage.

She was about to drive her other elbow into the belly of another of her attackers when she felt a prick on her neck. She knew immediately what it was. The adrenaline rushing through her body would delay almost all the pain; she hadn't felt anything in her elbow, yet she knew it would hurt in thirty seconds. But the prick on her neck was immediate; a needle had just pierced her skin. With her last strength she went for the elbow against the belly, but she adjusted it a bit lower so that it would hit the attacker's crotch. It was the last thought she managed to have.

After that, it was all a blur.

And then it was all black.

"Both packages secure," one of the CIA agents said.

"Any news about the third package?" the CIA agent asked.

"No."

"Ok, bring both packages to the extraction point."

"Confirmed. ETA six hours."

The CIA agent nodded to the driver, who was looking in the rear mirror of the black town car. It was a signal that the driver should take them to the airport. He had been a bit worried about letting the Brisbane team complete this operation unsupervised, especially after all the errors they had managed to rack up at the Royal Albert Hospital of Brisbane a few weeks earlier. But they seemed to have been up to the task. The girl, Cameron Mullins and the only loose end from the failed Brisbane operation, the nurse Nina Winter, were now both in the agency's custody. The Brisbane team had wanted to tie up the loose end in Vietnam, but the CIA agent had put his foot down. It was best if they brought both Nina Winter and Cameron Mullins to the US. Adam Mullins was still at large and they didn't know what his relationship with Nina Winter had grown into after a few weeks on the run together. She could be another incentive for Adam to come after them. He stared out the tinted windows, lost in his own thoughts for a moment.

"Everything ok?" the side passenger asked.

The CIA agent got his act together and turned to face his passenger. It was an older man, grey hair and big square glasses. He had always reminded the CIA agent of Alan Greenspan, the old FED chairman most people blamed for the housing bubble in the US.

"Yes, we have the daughter, but Mr Mullins and Patient F are still at large."

"Forget about Adam Mullins, he is a nobody. But you need to get hold of Patient F as soon as possible. The clock is ticking."

"I know," the CIA agent said.

He was all too well aware of the clock ticking.

-80-

Adam moved almost without a sound through the dense jungle terrain. He was crouching down as he closed in on the straw hat Ahn had spotted a few minutes earlier. If it turned out to be a person, it would most likely be a hostile, and Adam wouldn't want to be trapped on the path without any weapons. His plan was simply to get a better view of the straw hat, and then to reassess the situation. They could always take a detour and walk around whatever threat was in front of them, it wasn't like they were walking the tourist trail anyway.

He moved slowly, took his time and checked the ground for any sign of booby traps before making the next step. Suddenly he stopped in his tracks. He turned his head and studied the ground. Was that smoke he could smell? He barely moved half a meter to the side. Then he brushed aside some leaves. It wasn't much, but some smoke seemed to seep out from a tiny hole in the ground. He crouched down to a little ball and tried to listen. He had read that the Viet Cong used to position the air tracts quite a distance from the entrance of their tunnels, so that the Americans wouldn't know where the entrance would be even if they located one of the air tracts. And that's what he had almost stepped on, an air tract from one of the old VC tunnels. The problem was that it was emitting smoke. That meant somebody was down there. Why the hell would someone be down in one of the old VC tunnels?

Adam turned his body one hundred and eighty degrees. He tried to be as silent as he could, but he could hear that he made some noise. They needed to get out of this area as soon as possible. They had no real weapons, just a couple of knives. If someone went to the trouble of hiding underground in one of the old VC tunnels they couldn't be up to any good. If Hayburner had walked into this area nine days ago, unarmed like Adam and the boys, then he was most likely dead or taken hostage.

Adam decided to abort the operation. He would have to find the Shaman without Hayburner's help. This area was simply too dangerous. He didn't like the fact that he had to disappoint Ahn, and he didn't like the fact that he couldn't help his old friend. But he had other, more important people in his life now. He had to focus on finding this mysterious Shaman so that they could figure out why the CIA was hunting Cameron, Nina and him.

Suddenly the silence of the jungle erupted into a cacophony of sounds. It was the sound of screaming soldiers. Adam could only sit and watch as seven Vietnamese soldiers, all dressed in camouflage outfits, machine guns raised in their hands, came barging out of the jungle.

Ahn and his friends immediately froze. Then they slowly stood up, hands above their heads.

Good, Adam thought. At least they had the sense not to panic, not to attempt an escape. If they had, they would surely be dead by now.

He was even more impressed when he witnessed how they acted in front of the soldiers. The soldiers slapped their faces, hit them with the butts of their machine guns and screamed at them continuously. Adam had no idea what they were screaming, but it was obviously no friendly banter.

Ahn and his friends just took it, they took it like men. They didn't even glance over towards the spot where Adam was hiding, they didn't try to trade their way out of the situation.

Twenty minutes later, Adam watched as Ahn and his friends were tied together with thick rope. It appeared that the soldiers intended to take them to another place. It gave Adam a bit of relief, when the screaming and hitting was at its worst he had feared for their lives. Yet there had been nothing he could do. He couldn't launch himself on seven heavily armed Vietnamese soldiers, armed only with a knife. That would have been certain death for all of them.

At least if they were taken to another place, there could possibly open up an opportunity to help them. Adam shook his head. He didn't owe Ahn and his friends anything. Eventually Ahn would have gone looking for his father. The only reason he had done it so quickly was because his own mother had sanctioned it. She had believed Ahn would be safe with Adam, Hayburner's old army friend. Well, she had been wrong. Adam hadn't been able to lift a finger. Was he out of practice? Had it been reckless of him to agree to this search party without bringing any weapons?

Well, there was nothing he could do about it now. The only thing he could do now was to follow the Vietnamese soldiers, to track them to wherever they were planning to go. Probably a remote place where they could interrogate and execute Ahn and his friends, a place where no one would ever find their remains.

At least he could follow them there. And if the opportunity

arose he could try to take out the soldiers. If not, he would at least know where their remains where buried.

He could give Ahn's mother a grave to go to.

-81-

D r Drecker gently put his feet on the ground to stop the rocking of his chair. Slowly, he got up on his legs. He had been observing the death row prisoner Andrew Mortimer for the last fifteen minutes, the person whom the CIA agent just referred to as Patient A.

Patient A had hardly moved for most of those fifteen minutes, but for the last thirty seconds he had been busy rearranging the scrabble letters that Dr Drecker had sent through the drawer. Dr Drecker moved closer to the glass wall separating them. Patient A had set himself up in the middle of the cell and it was hard to see what he had done with the letters from so far away. Dr Drecker almost had to touch the glass with his nose to be able to see what Patient A had done.

"I am Andrew," the first line of letters said. "I am a prisoner," the second line read.

Dr Drecker could hardly conceal his enthusiasm. He had managed to open up a line of communication with the death row prisoners, and it had been perfectly simple, perfectly logical.

He had remembered studying the work of Dr Roger Sperry during his early days of med school. Dr Sperry, who had worked with epileptic patients, had been a co-recipient of the 1981 Nobel

Prize in physiology and medicine for his split brain research in the 1960s and 1970s. An interesting part of Dr Sperry's work had been to try to figure out what would happen if one severed the connection between the right and left brain hemispheres. As long as patients had both eyes and both hands available to perform tasks, they were generally ok. But when only one eye was allowed to read a word or only one hand was allowed to feel an object, interesting things started to happen.

It turned out that the left hand and eye were connected to the right brain hemisphere and vice versa. Thus if one showed a patient the name of an object to his left eye, he could pick it up and identify it with his left hand. But if asked what word he had been shown, he was unable to explain it, or even explain why he was holding the object in his hand. The reason turned out to be that spoken language, it seemed, was centred in the left hemisphere of the brain, whereas the ability to analyse and comprehend was located in the right.

By showing Patient A the question "Who are you?" to only the patient's left eye, and then giving him scrabble letters to enable communication without the use of spoken language, Dr Drecker had given him the ability to communicate without involving the left side of his brain. Could it be possible that the DMT had caused a growth spurt in the pineal gland that had caused severe damage in the death row prisoners' brains? Could it even have severed the connection between the two hemispheres, like in the case of the split-brain patients of Dr Sperry?

Dr Drecker walked back to his rocking chair and picked up the pen and paper that were lying beside it. He scribbled a new question before walking back to the glass cage.

He held the note up to the glass wall, as Patient A looked back at him.

The patient was still holding the black cloth over his left eye.

Part 4

-82-

dam's hands were trembling as he watched Ahn and his two friends being led towards three holes in the ground. It appeared that the Vietnamese soldiers had prepared three graves for them. Adam knew that it was hopeless. There was nothing he could do. He had managed to track the soldiers unnoticed for the last two hours, and they were now deep in the jungle, way off track. Palm trees covered the sky and the sounds of the jungle were everywhere. It would be dark in less than an hour, and not only had Adam not spotted an opportunity to free them, but things had gotten more difficult. The initial group of seven soldiers had now increased to nine. Adam assumed that the two new ones had dug the graves.

Adam crawled closer on his elbows. He knew it was most likely a suicide mission. But he couldn't just sit there and watch three teenagers be executed. He had to do something. What if Cameron had been one of those kids? Would he have just hidden behind some bushes? Waited for the terrible deed to be over and done? And then cowardly brought the body back to civilisation? No, it was unthinkable.

His only chance would be to get hold of one of the machine guns. If he had a weapon, he would at least have a fighting chance. Maybe he could take down two or three of the soldiers, cause some commotion that Ahn and his friends could use to attempt an escape. At least he would have given them a chance. He didn't like his prospects though. He had observed how the Vietnamese soldiers carried their weapons. This wasn't a gang of drug dealers, these guys had serious weapons training.

Oh, fuck it. He knew the decision was already made for him. He wasn't built to sit it out. He had to give it a try.

He studied the perimeter. The three graves had been dug in a small clearing, and Ahn and his friends were kneeling down about seven metres from the graves. Black bags covered their heads, presumably so they wouldn't be able to tell where they had been. Initially Adam had thought that was a good sign. The fact that the soldiers wanted to conceal their own identities and not reveal their location could mean that they would potentially let the prisoners free. But as they were kneeling in front of three empty graves he understood it had been wishful thinking. Ahn's and his friends' fates were already sealed.

But what were the soldiers waiting for? They had been standing around now for more than ten minutes.

It didn't really matter though. Adam had to act now. This was his window of opportunity, and it was closing fast. The soldiers had just finished a two-hour-long walk, they had the prisoners at the execution site, somewhere deep in the Cu Chi jungle. They had let their guard down. Some of them were having a cigarette, their machine guns leaning up against the base of a tree. Two of them still seemed focused though, machine guns pointing from their hips, scouting for any suspicious movements. But the rest seemed to have let their guard down.

Adam decided that his best bet would be to move up behind

the soldier sitting straight ahead, about thirty metres in front of him. He seemed to be busy eating, and his machine gun was lying on the ground next to him. Adam would sneak up from behind, cut the soldier's throat with a swift movement of the wrist, ditch the knife, and start shooting. The first bullets had to take out the two soldiers with the machine guns still on their hips. If he got them he could still have a chance of surviving as the remaining six soldiers would all use a couple of seconds to get to their weapons.

He had no idea whether there were more soldiers in the area, and he silently cursed Ahn for telling him the blatant lie that soldiers didn't venture into the jungle, that it was considered too dangerous for them with the uncleared landmines and all.

Well, there were soldiers there, heavily armed soldiers. And now Adam had to kill nine of them if he was to have any chance to save Ahn and his friends.

Nine against one. He had survived worse odds, he thought, as he slowly approached the soldier scuffling down his dinner.

-83-

Cameron opened her eyes. She had a throbbing headache. With dopey eyes she glanced over her shoulder and saw that Nina Winter was sitting in the seat next to her. She appeared to be sleeping. Cameron tried to move her arm, but soon realised that she had been restrained. Both her hands were strapped to the armrests.

She couldn't recollect what had happened. Her last memory was of a big white flash. She had gotten out of bed to see what all the commotion in the street was about, and then before she even knew what was going on, a big white flash had come out of nowhere.

A stun grenade, they must have thrown a stun grenade into the bedroom.

She tried readjusting her body, every part of it ached; it was as if she had been beaten up by a gang of gorillas. Perusing the other passengers she realised that her assessment probably wasn't too far from the truth. They were in what appeared to be a private jet. It had six rows of seats and looked relatively luxurious, but not overly. More business luxury, conservative discreet luxury.

Two guys in black pants, black leather shoes and white shirts, two buttons undone, sat straight opposite her. They were observing her.

"I think she's awake," one of them said.

Fucking geniuses, she thought.

The guy who had made the stellar observation that she was awake got up from his seat and walked to the front of the cabin. He seemed to whisper something to a guy sitting there before returning to his seat.

Cameron leant to the side, but it was hard with the restraints restricting her ability to move her body. She couldn't get a glimpse of the guy in front, couldn't even see the back of his head through all the expensive leather of the seats.

A private jet.

Neatly dressed guys, American-looking.

She wasn't sure, but she assumed it had to be the CIA who had taken her.

At least that was good news, the CIA didn't kill people.

If they thought Cameron and her mum had anything to do with the airplane crash, had anything at all to do with the crash of flight SQ183, Cameron would be able to clear that mistake up straight away.

"Can I have some water?" she asked the guy sitting opposite her. He had just returned from his chat with the guy in the front.

"Sure," he said and got up. "Ice or no ice?" he asked.

Damn polite kidnappers, she thought before requesting ice.

"Where are we going?" she asked the remaining guy.

"You'll know soon. We'll be there in a couple of hours. Just try to relax, and enjoy the flight," he said, smiling.

When she noticed, it was already too late: The guy who had gotten up to get some water, had positioned himself right behind her. Before she had time to react, he had injected a needle into her shoulder. She could feel the prick, followed by a rush of fluid going into her muscle.

The effect wasn't immediate, but she could feel herself getting tired, her eyes struggling to stay open.

"You, fuuckkers...." She managed to yell before her head dropped forward and her jaw hit her breastbone.

She was out.

-84-

"Drop your weapons!" Adam shouted. He had made a last minute change in his plans. The blade of his knife had been so close to the main artery of the dinner-eating Vietnamese soldier that he would have been able to smell the metal. Instead of slitting his throat, though, Adam had decided to try get out of the situation without the loss of human lives. He stood upright, machine gun pointing towards the two soldiers with their machine guns on their hips. They didn't seem to flinch. Adam had one advantage, he had a knife against one of their comrades' throats, but he soon realised that he could have overestimated their sense of camaraderie. Instead of dropping his weapon, one of the Vietnamese soldiers turned his machine gun towards the three boys kneeling on the ground. Adam could see his trigger finger gently putting pressure on the trigger.

"Nobody needs to die here," Adam said. "Just let me and my friends leave and we will not be a problem. We will forget we were ever here. You have my word."

"We can't do that," the Vietnamese soldier said with perfect English pronunciation.

"No need to be a hero. Just look the other way."

"I wish it was that simple," the Vietnamese soldier said.

"It is that simple," Adam quipped.

The Vietnamese soldier shouted an order, and the other soldiers jumped to their feet, machine guns in hands. They were all pointing their machine guns at Adam now, except for the soldier who had given the order; his machine gun was still pointed straight at Ahn and his friends.

This is not going to end well, Adam thought as he steadied himself for what was about to come. He decided it would be best to attack, at least then he would be able to take some of them down with him. He took a deep breath and increased the pressure on the trigger slightly.

"Can't stay out of trouble, can you?" a voice called out from the dense jungle.

"Hayburner?" Adam asked, and turned his head slightly to the right to see where the voice came from. He still kept the knife against the soldier's throat and the machine gun was squarely aimed at the other soldiers.

"Haven't called or sent a letter in ten years, and then you show up here like this." Hayburner gave a wave with his hand and, as if on cue, all the Vietnamese soldiers lowered their weapons.

Adam relaxed a little bit and let the soldier he held at knifepoint go, he still kept the machine gun pointed at the other soldiers though. The soldier who had been held at knifepoint stumbled over the others, covering his throat, coughing like he had choked on a fishbone.

"I need your help," Adam said.

"I can see that," Hayburner said. "You need to work on your math skills. One against nine. That never ends well."

"It did in Mogadishu."

"That was a lucky break," Hayburner said, and walked up to

Adam. Adam finally relaxed enough to lower his own weapon.

"What are you doing here?"

"Your son." Adam nodded towards the boys with black bags over their heads. "Your son was concerned for you."

Hayburner swore before walking over to Ahn, ripping his head bag off.

He looked back at Adam with gratitude in his eyes, before lifting his son from the ground.

"It will be dark in less than half an hour, we'll have to move now," he said.

Two of the Vietnamese soldiers walked over and pulled off the other two boys' head bags and released their ropes. When one of them saw the empty grave in front of him, he almost broke down. He hadn't realised how close he had been to ending his life there in the jungle.

"You can trust them," Hayburner said to Adam. "They're working for me."

"Working for you? What the hell have you gotten yourself into?" Adam asked.

"You'll have to wait and see. I think you'll be pleasantly surprised," Hayburner replied.

-85-

The CIA agent walked up to the glass cage holding Dr Drecker and knocked on the window. Dr Drecker got up from his desk, and walked over to the glass wall.

"I heard you took some liberties when I was away," the CIA agent said.

"You authorised it. You told me I was allowed to let Cody see the sky for one last time."

"The authorisation was to take him outside in the garden. You took him up to the roof."

"The place wasn't specified in your written approval," Dr Drecker said.

"I acknowledge that. But I instructed you to take him out in the garden."

"No harm done. There was never any risk he would jump of the roof or escape. We had a cigarette, then we walked down again. That was all."

"You disobeyed my orders."

"I'm sorry for that. I just thought the roof would be nicer. A bit closer to the blue sky."

"If you break the rules one more time our deal is off."

Dr Drecker nodded. He knew the deal being off didn't have the normal meaning in this place. It didn't mean that Cody wouldn't be let out under Dr Drecker's supervision, because that would never happen anyway. If he crossed the CIA agent one more time it probably meant immediate death. Immediate death for both him and Cody.

"Understood," he said.

There was a silence between them before Dr Drecker continued.

"Did you locate Patient F?"

The CIA agent smiled. "No, but it is not a problem anymore."

"How so?"

"I've got somebody else,"

"Who?" Dr Drecker asked.

"None of your business, but you asked to see me. I hope there was a purpose for it. I have a busy schedule."

I'm sure you do you fuck, busy schedule scheming how to kill people, Dr Drecker thought.

"Yes, I think I may have an explanation of what DMT does to the patients. I think I may have solved the problem."

"Ok." The CIA agent leant forward. He hadn't expected Dr Drecker to come up with anything. He was there to make Cody useful. But then again he was a neurologist, a specialist on brains. They had focused broadly in their studies of the death row prisoners, but it was the first time a neurologist was part of the team.

"What's your thoughts? What do you think you have found out?" he asked.

"I would like to present my findings to the other scientists as well," Dr Drecker said. "I need constructive feedback. And frankly just you and I talking isn't going to cut it."

The CIA agent studied Dr Drecker. He was either stupid or very brave, requesting a meeting with him and demanding to present his solution to the rest of the scientists.

The CIA agent scratched his chin. The clock was ticking, and he needed to keep the scientists occupied for a few more days. Maybe a presentation from Dr Drecker could be a welcome distraction. Something that could divert their attention. Some of them had gotten visibly nervous lately. It was as if they sensed something was going to happen, something very bad.

And some of them knew about the timeline, about the date.

Any distraction at all would be good, he decided.

"Ok, I'll organise it. You can present your findings tomorrow."

"Thank you," Dr Drecker said. "Thank you."

-86-

"So you knew I was coming?" Adam asked.

"Are you kidding me? Did you think you could walk around in Saigon, asking questions unnoticed?"

"In all honesty, yes," Adam replied. "I didn't think you were such a hotshot that everybody knew your name."

Hayburner laughed. "You're right. It wasn't my name that set off the alarm bells."

Adam studied his old friend.

Hayburner nodded. "You've been asking around about a ghost."

"The Shaman?" Adam asked. "Do you know where I can find him?"

"Depends," Hayburner replied.

"Depends on what?"

"Depends on why you want to speak to him."

"I have information he would like to hear."

"Well, he does have a soft spot for good intel, but I don't think he will see you without credentials."

"Can you vouch for me?"

Hayburner shook his head. "I'm not part of the inner circle.

I've only met him a couple of times. I'll get you out of the trouble you're in. I'll explain that you, and Ahn and his friends are no threats to him, but after that you have to leave. You have to leave Vietnam and never return."

"I can't do that," Adam said. "There was a reason my wife risked getting caught. The Shaman is important. I don't know why, but I need to see him. For Cameron's sake."

"I can't believe that Mimi would do something like that. Kidnap Cameron and disappear for seven years."

"Well, it happened."

"Do you have any idea why?"

"I do," Adam said. He opened his left breast pocket and pulled out the brown envelope he had found in his wife's sailboat. It had been hidden among all his letters from Afghanistan.

"What is that?" Hayburner asked.

"This is the reason Mimi ran away," Adam replied, and handed Hayburner the letter.

Hayburner called for a break, and everyone stopped walking.

Adam and Hayburner sat down next to each other. Adam studied his surroundings while Hayburner read the letter.

It was now dark, and they had to use flashlights to see the path, or what was supposedly a path. It was more like dense jungle.

Adam was glad they had Hayburner and his crew to guide them; there was no way he would have been able to navigate this area at night by himself.

"I don't understand," Hayburner said after having finished reading the letter.

"They wanted to test Cameron's blood," Adam said.

"Yes, and so?"

"Cameron isn't my daughter, she doesn't have my blood."

"And what has this to do with me, what has this to do with the Shaman?"

"I just want you to tell him I want to speak to him. Tell him I want to speak to him about Patient F."

"Patient F? None of this makes any sense, Adam. What the hell are you going on about?"

"Just tell him, Hayburner. Just tell him."

=87=

"So what do you think the patients are talking about? Do you believe they travel to a different world, a parallel universe when they are injected with DMT?" the CIA agent asked.

"It's a tough question," Dr Drecker started. "If you asked me a few weeks ago what psychedelics do I would just have answered that psychedelics fire off certain neurons in our brains, and those neurons are responsible for the visions people experience under the influence of psychedelics."

"And now. Have you changed your mind?"

Dr Drecker shook his head. "I haven't changed my mind. But I have realised that this is a much more complex problem than I thought. People who smoke, drink or inject themselves with traditional psychedelics like LSD, mescalin and Yage, can be said to share a lot of similar experiences: The separation of the body from the consciousness, the feeling of dying, the feeling of hovering over your own body, seeing a light in a tunnel. Even visiting alien worlds, and being probed and examined by humanoids or aliens." Dr Drecker paused deliberately before continuing. "But the reality is that you can re-create a lot of these experiences by simply starving the brain for oxygen. Reduce the flow of oxygen to the human brain and people can have out-of-body experiences, they can see a light in a tunnel, even experience that they are being abducted by aliens. It is all the creation of this fabulous machinery that sits on top of our bodies: our brain."

"So what is different with DMT?" the CIA agent asked.

"Well, if administered at the correct level, at Phi, it appears to cause a growth spurt in the pineal gland, and it seems to have some sort of self-healing effect on the test subjects. The self-healing effect gradually disappears, but is replaced by a more permanent effect: The body stops aging, or at least slows down the rate of aging dramatically."

"Any theories why?" the CIA agent asked.

Dr Drecker shook his head. "Not yet. And of course we have the additional mystery of why the test subjects die or commit suicide almost immediately after the DMT injection, only to resurrect three days later."

"And die again," the CIA agent followed up.

Dr Drecker nodded.

"That is the big problem. Who are they? These people who take over the test subjects' bodies when they die for the second time, 49 days after the DMT injection? Who are they, and where do they come from?"

"Well, that's the reason you are here today. You mentioned that you have come up with a possible theory," the CIA agent said.

Dr Drecker nodded.

"I believe they are still the same people they were. That it is just something inside them that has taken over."

"You propose that they have become schizophrenic?" the CIA agent asked.

"Not schizophrenic. Schizophrenic means that there are several personalities struggling to take control over your mind. I propose that it is just the power struggle between the left and right brain that finally has had a victor."

"Please explain," the CIA agent said.

"Have any of you heard about the split brain paradox?" Dr Drecker asked.

Some of the scientists shook their heads, but some also nodded. Dr Drecker decided it was best to give them a proper explanation.

"The split brain paradox is caused by the human brain having two nearly identical halves. The left and the right. Why this redundancy? The brain can operate without either one of the halves, so why do we have this duplication?"

"Because they are not exact copies. The left and right brain have different duties. The left brain is more analytical and logical, and the right brain is more holistic and artistic," one of the scientists said.

"Correct. But the left brain is the dominant brain in all humans. It makes all the final decisions. Commands pass from the left brain to the right brain via the corpus callosum. In reality the right brain is a prisoner of the left brain."

"So you believe that the DMT injection lets the right brain take over?"

"I believe that the DMT experiment may have changed the power balance in these patients' heads. They are not schizophrenic, they only have one personality, but it is distinctively different from the one they had before they were affected by the DMT injection. They also claim that they are prisoners in these bodies, that they are not their own. This could be explained by the left brain now being suppressed by the right brain. This is not a normal situation for the left brain and could thus explain the constant feeling of being stuck inside a head but unable to speak."

"It is an interesting theory Dr Drecker. But it doesn't explain why the patients initially gained the ability to self-heal, why they don't age or why they talk about this coming apocalypse, this alien invasion."

"No, it doesn't. And to be able to provide some answers to those questions I will need to study the death row patients more closely."

"But do you have any theories at this point in time?"

Dr Drecker scratched his chin. It was essential that he got his points across. "We are trained to think about abnormalities as special gifts. I went to University with a so called autistic Savant. My friend Simon had an accident when he was four, got hit in the head by a golf club. And from that day on he could remember every conversation, every meal, every single little detail in his life. I could call him right now, and he would be able to tell me what the temperature was on the third Sunday of July in 1987. He once told me that the key to his ability maybe wasn't a brilliant brain, because he didn't feel like he had a one, not at all. He asked me whether it could instead be the inability to forget."

"So instead of looking at these abilities, these special skills that the DMT patients acquire, as an improvement, we should look at them as a handicap?"

Dr Drecker nodded.

"We should look at whether the growth of the pineal gland has caused damage to part of their brains, and whether this is not some alien mind having occupied the patient's heads, but plainly, damaged brains."

"But the ability to see this world they are talking about, they all talk about the same specific world. How do we explain that?"

"If it is true that the right brain has taken over control of the DMT patients, then this world they all talk about could be a place, or a plane of existence, where the right brain normally lives, normally exists."

"Are you saying that the right and left brain exist in different dimensions? That all humans live in two different worlds?"

"I don't know. Dreams are a way of sorting out our memories. Like running a disk cleaner on a computer hard-drive. Maybe the right brain has been dominated for all these years, and when it first takes over it also dominates the dreams. "

"And the prophecy? Why did they all start praying for this Saviour to come? Why did they suddenly stop talking and only recite the prophecy?"

"One of the side effects of psychedelics is that the user generally believes he is part of something bigger. It could also be described as a religious experience. It is not impossible that by giving the patients the exact same dosage..."

"The dosage of Phi, the divine number," one of the scientists interrupted.

"Phi is not a magic number. The magic is that the patients were given the exact same dosage. The point is that it is not impossible that their experiences are similar because they got the exact same dosage. The damage to their brains would therefore also be identical."

"That makes no sense. Before they stopped talking they talked about a different world. Their own world."

"The world where the right sides of their brains have been living all these years. You don't see any animals worship gods. You don't see any animals pray. Yet humans across the world, even in remote places that have never been in contact with other people, have through all times created their own gods. Being religious is ingrained in humans. It's almost like it is in our DNA. The reason could be that we are born to be religious. If you have a split brain, you could potentially both be religious and an atheist. Your so-called conscience, the one that is displayed when your right and left brain halves work together, could be different from the one that would materialize when only the right brain half would be dominant."

"Do you have any evidence at all, Dr Drecker? Or is all this just speculations?" one of the scientists asked.

"I do have some evidence. I have gone through the files of all the patients. And without exception they are all left-handed."

"That's your evidence? That all the patients are left-handed?" the scientist was laughing when he asked.

"None of them were left-handed before they were injected with DMT," Dr Drecker said, and the room turned silent.

The older man took the word. "So what are your requirements, Dr Drecker? I understand that you have only been here for a short time, and we do not expect you to have all the answers. But all the things you have presented here today are mere speculations. Speculations without proof. So I guess the true goal of today was to ask us for something, am I right?"

Dr Drecker nodded.

"Yes, you are. As you understand, I have a lot vested in finding a solution."

"We are aware of your situation, yes," the old man replied.

"To be able to test my hypothesis and progress, I will need to inject some of the death row prisoners with a new dosage of DMT."

"We can't allow that. We don't know what they are. The security protocols in this building have been put in place to ensure safety for the rest of the population. If the patients really are from another world, we can't risk opening up the gates to this world," the CIA agent said.

"You have had these patients locked up for decades. As far as I understand they haven't done a lot of damage in those years. No attempted breakouts, no violent riots. No deaths. I think the risk is acceptable."

The CIA agent glanced over at the old man, who seemed to be considering Dr Drecker's proposal.

"We can't do it," the CIA agent said silently.

The old man just raised his hand.

"I understand that you have volunteered to enter the cells, and that you know the consequence of this action."

Dr Drecker nodded.

"I don't think the experiment will give us any new information, but if there is a chance we can save your boy I think it is worth it. I will allow you to inject one patient with DMT."

The CIA agent stared at the old man with distrust.

"Thank you, Sir," Dr Drecker said, before leaving the room.

After the other scientist had also left it was only the CIA agent and the old man left. "Are you crazy?" the CIA agent asked.

"Calm down. I'm not going to give him access to any DMT."

"You're not? Because it sure as hell sounded like you promised it."

"The date is approaching and we need to know if our serum will work."

"You intend to give him the serum instead of DMT?"

The old man smiled. "We need to know if it will work. And Dr Drecker seems to have struck up a relationship with Patient A. If he trusts him we can get the serum tested without any risks."

-88-

It was almost midnight when they arrived at what appeared to be the Vietnamese soldiers' headquarters. It wasn't a camp as Adam had expected however – it was a tiny hole in the ground. "After you," Hayburner said.

"Are you kidding me? I won't fit," Adam said.

"You'll fit. Just don't panic. You can't turn around once you have started descending."

"Descending?"

"Yes, the tunnel is built in three levels. The upper one is just for transport. We need to get down to the lower levels, where we have our living quarters."

"Fuck," Adam blurted out. "He wasn't afraid of any of the usual things. Spiders, snakes, heights, even death, none of those things scared him. But he wasn't particularly fond of closed spaces. Of not having anywhere to run, of totally exposing himself. He did trust his old friend, Hayburner, but if this was a trap, if this was an ambush, then he would have nowhere to go. Once he entered these tunnels he was at Hayburner's mercy.

He sat down on the edge of the entrance to the tunnel, feet dangling into the hole. With a swift move he put the palms of his hands on the ground and lifted his legs into position before lowering the rest of his body into the hole. He had to stretch his hands above his head to fit through the entrance; the tunnel opening was obviously not built for broad-shouldered westerners. He turned on his flashlight, faced it towards the black abyss in front of him, and started crawling forwards.

After about ten minutes of tedious crawling, he estimated that they had moved about thirty-five metres forward, and eight metres downwards, but he could be way off. It was difficult to keep your bearings underground, the pace was slow, it was insanely hot and claustrophobic, and there were no reference points. Every turn looked the same. It was like fucking suburbia, Adam thought.

Up ahead, about five metres in front of him he could see the tunnel open up. There had been a soldier in front of him the whole way, and Adam had basically focused on his back, just to stay on track. But now the soldier's back was gone and a dim light had replaced him.

Adam crawled out of the tunnel and entered something that appeared slightly more comfortable, although still far from spacious. The tunnel opened up into a small hall, about six by six metres, and on the dirt ground there were placed a couple of mattresses, some chairs and a table. Adam couldn't stand up straight, but if he bowed his head he could move around freely.

"What is this?" he asked Hayburner, who had just exited the tunnel behind him.

"This is your quarters for the night," Hayburner replied.

"Is the Shaman here?"

Hayburner shook his head.

"He is not here. I'll keep my promise. I'll convey him your

message. But if he doesn't want to meet you, you'll have to promise me to leave Vietnam and never return."

Adam considered the proposal for a second before replying.

"Scout's honour," he said, and stretched his hand out.

Hayburner laughed and shook Adam's hand. "You've never been a bloody scout. As far as I can remember you were terrible at tracking."

"I tracked your guys today without any problems," Adam said.

"I knew you were coming, remember."

They both laughed.

Ahn was the next one to come through the tunnel. He walked straight over to one of the chairs, and sat down, mulling.

"You've got a good boy," Adam said.

"He should never have come here," Hayburner replied, looking strangely serious for a moment.

"He is his father's son. I bet you wouldn't have stayed put if your dad went missing either."

"He should never have come," Hayburner repeated.

-89-

"**W**elcome Cameron," the CIA agent said. He was standing in the door entrance, neatly dressed in a black suit.

Cameron looked up at him with disgust. It was the first time she had seen his face, but she knew this was the guy from the airplane, the guy with the back to her who had ordered his colleague to inject her with some sort of tranquiliser. Her head and body still ached like anything, a side effect of whatever they had injected her with, she thought.

"Where is Nina?" Cameron asked.

"She is safe; she is just down the hall."

"I would like to see her."

"That can be arranged, but it will have to be later."

Cameron sat up in her bed. She looked around, it appeared that she was in some sort of hospital, but it looked more like a prison cell than a hospital room. There were no loose items, every piece of furniture was either bolted down or part of the structure itself. The walls were made of glass.

"Where am I?"

"You are at a research facility in the US. We are here to help you."

"I don't need any help," she quipped.

"Yes you do, Cameron. You may not know it, but you are changing."

"I'm totally fine," Cameron said.

"In the last month you've survived an airplane crash and a car accident. None of the other passengers survived. Don't you think that is a bit strange?"

"I've been lucky. Is that a crime?" Cameron replied.

"Luck has nothing to do with it," The CIA agent said. "You killed those other passengers."

"Bullshit. They were accidents!" Cameron screamed. She was scared now, scared that he was right, scared that he knew something she didn't.

"You are a special girl, Cameron, you have special gifts."

"I'm normal. There is nothing special with me. I'm perfectly normal," she screamed.

"Far from," the CIA agent said.

He took a step closer.

"Do you remember anything from the crash of the semi-trailer?" he asked.

"No, I don't," she replied. "I woke up in a field. That's all I remember," she said, wondering how the agent knew about the accident. Nobody had seen her inside the truck.

The CIA agent understood what she was thinking. "We found your DNA on the crash site."

He leant against the wall before continuing.

"The local police couldn't figure out why the semi crashed. There were no skid marks, the driver just seemed to have steered off the road on a straight stretch. Why would he do that?"

Cameron knew why he had done it. There had been another passenger in the cabin, in the sleeping cabin. When they had started to drive he had jumped down in the seat next to Cameron. He had been a sleazy-looking guy, and Cameron had seen it coming a mile away. The hand on her thigh, the look in his eyes.

"It was an accident," she said. "He tried to rape me. I defended myself and the driver lost control of the truck."

"It wasn't an accident."

"It was!"

"When did your mom first start teaching you about bombs?"

"My mom wasn't a terrorist, she was never a terrorist!" Cameron screamed. She was on the verge of crying.

"I know," said the CIA agent. "Your mom did nothing wrong, she was a good woman."

"Then why am I here?"

"You were the one responsible, you were the one who blew up flight SQ183," the CIA agent answered.

-90-

A dam woke, covered in sweat. It hadn't been one of his best nights. For the first time in years he had experienced nightmares about his time in Afghanistan. Maybe it was the reunification with Hayburner that had brought the bad dreams back? Maybe it was the sight of the soldiers getting ready to execute Ahn and his friends? Adam sat up on his mattress. Hayburner hadn't mentioned anything about the incident, and Adam hadn't brought it up. Had they really been ready to execute those kids, or had it all been part of a scare tactic? To scare the living lights out of some local teenagers so that they never ever again dared venture into the Cu Chi jungle. Hayburner had said that he had expected Adam, but he had seemed genuinely surprised by seeing his own son. That meant that they probably hadn't kept eyes on Adam in Saigon. It was most likely one of the many traders at the market who had talked. Let them know that a westerner made enquiries about the Shaman.

Adam turned on his flashlight. His watch told him the time was four am. He made his way over to the entrance and for a second he considered whether he should go by himself or wait for someone to join him. He didn't know the way through the tunnels. He had just followed the soldier in front of him. If he took the wrong turn he might end up in a dead-end, or worse; he might crawl straight into a booby trap.

A hand on his shoulder solved the problem. It was Hayburner's.

"Jeez, have you been swimming?" he said, removing his hand from Adam's wet shirt.

"Just a bad dream," Adam replied.

"Welcome to the club. You wanna get some fresh air?"

Adam nodded in the dim light of Hayburner's flashlight, and followed him into the tunnel.

When they arrived at the surface, Adam took the deepest breath he had taken in years. Although he knew it probably wasn't, the air in Vietnam felt the freshest he had ever felt.

Hayburner laughed.

"Why do you hide in the tunnels?" Adam asked.

The Government does the occasional fly-by, or points their satellites in this direction. Can't detect us if we're underground, can they?" he said.

"Yes, but why do you need to hide?"

"You don't need to know. It's just business."

Adam shrugged. He didn't really care. He understood that whatever Hayburner was involved in, it probably wasn't legal. He had probably lied to his son. It was most likely drug-related.

"So when do I get to see the Shaman?" Adam asked.

"When he wakes up," Hayburner replied.

"I thought you said he wasn't here."

"He wasn't. But I got your message to him last night, and he must have thought it was important because he arrived during the night. He is in another tunnel a couple of hundred metres from here."

Adam nodded.

"Hungry?" Hayburner asked, and walked over to the base of a tree. He sat down and pulled out two plastic containers. He handed one to Adam and started eating out of his own, with his fingers.

It was just plain rice.

Two hours went by, and most of the other soldiers had arrived from the tunnel. They scattered around, resting against trees, cleaning their weapons, or just simply squatting. It reminded Adam of how much time went by doing nothing in the army, how much time was spent waiting.

Suddenly they all seemed to get busy; they jumped to their feet and dispersed into what seemed as prearranged positions around the clearing.

"What's happening?" Adam asked.

"The Shaman is on his way," Hayburner replied.

Adam studied the soldiers' faces as the Shaman walked into the provisional camp they had organised; they all looked down, didn't dare stare at his eyes. They had brought up three tiny plastic chairs from the tunnels and placed them in the middle of the clearing. The so-called Shaman was nothing like what Adam had expected, though, and he could hardly conceal his disappointment. Adam had believed that the Shaman would be the mysterious Patient F, the person who most likely was Cameron's real dad. That the reason his wife had travelled around Southeast Asia for all these years was to find Cameron's biological dad.

When he looked at the frail figure of the person walking

towards him he knew it wasn't so.

This so-called Shaman couldn't be Cameron's dad.

This so-called Shaman was only a teenager.

Hayburner indicated to Adam that he should sit down in one of the chairs. He obliged. He couldn't be impolite; he had to wait for the right moment to explain this was all a misunderstanding. He hoped this didn't affect his, or Ahn's and the other boys' safety. He had no idea what sort of illegal operation this Shaman, this teenager was running, but he knew he wasn't the person Adam's wife had been looking for.

The Shaman walked over and sat down in the chair opposite Adam.

His skin was white, almost see-through white. He had a wrinkle-free, childish face. Adam had expected to meet a guy in his fifties, a hippie, an Indian guru clad in robes with a long beard and Rastafari hair. Instead he sat across from this teenager, this tiny teenager with the most innocent face he had ever seen.

"What is your name?" the Shaman asked in an American accent.

"Adam."

The Shaman put his hand on Adam's arm. It felt warm, incredibly warm.

"Why do you seek me?" the Shaman asked.

"It was a mistake. I'm sorry, I was looking for someone else," Adam said, and readied himself to get up.

The Shaman increased the pressure on Adam's arm and it was as if his entire body was instantly immobilised.

"There are no mistakes. Everything happens for a reason."

Adam didn't know what to say. The kid had an almost hypnotic look in his eyes, and although he didn't seem to put any weight on Adam's arm, Adam strongly doubted whether he could actually get it loose. What the hell was going on?

"I was seeking a special person, a person who went under the name Patient F a long time ago. My wife thought she could find him here in Vietnam, and so I thought the same."

"A long time ago. Indeed, it has been a long time ago since anybody called me by that name. Now I want you to tell me exactly why you wanted to talk to me," the Shaman said, and applied some more pressure on Adam's arm.

It was as if somebody had placed a truck on top of his arm, the weight seemed so unbearable.

Adam looked at the white face in front of him. And for the first time in his life he was afraid. This person in front of him wasn't human, he was something else.

-91-

"No, I didn't. I didn't blow up the plane," Cameron screamed. She was almost hysterical now.

"Do you remember anything from the crash of the semi-trailer, anything at all?" the CIA agent asked.

Cameron remembered everything. The sleazy guy who put his hand on the inside of her thigh. She had pushed it off, but he had just put it back there. Then she had hit him, hit him hard."

She shook her head.

"The local police couldn't figure it out. They couldn't figure out why the driver and the passenger died from that crash. They shouldn't have. They hardly had any visible injuries."

Cameron shrugged her shoulders.

"Both their necks were broken, clean breaks. Just above the fifth cervical vertebra. The passenger hung on for a few days before he died. But he never had a chance," the CIA agent said.

"What are you implying?" Cameron asked.

"There was another casualty in Brisbane three weeks ago with the exact same injury. A security guard from the Royal Albert Hospital. The staff found him in the kitchen, with a broken neck. Fifth vertebra."

Cameron's eyes narrowed, it was as if the black in the pupils turned into a black hole, a black hole that threatened to suck everything in the room into them.

"I know what you are, Cameron. There is no need to play games with me," the CIA agent said.

Cameron looked away, she didn't want to look at him, didn't want to hear what he had to say.

She had lied when she said that she didn't remember anything from the airplane crash. She had been plagued with vivid dreams about it ever since the accident. The dream was always the same. She would feel her body heat up, that she got hotter and hotter, and there was nothing she could do about it. Her mum was sitting next to her, first consoling her, then getting scared, then screaming, her whole body on fire.

Then, a loud explosion.

-92-

"I'm telling the truth," Adam said. He was struggling to keep a calm face. His arm felt like it was being crushed.

The Shaman let go of his arm and Adam let out a breath of relief.

"I believe you," the Shaman said.

"So is it true? Did Dr Middleton take the sperm samples from you? Is it possible that you are Cameron's dad?"

The Shaman looked at Adam, he looked straight through him.

"It is correct that Dr Middleton took a sperm sample all those years ago. He was a good man, Dr Middleton, and he realised what potential I had. He realised before I did."

"Who are you? And what is the connection? Why did both you and Cameron survive terrible accidents?"

"The question is not why we both survived terrible accidents. The question is why those terrible accidents happened," the Shaman said, and rose up from the chair.

"Come with me, I need to show you something," he said.

-93-

"So you have interviewed the new patient?" the old man asked.

The CIA agent nodded. "It went as expected. She didn't reveal anything."

"Do you think you will be able to get her to talk?"

"It doesn't really matter," the CIA agent said.

"What do you mean it doesn't matter? He is still out there, Patient F is still out there."

"But soon he will be here," the CIA agent said.

"And why is that? He hasn't shown himself in over thirty years. And now you tell me he's been living underground, that he's been hiding in the old VC tunnels in Vietnam all this time. If he has gone to that extent to stay hidden, why would he expose himself now?"

"Because he now has a purpose. Cameron is his daughter, and Adam Mullins is going to convince him of that fact."

"You're assuming Adam Mullins gets to him alive. That he is able to walk straight into Patient F's dungeon without getting killed. Have you forgotten how it was in Nam, how the damn VC almost wiped us out?"

"I haven't forgotten, my old friend, and that's the reason I let Adam continue on his own. If we had tried to track down Patient F he would have wiped us out without breaking a sweat. My father fought in Cu Chi, he never made it back."

"So what if Adam Mullins manages to convince Patient F that we have his daughter. That's not going to change anything. He wouldn't have a clue where we keep her. He would have no incentive to come looking for her. He would just have an even stronger incentive than usual to keep up his acts of terrorism."

The CIA agent smiled. "Luckily your minions in the army are quite predictable. Adam Mullins was obviously scared of losing his daughter again, so much so that he put a tracking device on her." The CIA agent held up the watch Adam had given to Cameron after they landed in Ho Chi Minh City.

"Do you think he is stupid enough not to understand that we would find this?"

"It is not a question about stupidity; it is a question about desperation. Adam Mullins has been out of service for seven years, and he has acted opposite of what we expected on several occasions. He is not making decisions based on rationality; he is making decisions based on his love for his daughter."

"A daughter he now knows isn't even his."

"I don't think whose blood she has will matter. A father's love is stronger than that."

"So you think we can lure him here, trick him into walking straight into an ambush."

"Patient F won't be thinking as a commander either, he will be thinking as a father. We have two fathers, punch-drunk on love. I am certain they will walk straight into our trap."

"So what do we do? This building is not ideal for setting up a trap, and we have the added risk that he might succeed. That he might be able to fight back your ambush. What then? What if he is successful in breaking into MKULTRA?"

"He won't be breaking into this building. He is following the tracking device. We can place that wherever we want to."

The old man smiled. "I know where you have in mind."

The CIA agent nodded. "New Mexico it is."

-94-

Patient F waded into the dirty river, splashing water over his body. Adam followed after, his feet sinking into the muddy bottom.

"This is a good spot to catch crabs," Patient F said.

He was standing knee-deep in a clearing that opened up in between the palm trees. The clearing looked like a small lake, an oval-shaped lake.

"Do you know what caused this?" Patient F asked, pointing at the clearing.

"An American bomb?" Adam asked.

"Yes," Patient F replied. "An American bomb. The shell landed in the middle here and made a crater of five by seven metres, three metres deep. They bombed this whole area for five continuous months. But still they never managed to destroy the tunnels. The Viet Cong just built them deeper. The harder they got hit, the deeper they dug."

Adam nodded.

"This was a war without a purpose. The Americans chose to fight the North Vietnamese because they were afraid that communism would spread like a virus if they didn't crush it in its infancy. They failed to realise that you can't manipulate the forces of nature. Communism would have failed anyway, it wasn't a sustainable model. But by fighting every threat the US is only ending up with more enemies."

Adam nodded again. He had been fighting the Taliban in Afghanistan, and Saddam Hussein in Iraq. They had not been replaced by peace-loving democracies, that was for sure.

"You want the world to stand on the sideline. To witness genocides without doing anything?"

"It is not America's responsibility to be the world police."

"Then whose is it?"

Patient F didn't answer. He just stood there looking out over the oval clearing.

Suddenly Adam heard something behind him, it sounded like footsteps. He turned around and saw Hayburner carrying a tiny baby in his arms. The baby was screaming.

"What is happening?" Adam asked.

"Just watch," Hayburner said as he placed the little baby in front of the Shaman, in front of Patient F.

-95-

D r Drecker was preparing the IV with the DMT. He had explained the procedure to Patient A, Andrew Mortimer, by writing down everything he was about to do in a notepad, and had let the patient keep it overnight. Patient A seemed relaxed. He was holding the black cloth in front of his eye when he re-read the instructions, before lying down on the bed.

Dr Drecker was convinced that he was right. These crazy old MKULTRA agents were no scientists. They believed in telekinesis, parallel worlds and other pseudo-science. The boring truth was that most things had a natural explanation. The death row patients had never visited an alien world where their bodies were taken over by an extra-terrestrial being. That was just ludicrous.

The death row patients and Cody had simply been given an extraordinarily large dose of a substance that was found everywhere in nature. Both plants and humans produced DMT in small quantities.

MKULTRA and Dr Kovacks had simply stumbled upon one of nature's incredible wonders – a way to make the body heal itself more rapidly and age much more slowly than normal. We knew so little about the brain that it was no wonder the MKULTRA guys had been scared. The human brain only weighed around three pounds. It used less energy than a lightbulb and raised the body temperature by a paltry few degrees. And best of all; it only needed a couple of slices of pizza to keep going. Yet, if humans wanted to build a computer that could replicate some of its calculations, that computer would have to be the size of New York City.

Dr Drecker administered the DMT into the IV and put a hand on Patient A's head. "Just relax, Andrew. Don't fight it."

The CIA agent had queried why the DMT injection caused the death and resurrection of the patients, and Dr Drecker hadn't been able to come up with an answer. He did have a theory about what the consequence of the death and resurrection was, though. Aging was a result of the build-up of errors at the genetic and cellular level. Not all cells in the body reproduced, but most did. And although some cells like the heart and nerve cells could live for decades, most cells reproduced or were replaced by other cells in the body continuously. The problem with continuous reproduction of cells was that errors snuck in when a cell split and made a copy of itself, and those errors accumulated. One might imagine taking a photocopy of an image, and then repeating the process. Eventually, one would find errors in the photocopied image.

So how was it possible for a middle-aged couple, often riddled with cancer and old-age diseases, to produce a perfect little baby? Well, most babies looked very much alike when they were born, it was almost impossible to distinguish their sex based on their facial features. A twenty-year-old man, however, was often very unique, wrinkles and all. Thus it would be more complex to replicate a twenty-something than a newborn baby, and this lack of complexity, or fewer degrees of freedom to use the appropriate term, made it possible for the middle-aged couple to produce such a perfect baby.

Dr Drecker had read about a 29-year-old man in Florida who had the body of a 10-year-old, and a 31-year-old Brazilian lady who looked like a 2-year-old. Their bodies hadn't stopped aging; they had just started aging at snail's pace. A human cell could only divide about 50 times, something which was called the Hayflick limit. Other animals had other limits. The cells of a Galapagos tortoise could divide about 110 times. So aging was a function of cell division, of increasing disorder. If we lived long enough we would all die of cancer. But if the DMT injection had not only affected the brain of the patients, if it also had slowed down the division of cells in the bodies of the death row patients, that could possibly explain why they had seemed to stop aging.

They had died exactly three days after the first injection of DMT, and then died again exactly 49 days after the DMT injection. The same forty-nine days total that The Tibetan Book of the Dead claimed illustrated the exit of the spirit from the body.

Was it possible that their aging had slowed down to a snail's pace because their spirit had left the body? Was the human spirit such a complex thing that it increased the entropy and caused aging?

The reality of aging was a complex interplay between the environment and the cells in the human body. Over time, cell deaths outpaced cell production, thus leaving the body with fewer cells to repair wear and tear of the body. Free radicals and all the toxins humans took in just through living, eating and breathing, took their toll and caused people to age. But the death row patients had been held in complete isolation for a good forty years. They exercised in their cells and were fed healthy food. Could it be that they hadn't stopped aging? Could it be that their bodies' cell-splitting had slowed down to a snail's pace?

"Ahhhh. Rrohh. Ahhe." Andrew Mortimer, the death row patient who had so casually killed his own ex-wife arched his back and screamed. Dr Drecker couldn't make out the words. The sounds were probably not words anyway. He grabbed the patient's arm and held it down. Something was wrong. This was not the reaction he had expected from injecting the patient with another DMT shot. Dr Drecker had expected that the patient would have a natural trip this time. A trip back to whatever fairy-tale place people went when they were injected with a Phi dosage of DMT. Instead, it looked like the patient was about to die.

This couldn't be right.

There was no way the patient would die again.

-96-

Adam couldn't believe his own eyes. If he hadn't witnessed it himself he would have thought it was a lie. A made-up story. A made-up story like the ones in the Bible.

Hayburner had placed the little girl in front of Patient F. She was covered in a white cloth and only her head was sticking out. She had a full head of hair, a beautiful face, and stopped screaming the instant Patient F approached her.

Adam couldn't help it, he had to stare. The little girl didn't have any eyes. Where her eyes should have been there were only two dark holes.

"Agent Orange," Hayburner said. "The locals are still struggling with the aftermath."

"She was born without eyes?" Adam asked.

Hayburner nodded. "Now let's let the Shaman do his work. In the meantime I'll explain what we are doing here."

Hayburner placed a hand on Adam's shoulder and led him away from Patient F, who was carrying the little child out in the water. The child had turned completely silent.

"What were you going to do to those kids? Were you going to

kill them?" Adam asked.

"My son and his friends?" Hayburner laughed. "We weren't going to kill those kids. Just scare them,"

"It looked pretty real to me. Your men had three graves prepared."

"We are doing something important here. We can't allow it to be jeopardized by adventure seekers. On average we catch some kids every few weeks in this jungle. They are everything from drug smugglers to illegal immigrants. We can't just tell them to go home. Eventually they will talk. We have to make sure that they never come back. Make sure that they never talk about this place."

"And you do that by mock executions?"

"Among other things, yes," Hayburner replied.

"So what exactly are you doing here? If it's not drugs, what is it? Weapons?"

Hayburner laughed. "You've got it all wrong, Adam. I bring sick people to the Shaman, and he heals them. That's all we do."

Adam studied his old friend. He seemed to be telling the truth, but it didn't make any sense.

"You bring sick people to the Shaman?"

Hayburner nodded. "I've been doing it for years. He's got special powers. He can heal people. He was supposed to heal this little girl a week ago, but sometimes he gets very weak after a healing. That's the reason I didn't return as planned. I was never in any danger. This is the safest place in Vietnam. We're in the company of the closest thing there has ever been to a god."

Hayburner had barely finished his sentence when they heard the little girl scream. They turned around and walked into the water. Patient F was struggling to stand up, as he held the little child in front of him. Hayburner rushed to his side and put an arm around his shoulder. Adam grabbed the little girl from the Shaman's weak hands.

As Adam walked back on shore he looked down at the little girl in the white cloth. And he couldn't believe his own eyes. The black holes in the baby's face were gone. Instead two beautiful green eyes had taken their place.

The little baby was blinking and focusing. It looked like Adam was the first person she had ever seen.

-97-

"I don't understand how this could happen." Dr Drecker was teary where he sat inside his cell. He had almost managed to kill Andrew Mortimer, Patient A. He was now fine, but it had been a close call.

"We gave it a shot. I'm sorry it didn't work out," the CIA agent said.

"I was so sure I had figured it out."

"We've all been there," the CIA agent replied. "The problem is that we are dealing with something no one else has ever dealt with before. We can't rely on our common sense. We can't even rely on our senses."

"I just don't believe that these people are aliens. I just don't believe it. The DMT injection must have done something to their brains. It must have done something on a cellular level to their brains and bodies. There has to be a scientific explanation for this."

"Trust me, Dr Drecker. We've been studying these patients for almost forty years. They are what they are. And it is not human."

"Don't you think it's strange that they have all become hyper-religious? That they talk about an apocalypse and a utopian world somewhere else? All prophets in history have done the same.

Don't you find it strange that this apocalypse they have predicted is supposed to come in their lifetime? That their utopian world is supposed to come in their own lifetime? There is nothing original about it. They are just copying every other prophet who has lived. I don't doubt that they believe it, but it is all a made-up fantasy inside their heads. The heads you guys fucked up by injecting them with DMT."

"You injected your own son with the same," the CIA agent said.

"And I will never be able to forgive myself for having done that. But we can still save him. We can still save all of them."

"How?" the CIA agent asked.

"We humans are nothing but complex machines. The only difference is that we have wetware instead of hardware. Our brains can be rewired just like any computer. I can bring back the death row prisoners' original personalities, and then you'll see that I'm right. They are not aliens. They are just like you and me."

"I'm sorry, Dr Drecker. We tried. But enough is enough. Good bye," the CIA director said, and turned around.

Dr Drecker stood inside his own glass cage, staring at the glass wall. In the next door cell was his son Cody.

Cody couldn't see it, but Dr Drecker was crying again.

The CIA agent pulled out his phone and dialled an internal number.

"How did he take it?" the voice on the other line asked.

"As suspected. I don't think he'll be of much more help to us. Not that it is needed anyway."

"And the patient?"

"He responded to the poison as we had hoped. It targeted the brain cells. We only gave him a minimal dose, but he was heavily affected. I'm sure it will be effective."

"Good. We will have to come up with a new method of delivery though. IV won't work again."

"I've got it under control. A new delivery method has already been selected. It will minimise risk and be highly effective."

-98-

It was mid-afternoon and Adam was sitting next to Hayburner, who was cooling the Shaman's forehead with a wet cloth. The Shaman was lying down on the ground, his face even paler than before.

"Is he going to be ok?" Adam asked.

Hayburner nodded. "Healing a person drains him of energy. He'll be ok in a few days."

"Do you think I could ask him some questions?"

Hayburner shook his head. "He should rest. Wait until tomorrow. He'll be better by then."

"It's ok. You can ask me now," Patient F said, sitting up. "You've come a long way to talk to me. So it must be important. What is it that you want?"

"Do you know why my wife sought you out? Why she was looking for you all these years?"

Patient F nodded. "I have my suspicion, yes. My powers didn't manifest until later in life. You said your daughter was a teenager. How old is she?"

"She is sixteen. She was sixteen on the day her mother died. On the day of the accident."

"It happened earlier for me. On the day I hit puberty.

Something happened that I can't explain. I died that day, and I was born again three days later."

"You're talking about the train crash in Melbourne, the one where eighty people died?"

"Yes. The crash was my fault. I don't know why or how. All I remember is that I got so hot, so incredibly hot. My minders tried to cool me down, but it was impossible. I could see everything around me catching fire, and then the train tipped over."

"You're saying you were responsible for the train crash?"

"I believe so, yes. I was responsible for all those people's deaths."

"So you're saying that Cameron was responsible for SQ183 crashing? That she caused the plane to explode?"

"You will have to make up your own mind, Adam. I'm just telling you what happened to me."

"But why was my wife trying to find you? Why would she risk getting caught trying to find you?"

"I believe she may have wanted to know how I've been able to live with my powers all these years. If it would be possible for Cameron to live with these powers."

"Hiding underground. Hiding in tunnels. Is that the life that awaits Cameron?"

"There is a reason I've been hiding. When Dr Middleton let me out of that hospital in 1980, he saved my life. I had been held a prisoner since I was one year old by an organisation called MKULTRA."

"MKULTRA? The CIA stopped funding MKULTRA in the 70s."

Patient F shook his head. "So they want the world to believe.

But it was never shut down. Instead of growing up with a mum and a dad, I grew up in a maximum security prison. My friends weren't kids my own age, they were scientists and death row prisoners."

"Death row prisoners?"

"It's a long story," Patient F said. "All you need to know is that your wife did the right thing keeping Cameron hidden. MKULTRA getting hold of her would mean a destiny worse than death."

"I think that's enough for today," Hayburner said, and put a hand on Adam's shoulder. "The Shaman needs rest."

Adam thanked Patient F for the session, and rose to his feet.

Outside the small hut, he turned towards Hayburner and started sobbing.

"Why didn't she tell me? Why didn't Mimi tell me? I could have helped. I could have helped keep Cameron safe."

"It's impossible to say, Adam. Back then you were a patriot. You would do everything for your country."

"I would never give up my own daughter."

"But Cameron wasn't your own daughter. At least not in blood. Mimi could have been afraid of your reaction when you found out she had tricked you into believing you were Cameron's biological father."

"I am her father. Her blood means nothing. I've always loved Cameron as my own daughter, and I always will."

"I know, I know," Hayburner said, patting Adam on his back.

"Excuse me Hayburner," one of the Vietnamese soldiers said.

He was holding a small note in his hand. "We have news about the girl."

"What is it?" Hayburner asked. He could see by the look on the soldier's face that it wasn't good news.

"They were taken yesterday morning."

"Taken?"

"Abducted."

"Government soldiers?"

"No, it looks like it was Americans."

"Shit," Hayburner said.

"What is it? Has someone taken Cameron?" Adam asked.

Hayburner nodded.

"I know where they are going," Patient F said. He was now standing up, although he hardly looked like he could stand up straight. His skin was so pale one could almost see straight through it.

"You know where they are taking her?" Adam asked.

Patient F nodded. "Do you know how to get in contact with them?"

"I do," Adam replied.

"Then offer them a swap. It is me they want. Offer to swap me for Cameron."

"Shaman, you can't do this. They will kill you," Hayburner said.

"It has already been decided. Organise the swap."

PART 5

-99-

Two weeks later
Somewhere in the US

Adam was standing on a crest overlooking the valley in front of him. He removed the gloves and raised the binoculars to his eyes. The metal felt cold against his skin, and his breath fogged the lenses. He wiped them down using one of the gloves he had just removed.

"What do you see?" a voice behind him asked.

"It looks like an old concrete building. It is surrounded by a metal fence. I estimate it is about three metres high."

"Can we get in?"

"Depends on security. We have one advantage though; they don't know we are coming. But it will have to be a stealth attack. There will be no room for error."

"My men don't do errors," Patient F said as he exited the car.

He surveyed the valley in front of him. If this was where they kept his daughter, imprisoned like he himself was for all those years, then they would soon feel a wrath beyond imagination.

"Who are your men anyway? They seem well trained, well organised," Adam said.

"They go under the name The Orange Army. During the Vietnam War the US sprayed large parts of Vietnam with herbicides. The intention was to kill the crops so that the Vietnamese army would run out of food. Or at least that was the stated intention. As you would expect the strategy mostly affected the civilian population. Hundreds of thousands perished during the famine that swept the country, and the soil and water was polluted for generations to come. Kids were stillborn or born without arms or legs. My army is these kids, the deformed kids, the Agent Orange kids."

Adam glanced at the soldiers lined up behind the two trucks. They looked nothing like deformed kids. They looked like strong, well-trained soldiers.

Patient F understood from Adam's expression what he was pondering.

"They didn't look like this when they came to me," he said, and walked over to Adam.

He grabbed the binoculars and pointed them towards the building below. It was the right building.

It was under the cover of the Agent Orange victims Adam, Patient F and the soldiers had managed to sneak into the US. The American president had finally chosen to offer the people of Vietnam an apology for the Americans' use of Agent Orange during the war. It was long overdue, and almost part of a fad running across the western world. In recent years Australia had apologised to the stolen generation of indigenous people, and Japan had apologised for atrocities committed during the Second World War. Apparently asking for forgiveness made everything better. It didn't matter how delayed it was.

Adam didn't hold his breath for the US to ever apologise for MKULTRA's actions though. The killing of all those people at the Royal Albert Hospital of Brisbane would never be publicly acknowledged. Some things were just too evil to ever be admitted.

But the president had admitted that the US committed a crime against the Vietnamese population during the war, and he would publicly acknowledge this in six days. Adam, Patient F and the others had been smuggled in on the private jet the Agent Orange victims had been provided. And as the Agent Orange victims had been lodged in a luxury hotel in New York, eagerly awaiting their public appearance in front of the United Nations building, Adam and Patient F had snuck out from the private jet and hid in the hangar.

They had managed to get into the US, but the charade would be exposed on the day of the public apology. Because half of the Agent Orange victims would be missing. They were with Adam. They were the attack force Patient F had provided him with.

-100-

Yet again the CIA agent found himself outside Dr Drecker's cell. He had thought their last encounter would be the final one. He had even said his goodbyes, although Dr Drecker probably hadn't picked up on it. The CIA agent had been very subtle.

"We don't have to do this," Dr Drecker pleaded. "It's a mistake. They are not what you think they are."

"We have studied these patients for forty years, Dr Drecker. You have been here for a month and a half. Who do you think knows them best?"

"But you have been looking at the problem the wrong way. You have been looking for evidence that they have bad intentions, that they are aliens hiding in human bodies."

"And you claim they are not. You claim that all their extraordinary abilities can be explained by physiological changes in their brains. It is ludicrous, Dr Drecker. You are grasping at straws."

"I'm not. And I can prove it, I just need a few more days."

"We don't have a few days, Dr Drecker. Today is the first of June. If you had paid any attention at all to what has happened here over the last few weeks, then you would understand what this date signifies. The event is only a few days away."

"What you believe this date signifies!" Dr Drecker screamed. "You have no evidence to support your theory that they are aliens, you have no evidence that they are planning an attack on Earth."

"I don't have the privilege of waiting and seeing if I'm right. If I hesitate, then we will all die."

"How can you even claim such a thing?"

"Enough," the CIA agent said. He turned around to face the armed guard who stood next to him. "Seal off the room. For the next twenty-four hours no one goes in or out."

Dr Drecker looked at the CIA agent with desperation in his eyes. It wasn't just the fact that the CIA agent had so easily condemned him to die with the others – that had probably been his plan from the start. Dr Drecker had known that for weeks. It was the sheer reluctance to look at the evidence Dr Drecker had accumulated. The death row prisoners weren't different persons, they weren't empty bodies taken over by an alien life form when they visited an unknown dimension under the influence of DMT. They were the exact same persons they had always been. They were just hidden inside damaged brains.

Dr Drecker looked at his son, Cody. He walked over to the glass wall facing his cell and held his hand up against the glass.

Cody walked over and did the same.

The CIA agent shook his head and turned around.

Over his shoulder, Dr Drecker could see the neatly dressed CIA agent leave the room with the guard. And he instinctively knew it would be the last time he would ever see the CIA agent.

-101-

The CIA agent pressed the button for the conference call, and a screen lit up on the wall. A few seconds elapsed before the screen divided up into six squares. Four of them had people sitting in front of them. One of them was black and one of them showed a big, concrete building.

"Have we got visual confirmation?" the CIA agent asked.

"Negative," a voice answered. "We have detected movements around the perimeter, but we have no visual confirmation of the target."

"Ok, I want the birds in the air in five minutes. Give me an update when the payload is ready to be delivered."

"Roger."

"Roger, out," the CIA agent said, before fixing his eyes on the third quadrant of the screen.

"Everything is going ahead as planned," he said.

"And you can guarantee it will be simultaneous?" an old man with greying hair asked. He was dressed in a shiny blue suit.

"I can guarantee that it will be as good as simultaneous. There is always a risk that one incident will occur before the other, but there will not be enough time for any reaction. For all purposes the processes will be simultaneous."

"Good," the old man said. "We can't afford any surprises."

Adam moved with ease through the flat terrain. It had been more than seven years since his last active operation, the infiltration of a Taliban-infested village in Afghanistan. But it felt like it had been only yesterday. He felt comfortable in his camouflage outfit. He felt like he was finally home.

"We only have one chance at getting inside. Once the alarm goes off, it will be total chaos."

"Are they all still there?" one of the Vietnamese soldiers asked.

Patient F nodded.

The group moved closer to the fence and Adam pulled out an Uline 36-inch bolt-cutter from his backpack. He cut an opening, just wide enough for a person to move through, and signalled to Hayburner that he should go first. Hayburner moved with grace through the hole and positioned himself behind a big rock, before the next person followed.

The assault team consisted of sixteen people in total. It was a small group, but sufficient for the purpose. It was easier to move undetected when you moved in a small group, and that was the only advantage Adam and his team had – the element of surprise. Nobody would expect them to be stupid enough to try to free Cameron and the other prisoners with a sixteen-man team.

Sixteen men against the mighty force of the CIA.

"Something doesn't seem right. There are no guards here," Hayburner said.

"That's part of MKULTRA's strategy, they hide in plain sight. If they had built these premises on military ground, some foreign government would eventually have found out. When it looks just like any other industrial park, located in close proximity to a residential area, it is much harder to guess that it is actually military property," Patient F said.

"So you don't think we will encounter any guards?"

"We will encounter plenty of guards. They may keep up the pretence that this is not a military installation, but they will do their utmost to protect it.

We will meet the best of the best the US military can provide, but they will all be on the inside of the building."

"So all our men have been removed from the site?"

"Yes, they were all evacuated two days ago," the CIA agent replied.

"But won't that alarm them? They would hardly believe we left the prisoners unguarded."

"It is a risk we will have to take. We couldn't allow any soldiers to be sacrificed in the operation. There is only one outcome here. That building and everything around it will be destroyed today. To mitigate the risk of alarming the attackers, we have however put in place a range of automated processes. To an outsider it will appear there is plenty of movement and activity inside the building. But it is all a sham."

"Do you have your men in position?" Adam asked.

Hayburner nodded. His team was well versed in combat; they had executed several missions shutting down drug operations along the Vietnam-Cambodia border. But they had never faced an enemy like this. This would be like David's fight against Goliath. Fortunately Hayburner knew the truth behind the David and Goliath story, he had read about it in a book by Malcolm Gladwell. It had never been a fair fight. Goliath had expected a warrior like himself to fight. A warrior clad in heavy armour, a fight with sword and spear. Instead he had met a boy, a shepherd, with a sling and some stones. According to traditional thought David had won the battle against all odds. The problem with the traditional story was that the odds had never been in Goliath's favour. The odds had always been in David's favour. How was a warrior, carrying a hundred pounds of armour, and only armed with a spear and a sword, supposed to protect himself against a professional stone slinger? It would be like sending a wrestler to fight a guy armed with a sniper rifle. The outcome had already been decided before the fight even started. It had always been David who had the odds on his side. And in the same way it would always be the Orange Army who had the odds on their side in the fight against this enemy. They were a small unit, they moved with speed and deadly precision. They were all allowed to make independent decisions, and they were all willing to sacrifice their lives for the mission.

Today the Orange Army would succeed. It didn't matter how many security guards were inside that building, it didn't matter what sort of weapons they would encounter. They would always be faster. More agile. More deadly.

"What was that? Focus the camera on sector G," the CIA agent said.

The sixth quadrant of the screen shifted to a different camera and he could clearly see movement on the ground. The outlines of three bodies slowly crawling along the ground.

"It's in motion. Tell the birds to be ready for updated orders," he said.

The guy standing next to him nodded, walked over to the phone, and spoke briefly before putting the receiver down.

"ETA for drop zone is five minutes. Awaiting your orders, Sir."

The CIA agent dismissively held up his hand. He still didn't have visual confirmation. He needed that before he was authorised to give the order. The two stealth airplanes would be in position over the building in less than five minutes, before that happened he needed confirmation though. Confirmation that Patient F was part of the attack team. If he didn't exterminate them all in one hit there was no point. If only one of them got away that could be enough, enough to know about Earth's intentions, enough to start a war. Enough for the prophecy to be fulfilled.

He picked up the phone from his desk.

"This is Moses. Await my instructions. Be ready to execute order within the next five minutes."

Cameron was resting on the floor, lying with her head on a pillow and legs stretched out. It was still pitch-black in her cell, although she knew it was almost mid-morning. Something was about to happen, she could feel it in her bones. Suddenly there was a mechanical click from up under the ceiling of her cell. She jumped to her feet. But she couldn't figure out what it was that had made the sound. It had come from near the ventilation system, though. It had sounded like something was being opened, like a hatch or something. She sat down again. She missed her mum. She missed her mum so much that she didn't even know how to express her longing. She was fully aware that she was never going to see her mum again, but sometimes it almost felt like she was there with her. Looking after her, watching over her.

Her mum had been able to keep her safe for all those years. There had been times when she had doubted her mum, doubted that their lives had been in danger. Now she felt angry at herself for ever allowing herself to feel that way. Her mum had always been right. There had been people after her, people with bad intentions.

And now she was stuck in a prison cell.

All by herself.

She wondered where Adam, her father, was.

She hadn't spent enough time with him to really trust him before she got taken. She had wanted to tell him about what happened in the semi-trailer, how she had hit that guy and caused the accident. She hadn't intended to kill him, just hurt him, hurt him so badly that he would never again try to put his hand on her thigh.

She hadn't intended to kill that security guard either. But he had pulled something from his belt, and she had panicked, she had thought it was a gun. Only afterwards had she seen it was a Taser, a simple Taser gun.

Most of all she had wanted to tell him about the airplane crash. How she was the one who had killed her mum, how she was the one who had killed all those people.

She hadn't intended to, she hadn't even known what was happening to her. She had felt a pain in her stomach and she had gone to the toilet. There she had noticed the blood. Her undies were filled with blood. She had quickly cleaned herself up. Her mum had told her about the day that this might happen. How she soon would become a woman.

She had hurried back to her seat, eager to tell her mum that she had had her first menstruation.

But on the way back she had gotten dizzy, she had felt nauseated and lightheaded.

She had sat down next to her mum, who nervously had grabbed her hand. They weren't supposed to know each other, Cameron was using a stolen passport, but her mother hadn't cared. She had understood something was wrong.

Her mum had looked her in the eyes, almost as if she knew what was about to happen. Then Cameron had started to feel warm, so incredibly warm.

Her mum had wanted to hold on to her hand, tears streaming down her cheeks, but she couldn't, and she had pulled her hand away.

It had turned red, with small white blisters mushrooming on it.

Then her mum's pants had caught fire.

Then everything around her had caught fire.

Then she had heard all the screams.

All the terrible screams.

-102-

"We are in position in T minus two minutes," the voice from screen six said. "What are our orders?"

"Await situation," the CIA agent replied. He brushed his left hand against his upper lip, and with surprise he noticed it was moist. He was sweating like anything.

They now had eyes on seven unidentified persons, all approaching the MKULTRA installation in New Mexico. He had to make a decision soon. If he couldn't get a positive identification, he had to make up his mind whether to still proceed with the plan or to abort. He had already made up his mind, though. An abort order was out of the question. It would be too dangerous. Today was the date they had set. They had made the decision almost twenty years ago that no one could live through the next couple of days. The only remaining question was whether he could get them all, or if Patient F would still be at large.

He surveyed the screen again. There were seven unidentified persons, and it was impossible to gauge the identities of any of them. MKULTRA had littered the surrounding area with high-definition cameras, but without exception the men crawling on the ground had been successful in avoiding them. They were obviously professionals. Thus the only eyes the CIA agent now had on the intruders were the eyes of the satellites and a lone drone flying in low orbit high above the premises.

"What is that?" he said, staring at the corner of the screen. There was an eighth person coming into view. He looked smaller than the others, frailer, almost like a kid, a teenager.

The CIA agent grabbed the receiver. "Bird One. You have permission to drop payload in T minus one." With a burst of excitement he realised that they had him, he realised that they finally had him. The smaller person had to be Patient F, there was no other possibility.

"Roger," the voice from the screen replied.

The CIA agent knew what those words meant. In exactly one minute Bird One, a stealth fighter flying 50,000 feet up in the air, would drop a GBU-57/B, popularly called a MOAB, The Mother Of All Bombs, on the empty premises below. Patient F and his band of terrorists wouldn't have a clue what hit them.

But one thing was for sure; Patient F wouldn't be able to resurrect from this one.

-103-

"All men in position," Adam said. They were now fifty metres out from the building. They had split the group into two teams of eight people, and were slowly making their way towards the building.

In the CIA agent's office all eyes were fixed on the screen in front of them.

"Payload has been delivered," a voice from the screen said. It was the confirmation that the stealth bomber had dropped its "mother of all bombs." Impact would be in less than thirty seconds.

"Initiate the process," the CIA agent said into a microphone. Screen five burst to life and it showed the image of the inside of one of the death row prisoners' cells. The camera was set to night vision as the cell was pitch black. He could clearly see the prisoner staring at the camera, his eyes glowing like two green marbles. Then gradually the vision got blurrier.

"Can we change to another camera, the gas seems to interrupt the view," the CIA agent said.

A man in a grey suit pressed some buttons and a camera on the other wall was activated.

The agent could see the death row prisoner moving towards the first camera, his curiosity awakened by the mysterious hissing sound from under the ceiling. Then he moved backwards. Realising that it was gas that was being emitted trough the ventilation system.

The death row prisoner stumbled over towards the glass wall of the cell, and started hammering on it with all his strength.

The CIA agent could hear the hammering in his office now, they were all hammering on their glass walls.

All the death row prisoners, all the patients.

"Change to J," he said.

The man in the grey suit pressed some buttons, and a new cell was shown on the screen.

The CIA agent could see Cameron lying on the floor, her head as close to the ground as possible. It looked like she had wrapped her bed sheet around her mouth.

She's got the will to live, I'll give her that, the CIA agent thought. But there would be nothing saving her. In a few minutes the gas would be covering all of her cell.

He focused on screen five again. The screen had a timer that was counting rapidly downwards. Time to impact nine, eight, seven...

He caught a quick glimpse of the eight intruders. They were almost at the wall of the building now.

Four, three, two, one.

Then screen five and six went black.

Impact.

It was all done, they had succeeded. They had killed Patient F.

There was no cheering in the room though, no celebrations.

They still had work to do. It would take a few minutes for the other patients to expire from the gassing.

And then they would have to do the clean-up afterwards.

The CIA agent asked for screen 4 to show the cell of Dr Drecker.

But before the guy in the grey suit had punched in the command, a red light started flashing in the ceiling.

"What the hell is that?" the CIA agent asked.

"There's been a breach in the southern end of the building," the guy in the grey suit replied.

"Impossible, show me the camera."

Two seconds later, the camera of the southern end of the building was shown on the screen, and the CIA agent stared with astonishment at a bunch of camouflage-clad people storming in through the door.

"Impossible," he repeated, before recognising the face of one of the intruders. Adam Mullins, the ex-army guy.

The guy in the grey suit turned towards the CIA agent, and with a nervous voice he said, "Sir, we just had a breach at the northern end too."

-104-

The CIA agent ran to the door. He stopped in the doorway, almost as frozen. The sound of gunshots rang through the halls of the building. He took a deep breath before turning around and closing the door. He then walked the eight meters over to his office chair.

"Bring up cameras 3 and 4," he said.

The guy in the grey suit did as ordered, but he was clearly nervous.

"Shouldn't we arm ourselves?"

"There is no time," the CIA agent said.

In front of him he saw Dr Drecker in his cell. Dr Drecker was sitting on his bed, the cell almost covered in fumes from the gas, but Dr Drecker was clearly smiling.

"That bastard," the CIA agent blurted out. Suddenly he understood what had happened.

Dr Drecker had planned it all. He had told the CIA agent where Patient F was hiding, he had told him to travel to Vietnam.

How had he been able to know where Patient F was hiding? He had asked Cody what he saw. And Cody had seen the inside of the Cu Chi tunnels, the tunnels that Dr Drecker had recognised from some documentary on Discovery Channel.

But when the CIA agent had returned from Vietnam he had been briefed about a breach in protocol. Dr Drecker had taken his son Cody up onto the roof. Let him have a glimpse of the sunlight, some fresh air. The CIA agent had seen the video. They hadn't spoken when they stood up there on the roof. Dr Drecker hadn't said a word. It had all seemed so innocent. But of course it hadn't been innocent. Dr Drecker had let Cody see his surroundings. He had walked Cody over to the southern end of the roof. That hadn't been an accidental walk.

From the southern end of the roof they could see straight over to the local bottle factory. The factory had its company logo written in big letters on the side of their building.

He had taken Cody up onto the roof to show Patient F where they were being held.

The CIA agent swore. He had thought he could lead Patient F and his soldiers to the empty building in New Mexico, the building that had been struck by a MOAB bomb only a few seconds ago. He had been sure that Adam and Patient F would be tricked by the tracker he had placed there. Adam had sent a proposal through to Matt Parks. It had been obvious that he knew the shared file was being monitored. He had just deleted the whole document and replaced it with a proposal for a swap – Patient F for Cameron.

He had walked straight into the CIA agent's trap. He had acted exactly as the CIA agent had expected. He had been given the time and date for the swap, and the location of the empty MKULTRA premises in New Mexico. The CIA agent had known that Patient F and Adam weren't stupid enough to believe that they would actually be able to trade Cameron free. But he knew he could make them believe they had a chance to free her. He had placed Cameron's watch in the building. Adam would be able to pick up the signal and read that as a confirmation that she was actually being kept in the building. And then they would probably attempt a morning attack. Everything had played out as predicted.

He had played them like puppets.

At least that was what he had thought.

Instead it was he who had been played, he who had been tricked.

"Is there any way to increase the speed of the gas being distributed?" he barked to the guy in the grey suit.

The agent in the grey suit shook his head. "There is only one distribution speed, Sir."

-105-

Abullet whizzed past Adam's head. He dove to the ground, rolled to his left, and quickly assessed the situation. They were outnumbered, maybe three to one. Their eight men against maybe thirty trained agents. He didn't know what the situation was on the northern end of the building, but he assumed Hayburner's team's odds were a bit more even. It was obvious that Adam's and Patient F's team had entered the lion's cage. This had to be the place where MKULTRA kept Cameron and the others.

"Are you hit?" Patient F yelled through the gunfire.

Adam shook his head. "Isn't it time to use some of your special powers?" Adam yelled back.

Patient F smiled. He knew that the power of healing, the power of not aging would be of little help in the situation they found themselves in.

But he had one advantage. He had been a prisoner of this building for fifteen years. He had never seen the outside of the building, but he had been around most of the inside before they sent him to Australia. And he had memorized every corner down to the most miniscule detail.

"The cells are straight ahead. We need to get past this hallway and up those stairs." He pointed to a large, steel staircase at the far end of the hallway. "Once we break through that door, we will have access to the cells."

"How do we open them?"

"Hayburner will handle that for us. The control room is in the northern end. Once he knocks out the main power and the backup generator, all cells should automatically be opened."

Another bullet whizzed past Adam's head, closer this time. It was time to move. He stood up straight and leant against the door, splinters of concrete flying in front of his eyes. He counted the bursts. The agent was clearly panicking, just keeping his finger on the trigger, emptying his machine gun without any purpose. He would soon have to reload, and that would be Adam's chance. The gunfire stopped and Adam heard a soft click. Without hesitation he jumped out from cover and ran towards the far end, spraying bullets in every direction of the wall. He knew that the agent would have been trained by the US army, trained by the same guys as himself. Always trained to duck and roll left. He shifted the position of his aim slightly and released the pressure on the trigger. Then he pressed it again, just as the agent rolled out from his cover. Adam could see the burst of bullets hitting him straight in the face; he didn't even have time to shoot back.

Adam pointed the machine gun towards the mezzanine, where more agents appeared from their hiding places. He aimed as well as he could, but it was hard firing and running at the same time, and he had another five metres before he could duck for cover again. With a sense of fear he realised he wasn't going to make it.

Then he heard a large blast, just before he was thrown to the ground by the sheer force of the blast itself. One of the Vietnamese soldiers stood in the middle of the hallway with a bazooka on his shoulder. When the smoke settled, Adam could see that the mezzanine with the US agents was blown to pieces, only bent and torn metal remaining.

He got up onto his feet and jumped the stairs, three steps in one, until he got to the top. He rested his back against the wall, and took a few deep breaths before attaching a charge of C-4 to the door. He moved back and just managed to get some proper cover before the doors blew inwards.

The CIA agent heard the blast and turned his head.

"That was close," he said.

"The safety door to the cells is compromised," the agent in the grey suit said. He was staring at the screen in front of him. It was full of smoke, but one could clearly see people moving through what had used to be the safety door.

"Redirect Bird 2. They need to drop a bomb on this place."

"Are you crazy? We won't be able to get out in time."

"Redirect it. This is more important than our lives. If we don't stop them all of humanity is doomed."

The agent in the grey suit got up from his chair, clearly distressed. "I can't do it. My family would be in the blast zone."

The CIA agent picked up the gun from his desk and pointed it at the other agent. "Too bad," he said before shooting him in the head.

He then picked up the receiver.

"Come in Bird 2."

"Bird 2 responding."

"This is Moses. New target. Coordinates are 37.407229,

-122.107162. Please confirm."

"I have not been authorized for new target," the pilot answered.

"Override of initial order has been granted as per the president's executive order 8367. Code for initiation: Project Black Swell. Please confirm ETA for payload."

The line went silent for almost ten seconds, as the pilot verified the new information. Then he finally responded. "Coordinates are for a civilian area. Please confirm."

"Coordinates are correct, Captain. All civilians were evacuated from the area forty-eight hours ago. Area is clear."

"Confirmed. ETA for payload is T minus ten minutes."

The CIA agent put down the receiver and sighed. He looked over at the control screen. Most of the quadrants were now just transmitting static noise, as they were shot out by the approaching Vietnamese mercenaries. The camera from 'Bird 2' lit up one of the screens and the CIA agent could see the pilot was turning the plane around. Turning it towards the MKULTRA building. In less than ten minutes he would drop a thirty thousand-pound MOAB bomb on top of the building. It would cause a tremendous loss of life. The CIA agent had lied about the civilian population having been evacuated. They were still there. They had been MKULTRA's cover during all these years. Nobody would have expected the US government to hide the greatest threat ever to humanity in the middle of a quiet suburban area, but that's what they had done. And it had worked.

The CIA agent had run the simulation before. A minimum loss of ten thousand human lives, and several tens of thousands with horrific injuries. The innocence of America would be lost forever. A massive bomb attack in the heart of the country. The consequences were impossible to predict with certainty.

But it had to be done. They had already worked out the media response several years ago. A terrorist cell had finally succeeded in smuggling a bomb past America's border. An Islamic Purist Terror organisation had finally achieved what they had been attempting for all these years. It would be easy enough for MKULTRA to direct the attention towards one of the known terrorist organisations.

It would be easier that way.

With a traditional enemy.

The world wasn't ready to know what enemies they were really facing. They weren't ready to face the reality that we weren't only facing earthly terrorists. That the real threat in the coming decades would make Al-Qaida and Taliban look like kindergarten kids.

The CIA agent closed his laptop and looked at the screen for the last time. Seven minutes. He could still make it.

Adam burst through the door. He looked down the hall, but could only see smoke. He ran towards the end of the hall, and then he saw it. Two rows of glass cages. It was hard to tell for sure. But he thought he could see a body moving inside one of them.

"They are gassing the prisoners!" he hollered. "They are gassing the prisoners. We need to get down there."

Two Vietnamese soldiers came through the door immediately after Adam. One of the Vietnamese soldiers attached a hook to the railing and lowered himself down to the floor with the prison cells. He pulled on his gasmask and started shooting at the glass of the prison cells. Adam could hear the glass shatter as he ran towards the stairs.

The CIA agent could hear the glass of the prison cells break as he ran towards the secret doorway. He had underestimated the American soldier, Adam Mullins, and Patient F. They had penetrated the MKULTRA building with ease. Only sporadic gunshots could be heard throughout the building now. It probably meant that the MKULTRA agents had been overrun. It was one of the problems with hiding in plain sight. They couldn't have too many military personnel on site. That was deemed to potentially arouse suspicion among the general population. Well, there was nothing he could do about that now. And most of the population they had tried to hide from would be dead in a few minutes anyway, when the second stealth plane dropped its MOAB on top of the MKULTRA building.

-106-

"They are all dead, Sir," the Vietnamese soldier said. He was dragging a patient out of his cell. "We must have been just a little bit too late. Their bodies are still warm."

"Have you found my daughter yet?" Adam yelled.

"No Sir, she isn't in any of the cells. Everybody is dead here."

"She can't be. She must be somewhere else," Adam said, running past the soldier.

Hayburner appeared with the survivors of the team who had attacked the northern part of the building. "The northern part is cleared," he said.

"We will have to leave now, Sir. We have lost contact with our dummy team at the New Mexico site. It appears from the reports we have received that MKULTRA dropped a massive bomb on the site. If that is true, they may not even bother sending additional teams here. They may just drop a bomb on this site too."

Hayburner stood emotionless and listened to the information. His own son, Ahn, had begged to come along and Hayburner had buckled under the pressure. They had needed an extra person for the dummy team. He had thought they would be safe. They were just a distraction and would abort the mission as soon as they were identified. Now he realised that his son was most likely dead.

"We are not leaving without my daughter. There is no way we are leaving without my daughter," Adam said.

"Adam is right. We're not leaving without Cameron," said Patient F. He was standing on top of the mezzanine level, with one Vietnamese soldier on each side of him. He looked like a ghost, a pale ghost surrounded by smoke.

Hayburner nodded. He had just lost his son. He knew how they would feel. "As you wish, Shaman. We will continue the search."

"Over here," one of the Vietnamese soldiers cried.

Adam and Hayburner ran over, as fast as they could.

"There is another hallway down there, with more cells. They must have had a system in place where they could keep certain patients separated from the others."

"Let's go," Adam said.

"There are two more rooms with cells," Patient F said. He had now arrived down at the ground floor. "They never used them when I was here, but they may well have been using them to lock up Cameron and her friend."

Adam and Hayburner took the lead. Patient F was still weak and the two Vietnamese soldiers didn't leave his side.

"Over here," Adam yelled as he ran into the second room. Frantically he started to gaze into the cells. Some of them were empty, and didn't seem to have been gassed. But the two cells at the end of the line were filled up with gas. Adam placed a small charge of explosives onto each door and took cover. When the charges detonated, the glass rained down onto the floor.

"There is someone in this one," Hayburner said as he dragged a dead person out of the cell. It was the janitor from Brooklyn who had been the unfortunate victim of Dr Kovacks' deadly DMT injection. Adam dragged Dr Kovacks out of the other cell. He was dead too.

"Last chance," Adam said, and ran towards the door to the next room. The last room of prison cells. He placed a charge onto the door and detonated it. As soon as the door came flying through the room, Adam ran through the opening.

And then he stopped.

The floor of the room was partially collapsed. Inside were two rows of glass cages, but the row on the left side was partially destroyed. It appeared that the floor had collapsed underneath it.

"What's happened?" Adam asked.

"It must have been the charges my team set off when we went through the outer wall. The charges must have collapsed the floor," Hayburner answered.

"Is that a tunnel down there?"

"It looks like it."

Adam was looking down the hole in the floor. If the floor had collapsed when the northern team blew the wall, then there was still a chance whoever was in the cells at the time was still alive. The dead prisoners had still been warm. That meant that the gassing must have started around the same time Adam's and Hayburner's teams breached the building.

"Get me down there. I need to see what's down there."

"Ok," Hayburner replied, and pulled out a rope.

He tied one end of the rope to the wall behind him and gave Adam the other end. "Be careful," he said as Adam started to lower himself down into the crater.

"Listen," Hayburner said to the five remaining Vietnamese soldiers. "The Shaman will come with me and Adam. The rest of you return to the vehicles as planned."

"It's not necessary," Adam said, dangling from the rope. "I can do this by myself."

Hayburner smiled. "You wouldn't survive in those tunnels for more than two minutes without me and the Shaman."

"Ok, let's move!" Adam yelled.

-107-

It was dark and hot in the tunnel. Adam's thoughts drifted back to his brief encounter with the Cu Chi tunnels. They hadn't been much different. But at least this tunnel was built for westerners. He had to crouch, but he didn't have to crawl. And the tunnel was wide enough for two people to move side-by-side.

"What is this?" he asked.

"I have no idea," Patient F replied. "But when the Vietnamese built their tunnels in Cu Chi, they built them with the intention of survival. They never meant them to be a weapon, only a means to help them survive the war. It was the war that turned them into weapons. I believe that MKULTRA may have built this tunnel as an escape route if their premises were ever compromised."

"So this would take us out of the area?"

"I believe so."

"Then there is a chance Cameron and Nina are still alive."

"They could also have been held at the other site. The New Mexico site we sent our dummy team to. The team picked up the signal from Cameron's watch there."

"No, that would have been too obvious. That site was always a trap. They wouldn't have kept anyone there. Cameron is in these tunnels. I can feel it," Adam said as he crouched down and continued forwards in the tunnel.

Hayburner and Patient F followed after.

The CIA agent couldn't believe his eyes. Above him the tunnel opened up into a gaping hole. It was the room that had once held ten glass cages, the room that had contained the cells that Cameron, Cody and Dr Drecker had been held in. It appeared that the floor of the room had caved in, and in the process some of the glass cells had shattered. Was it possible that Cameron and the others had survived? Was it possible that they had survived the gassing? The CIA agent swore. If that was the case, then they could possibly manage to escape. He checked his watch. The stealth bomber was still five minutes away. Probably not enough time for them to get away unharmed, but he couldn't afford to take any chances. He started running.

"Did you hear that?" Hayburner said.

Adam stopped and tried to listen. It sounded like somebody moaning.

"Cameron! Cameron, are you there?" Adam yelled. He started running towards the sound, his machine gun raised.

Hayburner tried to keep up the pace, but he was being slowed down by Patient F, who looked even paler than normal.

"Wait for us, Adam. It could be an ambush."

I'll take my chances, Adam thought as he disappeared around the corner.

The CIA agent froze when he heard the voice. Someone had just yelled out "Cameron". It had sounded very close. Maybe only a few hundred metres ahead in the tunnel. Could it be Cameron's dad, the army guy Adam Mullins? The CIA agent clicked the safety catch on his gun, and increased his walking speed. He needed to end this today. There was no other way.

"Dad!" Cameron yelled out as she saw Adam coming around the corner. She was shouldering an older man with what appeared to be a broken foot. On the other side of her was a twenty-something kid. His eyes missing from a face covered with blood. Next to him was Nina. They all looked like they had been through hell, torn pieces of white clothing covered in blood and dust. "We need your help. This is Cody and his father, Martin Drecker. They were locked up in the cells next to me."

Adam grabbed Cody's arm as Cameron stepped aside. He looked like he had lost a fair amount of blood, but he was still conscious. Adam ripped off a piece of fabric from his shirt and tied it around Cody's eyes. It looked like part of the collapsing glass cage had come down on his face. His eyes were gone and he had several cuts across his body.

Adam handed his machine gun to Cameron and asked if she knew how to use it. She nodded, then turned around and pointed it in the direction of the corner Adam had just come from.

"No!" Adam screamed.

The CIA agent was fast approaching the shadows in front of him. He could hear the taller guy comforting the shorter one. Saying that they had to keep moving. Then he heard a loud "No!"

Adam jumped forward and put a hand on the machine gun,

forcing Cameron to lower it. Around the corner came someone she hadn't seen since she was a little kid. Hayburner, her dad's old army friend. He was holding up a teenager who looked pale as a ghost.

Cameron laid the machine gun onto the floor and ran over to help Hayburner with the hurt teenager.

"We need to stop for five minutes, Adam. The Shaman is very weak," Hayburner said as he laid Patient F down on the floor of the tunnel.

"Ok, we'll take a two-minute break to patch up any wounds. Then we move on," Adam said before walking over to Cameron and giving her a big hug. "I thought I had lost you," he said.

Patient F was watching the scene in front of him and a tear formed in the corner of his eye.

Then a shot rang out. And Hayburner fell to the ground, the front of his skull blown out.

"Are we having a family reunion?" the CIA agent said as he approached the group in front of him. Adam glanced over at the machine gun that Cameron had placed on the ground. It was too far away. The only one in reach for it was Cody, and he was blind as a duck and of little use. "Don't even try," the CIA agent said as he looked Adam in the eyes.

They were all unarmed, but they were five people. The CIA agent only had one gun. If Adam jumped him, some of the others might be able to wrestle the gun from him. But who? Patient F and the guy Cameron had introduced as Martin Drecker were both in a pretty bad state. Cody was totally incapacitated. That left only Cameron and Nina winter. The risks were too great. He couldn't allow it.

The CIA agent glanced at his watch. Time was working for him. They hadn't managed to get very far. They were still underneath the MKULTRA building, and in three minutes the bomb would hit. It was a small sacrifice for him. His life for the safety of humanity.

His life for America.

He aimed the gun at Patient F.

"Welcome back. It's nice to see you again," he said.

Patient F didn't reply. The anger and hate darkened his eyes, and made them look like two small holes in the pale face.

"I never got the chance to tell you when you were our guest..." the CIA agent started.

"Guest? I was one year old when you locked me up. I was never a guest. I was a prisoner," Patient F said.

The CIA agent, unfazed by the interruption, continued. "As I was saying. I now understand why you have been hiding for all these years in Vietnam. Hiding under the ground like a rat. Trying to repent for your father's sins, for his war crimes."

"You should do the same one day. It helps," Patient F said.

"It's just that...." the CIA agent scratched his chin with his free hand before continuing. "It's just that your father never did the things they said he did. He was innocent. We didn't discover until a few years after he had been sentenced to death. Five other soldiers in his platoon were responsible for the murders your father took the rap for. But your father sympathized with the communists. So we buried the case. A good commie is a dead commie, right? Just the way you and your daughter will die today," he said, looking over at Cameron.

"What is he talking about, Dad?" Cameron asked Adam.

The CIA agent shook his head. "Wrong dad. The pale ghost in front of you is your real dad. A terrorist like yourself. Like father like daughter," he laughed.

Cameron looked with fear in her eyes at Adam.

But Adam didn't look back. He had noticed that the CIA agent kept checking his watch. It was obvious he was just stalling for time. What was he waiting for? Were there more agents arriving soon? Or was something else about to happen?

Whatever it was, Adam had to take action. He couldn't wait.

-108-

Adam was about to charge the CIA agent when he noticed a movement in the corner of his right eye. It was Cameron flying through the air. She had obviously had the same thought, but she hadn't hesitated as Adam had. Before Adam managed to react he heard the first shot. It hit Cameron in her left shoulder and knocked her to the ground. Blood splatter covered the wall behind her.

The CIA agent traced Cameron's body with his gun as it fell to the ground. He prepared to finish her off. Adam heard the second shot while he was still in the air. He had been too far away to make an attempt for the CIA agent's gun. His only option had been to go between the CIA agent and Cameron, to take the bullet intended for his daughter. He could feel it cutting through the flesh of his neck as he landed on top of Cameron. He was wearing a bulletproof vest, but that was of no use.

He opened his eyes and felt Cameron's warm breath on his face. She blinked, she was alive. He had caught the second bullet.

But he knew there would be more to come. With a burst of strength he rolled around to face the CIA agent. But what he saw was nothing like he had expected.

A third shot rang out and instead of feeling the pain of another bullet in his body, he saw the long and lanky body in front of him dropping down on his knees. In front of the body lay Patient F, with a bullet hole in his head. He seemed to be smiling, as his eyes rolled up in his head.

The body of the CIA agent swayed in a kneeling position, for a second, before giving in to gravity and collapsing forward. A gaping hole in the forehead the only witness of what had happened. Then he dropped his gun to the floor.

Dr Drecker rushed forward to hug his son Cody, who was standing with the machine gun in his left hand, smoke coming out of the barrel.

"How?" Adam asked. Confused.

Cody just pointed to the dead Shaman on the floor. "I saw through his eyes," he said.

The eerie silence was broken by the sound of a crackling radio. It appeared to come from the dead CIA agent's pocket. Adam got up on his feet and walked over to the dead agent. He rolled the agent's body over on its side and pulled out the noise-making radio.

"Come in Moses. Bird two in position. Payload ready to be dropped in T minus ten seconds," the voice on the radio said.

Adam pressed the microphone button on the radio, and with all the calm he could muster he said, "Abort mission. I repeat abort mission. Area not cleared for civilians."

"Who is this?" the pilot of the stealth bomber asked. He was clearly aware that it wasn't the CIA agent giving him the counter order.

"This is US Army Captain Adam Mullins, I'm retired now, but

I used to be in the army. I've done three tours in Afghanistan for my country, and I've seen some bad shit, believe you me. But nothing will compare to what you're about to do. I repeat: Abort mission. Area has not been cleared. Tens of thousands of American citizens will die if you drop that bomb."

"I have been cleared to drop the payload. I need official confirmation that the order has been changed. Please put Moses on."

"Moses is dead. He just caught a bullet in the head. Listen son, I know you've been trained to execute orders. But this order has not been sanctioned by the president. You are about to drop a bomb on innocent American citizens. It does not matter what your order was. Use your common sense. Do you want to become the most hated person in America?" Adam said, and turned off the radio.

He knew the pilot wouldn't drop the bomb. If a soldier was given the opportunity to think for himself, he always made the right decision.

-109-

Two days later
3rd of June, 2012
Somewhere in Mexico

Adam squinted as he was trying to read the sign in front of him.

"Are you getting nearsighted, Dad?" Cameron laughed as she read the sign out to him, a pair of binoculars in her hands. It read 'Bomali Bay'.

They had been sailing for five hours straight, and Adam could feel the skin on his back burning. "Am I getting red? I feel like my back is burning," he said.

Cameron peaked over the cabin. "Nah, you're not red. You're lobster-red." She laughed again.

Adam squirted out some more sunscreen. Factor thirty. The sun was strong in Mexico. After they had escaped the MKULTRA building he had asked Cameron what she wanted to do. He realised they would never be safe. There would always be somebody searching for them, hunting for them.

Cameron hadn't even had to think.

"I wanna be on the ocean," she had said.

Hearing how her biological father had been hiding underground for all those years had made an impact on her. And Adam could understand her. Patient F had chosen a life of suffering to make amends for something that wasn't even his fault. He thought he had been making repentance for his father's sins. But it turned out his father had never been a sinner. Maybe that's why he was the only one of the death row prisoners who had never resurrected. Maybe he had been the one going to heaven, and the other ones had been condemned to live on Earth. To live their own hell on Earth. Eternity in a glass cage.

Adam had no idea. He didn't know what to believe in, or not anymore. And he didn't care.

He had his daughter Cameron.

They were together again, and that was all that mattered.

He turned the wheel on the sailing boat, and 'Mimi', the name Cameron had come up with for their forty-two-foot monohull, got up on her keel and sailed into the sunset as Nina Winter arrived up from the cabin.

-110-

Another three days later,
6th of June, 2012
Somewhere in Mexico

D r Drecker was observing his son Cody eating breakfast in front of him.

They had said their goodbyes to Adam and Cameron a couple of days before. They had been helpful in getting Dr Drecker and Cody across the border. Somehow this Cameron girl was an expert in avoiding police and the authorities. She knew all the tricks in the book.

Dr Drecker smiled to himself. He had never really appreciated Cody when he grew up. When he was a little kid it had been different. Dr Drecker had enjoyed spending time with Cody before he became a teenager. It had been easier back then, less pressure at work, more time to spend with the family. And he hadn't yet started to resent his ex-wife.

Had still enjoyed being at home.

Dr Martin Drecker thought back on the many Saturdays he had spent building LEGO kits with Cody on the cold, tile flooring of their Queens apartment. Life had been so easy back then. Cody had been so easy.

Cody had looked up at him, with his big innocent green eyes, and told him that he loved him. Really, really loved him. And Dr Drecker had said "Ditto."

Now Dr Drecker realised that he should have treasured those moments more.

He should have treasured those moments, those little precious moments.

Instead, he had spent most of his adult life working, chasing material possessions and respect from people he didn't care about.

He looked at his watch.

9:32.

It was almost time.

It was only two minutes left until the exact time and date when Cody's heart had stopped 49 days earlier.

They had talked about this moment, Cody and he.

There was nothing Dr Drecker could do, nothing he could say.

He had tried everything, tried to find a cure, tried to find a way out, but there was none.

In exactly two minutes Cody would die.

He would leave Earth behind and be replaced by something else.

Dr Drecker's only hope was that he would be able to do what he had promised – to rewire Cody's brain so that he would get his old personality back. He promised himself, Cody was never going to be a prisoner inside his own head. Cody would be free. Always be free.

"Don't worry, Dad," Cody said, and pushed the plate of breakfast away.

"How can you eat now?" Dr Drecker asked.

"I was hungry."

Dr Drecker laughed, before his smile stiffened and his face was filled with sorrow.

"I'm so sorry Cody," he said. "I wish there was something I could do."

"There is nothing to be sorry about, Dad. I'm not afraid. I have been there before. I'm not scared."

"I just wish we had more time."

Cody nodded. "Me too. But I'm grateful we got the time we got. I'm grateful we got to know each other again."

Cody got up from his chair and walked around the table to where Dr Drecker was sitting. Dr Drecker also got up and put his arms around his son. He closed his eyes and squeezed their bodies tighter.

"I love you, son," he said, while slowly opening his left eyelid to get a glimpse of his watch.

Three seconds.

Two seconds.

One second.

And Cody was gone.

Dr Drecker could instantly feel it.

Cody's body going limp in a blink.

The warmth suddenly disappearing.

His heartbeat stopping.

Cody was no more.

Dr Drecker cried.

He screamed as loud as he could.

But he knew there was no point.

There was no way to save Cody.

There never had been a way.

Death was the one sure thing in this life.

The one constant that never changed.

And now it had taken Cody.

Suddenly a jolt of angst went through Dr Drecker's body. He didn't want to, but he couldn't avoid looking at the TV in the corner of the cheap hotel room. He picked up the remote, which was lying next to Cody's still-warm body, and turned up the volume. It was a news report from New York, outside the UN building. Tens of thousands of orange balloons were floating up in the air. The reporter said the balloons were released in the memory of the millions of casualties of the Vietnam War, in the memory of the generations ruined by the pesticide Agent Orange. The broadcast cut to old footage from the Vietnam War. An American soldier was seen dropping a hand grenade down the entrance of a Viet Cong tunnel in the Cu Chi province of Vietnam.

"Those tunnels are as close to hell as you can get," he said before the broadcast cut back to the reporter again. The next report was from New Mexico, where it was reported that an Islamic terrorist cell was suspected of deploying a dirty bomb on American soil for the first time in history. In several places the ground was still burning and dead animals could be seen littering the area. Luckily enough there had been no confirmed human casualties.

A shiver went down Dr Drecker's back.

'Millions of souls will fly into the sky'

'The army of undead will rise from the depths of hell'

'The earth will burn'

Dr Drecker looked at the date on the TV. The sixth of June.

'On the eve of Venus' second passing of the sun'

'Our saviour, the long lost son will return'

'On this blessed day our saviour will return and we will be free'

'Oh how we long for our revenge'

'His eyes cut out by evil, his soul darkened by injustice'

The death row prisoners had never talked about Patient F when they spoke about their saviour.

They had never spoken about a returning Son.

Who was it who had led them to Patient F?

Who was it who had made them all die?

Who was it who had killed the CIA agent?

They had talked about the resurrecting son, the one with eyes of darkness.

The sixth of June was today. The eve of Venus' second passing of the sun was today. An event so rare that it occurred only once every century. The first passing had been in 2004, the second was today. Then it would be another 105 years until the next one. A coincidence?

A drop of salty water fell down on Cody's sheet. It was a tear from Dr Drecker. He looked down at his son, the warm body turning colder with every second that passed.

With sorrow he rose from his chair and walked over to the window. He pulled the curtains open and let the sun stream in.

Then he picked up his overnight bag. He unzipped it and stared at the contents for a while. Adam had insisted that he accept it. They were in Mexico, after all. Dr Drecker picked it up and walked back to the bed.

When he saw Cody's finger move, he knew what to do.

He cocked the gun and looked away.

AUTHOR'S NOTE

Thank you so much for taking the time and effort to read 49 Days. It is truly appreciated.

If you also decide to leave a review on Amazon or Goodreads, or simply spread the word to your friends and family, I would be eternally grateful.

Erik